Soul Catcher

By
Vivi Dumas

Soul Catcher

Rachel at Happily Ever After Reviews: ...I really enjoyed this read and look forward to the continuation of this saga. The secondary characters promise to be as interesting as Angel and Jacque, and I can't wait to read on. I'm definitely recommending this read to everyone!!!

5 Tea Cups plus a Recommended Read!

To read the full review go to HEA Reviews.

By Blogging by Liza: ...SOUL CATCHER was the first book I read by Vivi Dumas, but won't be my last. I liked the pacing of the book and loved the character development of not only the main characters, but the supporting ones.

To read the full review go to Blogging by Liza.

Pen and Muse Reviews

...Vivi Dumas offers a butt-kicking take on paranormal romance in her latest novel 'Soul Catcher.' The beginning veers back and forth between some well-timed flashbacks to bring readers into Angel's dilemma. Dumas' effectively crafted writing helps readers transition from each character's point of view with clarity. Tight writing and excellent pacing guide the story through the hell of Angel's plight.

To read the full review go to Pen and Muse Reviews.

Copyright © 2012 by Vivi Dumas
Cover by Hot Damn Designs
VPG Publishing
ISBN: 978-1620508534

~DEDICATION~

*To those who supported me through the good and the bad.
To those who allowed me to be me, even when they didn't
understand.*

Prologue

Lucifer crouched on the ledge of the observation deck of the Empire State Building like a medieval gargoyle frozen in time waiting to be released from its stone prison, overseeing his minions below.

The street was empty, quiet.

He had waited centuries for a power like her to surface, someone strong enough to do his bidding and succeed. She was special.

The cars approached and his opportunity arose. As the vehicles got closer, he waved his ebony talons and both lights turned green. Neither car had a chance to brake in time.

Wheels screeched. The Toyota slammed into the Mercedes. The crushing of metal ripped through the night's silence. The sleek, black car rammed into a light post. Glass exploded and scattered across the street. The Toyota spun in the middle of the road like a child's toy.

Angel Dias flew halfway out the windshield of her Mercedes, only the dashboard impeded her projection out the car, pinning her legs against warm leather of the seat. She lay plastered to the hood of her car unable to move while he observed the chaos unravel around her.

Lucifer leaned over the ledge of the building and smirked at the destruction he created. A familiar light appeared behind him.

"Up to your old tricks, I see," the Light's voice rumbled.

Lucifer glanced its way, his horns appearing for a second as he struggled to maintain his human form. "I don't know what you're talking about."

"She isn't yours to take."

He shifted his head slightly. "You're wrong." Lucifer grinned a grin of death. "Her family has always belonged to me."

The Light grew brighter, blending its soft aura with the illumination of the moon above. "Not all of them. She doesn't know about her lineage."

Lucifer shrugged. "Once faced with a big enough problem, humans always revert to their true nature."

"You think she'll call on you?"

"I know she will." Lucifer focused back on the scene of the accident as the Light disappeared. He listened in to the activity below.

Sirens sounded. A paramedic jumped from the ambulance and ran towards Angel. Her face smashed against the black hood. Her legs remained trapped by the dashboard, restricting her movement. She groaned and reached her hand out to the paramedic, causing him to suck in a sharp breath. His touch grazed her hand. A soft cry caught in her throat.

"She's alive," he shouted to the other paramedic.

Chapter One

Angel reclined in her seat, closing her eyes, wishing the attendant would bring her another drink. Her mind was trapped in the reoccurring dream haunting her. She lifted her head, wanting to get up, but her body refused. As she reached for her rescuers, the dark shadow watched her from across the street. His skin sparkled under the streetlight. The intensity of his eyes drew her to him. His sinister grin warned of danger, causing her to turn away. The light faded as she grew too tired to hold up her head. The darkness called, whispering her name. She relinquished herself to its mercy.

She opened her eyes and sighed as a man in the pinstriped suit squeezed past her to get to his seat. First class was more her style. She hadn't worked since the accident, therefore she settled for economy. The hefty guy in front of her smelled of beef jerky and stale cigarettes, and he leaned back on her lap as soon as the plane took off. Angel envisioned stabbing his fat, grimy neck with the heel of her Prada.

She turned and glanced across the aisle, where a red-haired woman pleaded with her daughter to be quiet. The brat had screamed for the last hour and a half. Angel prayed they would land before she snapped, taking out the kid and the fat guy in her lap.

"Mommy, whas wong wit her face?" The little girl with pigtails pointed at Angel.

"Shh...it's rude to point at people," her mother whispered.

"Mommy, is she a monster?"

Angel scoffed and stared ahead, trying to ignore the little girl. The same question crossed her own mind when she first viewed her face in the hospital after the accident and each time she stole a glimpse of herself in a mirror. People's fear of her grotesque disfiguration consumed her existence. She slid down in the seat until her ass hung off the edge and pulled the Knick's cap lower and her hair closer around her face. With her eyes closed, she drifted back to the first day she awoke in this nightmare.

"Ms. Dias? Ms. Dias, can you hear me?" an unfamiliar voice had called out to her. Excruciating pain had throbbed behind Angel's forehead. A vise grip tightened at her temples as she struggled to focus on the person who beckoned her back to reality.

The next time Angel came to, the bright light above her bed blinded her. As her pupils adjusted, she scanned the room, noticing she was in a hospital, but how she got there was a mystery. Feeling around the bed, she found the call button and rang for help.

"Ms. Dias. Glad to have you back with us." The white-haired male stood over the bed, flashing another glaring light into her face. "You've been out for a while."

"How long?" Her parched voice cracked.

The cold stethoscope touched her skin, causing her to jump and pain to shoot through her body. "Hmm. Well, you've been with us for about a month."

Angel blinked and tears rolled down her cheeks. "Month? What happened?"

"You were in a car accident."

Staring blankly at the ceiling, Angel asked, "Where's everyone?"

Why was she in the hospital alone? She expected at least her family or Jackson to be there with her. Her mother and sister should've come up from New Orleans.

"Your sister went home a couple of days ago. She said to call her if anything changes. I'll give her a call."

Angel pushed the button and raised the head of the bed. The pounding in her skull increased as she sat up. She fumbled with the gauze, which may have been the only thing keeping her brain from exploding in her skull. "What's wrong with me?"

"You went through the windshield and got cut up pretty badly." The doctor began to unwind the bandage from her head.

Cool air whispered against her skin when he freed her from the constraints of the bandages.

"I want to see." She stared at the concerned look on the doctor's face.

"I'm not sure if it's such a good idea this soon. You need to gain your strength back."

"I want to see *now!*" Angel's throat burned when she tried to yell.

The doctor picked up the small mirror on the nightstand and handed it to her.

Trembling, Angel peeked at her reflection. When she witnessed the horror of her mangled face, she threw the mirror across the room, smashing it into a thousand pieces.

The sharp cackle that escaped Angel as she thought about the things she'd lost this year startled the guy in the pinstriped suit in the seat next to her. The laughing stopped the tears. Her whole world imploded on the night the drunk driver hit her. She hung her head, biting hard into her lower lip. The pain and the taste of blood were the only things keeping her from expelling the horrific scream trapped in her heart.

"Here."

Mr. Pinstripe handed her a miniature bottle of Smirnoff. "I think you need this more than me."

She stared at him, anchoring herself back into the real world. His warm brown eyes smiled at her, showing mercy. He played two roles. The starkness of his power suit and the lightness of his voice contradicted one another.

"Thanks." Angel trembled as she gratefully took the bottle.

"They should ban them from flying."

"What?"

"Kids. They shouldn't let them fly. They're a pain in the ass."

Angel grinned. "Yeah. That they are."

He leaned back in his seat and crossed his arms. "Are you vacationing or running?"

"Running. Can't you tell?"

"Man troubles or family?"

Angel's troubles traveled in packs. She stifled a cry, her mind once again wandering back over the past year.

She'd spent a total of three months in the hospital after the accident. On her release day, she'd sat on the bed with her bags, waiting for Jackson to pick her up. She curled in the small armchair, gripping her release papers, for two hours. No one ever showed.

The nurse walked in, a sad smile on her face. "Is there someone you want me to call?"

"I've left a couple of messages. He probably got caught up in a meeting." Angel forced a smile. "Can you just call me a cab?"

"We usually don't let people check out without having someone with them."

"It looks as if I'm on my own. Please just call me a cab." A tear fell down Angel's face. The papers she gripped in her hand rattled as she shook.

The cabbie pulled in front of her building. He diverted his eyes from her face when she caught him staring. Angel handed him a twenty and hopped out the back. Her doorman refused to look at her, saying good morning to the ground. In the elevator, her upstairs neighbor and the lady down the hall whispered in the back. Angel pushed the button for her floor again, praying it would make the ride faster.

Inside her apartment, Angel closed the door and slid to the floor. Holding her head in her hands, she allowed the tears to flow. After pulling herself together, Angel glanced around the room. All of Jackson's things were gone. He had moved out while she was in the hospital waiting for him.

Angel dug the vodka out the freezer and downed two Percocets.

Now she turned a tiny bottle over in her hands, wondering where the flight attendant had disappeared to. She could use some ice to go with the gin. Then it hit her. The worst scars were on the right, and this stranger hadn't seen them. She leaned forward, as far as the seat back in front of her would allow, and twisted toward him. "Both man and family troubles. Look at me."

He pursed his lips. "What happened?"

"Car accident."

"Life's a bitch—"

"I'm a bitch, too, or at least I used to be. Falling from Diva status is hard. It's like going from Nordstrom's to the Dollar Store." Her smile pushed at the edge of her scar. She held out her hand. "I'm Angel by the way."

He eyed her. "You look familiar. Were you on T.V. or something?"

"Sometimes. Magazines mostly. I'm surprised anyone recognizes me like this."

He shrugged. "Don't worry. I can tell you used to be beautiful. You said you were running. Wanna tell?"

"I haven't talked about it to anyone. I'm not sure a stranger on a plane is a good place to start."

"If talking to your family or your man had helped, you wouldn't be here with me. Honey, I'm a gay civil rights lawyer—problems and drama are my business. Let's have it." He rattled around in his bag and pulled out two more little bottles, handing one to Angel.

She threw the fiery liquid down her throat. "I used to be a model until I got in the car accident last year. Now, I look like something from a carnival freak show."

He shoved another bottle in her hand. She cracked it open, downed it, and cringed at the heat in her chest.

"No shit! You really did need to run away. Where's your fam?"

"New Orleans. My mom's draining what little money I have left and my sister's busy trying to keep her out of trouble."

Angel's hands trembled, remembering the mess she called a life. Acid churned in the pit of her stomach when she recalled her mother dragging her from one plastic surgeon to the next.

"Sit up straight. Bad enough you look like a monster, I don't need you looking like a slob, too." Angel's mom straightened her suit as they sat in the waiting area.

This one was a replica of the twenty others they had visited, bad wallpaper and uncomfortable chairs. Each time the answer was the same. "No, there's nothing we can do." Why should this time be different?

After the examination and review of her prior surgical records, the doctor crouched behind the massive desk and stared at her with pity in his eyes.

"I'm sorry, Ms. Dias. There's nothing else we can do for you. You have had everything technology can offer. At this point, another surgery will only make things worse."

"What'da you mean? You can't leave her like this. She's a model, not a fucking freak!" Her mother's voice echoed in the large office.

"I'm sorry." The doctor handed Angel the thick file she brought with her. "If there was anything I thought would work, I would try."

"Thank you for your time." Angel stood, pulling her mother up with her.

"We can find someone else," Elise muttered.

Angel guided her by the elbow. "With what, Mother? You've depleted most of my money already. We're out of options."

The next day, when Angel awoke, Elise was gone. She'd tossed Angel aside like a bad pair of Payless shoes and hauled ass back to New Orleans.

After thirteen surgeries, the deep gash still mangled the right side of her face. Angel ran her fingers along the rigid terrain. The scar jetted from her temple to her chin, in twisted ridges like a 3-D topographic map. No more invitations from *Vogue* for her.

Angel turned to her new friend. "Enough about me. What're you going to the island for? R and R?" Angel studied him, noticing his smooth skin and perfectly arched brows.

The corner of his mouth slid up to a sly grin. "Meeting my man. Every couple of months we try to get away and spend some time."

"That's nice. Why isn't he flying with you?"

"We don't travel together. He has other obligations to take care of before he comes."

"Is he one of those workaholic types?"

Turning his head, he murmured to the window, "No, one of those married types."

"Oh...." Another bottle appeared in her hand. She downed it with no trouble.

"Like we said, life's a bitch." The sadness in his eyes negated his smile. "So, Ms. Angel. What finally made you run?"

Angel shivered. She had stopped by the agency trying to find out about the check from her last shoot. As she rounded the top of the stairs, she caught Jackson in the hall leaning over Gisele and pinning her against the wall. They turned to look at her, and the girl giggled. Jackson kissed her on her neck, the same way he used to kiss Angel. She wondered how long this had been going on. Was he seeing her before the accident?

On her way home, Angel stopped for her prescription of Vicadin and a gallon of vodka. She poured a drink and popped two pills. Feeling nostalgic, she waded through the clothes in her closet. Angel slid on her best Dior gown and matching shoes and then pumped up the music.

Angel danced and drank. She awoke to the feeling of something cold and wet against her face. Her head pounded almost as bad as when she awoke from her coma. The room spun. She laid her head back on the smooth, cool object.

The next time she pried her eyes open, the room was dark. She sat on the floor of her bathroom with a half a gallon of vodka between her legs. She must've drunk the other half. And scattered about on the lid was the Vicadin she just picked up from the pharmacy. Resting her head on the cool porcelain of the toilet, she tried to forget the events leading her to hit her bottom.

She crawled off the floor. Steadying herself on the sink then holding on to the wall, she stumbled to the living room. Checking her cell phone, Angel realized she had been on a two-day binge.

Angel chuckled as the scene replayed in her mind. It scared her straight into something just as stupid. "I finally cracked."

"You didn't think to call a shrink?"

"Thought about calling Dr. Drew and see if I could get on *Celebrity Rehab*." Angel gave him a sideways grin and felt the rugged edges of her scar. "I came to my senses and figured out I didn't want a monster plastered all over T.V. Been there, done that. And watching your life fall apart in front of millions of people isn't therapeutic." She shook her head at her own bad joke.

Two more bottles rattled in front of her. "Last round. Then we sleep."

She polished off her share and nestled back into the seat. The cabin of the plane spun slowly in her mind. She regulated her breathing to keep from getting sick. Closing her eyes, she visualized her new life, which closely mirrored her old one, fabulous. She wanted to shed the shards of the last year. Angel missed walking by the newsstands and seeing her face on the covers of *Elle, Vogue,* or *Glamour*. She craved the strong arms of a man wrapping her in safety. Even her mother pretended to love her then. Her heart remained an empty shell of her previous life. Out of options, she stepped into the realm of dark magic, risking her faith, sanity, and life, but nothing could be worse than the hellish nightmare she currently lived.

Beef Jerky Guy coughed and pressed the seat farther back; his putrid smell of sweat and old tobacco made her want to gag. The gin she consumed sat burning in her chest and belly, waiting for Angel to make the wrong move so it could resurface. She molded her body into the hard foam of her seat and clutched her Louis Vuitton tote, stroking the leather bound book within. Her fingers traced the etched gold letters across the front, which read "Laveau Family Heritage." *Who would've thought I was related to the Voodoo Queen?*

Two planes, seven hours of layovers, and six hours in the air later, she arrived in St. Croix, hot, annoyed, drunk, and tired. As Angel deplaned, her demeanor changed. The exquisite beauty of the island robbed her of aggravation. The sun shone like a canary diamond against an aquamarine sky. The warm breeze embraced Angel, enticing her to relax. She waved goodbye to her new confidant. He gave her a nod and slid into his cab.

The driver carried Angel's bags to the car. They rode twenty minutes to the house near Divi Carina Bay. The white Spanish style house appeared through the palm trees with the crystal blue ocean as its backdrop. The circular driveway wound its way around a Grecian style fountain, which always seemed a bit out of place to Angel. Lush vegetation and colorful blooms dotted the landscape, giving it life.

Angel's mother begged for the house as a hideaway from Gran. She only managed to come here twice in the last four years. It proved to be a better conversation piece at her mother's social events than a getaway. Her mother was always more talk than action.

A cool breeze from the open patio doors and palm-leaf shaped ceiling fan in the living room greeted Angel as she entered the house. She admired the white sand and blue waters draped across the backyard beyond the pool. The water could prove a delightful break from the unbearable heat, but Angel needed to unpack first. Kicking off her Prada sandals, she picked up her bags and headed to the bedroom.

The scent of freesia and bougainvillea drifted through the window from the flowerbeds outside. The smell comforted Angel and soothed her nerves. Her stomach flipped as she thought about her impending decision. Playing with magic was stupid and dangerous; playing with dark magic was lethal. She still questioned this method of achieving her objective. Nothing good came of messing with the Devil.

The sun set in magnificent hues of crimson, copper, amber, and sienna. Angel watched the sun hover over the indigo water and contemplated the ramifications of her actions. The beating of her heart was as loud as the crashing of the waves. There was no turning back after it was done, and there had to be a hefty price to pay. She had no idea what the going rate for beauty was these days. It couldn't cost more than her shoe collection.

Vanity was a minor infraction. She was willing to pay her moral dues. Was it worth any price? This question kept her up for the last several nights. She exhausted all her other options. She needed her face back. It was her livelihood. It was her life.

***

The moon shone full in the sky. On the back patio, Angel set the chest of items from her grandmother's attic on the ground. She knelt on the warm slate of the patio, removing each of the family heirlooms from the wooden box. She raked her fingers through her dark, wavy hair and smoothed down the hem of her black Prada slip dress over her knees. With love and reverence, Angel unlatched the strap around the Laveau Family book and opened it to the page with the spell.

She laid the incense to form a triangle and lit a red, rose-scented candle in the middle. Writing the name, Lucifer, on the papyrus paper, she rubbed it with manuka oil. She burned the paper with the ivory candle and mixed the ashes with water. Sprinkling the water and ash mixture around the triangle, Angel began her chant.

"O life beyond life itself,

Come forth as I call out to thee.

Find me through the worlds and come to me.

I call you to appear before me, Dark Father."

The night stood still and a deafening silence clung to the air. She waited and repeated the words again. As her chant dissipated to a faint murmur, a warm breeze stirred and a kiss of flames nipped at Angel's ear.

A heated whisper sang, "How can I be of service?"

The pounding of her heart droned out his words. A tremor quaked in her gut. Her first response was to run. Instead, she remained steadfast in her mission. Her stubbornness was a weakness. She stared at the figure before her in wonder. His beguiling beauty charmed her like a cobra coaxed from a basket by the snake charmer's Pungi. Lucifer's ebony skin glittered as if glazed with diamond dust. His deep blue eyes searched the depths of her soul. She felt the enchantment of his power, a power she vaguely remembered feeling before.

Lucifer's smile dazzled as he spoke. "This must be my lucky day. To what do I owe the pleasure of being in the presence of such beauty?"

"You're mocking me." The hurt in Angel's voice showed her vulnerability.

"No. I never mock. I speak the truth others are unwilling or unable to see. My eyes unveil the truth of you."

"You know why I called you here."

He reached out to touch her, stopping when she cringed and covered her face with her hands. "Of course I know. The question is...are you sure you want me here?"

At this point, I'm not sure of anything. How can the epitome of evil be so beautiful? Focus, Ang. This is not the time to not be on your "A" game.

Chewing the inside of her cheek, she met Lucifer's flaming stare before answering. "I can't say this was my first choice. My options are limited now. I need to know what this is going to cost me."

"Ah. I'm glad you understand my help comes with a cost. How much are you willing to pay for beauty?"

Her hands sweated and the blood rushed to her head, throbbing at her temples.

"I'm not sure. I don't think I can answer without knowing the price."

"I can restore your former beauty. I can do it now if you wish. It will cost you a small price. I've been searching for a special creature to help me bring home some of my wayward souls. I need someone who's cunning, intelligent, and beautiful. Do you think you can bring home my renegades for me?" He circled Angel as he spoke, bringing the fire so close the heat brushed against her like a caress.

Angel backed away, ignoring the sensation of pleasure lapping against her skin. "I wouldn't know how to catch lost souls. I'm sure it's not as easy as you make it sound."

"I'll ensure you get the needed training." Lucifer met her gaze. "I know you'll excel or I wouldn't ask this of you."

Her brows scrunched together in thought. "How long will I have to do this if I agree?"

"Well, you're still young yet. Twenty-two years is an infant in my world. Ten years. After ten years, you can go back to your life and retain your soul. But...if you should die while in service to me, then I keep your soul as payment of your debt. If you try to run from me, then I'll retract our deal and return you to your current state." Lucifer picked at a sharp claw on his right hand.

She straightened her posture and crossed her arms over her chest. "You're asking for a lot. Why should I take it?" Angel studied him as he gave his response.

"You called me. Take it or leave it. I don't care either way. But, I offer you your life back plus more. You'll find the Underworld can offer a multitude of rewards. I offer you two lives for ten years of one miserable life."

Angel relaxed her demeanor, leaned in toward Lucifer, and with a wide-eyed expression whispered, "Two lives. What do you mean?"

Lucifer slid closer and knelt beside her, his eyes twinkling. "There's a whole other world humans ignore. I'll introduce you to that world. I think it's one that'll bring you more excitement and pleasure than you can imagine."

Angel perked up at the thought of something new and exciting. She loathed the mundane. She was tired of normalcy. This was her opportunity. Ten years seemed a small price to pay for everything Lucifer offered. This sounded too good to be true. Shit. Anything had to be better than the life she lived as a monster. *What do I have to lose?*

"Okay. I agree to your terms. Ten years. I'll find your souls, but you'll provide me with the training and all the tools I need to do the job." Once the words escaped her lips, a sharp pain pierced Angel's heart.

Too late to turn back now.

Lucifer's hand caressed the side of Angel's face, tickling the scar. Heat smoldered under his touch. Angel felt her skin rejuvenate as his fingers trailed the lines of the damaged tissue. A shiver slithered down her spine as his lips grazed her cheek. Frozen in fear, she waited for him to move. When he stepped back, she released the breath she held and closed her eyes. She was whole again.

"Your beauty is more stunning than I imagined." Lucifer's smile revealed the jagged teeth of a beast. Angel wondered what lay beneath his beguiling exterior. Was his beauty the truth or a sweet lie hiding the monster he represented?

She shifted nervously, the stone patio rough on her knees. "What's next?"

"There's a club on the South Shore called the Night Haunt. Go there tomorrow night and someone will be waiting for you to begin your training."

"Who should I ask for?"

"They'll know you when you get there. Who could miss such beauty?"

"I guess it starts tomorrow then." Her heart dipped into her stomach, warning her of danger. She pushed it aside. She had what she wanted.

"Good night, my love. Hell awaits me," he whispered and he disappeared into the flames.

The night returned to its peaceful silence. Only the sounds of the rolling waves remained. Angel wiped the moisture from her hands along her thighs. Her toes tingled from sitting on her legs too long. She pushed herself up from the stone patio and ran inside to examine her face.

Once in the bathroom, she gripped the sink, paused, glanced at her reflection, and closed her eyes. Elation and apprehension twisted in a mangled knot inside her belly. Should she attend the meeting tomorrow? If she went, her life would change forever. If she didn't, she would risk losing the beauty she just regained or even worse. Death.

Chapter Two

"You know I hate being around humans." Jacque threw his sword on the cot in his tent. *This must be important since Lucifer came to deliver the orders in person.*

Lucifer brushed the dust from his shirt. "I know. I need the best."

"Laurent's just as good as I am."

"No, he's not, and he's on assignment Topside."

"I like it just where I am. I want to be in the field with my men. I told you my reasons when I left." Tossing his dust-ridden shirt onto the cot, Jacque sat in the small foldout chair by the writing table.

"You let a female drive you away. Get over Isabella. It's time to come home."

"She didn't drive me away. She drove me crazy. It was leave or kill her. I'm sure Lilith wouldn't appreciate me killing her daughter."

Lucifer tilted his head and shrugged. "What's one less female?"

"Yeah, right. Lilith would have both our heads. What's so special about this human?"

"Why do you think she's special?"

The corners of Jacque's lips turned up in a smile. "Ah. Now I see...female."

"I need you to go pick her up tonight."

"Luc, I don't want to deal with the human, especially now I know it's a female. Find someone else."

"You don't have a choice. You'll find her at the Night Haunt." The red glow in Lucifer's eyes intensified.

"Fuck! I'll go pick her up. How will I know her?" Jacque ran his hand through his hair in frustration. Luc wasn't going to give in.

"You'll know. And hands off."

"I told you. I don't do humans. Too many emotions."

"She'll be waiting for you at eleven. Oh. She'll be training with the new recruits."

Jacque rose from the chair, stretching his hands behind his back, feeling the pull of his tight, worn muscles. "Good. I'll drop her off at headquarters."

"You'll be training this class."

"Fuck me. You're killin' me here." Jacque wasn't ready to deal with Bell yet. He still carried the scars from their breakup. Going back to headquarters meant seeing her again.

Lucifer chuckled. "You're just not agreeable tonight. Make sure you have a drink or two when you get to the club to calm down. I don't want you scaring our new friend. Her name's Angelique Dias."

"The supermodel?"

"You know her?"

"What guy doesn't?" Jacque sat on the cot and pulled off his boots, half-smiling at the image of his new charge.

"Remember, you don't do humans." Luc's heat spread through the room.

"Don't worry. Too many headaches. I had enough problems with Bell, and she's a demon. I'm taking a break from females for a while." Jacque rummaged in his duffle bag, pulling out a pair of black jeans and a blue T- shirt. "All right, I gotta get going if you want me to meet your human on time."

Humans were fickle creatures, unable to control their emotions, especially the women. Their emotions put his equilibrium off kilter. He became nauseous thinking about the turmoil their hormones created. Jacque dreaded meeting Lucifer's new project.

***

The cabby honked his horn outside the house. Ten o'clock came fast. Angel hadn't taken this much time to get ready since before the accident. Tonight was her new debut. The cabby let out a whistle as she folded into the backseat of the cab.

"Wat be ya pleasure, miss?" he asked in a smooth island tone.

"To the Night Haunt on South Shore. Please." She rewarded him with a smile for the appreciation he'd shown. The night of her accident was the last time someone whistled at her. The attention made her giddy.

"Dat be a rough place for sucha fine lady. Maybe I take you to a bedda club, no?"

"No. I'm supposed to meet someone there. I'll be fine."

The cabby stole short glances in the rearview mirror throughout the trip. Once they arrived at the club, he jumped out of the cab to open Angel's door. She forgot how nice it was to have someone cater to her. She paid the driver, plus added a handsome tip.

The club resembled an old bayou juke joint. Angel feared she might lose a heel to the battered plank bridge leading to the entrance. She couldn't afford to replace a seven hundred dollar pair of Jimmy Choos, so she carefully maneuvered across the bridge. A wave of heat welcomed her as she opened the door. The tall blond-haired bouncer with a bronze tan filled the doorway with his body. Angel threw him a sultry grin and scanned the background. After paying the cover, she moved to the bar.

It was still early. Only a few people were inside. Angel slid into one of the empty stools at the old teakwood bar. The vantage point from her seat provided her with a full view, including the door. She ordered a White Russian and observed the crowd. It comprised of an eclectic bunch. A handsome couple cuddled in a corner. Two guys chatted each other up at the end of the bar. A few people swayed to the music on the dance floor. Angel noticed she was being checked out as she surveyed the crowd.

The bartender placed her drink on a napkin in front of her. His dark brown complexion and strong jaw line complemented his soft hazel eyes. A tight white tank showed off his muscular build.

"Hallo, lovely. Haven't seen you 'round before?" His slight English accent made him even hotter.

"Never been to this side of the island before." Angel skimmed her finger around the rim of her glass.

"We don't usually get your kind in her often. Who told you about this place?"

"What do you mean 'my kind'?" Her glass hit the bar with a loud clang.

"Human."

"What?" Her confusion generated a chuckle from the tall, dark-haired man behind the bar.

"I guess no one told you about this club. Are you meeting someone? If not, you might want to find another place to party."

She surveyed the room before answering. "I'm meeting someone. I just don't know who." Nervousness made the hair stand on Angel's arms.

The bartender's words faded into the calypso beat of the music. Across the club, a beautiful specimen of a man, even more beautiful than the male models from her past, stood paying the bouncer. His dark olive skin glowed under the pulsating lights. His black hair fell back in curls surrounding his face. He towered a good six inches taller than the bouncer, who must've been at least six feet. The blue T-shirt stretched tight across his massive chest and sturdy shoulders. The hint of a six-pack teased through the thin cotton. Piercing green eyes, the shade of emeralds, searched the room and assessed the surroundings. She caught his attention and he rewarded her with a toothy grin.

He crossed the room with long languid strides. Mr. Tall-Dark-And-Do-Me straddled the seat next to her and ordered a Grey Goose on the rocks. Once the bartender brought his drink, her new friend turned and soaked in every inch of her. Adjusting herself on the stool, she shifted her position to provide him maximum advantage.

"You must be Mademoiselle Dias, no?" He hovered close enough to inhale the scent of her soap.

"I am. And who might you be?" Her heart raced in her chest. In this moment, it was lust, not fear driving her.

"Excuse my manners. Jacque Toussant. I was asked to meet you here." He dipped his head in a slight bow and met her gaze.

Playing with the diamond necklace dangling between her breasts, she leaned into him. "Nice to meet you, Jacque." A strand of her wavy hair fell into her face. She smiled at him and brushed it back into place. She followed his line of sight as he traced the line of her neck and landed on the generous swells testing the elasticity of her red dress, which clung like saran wrap. This dress never failed to catch a man's attention.

"I hope you haven't had any trouble while you waited." He brought his gaze back to her face.

"No. I was having a conversation with this nice gentleman until you arrived." Angel tipped her head toward the bartender.

Jacque glared at him, prompting him to scurry to the other end of the bar.

"I see my uncle didn't tell you about the club. I'm surprised the bartender was the only friend you made. This is a Supe bar. I'm sure the Vamps got a good whiff of you by now."

"You mean all these people aren't *people?*" Angel's question was more to herself than him. "I hope you don't mind me asking. What are you?"

"You already know I'm Lucifer's nephew. I'm a Mutura Demon, a shifter. I'm a commander for the Legions of Hades or Hell, whatever you humans call it."

Angel scanned the room. "How much more shit is out there I don't know about?"

"Too many things to list right now. I know this is overwhelming for you. I promise to tell you all about the Supernaturals as we spend time together. It'll be pertinent to your work."

"What do you mean pertinent to my work? I'm just supposed to collect a few lost souls." Angel arched a brow, waiting for his response.

"I guess Luc left out a few tidbits of info. These 'lost souls' of yours are Supes that avoided their judgment. They were supposed to come to Hell as humans. Somehow they eluded Death by taking on supernatural forms." Jacque shook his head at Angel. "Humans.... You never ask enough questions when dealing with Luc."

Angel fumed in her seat. She pressed her blood-red lips into a thin line. Her body shivered as she swallowed what remained in her glass with one gulp. Squirming in her seat, she rolled the empty glass in her hand. When she shifted on the stool, the slit of her dress exposed her leg to mid-thigh. Angel glanced his way when a low growl escaped Jacque as he admired the view she provided him.

Jacque finished the rest of the Grey Goose in his glass, squelching the fire in his eyes. "If nothing else, this'll be interesting. You'll have to excuse any impropriety. I'm not used to being around humans. I try to stay as far away from your kind as possible."

Thunder clapped outside and she glared at him. "I'm sorry to inconvenience you."

"It's a job. I do as I'm told. We have a lot to get through tonight. I suggest we get started." Jacque cued the bartender, and he poured him another drink. He downed the shot, hanging his head and sinking down into his seat. The look was one Angel understood immediately: exasperation. It was the same look her doctors had when she came for her appointments.

Jacque covered the training regiment with her. She was to attend Supe Warfare Boot Camp for the next six weeks. He lucked out with a class starting the same time Angel needed to be trained. The recruits were in for a treat; he rarely took the time to work with the new recruits anymore. Training began bright and early in the morning. It was time to leave.

"Mademoiselle Dias, is there anything else you would like to know before we leave?" He kept his distance as if he was afraid she might bite.

The thought made Angel giggle.

She turned her attention back to the conversation at hand. "I'm sure more questions will come up. Right now, I'm still trying to digest the info dump you already laid on me. I guess there's no turning back, is there?" Angel propped her elbows on the bar and rested her chin in her palms, examining her reflection in the mirrored shelving behind the bar.

"I'm sorry, *mon chéri*. A deal is a deal. Too late to change your mind." Jacque's voice broke at the end. His face softened as he gazed at her. "I'll go back to your house with you to gather your things. You should contact your family and wrap-up anything you need to handle before we head out tonight."

"Are there many humans in Hades?" Fear caused her pulse to race.

"No. Not at this time. Occasionally, we get someone who messes up a spell and pops in. Or, like you, someone might come to train for a position they gotta fill. The magical energy's too much for any human to stay in the Underworld for too long." Jacque watched her as he spoke. Angel fought to maintain a neutral façade, hiding the fear overtaking her confidence. He smiled at her, slow and deliberate, as if he saw through her disguise.

"Come on. I'll take you home." He stood and helped her from her stool.

The air outside had cooled. It had been a long time since Jacque was Topside. The last time was the 1930's, if he remembered correctly. Although he belonged in the Underworld, Topside had its benefits. He welcomed the differing temperatures. A black sedan waited for them in the parking lot. The driver opened the door as they approached. Jacque helped Angel into the back seat and slid in after her.

The tension throbbed in Jacque's head. Her anxiety flipped in his stomach.

"What made you conjure the devil?" He caught the odor of regret surrounding her.

She diverted her eyes. "Problems."

"No shit. How bad could the problems be to ask the Devil for help?"

"You wouldn't understand."

"Maybe not, but I'm curious. I always wonder what the hell you humans are thinking, messing around with Luc." Jacque slid low in his seat, looking out the own window to resist the urge to stare at her lovely face.

"It's really none of your business. The deal was made, and now I'm here. What brought me here is irrelevant." Her voice rose an octave, warning him to back off.

Fire lit in his already queasy belly. He hated being around humans. They were so inefficient at guarding their emotions. His mother bore the empath gift. He inherited the ability from her bloodline. The frenzy of human emotions always caused him problems. Between experiencing every feeling, the nausea, and headaches, hanging out with top dwellers wasn't Jacque's favorite pastime. Angel would be with him for six weeks. He needed to find a way to block her out.

***

Staring out the car window, she watched the dark waters roll into the shoreline, creating frothy foam against the sand. A maddening silence lingered between her and Jacque. They couldn't get to the house fast enough. Angel sunk into the plush leather of the seat, mauling over the events of the past few days. She could kick herself for being so stupid. *I sold my soul to the Devil for a pretty face. My headstone will read, "Queen of Bad Choices."*

She studied his profile, wondering what training would be like with him in charge. A mixture of panic and intrigue bubbled in the pit of her stomach. Angel pushed the fear aside; she waited too long to be scared. She needed strength to survive this situation. This was something she would have to dig deep inside to find. It's not a quality she depended on very often.

Pulling back her hand, she stopped herself from caressing his strong jaw, which carried a hint of a five o'clock shadow. Other than having issues with humans, he wasn't so bad for a demon. Or was he? Jacque was the only demon she knew. She had no frame of reference to find out if she was correct in her assessment.

He made her so hot beads of sweat developed in the valley of her breasts. Angel knew she should stay away from Jacque. *Temptation is a bitch.* Did all demons pop off the pages of *GQ* magazine? She sank deeper in the seat and wiped her sweaty hands on the sides of her dress. He looked so delicious she could take a bite out of him. As she deliberated the outcomes, she thought better of it.

The list of her problems grew by the minute. Angel didn't need to add sleeping with a demon to that list. She thanked the heavens when they arrived at her house. Jumping from the car as if it was headed for a cliff, she ran into the white bungalow.

Jacque followed her into the place.

"Whose house is this?" Jacque called out.

"Technically, it's mine. I bought it for my mother. What a waste of money. She likes to talk about it more than actually come here," she shouted from the bedroom.

Angel strolled back into the living room, dropping a couple of bags on the floor. Her toes curled from the coolness of the ceramic tile. Her gaze darted from Jacque to the dazzling color below her feet. Approaching him, she watched him with each step. Without her heels, he stood close to a foot taller than her. Unlike many men, he made her feel petite.

"Um...can you help me?" She pointed to the back of her dress.

"Anything for you, *ma chère.*" The green of his eyes deepened a shade darker, highlighted by golden flecks, as they drank her in.

She turned her back to him, revealing the stuck zipper. "I need help with my dress."

"Sure. Come here." He grabbed the thin fabric and pulled her to him. A flash of heat overcame her as his fingers grazed her skin.

"Never mind, I'll do it myself." She tried to run. He caught her by the arm before she could get away.

"I don't mind undressing you," he whispered into her ear as he wrapped his arm around her waist and yanked her into him.

Angel froze with panic, feeling the solid wall of his body against her back. She wasn't sure what he would do. Shit. At this moment, she wasn't sure what *she* would do. He held her close to him for a second. It felt like an eternity. The warmth of his breath tickled the back of her neck. The smell of musk and fire infused around her. Before letting her go, his lips brushed the crook of her shoulder, warm and moist.

Jacque couldn't keep her that close to him without taking her right there on the living room floor. She smelled like vanilla and sex. Her skin glistened in the moonlight and held the texture of a rose petal against his lips.

He released her from him and clenched the top of the zipper. With a slight tug, the dress fell open, exposing creamy brown skin and a butterfly tattoo at the base of her back just above a perfect ass. Turning slowly, she faced him, holding the dress tight against her.

"Thank you," she whispered and backed out of the room. Her eyes reminded him of frightened prey.

It took everything in him not to follow her into the bedroom. He resisted with every ounce of strength within him. Nothing good came from involving himself with a human. His body craved her. Probably due to inactivity. He'd been in the field too long and missed a female's touch. Why couldn't they make demons like her? Angel — such a fitting name. He forced himself to go outside to wait.

As he checked his watch, she appeared in the doorway dressed in a pair of form-fitting jeans and a white tank top with her bags in hand. She relaxed her stance, such a difference from a few minutes ago when she crept out the living room half-dressed.

"I'm ready when you are." Her smile shined as bright as the full moon above.

"Let's not waste time." Jacque relieved Angel of her bags and headed to the car. The driver opened the trunk as they approached.

"Will it take long to get there?"

"The portal to the Underworld is outside the Night Haunt. That's why so many Supes hang there. Don't worry, Hell's not going anywhere." He flinched at the thought of taking her to the Underworld. Studying her, Jacque realized the next six weeks would present a new kind of hell for him.

Chapter Three

"Women...." She heard Jacque muttered as he carried her bags, heading to the field behind the Night Haunt. The waves crashing against the rocks at the edge of the beach were in tune with the feeling in the pit of his stomach. He trudged along as his boot laden feet sank into the sand. Not a great choice for the Caribbean. Once they rounded to the back of the Night Haunt, the rock beach transformed to lush greenery and colorful blooms.

Angel tripped over her own feet as she hurried after him. "Hey, can you slow down a bit?"

"Sorry. The portal's gonna close soon. I don't want to get stuck Topside." He continued his long strides across the field.

She studied Jacque as she scurried behind him. His jeans hung low on his hips and refused to hide the strength of his legs. His thighs made her think of tree trunks wrapped in denim. Angel imagined Jacque's long legs intertwined with hers in blissful union. Tripping, this time on a root, she snapped out of her fantasy.

A hazy fog lingered in the middle of the sand and tall grasses. Jacque murmured a few words in a language she had never heard before, causing an opening to clear in the cloud.

"That's us. Let's get going, babe." Jacque picked up his pace, sliding through the portal before Angel could say anything.

Angel hopped through the circle of energy, expecting to feel different, however nothing changed except the scenery. They stepped through the other side and stood on the banks of a dark, murky river. A warm mist hugged the air around her. Despite the tepid temperature, a shiver ran down her spine. In the distance, a dark form floated toward her and Jacque. Fearful, Angel ducked behind Jacque for protection, burrowing deeper against his back as the hooded figure moored the boat toward the shore.

"Charon, old friend, what's doing?" Jacque held up a hand to his silent companion standing on the boat. He loaded her bags in the front by the shadowy figure. Afterward, he hopped in and turned to help Angel.

Eyes wide, she reached for Jacque's outstretched hand. He sat in the back of the small gondola, patting the bench in front of him. She accepted her cue and situated herself between his legs. His body surrounded hers, making the boat feel small. The bulk of his mass brought her a sense of safety. Charon pushed the boat along the water toward the shore on the opposite side of the river. The black water rippled with each movement of his stick.

As they approached, bright flames danced on the branches of the trees in the black forest. They stood like charred guardians, dead — permanently consumed by the fire. She leaned back into Jacque and gasped at the sight. His arms circled her, containing the tremor tearing through her body. Ingesting the visions of Hell, she covered her face with her shaking hands as tears streamed down her cheeks. *I made a huge mistake.*

As the boat drifted onto land, Charon remained at the bow. Jacque leaped over the side, grabbing the bags out the boat. He then picked Angel up from her seat, placing her on dry land. She clutched his arm, refusing to let go. As he guided her away from the boat, her legs threatened to fail her. She glanced over her shoulder and contemplated turning back. Angel swallowed hard, leaned in closer to Jacque, and pressed on, sealing her fate.

A chariot waited for them at the top of the embankment. He climbed into the massive black carriage embellished in gold and pulled by two pitch-black steeds. He lifted her to him.

"Hold on tight. It can be a bumpy ride. I should've brought something more comfortable," Jacque mumbled to the ground.

"It's okay. I'll manage." She breathed in deeply as she locked her arms around his waist. Cracking the reins, they took off into the night.

***

Looming stonewalls appeared in front of them. Two metal gates arched unwelcoming against the orange-grey of the sky. Rooftops peeked out along the top of the stone barrier. Jacque came to a halt in front of the overbearing gates, motioning to the guards in the tower. The metal creaked as the doors opened and provided them access the Kingdom of Hades.

Angel sucked in a small breath and released it. The smell of sulfur burned in the air. Her arms circled closer around his waist as they rode the dirt path to the dark castle in the horizon. The dead, tattered and torn, stalked the streets. Some labored the chains of their misused lives. Others sat in the street gutters, praying too late for undeserved redemption. Tears wet his shirt as she buried her face into his back.

"Are you okay?" He glanced at her over his shoulder.

Her fingers dug into his side. "I don't know."

"It's not as bad as it looks."

With her face still buried in his shirt, she muttered, "You're probably right, but I don't belong here." She tightened her grip on him.

His large hands covered hers, minimizing the trembling. "I agree with you. Unfortunately, I can't take you home."

"Will you protect me?"

Jacque pulled her closer into him. "Protection isn't my area of expertise." He held her hand to still the shaking. "My job is to teach you to protect yourself."

"Now you're outside of my expertise." His muscles were hard and tense against her cheek.

"Maybe we can work on that while you're here." He cracked the reins, guiding the horses toward the castle.

Angel gave him a squeeze. "Thanks...."

"Don't thank me, yet. Let's see how you feel once training starts."

The chariot entered the gated courtyard and stopped in front of the formal entry. He tried to turn around, but Angel refused to let go. As she unwrapped her arms from his waist, he stepped away from her. He spun to face her and leaned against the chariot, keeping distance between them. Jacque peered into the depths of her eyes and swept a wayward strand of hair out of her face. She graced him with a half-smile, letting him pass by her. Once on the ground, he took her hand to help her from the chariot. Angel followed close behind him as Jacque strutted into the castle with a bag under each arm.

Gargoyles guarded the grand entrance. The interior contradicted the exterior view of Hades. The castle boasted an opulent grandeur. Marble columns littered the entry foyer and brocade draperies hung from floor to ceiling. The clicking of his heels echoed as he stomped through the hall. Angel clung to him, taking in every inch of scenery.

A petite female rounded the corner down the hall. When he recognized her, he dropped his head, hoping not to be seen. He wished he could turn and run the other way. Sadly, it was too late. She saw him.

A bright and dangerous smile crawled across Isabella's face. "Long time no see, Jacque."

"It's been a while. I see you're still as lovely as ever." He forgot how good Bell was at making men bend to her will. Her games, which had ripped his heart apart, never strayed too far from his memory.

"You should stop by after you put away your little toy." She sneered in Angel's direction.

The women glared at each other, ready to pounce. Angel's chocolate eyes challenged Bell. The scene was comical. He wasn't even sure if either of the women wanted him. However, each refused to back down. Competition brought out the worst in females.

"Angel. This is Isabella LaCoste, Lilith's daughter. Bell teaches Demonology at the academy."

"You make it sound so impersonal. He forgot to mention we've been dating for the last half-century." She shifted her eyes from him to scrutinize Angel. "I guess you're Lucifer's new plaything, right?"

Angel's eyes fired daggers. "I'm no one's plaything."

"Whatever. I guess I'll be seeing you around." Bell flipped her long blonde hair behind her shoulder and snorted.

"I'm sure you will," Angel retorted with a smirk, hesitating before saying more. She stepped a little closer to Jacque and hid behind him.

Alarmed, he took a step forward when Angel's breast rubbed against his arm.

Her reaction surprised him. She had more spunk than he gave her credit for, but messing with Bell was a mistake. Luckily, Angel came to her senses before it went any further. Bell played to win at all costs. Competition made her irrational. The last thing he needed was to be caught in the middle of a catfight.

"Let's go." Jacque caught Angel by the elbow. "I'll show you to your room. Bell...you can retract the claws." Pushing past Bell, he started down the hall.

***

Angel was pissed she allowed Isabella get to her. She didn't even know why she let the woman ensnare her into this frenzy. Jacque wasn't her man. She had no right to be jealous. Although it was crazy, she couldn't bring herself to stop fuming over Isabella.

Jacque picked up his pace. She had to half-run to keep up with him. At the top of a long winding staircase, they turned right down a narrow hall. After walking past three rooms on the left, he came to a halt and pushed open the wooden door.

Peeking into the room, she saw a massive cherry canopy bed with plum velvet draperies hanging from the rod at the top. The same plum fabric covered the window gathered back by gold cording. The old wood floor was covered with an antique oriental rug. In the corner of the room, a shadowy figure lounged in the armchair. Her heart sank when she realized who waited for her.

"I'm glad to see you made it safely, *my* Angel. I hope Jacque treated you well on your journey here." Lucifer's ebony skin sparkled in the darkness.

Her chest tightened and her eyes watered. "He took good care of me, unlike you who left out a bunch of information the last time we talked."

His black eyes danced with the flames from the fireplace. "I apologize. Some things just aren't relevant to me. If not asked, I tend to overlook the simple things humans find important."

"Excuse me. Is there anything else you need from me?" Jacque interrupted.

"No. You may leave."

Jacque dropped the bags by the four-poster bed. "I'll see you in the morning. Breakfast is in three hours."

The weight of the day wrapped around her shoulders, strangling the fight out of her. She needed sleep. Closing her eyes, she wondered what training entailed, expecting it to be grueling. Isabella definitely wasn't going to roll out the welcome mat for her.

"Isabella is less frightening than her bark," the Devil guffawed.

With her hands on her hips, Angel glared at Lucifer. "Now you're playing in my head?" The Devil rooting around in her mind was the last thing she needed right now. Her thoughts and emotions bubbled in a cauldron of confusion, especially her thoughts about Jacque. She didn't want to give Lucifer anything else to use against her.

Lucifer waved a hand as if to dismiss her comment. "It's not anything I do consciously. Thoughts just come to me."

"I'm tired. Is there anything else you need from me?"

"Of course...I'll take my leave. You need rest." Lucifer brushed the backs of his fingers across her cheek, sending a shudder down Angel's spine.

Before another word escaped, she was alone in the large room. Feeling trapped in a crazed nightmare, she longed for her grandmother's embrace and advice. Gran would've known how to get out of this mess. Stripping her clothes off and throwing on a T-shirt, she pulled the gold and black duvet down and plunged into the welcoming comfort of the bed. Weariness drew her into the dark abyss of sleep.

***

Loud banging drew Angel from a deep sleep. The force of the pounding vibrated the glass in the windows. She jumped from the bed, running to stop the ruckus before they woke the whole castle.

Still groggy, she swung open the door. *"What!"*

Jacque's expression jogged her out of her fog. "You're late. Get dressed. You need to be out in the courtyard in ten minutes."

She pushed her hair out of her face and leaned on the door jam. "Okay...fine. I'll be down in ten. Should I wear anything in particular?"

"Just a little more than what you have on now 'cause it'll be distracting to the others if you don't." Jacque turned and stomped away before she could answer.

As she steadied herself against the doorframe, she looked down at her outfit. She answered the door in a T-shirt and purple lace panties, her usual sleepwear. *Shit!* She slammed the door and snatched her travel bag off the floor. Grabbing a pair of jeans, her Saints jersey, and cosmetic bag, she headed for the bathroom.

***

Jacque's gaze followed her as she stepped out the front door. She blushed when she met his stare. Pushing through the crowd, she made her way to him. A tinge of pain pricked Jacque's heart as he watched the reaction of the guys she passed. Females weren't the only ones with a problem with competition. Another reason to stay away from her. The girl had trouble written all over her.

***

Angel's day slid further downhill when Isabella entered the room. Isabella strutted in with an air of confidence reserved for royalty. Angel met her glare as she sidled toward her.

"Glad to see you made it this morning. I was concerned when I didn't see you at breakfast." Isabella leaned against the desk across from her.

Angel's lips turned up in a smile. "I'm sure you were worried sick. It's okay, Jacque came and found me."

"Look, human... you don't want to play this game with me. He belongs to me. Always has, always will."

"No one wants your man. I'm here to train and afterward, I'm gonna go back home. But understand this...if I wanted him, I could have him."

"Jacque would never stoop so low as to sleep with a human. Even if he thought about it, he'd come to his senses when he realizes the consequences. You could never have him, no matter what you look like."

"We'll see," Angel mumbled as Isabella sauntered to the front of the room.

Isabella addressed the class. "Morning. I'm Captain LaCoste. We'll be together for the next few weeks learning Demonology. By the time you leave here, you should understand the weaknesses and strengths for most of the creatures in the Underworld and Topside."

Angel's head spun with all the information of demons and other creatures she thought only lived on the pages of books or on movie screens until now. Two and a half hours later Jacque's six-foot-five, muscle-bound body filled the doorframe. His black wife-beater and camouflaged cargo pants matched everyone else's. She was the only one without a uniform. He gathered and marched them outside to an obstacle course. Angel hated heights and several of the contraptions hung high above the ground.

Her heart raced inside her chest as Jacque's voice faded out of her head. Sweat covered her palms. The flip-flop of her stomach made her thankful she was too late for breakfast. She stared at the enormous tower in front of her. The class began climbing up the stairs one-by-one. Only after a couple steps, Angle froze as fear struck. The demon behind her persuaded her up the ladder with a small shove. Not wanting to back down, she inhaled a deep breath and continued. Her legs shook as she clutched each rung on the ladder. Keeping her eyes fixed above her, she inched her way to the top. When she reached the platform, she clawed her way to safety.

A hawk attacked the first cadet on the hand bridge. As she spun around to leave, the others caught her and pushed Angel to the front when it was her time to maneuver the course. She swallowed hard and grabbed the rope over her head, balancing her foot on the one below.

Angel gripped the rope so tight, the color faded from her hands, leaving them a pasty shade of white. She slid one foot in front of the other, refusing to look down. Trembling in fear and dreading the unexpected, she scooted in slow motion across the braided cords. She stopped when she began to sway with the wind. Tears stung her eyes and the braided hemp slipped in her sweaty hands. The squawk of the brown and tan creature approached above her head, forcing her to take action. She inched slowly, trying to make it to the other side. Her hands burned and the skin chaffed underneath as they slid over the cord.

When the hawk swooped millimeters from her head, she released the rope to swat at the bird. She fell unobstructed toward the ground. Nothing separated her from the hard compacted red dirt below. Her screams echoed through the air. Shutting her eyes, she braced for the impact. Instead of the crushing pain of hitting the ground, strong arms scooped her from the air and held her close.

Jacque stood still as Angel clung to him, burrowing into his chest and listening to his heart beat as fast as hers. He flew so fast she didn't even see him until she was cradled in his arms. She couldn't believe he caught her. She watched him allow a dozen other cadets hit the dirt. She wanted him to sweep her away, hold her close and take her to the safety of her room. When she lifted her head from the solid wall of his chest, she realized all eyes were watching them. Instead of sweeping her away, Jacque dropped her on the ground.

"This is why humans shouldn't be a part of training!" he spat. "Get back on the tower and do it again," Jacque demanded, leaving her to stare blankly after him.

Her body cried out for help. She ached all over from a combination of bumps and bruises earned throughout the day. Jacque pushed her harder and harder as the day continued. After shoveling dinner down her throat, she climbed the long stairway to her bedroom. Soaking in the tub, she closed her eyes dreading the punishment waiting for her the next day.

Chapter Four

The growls and snarls inched closer. Angel's feet pounded the dirt, kicking up red dust all around her. The barren trees provided little sanctuary. Her heart and mind raced as she tried to think of her next move. The skies darkened above, thunder rumbled through the thick clouds, and the air smelled of dampness.

How long had she been running? It seemed hours. Other than Noel, the other cadets were long gone ahead of her. Being human sucked when it came to supernatural warfare, but she refused to give up. Every day the class waited, watched, wondering when she was going to quit. Two of the others had already dropped out, and they were demons.

Noel passed Angel on the left, ducking through the low branches of the charred trees, cackling as he passed. Angel picked up her speed, her calves cramping and an ache developing in her side. She wanted to stop. Stopping meant quitting. Quitting was not an option. The hellish howls closed in on her.

Angel glanced over her shoulder and caught sight of one of the ugly beasts. Its long, rounded snout protruded from an enlarged head. Red eyes peered through the burnt trees, scanning the landscape. A ridge of ivory spikes ran down the monster's back extending from each vertebra. The dog-like fiend pounded through the forest on powerful, muscular legs, which carried its compact body. Outrunning them wasn't going to work. She had to come up with another plan. Surveying the terrain in front of her, the only place to go was up. The trees disappeared into the grey clouds. If she could climb high enough, maybe she could wait them out. Or maybe they would go find another victim.

She lunged for the closest branch, leveraged her foot on the tree trunk, and boosted herself off the ground. It took all her strength to hoist her weight into the tree. As she reached for the second branch, three hounds pounced on the trunk, clawing at her dangling foot. The dark-haired one's razor sharp teeth nipped Angel's ankle. Stretching for the next limb, she stared down just in time to see the dagger like claws of the reddish colored beast rip into her calf.

Scurrying up the tree, she climbed higher until she was out of reach of the animals. Angel perched on one of the higher limbs, praying it could hold her weight. She clung to the trunk and observed the creatures clawing the burnt bark off the tree. Slowly, deliberately, a hound dug its sharp claws into the wood, using them like spikes, and began to maneuver its way to her.

Tremors quivered through Angel's body, almost causing her to lose her grip and fall. Thunder clapped and lightning flashed. Ominous clouds gathered overhead, growing darker as the hound drew nearer. The animal swiped at Angel's bleeding leg, barely missing as she jerked it onto the branch she sat on. Electricity hummed in the air. Angel felt the energy gathering about her, a strange, eerie sensation floating on top of her skin.

The hound's red eyes glowed as it stretched toward Angel, drooling from its mouth and snarling. Angel stood on the limb, grabbing for the one above her. As she pulled on the branch, it snapped in her hand. She wrapped her arms around the trunk to keep from falling. The beast snagged her ankle, jerking its head, trying to yank her from her perch. Lightning flashed through the sky, hitting its target — Angel.

Angel closed her eyes as the pain she expected never came. Her body absorbed the energy and channeled it to the beast attached to her ankle. The smell of burning fur wafted to Angel's nostrils. The hound fell to the ground with a thud. The two other monsters sniffed its cohort and growled up at her. Angel redirected the remaining energy to the creatures below with deadly accuracy.

***

Hidden behind a tree, Jacque watched, impressed and amazed. Angel had more power than he imagined. It was clear why she was so important to Lucifer. There were very few people with the power to control the elements. She needed to learn to deal with her gifts better.

The sound of a branch breaking caused Jacque to focus back on Angel. The limb she sat on snapped in two and she plummeted to the ground, trying desperately to grab hold of anything to break her fall. The high pitch of Angel's screams ripped at Jacque's reason. Her body bounced off the tree trunk and crashed through the dark branches. Again, he raced to her rescue. Before Jacque could reach the tree, Angel's fragile body hit the ground.

He kneeled beside her and brushed the hair out her face.

"Hey. You took quite a spill," Jacque murmured.

Angel stared up at him and smiled. "Yeah. But I showed those hellhounds who's boss." She chuckled, grimacing as she held her ribs.

"Yep. You showed them. Doubt they'll mess with you again." He examined Angel, wondering if he should move her.

"Did I pass the test?" A tear rolled down her face when she tried to sit up.

He held her hand. "Look. I'm gonna pick you up, and it's gonna hurt. I'm sorry. I gotta get you back to camp and get you fixed up."

She bit down into her lip, waiting for his next move. "Okay."

"You let me know if anything hurts too bad." He slid his arms under her back and legs, lifting her gently.

She was light as a cloud in his arms, her head rested against his shoulder. As he made his way through the forest, she moaned whenever he shifted her in his arms. Jacque cringed, knowing he caused her pain.

"Sorry," he whispered in her hair.

Her hand caressed his neck. "I'm fine."

The warmth of her touch spread a tingling sensation to the back of Jacque's neck.

The campsite lay ahead. Jacque hurried through the brush. The other cadets waited, turning their attention to them as they entered the open area. He laid Angel on the back of the wagon with the equipment. "Bring me some Vamp Juice," he barked.

Everyone scattered, gathering items. The tall dark-haired cadet brought the Vamp Juice, and Noel handed Jacque the medical bag. Jacque sat on the back of the wagon and propped Angel's head in his lap.

Cracking open the bottle, he held it to her mouth. "You got to drink. Hey, let me see those big brown eyes."

She groaned and her eyes fluttered opened.

"Hi there." He smiled down at her. "Drink."

She drank the juice, choking on the thick liquid. Jacque cradled Angel in his lap, helping her with the juice. Her body relaxed and her breathing steadied as her pain subsided. He fought the urge to kiss her and turned to the others.

"What're y'all standing around here for? Pack up the equipment and let's get ready to head back." Jacque's voice boomed.

He prepared a pallet in the wagon for Angel to lay on for the ride back to the city. Jacque hated the bumpy dirt roads. A point for living Topside, at least most of the roads were paved. Angel hadn't fully healed. She took longer to regenerate since she was human. After ensuring Angel's comfort, he slid into the driver's seat and took the reins from the wide-eyed cadet.

"I got this." Jacque nudged the kid. The fair-haired boy hopped down, his eyes questioning. Jacque looked forward, not rewarding him with an answer.

The wagon bumped and trudged up the road. Jacque released a sigh of relief when the city gates appeared ahead. Angel slept soundly in the back. Her soft moans brought Jacque comfort during the journey. It told him she was still breathing and alive. The fall was rough, even for a demon. She was a fighter. She survived. Her agony twisted in knots inside of him, drawing him closer to her, making him want to take care of her. He ignored the feelings, writing them off as sympathy.

Jacque halted the horses at the front entrance, went to the back of the wagon, and lifted Angel out the bed. He pushed through the cadets on the steps, carrying Angel into the castle and up the stairs. He kicked open the door to her room, went to her bed, and laid her against the plush pillows. She smiled briefly. He opened another bottle of Vamp Juice and held it to her mouth. She drank, the color returning to her cheeks the more she consumed.

"You're looking better." Jacque took a seat on the edge of the bed.

She smiled as she pushed the hair out of her face. "I'm feeling much better. Stupid tree kicked my ass. To top it off, the ground jumped in to help."

Jacque was amazed she could joke about her trauma.

"I guess I failed the test." She took the bottle from Jacque's hand and downed the remaining liquid.

"What'd you mean? You killed three hellhounds and survived a sixty-foot fall, hitting every branch on the tree as you fell to the ground. You more than passed the test." He gazed into her dark brown eyes. To counter the urge to touch her face, he took the empty bottle from her and stood. "You need to get some rest. I'll have someone send you up some food later."

As he turned to leave, she grabbed his hand. "Thanks. You always seem to be around when I need you."

Jacque tightened his grip on her hand, enjoying her touch. "It's nothing. You can take pretty good care of yourself, especially with the ability to harness lightning."

"What's up with that? Did I cause it to happen?" She pushed off the pillows, lay back down, and grimaced, holding her side.

He realized he still had her hand and let go. "You didn't know you had active powers?"

"No." A mixture of fear and confusion filled her features.

"I'm sure Luc knew when he made the deal with you. There's not many Elementals around. It's a valuable power to possess."

Angel's fingers brushed the back of his hand, sending a tingle up his arm. "Interesting. Can someone help me figure out how to use it?"

"There's only one Elemental I know of. I'll see if Marie is around and can help." Jacque crossed the room, needing to put distance between them.

Angel sunk into the pillows and closed her eyes. "Thanks again," she replied in a hushed tone.

Jacque slipped out the door, closing it softly behind him.

***

Angel awoke refreshed and healed. The only reminder of her terrible fall was fading bruises all over her body. The marks of the hound's teeth also vanished. As she studied her face in the mirror, she smiled, proud of her accomplishments. She survived three weeks of training. Halfway done and she hadn't quit or gotten kicked out.

More of the odd occurrences during her childhood and as she became a woman began to make more sense to Angel. She always thought it strange the weather always seemed to match her mood. Never in her life would she have thought it was because she controlled it. Angel found several books in the library about the elemental powers. These gifts were passed through generations of witches, warlocks, and voodoo priests and priestesses. Angel inherited the powers from the Laveau lineage.

Jacque tried to contact her great-great-great-grandmother, Marie Laveau. She was the only other Elemental he knew. Marie wasn't expected for another week or two. Angel was anxious to meet Marie and learn more about her powers.

Once dressed, Angel went down for breakfast. An odd silence hung in the air. The other cadets stared at her as she walked to her table. Noel dropped his tray in front of her and took the seat across from Angel.

"Glad you're okay." He shoveled a spoonful of oatmeal into his mouth. Angel glanced up from her tray and narrowed her eyes. "Thanks."

"I see Commander Toussant came to your rescue again," he snorted.

"Yeah. He's handy that way." Angel dug her spoon into her grapefruit.

"He's never around to carry me or catch me when I fall."

She stabbed the spoon into the fruit again. "Maybe you should speak to him about it."

"I wonder if it's because you're a female or because you're human. Maybe, it's both." Noel grinned, showing jagged, yellowing teeth.

The sound of Noel's spoon scraping the bottom of the bowl sent shivers through her. "Like I said. Take it up with Jacque."

"Oh...you're on first name basis now. How close are y'all?"

"Go fuck off, Noel." Angel stood, picking up her tray, and left for formation.

As she waited in the courtyard, Angel wondered if everyone else thought the same as Noel. She decided she didn't care. Her time was short time here. She would never have to see these people again.

Jacque walked past her, not acknowledging her existence. A lump formed in her throat; swallowing hard she pushed back the tears. After yesterday, she expected more from him — her mistake. She thought they made a connection, even hoped he might care for her. She realized now Jacque was doing his job and nothing more. She was reading too much into his actions.

He called cadets into formation and marched them to class.

***

It pained Jacque to ignore Angel. The sadness in her expression stabbed at his heart, but he had to regain control over the cadets. It wasn't going to happen without him shutting her out. Not only did he need to regain control over the troops, he needed to rein in his emotions. This girl was under his skin, and he needed to purge her out of his system.

The cadets filed into the classroom. The scent of Angel's apricot and vanilla perfume teased him as she passed. Jacque inhaled the aroma, trying to keep her with him. She took a seat in the back of the room, her brown eyes filled with indifference. When he flashed a smile, she looked out the window. Shaking his head, Jacque snickered to himself. He was failing miserably at getting her from under his skin.

"Whatcha doing?" Bell tugged on the flap of his back pocket.

Shifting his eyes down to the petite blonde, he winked at her. "Nothing. Waiting on you."

Bell's high-pitched soprano echoed through the empty hall. "Hmm. I'm not sure if I believe you."

Jacque snorted. Bell was vain enough to believe his comment, even if he never said it. "You make sure to have a good day, Bell."

"Maybe, I'll see you later, and you can make it a good night." Her eyes traveled up and down the length of him as she backed into the classroom.

"I'll see you later." He winked at Bell, catching a glimpse of Angel in his peripheral. He turned away and ignored her haunting stare.

He had to push her away. They were no good for each other. Jacque walked down the empty hall, shutting down his emotions, severing his connection to Angel.

Chapter Five

Angel bounded down the stairs. She was in the best shape she'd ever been. Four weeks gone and only two more to go. This past week she focused on building her strength and practicing her newfound power. She was happy with her progress. Her only disappointment was Jacque's aloofness. Angel stopped and cringed at the bottom of the steps when Noel stepped out of the cafeteria.

He flashed her a crooked smile. "Hey, Dias. How's it hanging?"

"Luckily nothing's hanging today. It's still early though." She already suffered two cracked ribs and an assortment of other injuries the last few weeks. Thank God for the Vamp Juice—a mixture of V8 and vampire blood. It helped her bounce back. Taken in higher doses, it also provided more strength.

"You're getting pretty scrappy. I didn't know humans had it in them, much less a female."

"I'll take you down any time. Just bring it." Angel's nails dug into her hand.

"I'd hate to jack up your pretty little face. It would ruin my fantasies." Noel's tongue darted along his bottom lip.

"Fuck you!"

"Stop by any time. I'd be happy to oblige."

She rolled her eyes and shook her head. "Two more weeks in this Godforsaken place. I'm so glad this shit is almost over. I'm ready to be done with your dumb ass."

"We'll all miss you. It's been a long time since Hades has seen such a prime piece of ass. You should let me tap that before you leave," Noel mocked, raising a hand to slap Angel's ass. He froze in mid-swing when she glared at him.

"Fuck you, asshole. I wouldn't let you touch me if you paid for it." Today, she wished she could switch out the wooden practice sword for the real thing.

"I bet Jacque could hit it for free."

"I'll see you in the ring. Fucking prick."

***

Jacque observed Angel as she went through the breakfast line. The impact of her smile knocked him over like a blow from Thor's hammer. She had surprised him these past few weeks. He hadn't expected her to last this long. He already lost two of the regular recruits and expected another to drop out in the next couple of days.

Angel took a beating and kept on going. No one would've guessed an ex-supermodel, who showed up to training in her pink sweat pants with "Juicy" written across her ass, could survive the abuse. Something drove her to keep going, although Jacque had no clue to what it was.

He swiped an apple from the bowl of fruit on the salad bar and started in her direction. He flipped a chair backward and straddled the seat. Winking at her, he bit into the apple.

"Morning, Jacque." She smiled as she glanced back at her plate.

"Good morning, Ms. Angel. Ready for another day of combat?" Her lips twitched into a grin when he mentioned battle.

She reached over, wiping the apple's juice dribbling down his chin. "Yeah. It should be good. I plan to whip Noel's ass today." She crossed her arms across her chest and curled her lips back slightly to bite her bottom lip.

"I'd like to see that, since he has you by a good hundred pounds. A Level Three demon is still stronger than a human, especially a female."

Angel furrowed her brows and pouted. "I don't care. I'm gonna bring him down today. And what's with y'all and the whole female thing? It's becoming offensive. I might have to file discrimination charges against you."

Jacque avoided the urge to play with a strand of her hair. "Sorry. I just speak the truth as I see it."

"We'll see today, won't we?" She stood with her empty tray.

He took the tray from her and proceeded toward the exit. She strolled beside him, making small talk. They chatted about the various combat moves she should use. Jacque enjoyed Angel's company; she was easy to talk to. After getting to know her, he was even more confused about why she made the pact with Luc.

As they rounded the corner, a laugh crackled through the hall. Jacque caught Angel's arm and guided her toward the door. Bell leaned against the wall, talking to a large man with red hair. He had on dark brown fatigues, a red sash with gold stars, and a red beret. He was one of Jacque's soldiers home on leave. Bell twirled away from the guy when she caught a glimpse of him and Angel. Blowing her suitor a kiss, she headed toward them.

"You two look chipper this morning," Bell spat.

"Good morning to you, too, Isabella." Angel rolled her eyes.

"I see you have a new plaything," Jacque teased.

"If my old one would act right, I wouldn't need to find a new one. Until then, I have to keep myself occupied." Bell licked her lips as she stared into his face, ignoring Angel.

"Excuse me. I'll leave you two to your lovers' quarrel." Angel pushed past Bell and left out the front door.

Jacque glared at Bell with contempt.

"Do you always have to be a bitch?" He placed a hand on either side of her, trapping her against the wall.

Her fingers played with the buttons on his shirt. "I don't know what you're talking about."

"Bell, you and I are over. And we're not getting back together. We're like poison to each other." Aggravation ground like glass in his voice.

"I've changed. I know what I want now and you're it." She lowered her voice and her eyes fell to the floor. Jacque almost felt sorry for her, but remembered it was the act she pulled on him so many times before.

"Why now? Because you think someone else wants me? Afraid of a little competition?"

She met his gaze. "I don't compete with humans. And if I remember correctly, you don't do them. Or have you changed your mind?"

"No, nothing's changed. I'm just tired of this thing between you and Angel. Cut it out."

"Look. I'm me. This is what you get. You never had a problem with me in the past. I'm not changing because your human is sensitive." Bell traced a finger down his chest.

"This is why we broke up. You exhaust me."

"I also exhausted you in other ways. Maybe, I can help make your time more enjoyable while you're here." She ran a hand across his stomach muscles. "Remember how good we were together?"

"We're done. Let it go." He released Bell and stormed out to the courtyard to call the cadets into order.

***

Angel pushed the food around in her plate. She'd worked hard today, although she lost her appetite. She spotted Jacque heading her way with a tray filled with food. She had become fond of him over the last few weeks. His wit and humor were unexpected. He brightened her day when all she wanted to do was cry. And who could ignore his amazing physique?

She glanced up at him when he reached the table.

"Mind company?" Jacque gestured to the bench opposite her.

"For you, I'm always available." She flirted. It was a natural reflex when she was in the presence of a sexy man.

He set the tray down and took a seat. "You did great today. I'm sure Noel is going to be pissed for a while." His eyes twinkled with mischief.

"Aw. He'll get over it. He shouldn't talk so much shit." She smiled, remembering the punch to larynx that caught Noel off guard.

"Ms. Dias, training is almost over. I have to admit, you surprised me. I really didn't think you'd make it," Jacque said in between chews.

"To tell you the truth, I didn't think I was going to make it either. This is the first time I've ever did anything like this. The catwalk isn't quite what I consider dangerous. It felt great to kick that asshole in the balls and watch him fall to the ground." Angel beamed with pride.

"I can't believe you used such a low blow."

She licked the pudding from the back of her spoon and winked. "All's fair in love and hand-to-hand combat. I'm just a female. I have to use everything I got to win."

Jacque watched her tongue caress the spoon and wished he could switch places. He realized he was staring and snapped out of his fixation. Her every move screamed "Sex me!"

"What do you have planned for the night? No early morning wake up tomorrow." Jacque moved his eyes to the other side of the room and regulated his breathing.

"I don't know. It's not like y'all have cable down here. I didn't get much notice to pack so I didn't bring any books. Anyway, it's not like I had time for anything other than training before tonight. I've been so exhausted. I eat, shower, and go straight to bed." She scrunched her nose as she scraped the bottom of the pudding cup.

"I have some books in my room. You're welcome to come by and take a look to see if there's anything interesting." *This is a bad idea,* Jacque thought after the words came out his mouth.

"Oh? Great. Let me take a shower and I'll come by. See you in about thirty minutes?" She studied his face, waiting for his answer.

Jacque shrugged. "I'll see you then."

Picking up her tray, Angel said goodbye. Jacque stared after her as she left the cafeteria. He shouldn't have invited her to his room. He promised himself he wouldn't get involved with a human. His family had enough problems with Bell, and bringing home a human might kill his mother. Or his mother might kill them; it was a tossup. Not many people met his mother's standards. Anyway, humans complicated things with their need for commitments and relationships.

He told himself to catch her and tell her he changed his mind. Why? It was just a book. Reneging on the invite would be silly, but being alone with her worried him. They hadn't been alone since the first day he met her. The desire and passion she ignited in him still tormented and haunted him in his dreams. He longed to caress her soft, bronze skin. Every time he rescued her made him feel like the man he craved to be, a protector. He needed to find a way to block her out tonight. No longer hungry, he headed to his room.

***

Wandering up to her bedroom, Angel contemplated Jacque's invitation. His motives might have been innocent. Angel, on the other hand, had other plans. It had been almost two years since she felt man's touch. She missed the warmth of someone in her bed. Her body throbbed for Jacque every time he was near. He was a perfect solution to her dry spell. She was leaving in two weeks and would never see him again. It wasn't anonymous sex, but close enough.

After showering, she slipped on a royal blue tank-top jersey dress. It highlighted all her attributes. She slid on her DKNY flip-flops and checked her make-up in the mirror. Her hair trailed down her back, wavy and wild. Angel meant to entice him with her charms. She suspected Jacque had the same intentions. If not, she planned to change his mind.

She snuck down the hall, hoping not to run into anyone. A litany of thoughts ran through her mind. She was rusty. It had been too long since she was with a man and technically Jacque wasn't even a man. She wondered if they were even sexually compatible. She was observant enough to know he had the necessary equipment. And from their first night together, he was definitely interested.

Angel rapped on the dense oak door. No one answered so she knocked a little harder. Leaning against the door, she nearly fell through, as it swung open. She peered around the empty room. A large four-poster bed, much like hers, sat in the middle of the antique Persian rug. Navy blue curtains with gold fringe hung from the wooden frame of the bed. Heavy gold draperies over the windows shut out the world.

She stepped in the room and a deep smooth voice hummed a tune in the bathroom. Just as she went to leave, Jacque entered the room with a towel wrapped around his waist. Water beaded on his chest and his black hair glistened with moisture. Angel's jaw went slack as the muscles in his chest tensed when he saw her.

Her eyes roamed from his face, down the thick line of his neck, over the broad expanse of his chest, and down the taunt ripples of his abdomen. Gasping as the water dripped down his body, she followed the trail of dark hair from his navel until it disappeared beneath the towel. Her body responded as warm moisture spread between her legs. She took a step backward and crossed her legs, hoping to stop the heat pulsing between them.

Unable to take her eyes from him, Angel stammered, "Um. Sorry. The door just opened. I didn't mean to come in."

"No problem. Just give me a minute." He grabbed a pair of sweats and shirt out of the bureau, then disappeared back into the bathroom.

She admired the tight fit of his T-shirt as he came into the bedroom. A wicked grin pulled at the corners of her mouth as she remembered what lay underneath his clothes. He ran his fingers through his hair, pushing the loose curls to his nape. Sitting on the edge of the bed, he offered her the armchair.

"I see you don't have much more in this room than I do in mine. I would've thought permanent residents would have a bigger suite." She teetered on the edge of her chair.

"Oh. This isn't my permanent residence. I'm only staying here to train the class. I have a bungalow on the West End."

"I thought you stayed here. Huh. I wouldn't have pegged you for a bungalow type. More mid-town condo guy to me."

"Unfortunately, there are no mid-town condos down here. I'm one of the few lucky soldiers who live outside the castle walls. Are you a mid-town condo girl?"

Her words choked a bit coming out. "Naw. I lived in one for the last five years. I love New Orleans. I was happy to go back home." She missed her sister.

"There's some books on the shelf behind you, mainly theology and mythology. I love to read human versions of the Underworld. I have a lot more at my house. This is what I keep here." Jacque got up and crossed the room toward Angel.

"This is one of my favorites." He handed her the book about Hercules. She flipped through the pages as he hovered so close to her she could hear the beating of his heart. She stepped back into him, feeling the solid strength of his body against her back.

The aroma of apricots and vanilla drifted through his senses. Electricity shot through him when he wrapped his arm around her waist and pulled her tight to him. He inhaled the headiness of her perfume. Starting to lose control, he broke away from her and stepped back.

He was disregarding every rule he ever made about females. The first rule being — no humans.

"What's wrong?" she asked, her voice raspy with desire.

Everything about this female is telling me to run like hell. Her scent is like a drug. It's intoxicating and heady. Dangerous. Not easily purged out of one's system. I've already spent a decade erasing Bell from my world, learning to live alone.

"This is a bad idea. It might be best if you leave."

She turned to face him, running her hand over his chest, causing a burning sensation to spread in his belly. "What's so bad about this?" Her eyes smoldered beneath heavy lashes.

"I'm not a good guy for you. I doubt we have much in common. Hell, we're not even the same species." He took another step back, but ran into the chair.

A mixture of determination and lust exuded from her pores. "Lucky for you, I'm not looking for a good guy. And as tasty as you looked in a towel, who gives a shit what species you are."

"I'm not a commitment guy. I can't give you what you want. Once you leave, you won't see me again." *Shit. What's wrong with me? Man, you've been out of the game for too long if you're refusing a sexy female serving herself up to you. It's just sex. Just one night. Right?*

"How do you know what I want? I know exactly what you're offering. That's why I'm here. I don't want the complications of a relationship. I just need someone to remind me I'm a woman." She turned her back to him so he couldn't see her face, trying to hide her sadness.

He could feel the conflict boiling inside her as he fondled a long wavy lock of her hair. "Remember you asked for this. Just like your deal with Luc, there's no turning back."

Brushing a finger down the back of her neck and feeling her shiver under his touch, he folded her into him. Leaning down, he grazed his lips on her bare shoulder. Her body trembled. She bent her head to the side while he showered kisses up the length of her neck.

Angel longed for the taste of his lips. Turning in his arms to face him, she witnessed a hunger in the depths of his green eyes that matched hers. She caressed his square jaw, feeling the smoothness of a fresh shave. His soap smelled of the pine: refreshing and comforting. Stretching on her tiptoes, she brought her lips to meet his and was rewarded by a groan. His lips devoured hers. She melted into him as his tongue explored the sweetness of her mouth.

The spiciness of his aftershave infused in her nostrils. She craved him like a junkie jonesing for a hit. Fear struck. Her stomach quivered and her hands shook on his back. If she moved forward with him tonight, she wasn't sure if she would come back whole. The plan only worked in theory, and she missed a vital assumption–she liked Jacque more than she admitted. Her mind told her to pull back and break the connection. Commonsense told her to leave, but her body refused to cooperate. She needed him.

She tasted of mint and remnants of chocolate. Angel's tongue teased in and out, skimming the inside of his mouth. She strained on her toes to reach him. Her breasts pressed hard against his chest. Sensing her discomfort, Jacque picked her off the floor and carried her to the bed. His hand navigated up her thigh as he cradled her in his arms. They fell to the bed engrossed in one another. He skimmed the contours of her body as he slid his hand underneath the cotton dress. Her body tensed under the stroke of his hand.

He kissed behind her ear. "Are you okay?"

"I don't know."

"You want to stop?" His teeth caught her earlobe.

Angel's lips played along his neck. "No." She kicked off her flip-flops, hearing them clunk on the wood floor.

Jacque awakened everything inside of Angel. Her nerves tingled with each move of his body. His tongue left wet trails of fire along the neckline of her dress. He slowly pushed the dress higher as he caressed her curves. She sat up, lifted the dress over her head, and threw it to the floor.

With one swift move, he released her breasts from the black lace bra. He pushed her back onto the mattress. Sliding off the bed, he pulled her until her ass hung on edge. His rough hands traced her waistline and shifted to her breasts. Her nipples stiffened as his thumbs grazed over the peaks. He gave a slight squeeze to her left nipple, sending pain and ecstasy rippling through her body. She felt his mouth where his hand just left. His tongue circled her nipple, hot and moist over the hard nub. Angel writhed in pleasure when the sharp nip of his teeth caught the hardened tip. She tangled her hands in his hair and sank further into the bed as his lips explored her body.

"I want to taste every inch of you," he mumbled between kisses.

The sounds of her soft moans created a fury of desire inside him. He took her other breast in his mouth, sucking hard and kissing softly as he released it. He ripped her black lace panties off and his fingers, first one then a second, fondled the wet heat of her sex. His fingers worked her hot, moist flesh until she met his pace. He kissed a path down her flat stomach, lingering at her navel.

"Can I kiss you here?" Jacque used his thumb to caress the center of her desire.

She ground into his hand and moaned. "Yes."

"You sure?" He rubbed his thumb in circles around her swollen nub. Angel grabbed the duvet with both hands as if to anchor herself to the bed. "Oh, God. Please!"

He slid farther down until his tongue found her passion. His tongue and fingers stroked her until she raked at his back.

"Jacque. Please." She pushed back, climbing higher on the bed.

He caught her by the hips and held her in place. "Please what?" Another flicker of his tongue caused her leg to quiver. "What do you want?"

"I need you inside me."

His fingers filled her again. "Not until you come for me."

His mouth burned against her body. He quickened the pace of his strokes, making her want to scream. Her mind floated in agonized pleasure. Pulling away from the increasing fervor of his mouth, she heard herself whisper, "Oh, shit!" while she grabbed a handful of his silky black curls. Tremors shot through her spine as her body reveled in her release. She fell back onto the pillows, breathing heavily. Her hands still wrapped around a fistful of curls at the base of his neck, she growled, "Now!"

Finally giving in to her pleads, he slid up her body and brought his mouth down on hers once again. She felt the full weight of him and tasted her tanginess on his lips. The hard, thick length of his shaft rubbed against her begging for relief.

Leveraging himself on one arm, Jacque entered her gently, afraid to move to fast. Her velvety wetness wrapped around him. She was so tight as she arched to meet his thrust.

"Slow," he murmured into her hair.

He built a fluid rhythm until Angel rolled them over, straddling him. She picked up the rhythm, moving up and down along his cock. The motion of her hips massaged every inch of him. Grasping her thighs, he slowed her movements. She bent down and ran her tongue over his nipple. Ecstasy shot through his body. He grew harder inside her, thrusting his full length into her as she clenched around him. She stiffened as she took all of him into her.

"Are you okay?"

She shook her head, meeting his rhythm.

Angel bit into her lip as the thickness of his manhood stretched her. She'd never been with anyone so large, but the gentleness of his initial entry prepared her for him. As he picked up his strokes, she matched the fury of his passion. She wanted all of him. Riding him, she gripped his shoulders, using her thighs to glide along his swollen shaft. He throbbed inside her, pushing her to her climax. She quickened her movements. He guided her, his fingers digging firmly into her ass cheeks.

"I want you to come for me, baby." She kissed behind his ear and down his neck.

"Shit—" No longer able to control himself Jacque grasped Angel's waist, holding her for leverage. He thrust into her while she clung to him. She met the fervor of his thrust and her nails bit into the skin on his shoulders. The sweet wetness of her climax came down around him, causing him to shudder. She straightened, guiding him up with her. He wrapped his body around her, maintaining their rhythm. He sensed her desire for him, her longing. The intensity of her emotions drove him past the brink. The strength of his release shook through his body. He held her until they both collapsed in exhausted euphoria.

She shifted to roll off Jacque, but he stopped her. Snuggling her against his chest, he listened to the irregular pant of her breathing. He pushed her hair from her face and kissed her forehead. It had been a long time since he had been with a female. Angel was different. He never imagined the intensity he experienced with her could exist. He wasn't sure if she really came for the book or if she actually came for the sex. At this point he didn't care, just as long as she was with him. This situation entailed too many complications, but he didn't want to let her go.

Angel forgot how good it was to have the love of a man. Unfortunately, she remembered it wasn't love, just sex. Amazing sex, but sex all the same. He already made his position clear — not the relationship type. Anyway, she was leaving in two weeks. Talk about a long distance relationship. Wonder what it cost to call Hell? It was an impossible situation, too many obstacles. She got what she came for, so she would leave it at that.

Jacque rolled to his side, allowing her to slide onto the bed. He tucked her into his side and she laid her head against his chest. Listening to the beating of his heart, she drifted into a sound sleep she hadn't found for a long time.

Chapter Six

Like a cat, comforted and content, Angel stretched her arms above her head. She tried to roll on her back. An arm around her waist gripped her like steel. *Shit! Shit! Shit!* She fell asleep in Jacque's bed. Grimacing, she remembered the details of the previous night. The queasiness of regret and the heat of passion feuded inside her belly. She made a huge mistake and couldn't even blame it on alcohol. Sex without feelings was a difficult skill to master and she failed miserably.

She hadn't realized how much of an affect Jacque had on her these last couple of weeks. Sex wasn't what she craved. It was companionship and the security of being a part of something…someone. Jacque had become that someone she wanted to be with. He brought her security and confidence. Now she messed it up by involving sex. She squirmed free from his grasp, freezing when he mumble something in his sleep and reached out for her. *I am the Queen of Bad Choices.*

The amber glow of the hellish flames snuck in through the cracks in the heavy curtains. She scanned the room for a clock, wondering how many people would be awake. A strong hand grabbed her arm as she scooted to the edge of the bed. Turning to Jacque, she smiled at him tentatively.

He rubbed his eyes, trying to focus. "Where do you think you're going?"

"I gotta go. It's morning and people will be out soon. The last thing I need is to be seen coming out of here." She tried to move off the bed again with little success.

He lured her back to him, bringing her hand to his lips. "You were just going to sneak out without saying anything?" Jacque pulled her down to him.

"Kinda. I didn't want to wake you." His heart pounded in her ear as she absent-mindedly ran her hand across his chest.

"So, my Angel, what are we going to do now?"

"What do you mean? There's nothing to *do*. We had a good time. Now we go back to the way it used to be."

Jacque's brows furrowed. "Are you crazy? What if I don't want to go back to the way it used to be?"

"Hey. What happened to I'm not a commitment guy?" she joked, wanting to hear his answer.

"I'm not talking commitment. Why can't we just do some more of this?" He bent his head and his tongue flicked over a nipple, bringing it to attention.

Angel scooted away. "Last night was great, but this was a one-time shot. I'll be leaving soon, and I'm sure you have a life to get back to." Her throat tightened.

"We have another couple of weeks. I don't want this to be our only night together. Give me a chance to see how else I can make you moan." His fingers brushed the wetness between her legs.

"I can't. It's too much of a risk. I can't fall for you and give you up. Last night was amazing. But let's leave things on an up note." Angel sat up, hopped out of the bed, and rummaged around for her clothes.

Jacque watched her as she dressed. Hunting for the words to change her mind, he wished what she said wasn't true. As much as he wanted to be with her, too many obstacles stood in the way. He slung his legs over the edge of the bed and yanked on his sweats. Standing, Jacque caught Angel just as she reached for the door and secured her in his arms. His super demonic speed gave him an advantage over her. She went rigid then relaxed as he tilted her face to his, kissing her lightly.

"I didn't mean for it to turn out this way. But last night was better than anything I imagined for the past few weeks since I met you." He brushed his lips against her neck.

"What other way could it have turned out?" She hesitated. "But don't blame yourself. I knew exactly what I was doing when I came here last night. We both got what we wanted."

Standing on her toes like a dancer, she brought her lips to meet his. She wanted to embed him into her memory. If she couldn't have him, she would savor this moment. Angel struggled to break herself from his embrace. She never wanted to leave the safety of his arms. Reluctantly, she slipped from his grasp and fled the room.

Tiptoeing down the hall, she prayed she wouldn't run into anyone. She brushed her fingers through her hair and straightened her clothes, shooting for normal. Angel knew she wasn't going to fool anyone. She hadn't expected to stay the night, only make a quick booty call. Light banter floated from the end of the hall. *Fuck! Isabella.* Angel froze, debating her best move. Before she could make a decision, Isabella rounded the corner, eyeing Angel.

"You're out early this morning," Isabella announced in a singsong voice.

Angel plastered a shit-eating grin across her face. "Right back at ya."

"Huh. You're in the wrong hall, aren't you? Your room is on the west wing."

"Why is it any of your business what hall I'm in? I can go where I please. Why are you worried about what I do?"

"I only care about one thing. Unfortunately, you're interfering with my plans."

"Whatever. I have to get back to my room." Angel tried to move past Isabella.

Isabella grabbed her by the arm and said, "Look, I don't know what you think you're doing, but Jacque will never stay with you. You're a novelty, something new and shiny. You're not the first pretty little thing he allowed to distract him. Just remember, he *always* comes home."

"Seems like a personal problem between you and Jacque. I doubt he was thinking about home last night. I can't help it if you can't control your man. Believe me, you were the last thing on his mind when I left him." She snatched her arm from Isabella and retreated down the hall.

Running to her room, she burst through the door. In tears, she threw herself on the bed. Why did she let that bitch get to her? Probably because Angel knew what Isabella said was true. Building a relationship with Jacque wasn't an option and admitting the truth didn't make it more palatable. She wanted away from this place. This wasn't the deal she bargained for.

She snatched the towel off the chair and went into the bathroom. The hot water cascaded down Angel's back, rinsing the tension away. She needed to regroup. This was the 21st century. A woman could initiate a booty call. If Isabella didn't like her sleeping with Jacque, she should get tighter reigns on him. Angel only had a couple weeks left, and she didn't have to see any of them again. She leaned back against the cool tile of the shower wall and let the hot water stream over her head, dissolving the thoughts of Isabella out of her mind.

She refused to acknowledge any feelings for Jacque except lust and desire as she pictured him — muscular, sweaty, and naked. Her body shivered, remembering the passion invoked by his touch. No man ever delivered the pleasure he administered. Sex as great as last night deserved a warning label. Maybe it was a demon thing. Were all demons as skillful in bed as Jacque?

Wrapped in a towel, Angel stepped out of the bathroom. She shrieked when she turned to see Lucifer sitting on the bed.

She pulled the towel tighter around her. "Shit! You scared me."

"I didn't mean to." Lucifer watched her, taking lingering glances at her legs.

"Can I help you with something?"

"I'm disappointed."

"Disappointed? For what?"

"You had sex with Jacque last night."

Throwing up her hands, Angel demanded, "What the hell! Does everyone know? Did Isabella tell you?"

"No one needed to tell me. I know all things happening in my world. I had hoped you would save yourself for me. I should've thought it through before I asked Jacque to take this mission. Women tend to find him irresistible."

"Whether it was Jacque or someone else, it wouldn't matter. I'm not attracted to you." Angel blurted before she could stop herself.

He circled her, toying with a strand of her wet wavy hair. "You have yet to give me a chance to show you my talents. I think you'll find me to your liking. Regardless, you know you and Jacque can't be together."

"No one said we planned to be together. We had sex. We're not getting married." She backed away and pulled her hair out of his grasp.

"Jacque will be leaving at the end of the week. I need him back with the armies."

"Sure you do. Who's going to finish the last week of training?"

"The last week for you will be magic training. You'll be training with Marie."

She jumped as an invisible hand caressed her calf. "You know what. I'm done. Please leave now!"

"Call me if you need anything." Lucifer flashed the beastly smile and disappeared.

Mentally and emotionally, Angel was drained. Her heart broke at the thought of not seeing Jacque again. Her interest in him went beyond the physical. She had a talent for falling for unavailable men. Even when she was engaged to Jackson, she knew he didn't love her. At the time, a piece of a man was better than no man at all.

***

Jacque lay across the bed with his hands clasped behind his head. He knew he shouldn't have bedded Angel, but he couldn't resist, especially after he felt the lust exuding from her. Everything about her said, "Fuck me." He wanted to hold her in his arms ever since he laid eyes on her at the bar. He thought sleeping with her would satisfy his obsession. It just ignited the embers into a full-blown fire.

The knock at the door snapped him out of his thoughts. Jacque hid an amused grin, thinking Angel had changed her mind. Lucifer propped himself against the doorframe.

"What's up?" Jacque leaned on the door and smiled.

"You'll be going back to your army at the end of the week."

The words wiped the smile off Jacque's face. "Why the fuck would I cut training short?"

"Isabella can take over the training. She is more than qualified. Anyway, didn't you say you didn't want to be at headquarters and wanted to be with your soldiers?"

Jacque's hand pressed into the wooden door. He released it when he heard it crack. "What about Angel? You know her and Isabella have problems."

"Their only problem is you. Maybe when you're gone, they'll stop fighting." Lucifer disappeared before Jacque could comment.

Shit! He thought he would have more time to convince Angel to be with him. Luc was jealous. He wanted Angel for himself. Jacque figured let the best demon win. Competition was becoming a theme with Angel. Currently, she belonged to Jacque. Well, not completely, but he planned to fix that problem. He headed for the shower to get ready. He needed to go find Angel before anyone else got to her.

Another rap on the door interrupted him as he dressed to leave. He snatched open the door hoping it was Angel. But to his dismay, Bell stood in front of him with her hands on her hips. She shoved him aside and stormed into the room. Shaking his head, Jacque closed the door and followed her. He hoped to deal with her quickly.

"What the hell are you thinking?" Bell spat.

Fifty years of the bickering was getting old. "What're you ranting about now?"

"You fucked the human!" Her eyes cut through him like daggers.

"It's none of your business who I fuck anymore. We're not together, even when we were together, we did our own thing." Somewhere in his heart, he felt sorry for her.

"You know you belong to me. Sure, we fight, but we always get back together. It might take a decade or two, but we *always* get back together." Her voice was frantic.

"Bell, I care about you. We've been back and forth for a long time with nothing moving forward. We're no good for each other. Someone always ends up hurt. It's like eating too much chocolate. It's good while you're eating, but you pay for it in the end." He held her hand to soothe her.

"I know we're bad for each other, but you think you can make a life with this girl?" Tears glistened on her cheeks. This was the first time he'd seen her cry.

"I don't know what I can have with Angel. All I can do is test the waters and see what happens." Jacque wiped the tear as it slid down her cheek.

"What makes her so special?" Bell questioned.

"I don't know. It's what we had in the beginning. She's confident and independent, yet she still needs me. There is strength in her, yet she ended up here. I don't know."

Isabella smiled at him. She stepped into him, put her arms around his waist, and buried herself against his chest. Jacque held her close. They stood locked in each other's embrace when the door opened. Angel entered, pivoted, and ran in the opposite direction.

***

Running down the hall, she cursed herself for being so stupid. She heard the sound of Jacque's voice calling her and the echo of Isabella's mocking tone. She stopped by to say sorry for the way she left. It was apparent he was already over it. She burst into her room slamming the door. Tears flowed down her face as she slumped on the floor, propping her back against the bed.

Someone knocked on the door and pushed it open. Jacque filled the doorway. He crossed the room and kneeled beside her on the floor, reaching out for her.

She withdrew immediately and smacked his hands away. "Don't touch me!"

"I'm sorry. It's not what you think." He pleaded for her understanding.

"How do you know what I think?"

"I wasn't with Bell. I was just saying goodbye. For good."

She searched his face for reassurance. "Why?"

"Bell and I have a long history. She's having a hard time accepting it's over. I need her to understand it's over, and I want to be with you."

"We can't be together. You're leaving at the end of the week. Lucifer's pissed we slept together." Angel hung her head in her hands unable to look into Jacque's eyes.

"Luc's a poor loser. He hates that you chose me over him. His problem, not mine. He'll get over it. Yeah. I have to leave. All I'm asking is for you to give me until the end of the week. Let's see where this goes. If we can still stand each other by then, I'll figure something out." A mask of determination penetrated his face.

"I don't know."

"I wasn't good enough last night to make you give me a second try?" Jacque teased.

Heat spread inside her just thinking about the sex last night. "Okay. You got until the end of the week. Afterward, we go our separate ways. You're lucky you're good in bed." Angel chuckled through her tears.

"I'll make it worth your while. Last night was just a taste of my abilities." Jacque winked at her. "Come on. Let's get something to eat. It's been a long morning."

Chapter Seven

A hushed whisper spread through the cafeteria when Angel and Jacque entered the room. Most of the guys smirked in obvious acknowledgement of Angel's new status. Like most men, Jacque was oblivious to the attention his behavior attracted. He followed so close behind her they shared one silhouette. She nudged him with an elbow to create some space between them.

Jacque shrugged his shoulders. "What?"

"You gotta give me some space. You're crowding me, and it's attracting too much attention. Bad enough I'm the only human *and* the only female. Now they know we slept together. What the hell? Did someone Tweet it?" The words escaped without a breath in between.

"Sorry. I didn't notice." He dropped his head and moved the food around on his tray.

She needed something to take her mind away from the craziness. A good sword fight could release some of her anxiety. Too bad they didn't have training today. She and Jacque took a seat at the far end of the room. Everyone still glanced at them and whispered. Noel approached from the opposite end of the cafeteria with disdain written on his face.

"Finally given up hiding? I knew there was a reason you favored her." Noel glared at Jacque.

"You need to mind your own business. You're out of line." Jacque's gritty voice held an edge.

"You bust our balls all day long. Nothing we do is good enough, but you allow her to slack off because you're fucking her!" Noel's face glowed red with anger.

Before Jacque could move, Angel's hands locked like vise grips between Noel's legs bringing him to his knees. She trembled with rage. With shaky hands, she released Noel to fall flat on the ground groaning in pain. As soon as he hit the floor, her foot connected with his rib cage.

Straddling Noel, she grabbed him by his shirt. "Don't you *ever* disrespect me again! Next time you won't be lucky enough to pick your stupid ass off the floor." Angel dropped Noel back down, stomping on his knee as she stormed out the room.

Jacque smirked as he offered Noel his hand. *That'll teach him to fuck with Angel.* Jacque thought he learned his lesson the day before, but apparently Noel hadn't. He finished his breakfast to give Angel some time to cool off then strolled to her room and knocked on the door. The bulk of the door muffled her voice. When he entered her room, she lay on her back with her arms tucked underneath her head. Her beauty mixed with fury reminded him of an angry goddess.

"You kicked his ass back there. He'll never live this one down."

Her chocolate brown eyes sparked with rage. "He can go to hell for all I care!"

"Babe, we're already in Hell, but I think you showed him a new meaning for it. You know you can't go around injuring my soldiers."

"I didn't think. Just reacted."

His laugh rumbled through the room. "Don't worry about it. Noel will recover. At least I know not to piss you off."

Sliding on the bed next to her, Jacque pulled her in his arms. She nestled her head against his chest. Rolling over on top of her, he trapped her under him, tasting the saltiness of her kiss. Angel responded to his urgency. He tangled his hand in her hair, jerking her head back slightly, as he ground his hardness against her. She brought her lips just below his ear, languidly trailing her tongue down his neck. A deep voice snapped Jacque out of his haze of pleasure.

"I told you she didn't belong to you!" Luc spewed.

"Don't you ever knock? You've got to stop popping into my room!" Angel dropped back onto the mattress holding her head.

"This room belongs to me, just as *you* do," Luc corrected.

"She made a deal with you. She doesn't *belong* to you," Jacque challenged.

"Do you think she is yours?" the Devil countered.

"This is crazy! I don't belong to anyone! Both of you need to back off." Angel flinched at the pain reflected in Jacque's eyes.

Angel had had enough of everyone. She just wanted to be alone. Instead, mayhem broke loose before she could put them out. Jacque's curses burst from the flames enveloping him. Lucifer's blood-red eyes danced with fury as the flames lapped at his skin. Her screams mingled with his anguish. She couldn't tell if he cried out in pain or in anger. With one last bellow of her name, he disappeared, swallowed by the fire.

"What the hell did you do!" she cried out, falling to her knees on the spot where Jacque once stood.

"There's no need for you to worry about him. He won't be returning." Lucifer turned to leave. Angel snatched his shoulder and spun him around before he could leave.

"You *will* tell me what you did with him!" Her eyes narrowed, and her words contained the rasping of tears.

"I sent him back to his army. He serves me, and I no longer have a need for him. If you're so enamored with him, I'll be glad to make a deal with you." A smile crawled across his face.

"What kind of a deal?"

"You want to be with Jacque? I have a simple solution. Give up your soul and stay here. You can be with him for an eternity. How much are you willing to give up for him?"

"You're telling me my only option is to give up my soul and stay here? How do I know you're telling the truth? I might agree, and you'll still cause trouble for us."

"Are you willing to give up everything for him? I'll guarantee to let you and Jacque be together in peace."

"Can I think about it?"

"No. I need your answer now," Lucifer demanded.

"I can't give up everything for someone I hardly know. I have to get back to my mother and sister. But you promise you didn't harm Jacque?" Tears streamed down her cheeks.

Lucifer huffed, "Jacque's fine," and vanished.

She remained on the floor for some time, trying to understand what just transpired. She was in way over her head with no easy way out. If she made the right choice, why did this emptiness gnaw inside her? Her feelings for Jacque didn't justify giving up everything to be with him. Other than a few kind words, the most they shared was one mind-blowing night. Angel had to admit orgasms like the ones last night were almost worth being trapped in hell forever.

Tonight would be an early night. After the shower, she tucked herself into the thick covers on the bed. As she drifted into a turbulent slumber, she searched for Jacque in her dreams. His beautiful face haunted her in her sleep.

Screaming Jacque's name, she woke at dawn. Last night's events and lack of sleep put her in a foul mood. She needed coffee and lots of it. She threw on her black Baby Phat sweatpants and a pink spandex tank top and slinked down the stairs to the cafeteria. When she hit the door, the buzz of Jacque's departure already permeated the air. He was their hero, and she banished him back to the legions.

Grabbing her caffeine and some fruit, she snuck out of the cafeteria to avoid the prying eyes of her fellow cadets. When she turned the corner, she bumped into Isabella — the last person she needed to see right now.

Isabella leered mockingly. "I see you worked things out famously. Hope you're proud of yourself."

"I don't need your shit right now, Isabella!"

"I can't imagine what the hell the two of them see in you, but whatever. Don't worry. I'll take good care of Jacque when you're gone."

Before Angel could stop herself, her hand came across Isabella's face so hard it knocked her back a couple of steps. Hatred glowed in Isabella's eyes as she leapt on Angel like a tiger attacking its prey. The two tumbled to the stone floor ripping at each other's hair. Angel rolled on top of Isabella, raining blows to the side of her head as Isabella protected her face. Angel cried out in pain when Isabella bit into her thigh, forcing her to slide onto the floor. Isabella jumped to her feet and kicked Angel with a boot in the small of her back. Angel struggled off the ground. Finding her balance, she connected with Isabella's jaw with a back kick.

A crowd gathered in the hall. Instigated by the shouts of the crowd, additional blows rang through the castle. Noel yelled, "Stomp her human ass into the floor!"

A fist slammed into Angel's jaw. The iron-tainted taste of blood trickled down her throat. She tackled Isabella with all the rage burning within her. Once down, Angel snatched Isabella by her T-shirt and slammed her head into the cold stone underneath them until strong hands ripped her away.

Lucifer's voice boomed in Angel's ear. "I think you two have had enough."

"You keep the crazy bitch away from me!" Isabella shrieked.

"Maybe this'll teach you to better pick your battles, Isabella," Lucifer chastised.

"I think you've had all the training you need here. It's time for you to leave. I can't have you causing anymore trouble."

"Whatever. I'll be more than happy to get the fuck out of here." Angel's exhaustion rang true in her words.

Angel dragged herself back to her room. She took the Vamp Juice out of the mini-fridge and chugged it. She had more than her share of the stuff since she started training. It built up in her system, fortifying her with extra strength, giving her the ability to keep up with her supernatural classmates. Even with the Vamp Juice, she felt like a bulldozer ran her over. She began packing her belongings. She couldn't leave this place fast enough.

***

A couple of hours later, recouped and ready to go, a knock jogged her from a nap. A statuesque woman stood at the door, her hair bond in an African-style head wrap. Her skin was a shade or two lighter than Angel's, the color of a latte, but their features were similar. Angel realized the woman was her great-great-great-grandmother — Marie Laveau, Voodoo Queen. Even though it was told she died in her seventies, the woman before her couldn't be more than thirty. She looked the same as her photos in the family books.

"*Bonjour, petite-fille.*" The light sparkled in Marie's eyes.

"*Bonjour, Grand-mère.*" Angel graced her with the fullness of her smile.

"We have much to do, *ma petite*. We should be on our way."

"Where are we going?"

"We return home to New Orleans."

Angel picked up her bags and followed Marie downstairs to the waiting chariot.

Chapter Eight

The taxi drove through the gates of the large, historic brick house on Madison Street. They were back in New Orleans. Angel read the plaque on the brick wall, "Circa 1817." She wasn't sure why they were at this house. The lush garden and floor-to-ceiling windows encasing the colorful interior made her suck in her breath in awe and forget her concerns for the moment. She paid the driver, and he fetched their bags out of the car. The driver watched them the whole ride from the airport, sneaking peeks in the rearview mirror. She was glad to get rid of him — he had stalker potential. She lingered in the courtyard, waiting for instructions after the cab left.

Marie gazed around, taking in her surroundings with an approving smile.

"Lucifer never fails to provide adequate accommodations. Welcome home, Angelique. This will be yours as long as you are with Lucifer. Shall we go see the interior?" Marie headed into the house. Angel followed on Marie's heels, still dazed from realizing this house belonged to her.

Angel could never afford a house like this in the French Quarter even when she was modeling. The click-click of her heels on the cool marble floors echoed as they traveled through the light-filled hall. The windows framed the beauty of the courtyard and pool like Andrew Prokos photographs. The hall opened into an opulent living room, boosting hand-painted murals and an ornate fireplace surrounded by a mirrored wall. Dark wood beams decorated the ceiling, popping against the white. She suppressed the urge to touch every piece in the room, afraid to break something.

Marie was amused by the wonderment in Angel's child-like expression. She perched on the edge of the vibrant red settee with gold accents. Slipping off her shoes, she leaned back, wary from the trip. She surveyed the room and eyeballed Angel who turned in semi-circles, taking in the environment.

"*Ma chère*, we have much to do. Freshen up so we can go out shopping for the items we need. Do you have all my books with you?"

"No ma'am. There're still two books back at Gran's house." Angel still considered it Gran's house even though she passed away two years ago. Her older sister, Faith, and her mother lived in the house now. Faith took care of everyone, including their mother. She was more of a caretaker to Angel than their real mother ever was.

"You will have to go and retrieve them. We have a lot to do with such little time. I can only manifest in this solid form for about a week at a time. It takes many years to recuperate enough to attempt it again." Marie smoothed the folds of her skirt as she stood.

"I'll take our things to the bedrooms and get ready. Will you be coming with me to the house?"

"No, child. When you return, I will go with you to the shops. I can't believe I am home again. It's been over a century since I last saw New Orleans." Light reflected in her eyes as they darted around the room.

"I should get ready. I have to think though all the questions I'll have to answer. Faith is a force to be reckoned with. She won't let this go easily." Angel shook her head at the thought of confronting her family. She left to find her bedroom, shower, and change.

Although Angel was elated to be back in New Orleans, she missed Jacque. She enjoyed her time with him. She connected with him more than she had with any other man, including Jackson whom she knew most her life.

She hoped Jacque was okay. Lucifer promised he would be fine, but who could trust the Devil? Regrets and second-guessing was a norm in Angel's world. She added Jacque to her ever-growing list of "what if's." As much as her heart rooted for Jacque, she had to side with logic. Her heart had landed her in trouble too many times.

Angel descended the stairs dressed in a white sundress adorned with blue embroidered flowers. Catching her image in the mirror surrounding the fireplace, her heart skipped a beat. She never thought she would regain her former beauty. But as she ran a finger along her exquisite face where the scar once dominated, a pain still ached within her. She brushed it off as anxiety about meeting her family.

She air-kissed Marie on her way out the door. She waited on the street for the taxi. Even though it was only a couple of miles to the house, it was a difficult walk in her four-inch Christian Louboutins. The cab pulled up and Angel headed off to play twenty questions with her mother and sister. She practiced the story to herself during the short ride to her house.

Straightening her dress, she checked her make-up in the small mirror of her compact. She took a deep breath, turned the key in the door, and entered the house.

"Hello!" she shouted down the narrow hall. "Faith? Mother? Is anyone here?"

"Stop yelling!" Angel's mother hollered back.

Angel froze in the front parlor, waiting for them to greet her. Elise entered the room, sucking in her words when she saw Angel's face.

"*Mon dieu!* They did it! You found someone to fix you!" Elise exclaimed as she stared at her.

"I missed you, too, Mom." Angel blinked back the tears.

"What the hell did you do?" Faith said in a raspy whisper.

Angel was so engrossed with her mother's reaction she didn't hear her sister come in. She tried to smile, but failed to maintain her composure. "Hi, Faith. I'm so glad everyone's happy to see me."

Angel wiped the tears on the back of her hand. Why had she expected anything different? No one ever cared about her before, so why should they start now? She inhaled and released the air slowly. The tears retreated as she regained her composure and replaced the hurt with anger, which better suited her disposition.

"Don't worry. I didn't come back to stay. I just need to get my things." She turned to storm out the room.

"Wait, Angelique," Faith called after her. "Come back. We need to talk. I want to know what has happened to you."

"Faith, can we deal with this later? I don't feel like getting into it."

Faith caught her by the wrist and spun Angel around. "No. We need to discuss this now."

"Does it matter what happened or how? They fixed her. She can go back to work now. She might need to lose a few pounds, but nothing dieting and a trainer can't fix." Elise's smile danced across her face.

Faith's hand trembled against Angel's as she shot their mother a menacing glare. "Shut your mouth and think about your daughter for once, Mother! Can't you see Angel's in some kind of the trouble?"

The pain and fear in her sister's face made Angel cringe. She wanted to reach out for Faith and tell her everything. She wanted to plead for her help to right her wrong. She couldn't muster the strength. Instead, she ran up the stairs to her bedroom and locked the door. Angel threw her things in suitcases as fast as she could. Her sister banged on the door, begging to come in. Ignoring her, Angel continued to pack.

When she opened the door, Faith blocked her exit. The pain in her eyes bore into Angel like a laser.

"You can't win this, little girl. Turn around and sit down. You don't have to talk, but you will listen." Faith pushed Angel back into the room.

Angel backed up until she had no choice but to sit on the bed. "You're not my mother. And I don't care if you're eleven years older than me. I'm an adult and you just need to stay out of my business."

Faith took a seat next to her. She remained silent for a moment. Angel's heart raced in anticipation.

"I don't know who you conjured to help you, but it'll never work. All demons lie. They tell you what you want to hear. They find a way around the deal to keep you for themselves. Who did you call?" Faith hung her head low as if the burden of Angel's actions weighed her down.

Angel looked out the small window to avoid Faith's scrutiny. "I'm not sure what you are talking about."

"You know exactly what I'm talking about. *Who did you conjure?*"

"L-L-Lucifer," Angel stammered.

"Fuck! What have you done? You made a deal with the Devil himself!"

Self-defeat saturated Angel's voice. "I thought he was the only one who could help me. I didn't know I had other options."

"You never do anything halfway do you, sis? It has always been all or nothing. What was his price for this?" Faith leaned back on her elbows and stared at the ceiling.

Angel spent the next hour detailing the last several weeks for her sister. She described the deal, huffed through Lucifer's trickery, and shed tears about Jacque. She laid out the whole story. Listening was one of Faith's numerous gifts.

"This is a complete mess. I'm not sure how we'll fix it, but we'll try. Until we figure it out, you have to live up to your agreement. You said *Grand-mère* came back with you?" Faith exhaled a deep breath.

Angel laced her fingers with Faith's, squeezing slightly. "Yes. She's back at the house waiting for me. Do you think she'll help?"

"I don't know, sweetie, but we'll find out. Let's go. We got a crap load of stuff to do."

"At least everyone's singing the same tune." Relief resounded in Angel as she was engulfed in her sister's love. If anyone would stand by her, she knew Faith would be the one.

Angel dragged her bags downstairs. Faith went up to the attic to fetch the other books. When Angel reached the bottom step, her mother's soprano voice touched her ears.

"Angel, honey? Where're you going?" Elise's transparency clung to her like a cloak.

"I have a new place to stay, Mom. I told you I wouldn't be here long." Angel bit the inside of her lip to temper her words.

Elise lounged on the sofa sipping her drink. "Why? I've already called Jackson and let him know everything is back to normal. He's excited to see you again."

The rage choked the words in Angel's throat. "Mom, you and Jackson can both kiss my ass!" She grabbed her suitcases and dragged them out the house to wait for Faith. *My mother must be insane to think I would go back and work for the prick who left me when I needed him the most. I don't care if he's the best agent in New York*, Angel fumed.

Faith emerged from the house with her sandy-brown hair pulled into a tight ponytail at the top of her head. The worry weighed heavy in her light brown eyes. Faith's distress emphasized the dark sadness in her gaze. Outside of her concern, nothing else was out of place. The Ann Taylor ensemble lay perfectly on her slender body. Her Coach bag and Miu Miu shoes were gifts Angel had given to her last Christmas. If Angel didn't know better, she would think they were going to church.

***

They rode back to Madison in silence. Faith gasped when they pulled into the gates. Marie waited for them in the courtyard. Angel helped Faith out of the cab and gave Marie an apologetic half-grin. Marie seemed unaffected by Faith's presence. She greeted Angel's sister with a kiss on both cheeks and a lingering hug.

"Welcome, I am happy to see you, Faith. It's been quite some time since we spoke." Angel's jaw hit the ground before Marie could finish her words. "Faith...you've spoken to *Grand-mère* before?"

"You're not the only one who was curious about our family history. I found the books in Aunt Aimee's attic when I was about sixteen." A slight color rose in Faith's cheeks.

Marie's lips crawled into a wide grin. "Faith learned from me for almost a full year. I'm not sure what happened, but I never heard from you again."

"What distracts all teenage girls? A boy. I met my husband the summer I left you." Pain darkened Faith's features. James was on a call in the ninth ward when the levees broke. Even after five years, Faith still carried his picture in her wallet.

"I see. I can forgive love." Marie hugged Faith tight to her. "Ladies, shall we go in and figure out our plan?"

"What plan?" Angel asked.

"Faith wants to find a way to get you out of this deal with Lucifer. It will be difficult, but maybe not impossible." Marie looped her arm through Faith's and headed into the house.

"Now, that's a plan I can get behind," Angel acknowledged, following them inside.

The three ladies congregated in the dining room, pouring over the books of spells and potions passed through the family, generation after generation. They searched for anything to sever or work around Angel's pact with the Devil, but found nothing. The sun disappeared behind the courtyard walls, signaling the night.

The chimes of the doorbell startled everyone. Angel jumped up to answer the door. She didn't recognize the buff blond standing expectantly on the other side of the glass. She cracked the door and peeked out.

"Can I help you?" she asked, eyeing the stranger.

"Hi. I'm looking for Angelique Dias." His smooth, rich voice complemented his good looks.

Angel held the door tight as she questioned him. "And who are you?"

"My name's Laurent. I was asked to deliver a package to her."

Angel opened the door a bit wider. She wedged her body in the space and held out her hand. "I'll take the package."

"I'm only supposed to deliver it to Angelique."

"You've found her. Hand over the package," she huffed, tired of the games.

Laurent snorted. "I can see why you drove Bell so crazy."

"You know Isabella?"

"She's my sister, although most days I hate to admit it. Jacque failed to tell me you were so beautiful. I'll have to have a talk with him about holding out." A sparkle glittered in his eyes as he chuckled. His eyes were the same cerulean as his sister's.

"You spoke to Jacque?" Angel's heart pounded just hearing his name.

"Aw, shit! He got to you already. I've got to get on whatever welcoming committee he's a part of. He always gets the good ones first."

She blushed. "Laurent. You said you had a package for me."

"Oh, yeah. I almost forgot. Can I come in and explain what everything is?"

"Sure." She opened the door for him to enter.

Laurent came in and Angel introduced him to her grandmother and sister. Opening the package, he gave Angel a BlackBerry, car keys, credit cards, and safety deposit key. He explained she would get her target via email on the Blackberry with all the necessary details. He was also her Topside liaison. If she needed anything, she could contact him. Although Laurent refused to say it aloud, Angel knew his other duty was to report on her progress.

Angel escorted Laurent out to his car, a Lamborghini Murcielargo. It suited him.

She couldn't help but ask, "How's Jacque?"

Laurent shrugged. "Doing what he does best, being a soldier."

"Great." Her tone betrayed the excitement of her words. "I was just concerned. Lucifer was really mad the last time I saw Jacque."

"Hell. Jac and Luc fight every few decades. It's usually over a girl and eventually they get over it. It's just what they do." Laurent shook his head, an amused smile pulling at the corners of his lips.

"Oh," was all Angel could manage to say.

"Look. I'll come back around eleven to get you. I hope you're a night owl. If not, get some 5-Hour Energy or something. You'll need it for this job."

Angel waved goodbye and went back into the house. She wondered if she was just a conquest to Jacque. After she left, he most likely went back to Isabella and his old life. She had hoped he would try to reach out to her. She refused to chase after him. If he meant what he said, he knew where find her.

Chapter Nine

"Are you catching souls or a date?" Marie winked as Angel came down the stairs.

"I'm not trying to catch anything tonight, but it's nice to feel like a woman again. All the training and fighting kills all sense of femininity." Angel mused as she checked to make sure all the pertinent body parts were hidden in the dress. "Almost didn't get into this thing. If it wasn't for the last few weeks of training, I would've split it in two."

She straightened the edges of the deep V of her neckline and pressed them against the double-sided tape. The burnt-orange Baby Phat dress boasted a neckline which plunged to her waistline, disappearing under the belt. The dangling pave, diamond heart called attention to the swells of her breast. The dress was a little risqué, but not trashy.

"You'll definitely turn some heads tonight. What I would give to be young and alive again. I miss Earth and all its pleasures. I'll just have to enjoy the time I have now." Marie sighed wistfully.

Angel turned and met Marie's gaze. "You'll come back again."

Marie smiled reluctantly at Angel. "Maybe, you will find a way for me to be here with you."

"Were you able to find anything in the books to break this craziness I've brought on myself?"

"No, child. Nothing. Faith and I will keep looking. We have other books, but they were split amongst the family. She's going to try to retrieve them."

"*Grand-mère*, will I go back to what I looked like before, if we break the deal?" Angel glanced at her reflection in the mirrored wall of the living room, not knowing if she was willing to give up her beauty. *Wonder if vanity's one of the deadly sins? If it is, I might be in trouble. Hell, I made a deal with the Devil. I'm already in trouble.*

Marie clasped her hands behind her back and studied the painting on the wall. "Most likely, if we find a way out, all you get back is your soul."

"Oh...." The doorbell rang. "Laurent's here. Wish me luck."

"You'll do fine, *ma chère*." Holding her face, Marie kissed her cheeks.

The heels of Angel's Blahniks clicked on the tile floor, sliding a little as she made her way down the hall. When she opened the door, a well-dressed Laurent greeted her. His blue eyes twinkled as they skimmed down the length of her body, and he let out a slow whistle. Color flushed her face at his compliment.

"I'm *so* glad Luc kept Jac in the Underworld! We're going to have some fun tonight." Laurent took her hand and gave her a twirl.

"Laurent, you're gonna pull my arm off."

"Oh, sorry. Keep forgetting you're human."

"Not you too with this whole human thing?" She rolled her eyes at him. The fixation with her being human was getting old. Jacque struggled with her humanity, as if repelled by it. The thought of him caused her stomach to tense and the image of drowning in the deep green pools of his eyes surged at her with liquid fire.

"Not really. Humans are so fragile. We have to watch ourselves around you." Laurent shrugged.

"Makes sense. I don't know. With Jacque it seems like something more. Where are we going anyway?"

"Jac's complicated. He has his own issues with humans."

Angel was tempted to question further, but Laurent's tone discouraged her. "We're hitting a Supe club. It'll be fun. I'll introduce you to some people. People need to get used to you so the targets you'll be going after won't get suspicious when you start hanging around."

"Is it far?" she asked as she slid into the passenger seat of the small car.

"No. It's here in the French Quarter. You humans always think you have the monopoly on Earth." Laurent's toothy grin gleamed in the darkness.

It was a short drive to the club, but maneuvering the Bourbon Street crowd was tricky. People hung from the balconies, shouting to the street below, the beautiful architecture of the historic buildings littered with half-naked bodies. The hordes of drunken partygoers meandered through the street, ignorant to the hidden monsters lurking amongst them. Angel cringed when she remembered she used to be one of those people.

Laurent parked at the corner of Bourbon and Conti. The club was a block up Conti Street. The booming base of the music hit her before she reached the doors of Utopia. A long line of people slithered down the sidewalk, like a snake, waiting to get into the club. Angel surveyed the crowd, trying to differentiate the humans from the Supes without success. Hell, Laurent passed for human, but was all demon. He reminded her of Brad Pitt in Fight Club, just a bit bulkier — smoking hot. Too bad she preferred brunettes.

She and Laurent ignored the line and skipped straight to the bouncer. Laurent whispered something in his ear and pressed some bills into his hand. The rope fell and the bouncer let them pass, never taking his eyes from Angel's sparkling heart nestled between her breasts. *Works every time. Laurent could've saved his money.*

The music vibrated throughout her, causing her to sway to the beat. The club throbbed with people. Bodies writhed on the dance floor to the rhythm of the pulsating beat. Others lounged in the booths, performing acts better left to the bedroom. The strobe lights and hazy smoke gave the scene a hedonistic frenzy. Angel pushed through the crowd to the bar. Finding two seats at the corner, she slid onto the stool, crossing her legs. Laurent plopped down next to her, taking inventory of the dance floor. He swirled around when the bartender approach them.

"What you want to drink?" he yelled over the blaring music.

"Grey Goose Cosmo," Angel answered and then leaned back.

"Chivas on the rocks," Laurent called over his shoulder.

Laurent struggled to speak over the music. "What you think?"

"Looks like any other club I've been to, except with no ugly people. Can give a girl a complex." Her tone was hollow as the memory of her prior face flashed in her mind.

"What did you expect? We would be in here with our fangs out, tails wagging, and horns on blast? We have to blend in. It's the only way we can stay Topside without starting an all out war."

"What's the percentage of people verses Supes?"

"I'd say 75/25. Maybe, a little less Supes. Some of the humans know what we are. They come as dates. Others are just attracted by all the hotties in here."

"What's up with all the fabulousness anyway? *Everyone* in here is beautiful. It's a little intimidating."

"Beauty attracts beauty. Less attractive people would feel uncomfortable in here. No one wants to be the ugly friend, especially if they're pretty in normal circumstances. Everything is so superficial in your world."

"I know about being the ugly friend, and I don't want to go back there." No one in this world or hers would've given her a second glance a couple of months ago, especially someone as gorgeous as Jacque.

"You humans tend to forget beauty is only surface paint. In my world, everyone's born to beauty so you have to look for other qualities when seeking someone special. Physical attraction is a given to Supes. Do you think Jac would care two shits about you if he didn't like you on some other level?"

Her heart wanted to believe his words. Her mind told her if Jacque cared so much for her, he would've called by now. "First of all, Jacque and I hardly know each other. Secondly, who said Jacque liked me? Jacque does what men do best, try to get some."

"You're both stubborn. I'll let you two play your games. Anyway, if you're not interested in him, I want a shot. You snooze, you lose." Laurent's words faded into the sounds of "Bedrock" by Young Money and Lloyd. "Come dance with me," he said, pulling her to the dance floor.

As they danced, Laurent pointed out various creatures. The club contained a diversity of immigrants from the Underworld. Most of the clubbers were Demons and Vampires. Laurent spotted some Shifters and a couple of Ghouls. He also pointed out some Witches in the corner, although technically considered humans. With her family powers, Angel fell into the same category as the Witches.

Her feet throbbed in her five-inch stilettos as another song began to play. She and Laurent stumbled back to the bar exhausted. The bartender sat a drink in front of Angel, nodding to the opposite end of the counter. Someone had the nerve to send her a drink even though she was clearly with Laurent. She glanced at Laurent with an arched brow. She peeked down to the breathtaking guy at the end of the bar. His dark features set off his amber- colored eyes. Talk about *The Bold and the Beautiful*, he fit the mold perfectly.

"I think you have an admirer," Laurent teased.

"It doesn't bother you he sent me a drink? He doesn't know you're not my date."

"It would offend me if no one else wanted you. Why be with someone others find undesirable?"

"I swear, you Supes are strange people. I guess you're not people. What should I do?" It was her job to submerge herself into this world, make herself desirable.

"It's your choice. It would be beneficial for you to make friends in the Vamp society. They have strong connections and limitless resources. Etienne is one of the aristocracy in this area." Laurent downed the last swallow of whiskey in his glass.

She picked up the glass, took a sip, raising it and bestowing her benefactor her most seductive expression. The dark-haired suitor replied with a smile of his own, showed her a bit of fang. As he stood, he displayed the long agility of a swimmer's build. The Hugo Boss suit was cut to contour his body. He was a sharp contrast to the bulk of Jacque's brute physique.

"Thank you for the drink." The thumping bass of the music threatened to drown her out.

"It was my pleasure. Laurent, where have you been hiding this one?"

"It's good to see you, too, Etienne. Unfortunately, she's not mine to hide. I was just asked to introduce Angel into society. She's a friend of Jacque's."

"Well, where's ol' Jac? He left you alone with this beauty?"

"He's working as usual. Angel's Marie's granddaughter. She's learning the family business."

"I see. Are you taking your place as Queen of the New Orleans?" Etienne questioned.

"I like to consider myself as Princess. *Grand-mère* will always hold the crown of Queen." She gazed at him and batted her lashes, glad the conversation moved away from Jacque. She dusted off the skills from her dating days; it was like riding a bike. Men loved the shy, modest act.

"Beautiful and loyal. That's an admirable combination. Laurent, I'm having a party at my house Friday night. You must bring our Angel here so she can meet my coven."

"We'd be happy to stop by," Laurent answered.

Etienne touched the tips of her fingers as if afraid he might be shocked. "Will you be bringing Jacque?"

Angel flashed her brilliant white teeth. Improv wasn't her strong suit. "Jacque and I are taking a break since he finds his work more amusing than me." She and Laurent should have practiced their story before they left the house. She wished he had used someone other than Jacque as their cover story. The constant reminder of him was taking its toll.

"Jac has always been a fool when it came to women. Last time I heard, he and your sister were battling through eternity. I enjoy your sister, Laurent, but Jac made a mistake letting Angel go." The mention of Isabella's name darkened Angel's mood even further, drawing out jealousy and rage. She bet Isabella was digging her claws in Jacque at this very moment. Probably did a dance when Angel left.

Laurent nudged her playfully. "That he did. I'll make sure to relay your message. I'm sure Angel won't lack company in his absence." Laurent was good at altering the truth. Angel wondered if it was from practice or a part of his demon nature.

"Okay, guys. I'm standing right here. I wish you wouldn't speak as if I'm invisible." Angel pouted.

"I apologize for our rudeness. I hope you'll be able to make my party. I'm sure you'll be the talk of the town by then. And I can say I saw you first." Etienne bowed, kissed her hand, and disappeared into the crowd.

Laurent sat on the stool, shaking his head. "You rocked it. Couldn't have asked you to do better."

Angel sipped her Cosmo and shrugged her shoulders. "Maybe next time we'll leave Jacque out of the playbook. I don't like making up things about him."

"What happened between the two of you? He's really tight-lipped about it."

"Not much to tell. Girl meets demon, have a fling, gets banished by Lucifer, and here we sit." It sounded so simple in those terms. Her feelings for Jacque gnawed at her reasoning every day, creating turmoil and conflict.

"This is the first time he ever asked me to look after someone." Laurent slapped himself in the head. "Shit. Can you act like I didn't say that?"

"You're fine.... He probably just feels guilty he played with the fragile human. Nothing serious." She smiled at his questioning eyes. He didn't believe her and why should he? She hardly believed it and they were her words.

She danced so much, the five-inch Manolos made her calves clenched like butt cheeks at the county jail. Her watch showed 3:32, time to wrap it up. Angel was out of practice. She'd have to build up her partying stamina or lose her street cred. Tapping her watch, she signaled time to go. Laurent caught her hint and finished-up his conversation with the red-haired Fae who had came in while she danced with Etienne.

Angel dreaded the trip back to Bourbon Street. She debated the lesser of her evils — walk slow or run fast to get there sooner. The throbbing pain in her feet said neither would help. She winced with each step. Laurent stared at her and clucked his tongue. Before she realized what happened, he picked her up, hoisting her in his arms.

"Women and your impractical shoes. Why would you wear those things to a club or at all?" He gave her a little toss to adjust her weight in his arms.

"They're sexy. Men like to see women in stilettos," she argued, wrapping her arms around his neck. "Laurent, if my feet didn't hurt so bad I would demand you put me down. But right now, I have no fight left."

"Men don't care what kind of shoes you have on. It's just one more thing to take off. Women wear those things for other women, not for us."

She didn't have a response, couldn't argue with his logic. She remained silent until he placed her safely in the car, relieved. She kicked off her shoes. *He's right*, she thought resting her head against the seat. Women did things to impress other women. Getting the guy was the ultimate trophy. She knew exactly which trophy she wanted to mount. Laurent glanced over at her when she giggled, probably thinking she was losing it.

At the door, she thanked Laurent for a great night. She hadn't had this much fun in a long time. Before she said goodnight, she started to ask more about Jacque, but at the last minute decided against it. She had to close Jacque's chapter in her life before she lost herself in the fantasy. In the short time she spent with Jacque, he had won her over. She could be herself around him, no need for pretense. He had seen her for who she was, not the supermodel on the magazine cover, living a life not really her own.

Chapter Ten

The BlackBerry buzzed incessantly, jumping across the nightstand. "Who the hell's calling at this hour?" Angel cursed under her breath. The clock glowed 4:42 a.m. in neon green lights. She rolled from the middle of the bed, snatching the leather case and unsheathing the phone.

Shit. It wasn't a call. The message popped open and subject line read, *Your First Job*, prompting Angel to sit up and turn on the lamp. Rubbing the sleep from her eyes, she studied the message again.

From: Luc Devlin

Your First Job

June 20, 2010

Target: Antione Luison, Vampire

You have four days to complete this mission. Tell Antione I can't wait to see him again.

Missing you,

Luc

Lucifer is such an ass, she thought, staring at the brightly lit screen. Etienne's party would be a perfect spot to gather Intel on Antione. Laurent probably had information about this vampire. His brain was like her personal Google for the supernatural world.

The plush, suede-covered headboard squished under Angel's weight. She brushed her hair out of her face, leaning her head back into the billowy softness. She hadn't expected a job so soon. She just finished training with Marie last night. The last few days had been packed with combat, magic, and partying. When she wasn't practicing her Voodoo, Laurent swept her away to mingle in the spectacular and sometimes seedy supernatural underground. Her body hurt, her energy was drained, and her head pounded from too many Cosmos. Covers snatched over her head, she drifted back to the sweet bliss of her dreams where Jacque waited for her.

The sun streamed through the window warming her face, awakening her for the second time that morning. Like an agile feline, she hopped out the bed and headed to the bathroom for her morning rituals. Her hand shook as she brushed her teeth. She was disturbed by the new assignment, not sure if she was ready yet. Everything happened so quickly; she hadn't had a chance to process it.

She emerged an hour later, refreshed and radiant. The BlackBerry lay in the middle of the bed, where it landed after she read the message earlier. Picking it up, she scanned the numbers programmed into the contact list. She found Laurent's number listed just under Isabella's. The site of the girl's name twisted a knot in her stomach, and she hit *delete* to make it disappear. Dialing Laurent's number, she waited.

"Hello," a deliciously smooth voice answered on the other end.

"Hi. Laurent?" Angel couldn't quite make out who it was, yet it had a familiar ring.

"I'm sorry. Laurent's in the shower. Can I take a message?"

"Sure. Tell him Angel called, and I need him to call me back as soon as possible." The line went silent on the other end. Maybe the guy hung up. "Hello?"

"A-A-Angel?" His deep baritone had gone up an octave.

Her heart stopped as his name slipped from her lips. "Jacque?" She held her breath, waiting for his answer. His silence ate away at her like a river cutting through a canyon — slow but definitive.

"Yeah...how are you?" his labored breath whispered through the phone.

The phone shook against her ear, the sound of his voice evoked feelings she wish she could deny. "Okay, I guess. What about you?" She wanted to let him go, needed to let him go, but fate continued to throw him in her path.

"Good. Busy. Do you really need to speak to Laurent now? I can go get him."

"It can wait a bit. I'll see him later for the party anyway."

"Whose party?"

Chit chatting with Jacque as if nothing ever happened felt odd. She answered the question anyway. "Etienne Fouche's. I met him a few days ago at Club Utopia." This wasn't the conversation she needed to have with Jacque. She wanted to tell him she missed him. Wanted to know why he hadn't called. She was cracking. It was time to hang up.

"Oh. I hear you're the belle of the ball around New Orleans. Everyone's talking about you."

She thought she caught a hint of longing in his voice. "Well, we're just about wrapped up, which is good since I got my first assignment already."

"What do you mean you already have an assignment? Who is it?" Jacque demanded.

Angel calmed her voice, hoping to hide her fear. "I got the email this morning. I have to bring in Antione Luison. He's a vampire." She longed for the safety of his arms, but she gave up the right when she chose herself over their relationship.

"That mother-fucker! He's not planning to let you work out your agreement. Not if he's starting you with Antione."

"What're you talking about? You're starting to scare me." She collapsed on the bed as her legs wavered.

"Sorry, Antione's one of the most ruthless vampires alive or *undead* rather. He was a bastard when he was human. When he died, he should've come to Hell. But before Lucifer could keep him, he was turned into a vampire. He's been wreaking havoc for centuries."

"Leave it to the Devil to find a way out of a deal. Well, it's not like I got many options. I have to find him and bring him in."

Wood smashed in the background, and Jacque cursed under his breath. "I'll have Laurent come see you. We'll have to discuss a strategy on how to get rid of Antione. I'm going to kill Luc when I see him!"

"Okay. I'll wait at the house until I hear from him."

"Angel, please be careful."

Angel prayed the longing in her words were lost in the transmission. "I'll do my best. It was good talking to you, Jacque."

"I miss...you know it was good talking to you, too. I'll have Laurent contact you."

The dead air lingered several moments before she forced herself to hang up. The caress of his soothing tone beckoned her to open her heart to him. His beautiful face danced in her mind. The memories of his emerald-green eyes haunted her. She imagined her hands exploring his rock hard chest and washboard stomach. The scorching touch of his lips singed on her skin. His concern gave her hope — hope she couldn't afford to hold on to. Her heart was too fragile to sustain losing him again.

Against her will, Angel forced herself downstairs. She slumped into a stool at the granite island in the kitchen. Her forehead hit the counter with a thud.

"What's the matter, *ma chérie?*" Marie asked.

Angel jumped, realizing she wasn't alone. "Where do I start?"

"At the beginning, little one." Marie patted the chair next to hers and poured another cup of coffee.

"*Grand-mère*, how do you know when you love someone?" The words came out before she realized she said them. *Love?* Was this really what she felt for him?

"Ha. Love is an elusive creature. It has so many faces I cannot give you one answer to the question."

Angel tore off pieces of a napkin, making a small pile of confetti in front of her. "Can you love someone you hardly know?"

"I think some people have a natural attraction to one another. An attraction too difficult to break. If you couple it with emotional compatibility, the magnetism is undeniable." Marie reached over and squeezed her hand.

Her head hung low, Angel focused on the grain of the wood table. "I miss him so much. And hearing his voice again almost broke me."

"Who, *chère?*"

The thought of him forced a smile to her face. "Jacque."

"Oh, child. You don't do anything the easy way, do you? Of all the available men, you fall in love with an Underworld Demon. Lucifer's nephew, nonetheless." Marie shook her head, staring into the dark liquid in her cup.

Angel wiped the tears with the remnants of her napkin. It was time for her to toughen up. "I know I can't have him. It was stupid of me to fall for him. I know he's probably not thought about me since we…. Anyway, I made a mistake."

"You'll find someone who'll love you the way you deserve."

"Thanks for listening. I shouldn't be crying over a man. I have much more important things to think about. I got my first assignment today."

"Who?"

"Antoine Luison. I heard he's some badass vampire. Jacque was pissed when I told him."

Marie cocked her head to one side as she concentrated on Angel. "Was he now? You called Jacque?" Her eyes narrowed as she waited for Angel to answer.

"No. I called Laurent to let him know about Antione. Jacque answered instead. I guess hearing his voice has brought on all the crap about Jacque." She ran her fingers through her hair, pushing it out of her face.

"When will Laurent be here? I would like to run through a few more practices to make sure you have everything. Conjuring the elements is difficult. You're only the third person, outside of myself, who inherited the gift. It's a strong power to possess."

"I don't know. Hopefully soon." Leaning back in her chair, Angel released a deep breath, exasperated.

The dining room was staged as their ritual area. The table served as a makeshift altar filled with statues and candles. Angel chanted the protection spell with Marie. A haze of blue smoke surrounded her as she knelt before the eclectic array of items. She called upon the power of their ancestors to watch over Angel. The spell was supposed to be insurance in case her weapons failed.

Calling the elements required massive amounts of energy. The gift couldn't be used too often. She needed to learn to control this power. It was the only active gift she possessed. Fire was the easiest for Angel to control. Marie said each of them had a dominant element, which attached to their aura. Fire linked with passion and intensity. Angel examined her strengths. *I don't see those traits as my strong suits, but who am I to argue with fate?*

After her session with Marie, she went out to the backyard to practice her hand-to-hand combat, taking all her frustrations out on the punching bag hanging from the large magnolia tree. The neighbors probably thought she was a nutcase or martial arts crazy with all her training equipment out back. She also rented a place outside the city to practice with weapons. Too risky to have them around the house.

Stripping out of her workout gear, she changed and took a swim. The water relaxed her. She held her breath and dove to the bottom of the pool, skimming the smooth tile with her fingertips. The light refracted through the water and bounced off the multi-colored glass. She relished the beautiful serenity as she hovered along the bottom until she was forced to come up for air. When she broke the surface, Angel realized someone stood on the patio, blocking the sun. With her head thrown back, she pushed her hair and the water away from her face for a better view.

A smile broke across her face when Laurent threw a kickboard at her. She blocked the board with her arm and waded to the edge of the pool. As she pushed herself out of the water, another shadow caught her attention. At the sound of Jacque's voice, she almost fell back into the water.

"Hi, Angel."

Her stomach fluttered with nervous butterflies. Looking up, she desperately sought his face. The sun radiated behind him, making it difficult to see. "I hope you don't mind me just dropping by."

The sight of him stole the words off her tongue and melted her like an ice cream cone on a hot summer day. Penetrating green eyes smiled at her through dark-hooded lashes so thick it any woman would be envious. She sucked in a breath as she took in all six-foot-five inches of his masculinity.

His well-worn jeans hung low on his narrow hips with the bottom of his vibrate green T-shirt tucked just behind the silver buckle of his belt, showing off the tight expanse of muscles underneath. With the sun behind him, his olive toned skin and his dark brown hair glowed in the rays of light, likening him to a Greek god.

She tried to rise, but her legs were limp noodles, shaking beneath her. Laurent put his hand out to help her. Standing, she fought the urge to caress the beautiful face she thought was forever banished to her dreams. Her body failed her by reacting to his presence when her mind decided to block him from her heart, the same fickle heart, which pounded in her chest at the sight of him.

"Hi, Jacque. What brings you Topside?" Electricity tickled her spine when she said his name.

"You...of course." He stepped closer, filling the air with his spicy musk scent.

The answer caused her heart to sing, but she couldn't afford to waste energy on romance right now. "Do Lucifer and Isabella know you're here?"

"I didn't know I needed permission from them. Would you like me to leave? I don't want to be anywhere I'm not wanted." His eyes searched hers, making her burn from wanting.

Marie answered the question before Angel could respond. "You're always welcomed here, Jacque." Her graceful glide showed her poise and elegance. She kissed Jacque on both cheeks and greeted Laurent in kind.

Angel folded her arms across her chest in surrender. "Of course, you're welcome. You have to excuse me. I've had a long morning. It's apparently affected my manners. *Grand-mère*, will you entertain our guests while I shower and change?" She slid the towel off the back of the chair and wrapped it around her waist.

"Don't worry, *cher*. I'll take care of them. Would you gentlemen like a drink?" Marie took Jacque's arm and ushered him back into the house.

Angel snatched Laurent's arm, jerking him backward. "A little heads up would've been nice."

"And miss the look on your face?" A mischievous grin crawled over his face. "A pair of Johnston Murphy shoes — two-hundred fifty dollars. Look on Angel's face when she saw Jacque — priceless!" Laurent followed her as she stomped into the house, continuing to mock her as Angel picked up her pace.

***

She rummaged through the dresser for something to wear when a knock interrupted her. Jacque opened the door and entered the room, before Angel could answer. She tightened her hold on the towel, pulling it snug around her body, and looked away from him, shielding her from the magnetic attraction of his beauty. She wanted to crush herself against him, feel his lips on her, and lose herself in the headiness of his smell.

God, she missed him.

"You can't just burst in my room," she said with her back to him, hiding the longing in her eyes.

"I just wanted to talk to you." She felt his gaze burn a trail down her back.

"I'm getting dressed. Can't it wait until I come back down?"

"You act like I haven't seen what's under your towel. Believe me, there are no parts of you I'm not familiar with or have you forgotten?" She turned and gave him a sideways glance. "I just wanted to talk to you in private." He hung his thumbs in his pockets and studied his shoes.

"Because I gave into you once doesn't give you access to me whenever you feel the need. The first time was a huge mistake. What is it you need from me, Jacque?"

"You...." The word blew her away like a Category Four Hurricane. It sucked Angel into a whirlwind of emotions, ripping at the seams of her logic. She waited days to hear from him with no reward, just to have him show up today, expecting her to fall back into his arms. The unbalanced scales of her life toppled from the burden of his revelation.

In two quick strides, he closed the distance between them. The intensity in his eyes brought out the golden flecks embedded in the jewel-toned green.

She held up her hand to impede his progress. If she gave in again, she would be his completely, ensuring her destruction if he were to ever leave.

"We can't do this. I'm not going to give *it* up every time you feel the need be with a human. Don't get me wrong. The sex was great. Right now, I don't need distractions. And you? You're a big distraction." She repeated the words in her mind, to make sure they stuck. She had to convince herself just as much as him.

"Is that what I am? A distraction?" He granted her full access to the sadness in his eyes as he pushed the dark curls from his face.

"What do you want from me? What do you think we have?" Her harsh tone caused him to flinch, making her want to take those words back.

"I don't know what we have. All I know is I've missed you. I've tried to forget you, but it hasn't worked out for me. When I heard your voice this morning I knew I had to see you again."

"Did you have fun forgetting me?"

Jacque smiled at the accusation.

"Look, you stay in Hades and I live here. Lucifer will shit a brick if he found out we hooked back up. I don't have the energy to make this thing work."

"Okay. Tell me this. Have you thought about me since you left?" His shoulders sagged in defeat as he sat on the bed. It creaked under his weight.

Everything in her screamed *"Lie!"* Her heart was a traitor, betraying her as her defenses continued to waiver. She turned to evade his irresistible charm. Before she could escape, he reached out and caught her hand, drawing her close to him. His head rested against her stomach, which churned with a roaring inferno brought on by his touch. His long, muscled arms tightened around her waist, providing her the strength and security she lacked on her own. Gazing down at him, she brushed a curl from his forehead and breathed, "Yes."

Catching Angel's legs just behind her knees, he swept her into his arms. Cotton-soft lips closed on hers as he persuaded her lips to open to him. She surrendered to the sweetness of his mouth and circled her arms around his neck. Their tongues danced a fiery tango in his mouth. The fury of her yearning radiated through every extremity, causing her to shudder against the rock hard mass of his body.

His kisses felt like electricity, dynamic and stirring, as they trailed down her neck. She leaned back in his arms, exposing her body to him. With one snatch, the towel landed on the floor beside the bed. He ravaged her breast, his mouth hot and wet, while his hand traveled down the length of her taut stomach. Angel grabbed a handful of dark brown curls when his fingers plunged into the dripping heat between her legs. Burying her face into his chest, she stifled her cry.

His lips found hers again as she rolled her hips to the rhythm of his fingers, arching into his palm. Closing her eyes, she savored every beat of his stroke. When she opened her eyes, she found him gazing down at her with burning desire. She ached to have him inside her.

"I need you," she moaned in his ear. He groaned at her request, and his cock grew harder underneath her.

Tossing her onto the bed, he peeled the clothes from his body, teasing and taunting. Her hand played with her sex as she watched him undress. She stared longingly at his ripped abs, the sculptured hardness of his chest, the firm muscles defining his legs, and the impressive bulk of his manhood, which stood erect in its full glory. The friction of her fingers rubbing small circles against her center made her moan and lick her lips. Her mouth turned up in a smile when his shaft jumped in response to her pleasure.

The sight of her fingers fondling her sex was enough to madden Jacque. He had to have her, feel the warmth of her desire surrounding him. Bringing her ankle to his lips, he kissed it lightly, as he propped it on his shoulder. She trembled under his touch. His hand skimmed the long sleek expanse of her leg and grazed her moist folds. He sank two fingers back into her as she continued to caress her nub. Her leg quivered on his shoulder.

He was so hard he could explode.

"Please...." It came out more a command than a request, her voice thickened with lust.

"What do you want?" Jacque pushed his fingers as far into her as they would go. Her body tensed and her sex clutched his fingers.

"You...inside—" A third finger made her gasp.

She grabbed his arm, trying to pull him closer her. Arching in his hand, he could feel she was close to coming. He removed his fingers, bringing them to his lips, tasting her hot passion on his tongue. Her eyes grew wide as they followed his fingers as they slid in and out his mouth.

"I love the taste of you," he growled.

He couldn't wait any longer.

Just as she reached for him, he held her by the hips and thrust the full length of his manhood into her. The tight grip of her folds caressed him with drenched velvet. His body seized as molten liquid flowed through his veins, fueling his frenzied pace. He wanted to slow down for her, to stretch out her pleasure, but he waited too long. When she rolled her hips under him and moaned his name, he threw her other leg on his shoulder and thrust his cock deep into her sex.

His large girth stretched her. She forgot the painful bliss of him filling her womb. She absorbed every stroke of his fervent demand. With both legs across his shoulders, his manhood sank deep into her, setting her core on fire. Her need matched his. Arching up to meet his thrusts, she hung on the verge of orgasmic utopia.

"God, I missed you," Jacque groaned into her hair.

His movements were like lightning striking, fast, fierce and all consuming. As his long, thick shaft stretched her, he caught her nipple with his teeth. With his next thrust, Angel lost herself in the dark abyss of ecstasy. Jacque stroked hard into her again, trembling as the warmth of his seed mixed with her climax. Dropping her legs, he collapsed on top of her drenched in sweat. Her heart pounded in her ears as she tried to catch her breath.

He brushed his lips across her shoulder, up her neck, working his way back to her mouth. Their animalist hunger sated, their kiss lingered leisurely.

She was forever lost to him—irrevocably and undeniably his.

Jacque turned on his side, propping himself on an elbow. "Now that wasn't so bad, was it?" he joked.

"I never said the sex was bad. If I could bottle it, I'd be a millionaire." She sighed and played with his hair. "The other stuff is what worries me."

"I don't know where this is going. I can't make you any promises. Let's just see where this takes us." He brushed a sweat-soaked strand of hair from her face.

"I think this is a bad idea for both of us. I don't want to be hurt again and as you said, you can't make me any promises. Just know if I think for one second I'm going to get hurt, I'll run like hell. And I'm low on second chances these days. I just got back on my feet from being knocked on my ass. I won't let it happen again." What was she getting herself into? Warning bells sounded. Lost in her hopes of love, Angel blocked out the alarms.

"I would never intentionally hurt you." He drew her hand to his lips, kissing the tips of her fingers.

"Intentionally or unintentionally, I can't deal with drama. As soon as the shit hits the fan, I'm gone."

His lips covered hers, ending the discussion. She melted into the passion of his kiss. The promise of happiness found its way to her after what seemed like a lifetime of misery.

Chapter Eleven

Laurent's voice boomed on the other side of the door. "What the hell's going on in there?" His relentless banging could wake the dead.

Shit! Angel jumped up only to have Jacque grab her around the waist and wrestle her back to the bed. Struggling to get loose, she shoved against his chest.

"Knock it off, Laurent," she yelled, searching for her robe. "What do you want?"

He annoyingly rapped a drum solo on the door. "Are you two finished getting reacquainted? We actually came here to do work. Remember, Jacque?"

"Yeah, yeah, I remember," Jacque replied. "We'll be down in a minute."

"Am I forgiven now? We're good, right, Angel?" Laurent called.

"Whatever, Laurent. Get the hell away from my door." She giggled, still not convinced she forgave him. He landed her exactly in the middle of what she tried to escape — Jacque.

Jacque rolled out the bed and dashed into the bathroom. She debated following him, ultimately decided against it. They would never make it downstairs if she did. The mere thought of him and the steamy shower, the water and his touch caressing her, made her drip with anticipation. She bit her bottom lip to bring her back to reality.

Jacque strolled out of the bathroom, toweling his hair. "I left the shower on for you, babe, since you didn't join me."

"We have things to do. We can't stay trapped in this room having sex all day, especially with Marie downstairs." Her cheeks flushed red at the thought of her grandmother knowing what they were doing.

"I'm sure Marie understands." His smile flashed bright. "I'll meet you downstairs."

"Okay," she replied, studying the agile movements of his body as he dressed. The muscles flexed in his back as he pulled the shirt over his head, and the arms of the tee stretched tight over his biceps.

Showered and changed, she hopped down the stairs, humming a Keisha Cole tune. Her sensible side interrupted her momentary euphoria, reminding her of all the complications she and Jacque still had to overcome. Sex was easy, but building a relationship was much harder, especially between a demon and a human. Leave it to her to fall for an Underworld demon with an aversion to humans.

Laurent and Marie lounged on the red leather sofa. He winked at her and her grandmother snickered. Angel twirled her hair around her finger and smirked, like Sylvester on the prowl for Tweety Bird.

"What's on the agenda?" she blurted, trying to break the tension.

"Jacque and I tried to find out some more information about Antione before we got here. Not much out there to be found though. All we know is he's in the region right now, traveling between Mississippi and Texas, and passes through New Orleans a lot. We should be able to get some info from Etienne's party tonight." As Laurent filled everyone in, he took on a military stance, the demeanor of someone used to giving status updates.

"I ran into him a while ago when I was stationed Topside. He's powerful—a master vampire. It's not going to be easy to bring in." Concern resonated in Jacque's voice.

"Let's see what we can find out tonight. When we return, we can figure out a plan. What time are we leaving for the party?" After a glance at the setting sun, Angel checked her watch.

"I'll come pick you up at 10:30," Laurent answered.

Disappointment spoiled her good mood. "Jacque's not coming?"

Laurent didn't beat around the bush. As always, he was direct and to the point. "You told everyone you weren't with Jacque, which is a better situation to get information out of people. Men will open up to you. You're hot. Wear something skimpy and show a lot of cleavage."

"You're not going to put her out there like some cheap whore!" Jacque growled.

"This is her job. It's how we're going to keep her from Luc. If you can't do this, you need to go back home," Laurent stated matter-of-factly.

"I'm not going anywhere. You better take care of her. I'll be watching."

Angel turned to Jacque. "You'll be at the party?"

"Oh, I'll be there. Don't worry, babe."

"I'll come by and get you later. It's formal. I hope you have something to wear." Laurent picked up his keys off the coffee table, fingering the Lamborghini emblem on the ring. Angel watched him with amusement. *Men and their toys.*

"I was a model. I always have *something* to wear. Although shopping would've been fun. No time for that now. *Grand-mère*, do you want to come? It would be nice to go out together before you leave." There was safety in numbers. Angel wanted to surround herself with as many people as possible. Marie brought her comfort, gave her a sense of confidence she never experienced before. She believed Angel to be a smart competent woman, not just a pretty face.

Marie's eyes brightened with excitement at the idea. "I haven't been to a party in such a long time. Do you think it will be okay?"

"I think people will enjoy seeing the two of you together. Voodoo royalty should get people talkin'." Jacque stood in front of Angel and pushed her hair over her shoulder, his smile pensive as he gazed down at her. "Only if I could go with you."

"I'll see you there. You'll be dazzled when I make my entrance. I promise." She snickered, snuggled into his side, and hugged his waist. "It's all set. We'll see you at 10:30."

Transforming herself into a sinful temptation required time. Upstairs in her bedroom, she leafed through the dresses in her closet, finding most of them mundane, not worthy of enticing a ball full of otherworldly creatures. She passed by Dior, Armani, De la Renta, and Gaultier, needing something to make her stand out. Shock value, done the right way, can add a layer of intrigue to entice a man. She reached toward the back of the closet, shoving the other garments out of the way. She found her prize, an edgy gown by a new up and coming designer.

The clock glared 9:50 p.m. as the last roller slid out of her hair. She pulled the ringlets up, restraining them with silver combs highlighted with red jewels. A few curls fell, framing her oval face. Drifting to the bed, she picked up her dress, a masterpiece of leather, lace, and fine silk. She shimmied the dress along her curves, clasping the red leather corset to her breasts as she searched for help. The leather top, overlaid with black lace from France, tied in the back. The layers of black silk in the skirt whooshed around her bare feet as she shuffled down the hall.

Angel mused at her grandmother's girlish joy, silently watching her before entering the room. Marie spun in her royal-blue gown, admiring herself in the full-length mirror. "*Grand-mère.* Can you help me with my dress?"

"Of course, dear."

She turned her back to Marie, giving her access to the ties. Marie tightened the corset with apt skill, pulling so tight Angel lost two inches from her waist. The constriction also pushed her breasts until they almost busted out the top of the dress. The dress embodied sex and elegance at the same time.

"You look magnificent, *ma chère,*" Marie sang.

"Thank you. You do also. I hope I can breathe all night in this thing and nothing pops out." She inhaled and attempted to tuck the swells of her breasts farther into the corset. *Jacque is going to love this.*

"I see you and Jacque are no longer fighting."

"I guess you can say we are back together. We were never dating to begin with, I'm not sure what to call it."

"Demons are curious creatures. They can be insatiably passionate, irrationally loyal, and extremely possessive. You watch yourself."

"*Grand-mère*, it's not serious. We're going to take it slow and see where it goes. We have enough challenges to get through before we decide to make any commitments. Lucifer's going to be livid when he finds out. He sent Jacque away once. I'm afraid he might do it again." She cringed at the thought of being without Jacque, hoping Lucifer found a new toy to entertain him and forget about her.

"Just be careful, *mon doux* Angel. You play with fire. Everything in this world is dangerous, even love."

"I'll be careful, I promise." Wishing Marie could stay with her, Angel hugged her tightly. She needed someone who understood the insane world she had immersed herself into, someone who understood *her*; Marie was good at both.

"Shall we go down and wait for Laurent?"

"I just have to slide into my shoes, and I'll be down."

She slid the red leather Jimmy Choo boots on and they molded around her calves and knees. The boots served a dual purpose, a little more naughtiness and a place to hide her gun. The .9mm, filled with silver bullets, felt heavy against her leg. Silver was the way to go, since regular bullets were only going to get you one pissed-off Supe. Angel didn't plan to waltz into a house full of demons and vampires without packing. Even though the gun pressed hard into her calf, she rather be uncomfortable than dead.

She heard Laurent's voice in the living room. One final make-up check and she descended the stairs. Laurent's mouth hit the floor as she slowed at the bend on the landing.

"Holeee...crap! Jacque officially has competition tonight. You're fuckin' amazing. Like a Victorian dominatrix. You can beat me any time."

She blushed at his reverence.

"Why thank you, Laurent. May I say you look dashing, too." She curtsied like the southern belle she was and admired him in his Armani tux. She knew the cut well. It was the same one Jackson picked for their wedding. The black made Laurent's fair features stand out. His hair glowed platinum lying against the black jacket and the blue of his eyes had the depth of the Gulf.

"I'm a lucky son-of-a-bitch. I get to escort the two most beautiful women in New Orleans. Ladies, your chariot awaits." He motioned to a black stretch limousine parked in front of the house.

***

The massive white columns surrounding the porch of Etienne's colonial revival mansion announced the formality of the home as they turned off Charles Avenue. A line of limos waited to drop off their passengers at the front entrance. Gorgeous people dressed to the hilt emerged from car after car, reminding Angel of the red carpet show for the Oscars, all they needed was *Project Runway*'s Tim Gunn, to play host.

A boy dressed in a red valet jacket held the door for Laurent, who helped Angel and Marie from the vehicle. They each took his arm and strolled the walkway to the impressive front steps. The other guests stole whispered glances as the three of them entered the house.

At the head of the receiving line, Etienne greeted his guests. Several other vampires stood in the line beside him. A brilliant smile grew across Etienne's face when his saw her, and she returned the gesture. Angel nervously fidgeted with her dress as they waited their turn to greet the host and wished she could adjust the gun in her boot. As required, Etienne shook Laurent's hand first, showing his fangs, he dipped his head in a slight bow for Marie. Once finished, he focused his full attention on Angel, bringing her hand to his lips, letting them linger longer than necessary.

"May I say you look ravishing tonight, my Angel?" His eyes fell from her face and roamed to where her breasts threatened to escape from the corset. "Never have I seen such a lovely dress."

"Aw. This old thing?" She batted her lashes, dropping her eyes to the floor and hiding a smile. Flirting was an art Angel had mastered as a teenager. In high school, she could will her bidding with a flash of a smile or a longing glance. As she got older, she found grown men weren't much more difficult to persuade.

Etienne maintained his hold on her hand; his cool skin caused a chill through her. A young lady dressed in the purple Donna Karan bumped into Angel, breaking Etienne out of his trance. Noticing the anxiousness of the crowd, he brushed his lips across her knuckles and dropped her hand.

"Perhaps you'll save me a dance later, if Laurent is willing to share you." He smacked Laurent hard on the shoulder. "Marie, I'm so pleased you decided to attend. You've made my party the event of the year. Please enjoy yourselves."

The main ballroom hinged on ostentatious. The gold-leaf ceiling reflected the light from the five-tier crystal chandelier. The marble floor was inlayed with an intricate cherry design. Sapphire and silver brocade fabric covered the walls highlighted by the silver silk draperies, which flowed from ceiling to floor. People waltzed to the music from the quartet playing in the corner of the room. It was a scene from a regency novel or maybe *Gone with the Wind*.

Laurent bowed and asked Marie for a dance, leaving Angel alone to study the faces in the crowd, hoping to find Jacque. She recognized many of the guests from her prior week of partying. She struggled to remember their names as they greeted her. There was a bevy of people coming and going. Her head spun trying keep up.

"Who would leave such a beautiful lady alone at a party?" a male's deep voice asked from behind her. She stepped forward and turned to greet the man behind the voice. She recognized his face from a club two nights ago, however his name eluded her.

No woman would forget that face. Her inquisitor was soap opera sexy with mocha-colored eyes and skin to match. Only his opalescent sheen gave away his vampire DNA. Clean-cut and neat, he could have marched off a military compound. Many of the Supes held on to the styles of their human eras, keeping their hair longer. Mr. All-You-Can-Be's body strained to hide underneath the tuxedo. The baby-blue T-shirt he wore at the club revealed biceps she could hang a swing from and abs ready for the wash.

"Unfortunately, I'm sharing a date tonight, and my grandmother seems to have stolen him away," she said, giving him a coy smile.

"Your date must be blind or stupid — maybe both. I would've never left your side."

"Are you here to rescue me from my loneliness?" She touched the bottom of his sleeve, letting the warmth of her fingers graze his skin. She was here to work the crowd and get information, and she meant to find out all she could about Antione.

"I can ensure you're never lonely again." The heat in his voice hinted at danger. Angel couldn't complain; this is what she signed up for. "Would you like to dance?" Her suitor bowed, flashing his fangs as she took his hand.

He wrapped his arm around her waist, much too close for a waltz, and spun her across the room. As they glided over the floor, the coolness of his body transferred to her, causing her to quiver. She raised her voice above the music and said, "I didn't catch your name."

"Forgive my rudeness. It's Fabian Macion."

"Nice to meet you, Fabian. I'm Angelique Dias. Most people call me Angel."

His arm tightened around her. "Everyone knows who you are. You're the hottest thing on the streets right now."

Trying to adjust her body into a proper waltz hold, she countered, "I wasn't this popular even when I made the cover of *Vogue*."

They were on their third song when she begged him to stop. As Fabian spun her around, Angel recognized the cackle behind her. *Who the hell invited Isabella?* When she turned to see Isabella, she stumbled back into Fabian.

"What the fuck?" Fabian looked down at her as the words slipped from her lips. "Sorry." She gave him a half-grin, more of a grimace really.

On the dance floor, Isabella clung so close to Jacque, Static Guard wouldn't have released her. With Angel's fingers digging into Fabian's arm, she dragged him from the dance floor.

Jacque's gaze followed her as she hurried out the room. She had to get away to fight the instinct to scratch out Isabella's eyes. Poor Fabian shuffled alongside her, oblivious to the madness seeping into Angel's mind. In the hall, she thanked him for his company and excused herself to the ladies' room.

Her breaths came in irregular gasps. The pounding in her heart rushed blood to her head. She fanned back the water welling in her eyes, reminding her she had a job to do. She didn't have time to worry about Jacque and his tramp. Jacque was such an asshole. She couldn't believe he had the audacity to bring that bitch with him. She knew this afternoon was a mistake. She was weak, should've listened to her instincts.

Too late to cry over spilled milk, especially if you're giving it away for free as Gran used to say. If Jacque's going to parade his skanky ho in my face, I'm going to have as much fun as I can tonight. Game on!

Chapter Twelve

The bathroom door swung open and slammed into the wall. Marie jumped out of the way to avoid getting smashed by the dark mahogany panel. As soon as Angel saw Marie, the tears threatened to fall again. She inhaled a deep sigh and faked a smile instead. Her acting classes hadn't helped her land any commercials when she was modeling. Maybe they'll be useful in this career.

Marie watched Angel with concern in her light brown eyes. "I was looking for you, dear. Are you all right?"

"I'm fine. Just needed a moment. All's good." Angel's smile showed too much teeth. The same smile she used many years ago when she only dreamed of being a supermodel. Amazing how far reality drifted from the dream.

"I saw Jacque and Bell. I'm sure there's a good explanation. But now is not the time to discuss it."

"I could care less why he brought her. I'm here to do a job. I don't have the energy to waste on his bullshit. Excuse my language." Angel's chest tightened as she tried to convince herself of her own lie. "Anyway, I told him earlier, I'm out at the first signs of problems. Bringing some floozy with him to a party is about as much trouble as I need. Angel has left the building, and Jacque is free to do as he pleases."

Marie eyes twinkled as she spoke. "My, my, don't we have a temper? You remind me of me, during a younger time in my life. And like you, it was usually a man who brought it to the surface." She looped her arm through Angel's and headed back toward the ballroom. The silk of their skirts made a calming swishing noise as they walked.

Jacque and Isabella floated around the dance floor like feathers caught in the wind. Laurent hurried over to Angel, sweat beading on his forehead. His moist hand grabbed hers when he reached her side.

"Don't worry. There'll be no bloodshed tonight. I'm on my best behavior. See...." She forced a tight grin across her face, so tight it hurt her cheeks.

"I'm going to talk to him to see what's going on." He struggled to hold his voice steady, nervously watching his friend and his sister on the dance floor.

"No, there's no need to talk to him. We know what we came to do tonight. What he's doing really doesn't matter. We've got to find out about Antione. Have you heard anything?" She tore her eyes from Jacque, feeling the pain of rejection. She wanted so much to believe his words, to hold on to the hope of him truly caring about her. Like every other man in her life, he failed her.

"No, nothing yet."

"Okay. Let's spread out and work the room." Her blank face projected a mask of indifference.

Before they could leave, Etienne stopped them. "How's everyone enjoying the party?" he asked, placing a frigid hand on Angel's elbow.

"It's a wonderful party. However, some of your guests are questionable." She glanced in Jacque's direction. "I won't hold it against you though." Etienne followed her gaze.

"Oh. I'm sorry, my dear. I planned this party months ago, before I knew about you. Isabella and I go back a long time. She always shows for my parties. This is the first time she's brought Jacque in decades." He studied the couple on the other side of the ballroom.

"No need to explain. It's your party, you can invite whoever you want."

Isabella's curvy hips swayed to the rhythm of the music, drawing the attention of the men she passed. With her blonde hair swept up into a French twist, Angel could see the full extent of her beauty. The low-cut, navy, sequined dress sparked a fire in her blue eyes. The thigh-high split on the right side of the dress exposed her creamy white leg and sparkling silver and rhinestone shoe. If Angel were a guy, she'd want her, too.

Jacque towered above the crowd as they traveled toward her. His white jacket stood out in the sea of black, but he didn't need the jacket to be noticeable. His black pants boasted a crisp crease and his black shirt welded so much starch it could stand on its own. Angel's mind drifted to what lay underneath, and then she shut her eyes for a moment as she pulled herself out of the distraction. She had to stay focused.

Etienne greeted his old friends. "Good evening, Isabella. Jacque."

"Evening, Etienne. Good to see you again. It's been a while," Isabella answered. "Good to see you, too, Angelique. You left in such a hurry, you forgot to say goodbye."

The urge to slap the sappy smile from her face pulsed in Angel's hand. "Next time I'll be sure to leave you a note. Nice to see *you* again, Jacque. I see you're doing well."

"Thanks. You look like you're having fun tonight. I'm surprised Laurent allowed you to leave the house barely dressed. I'm not sure if I could've let Bell out of the house with such a revealing dress on." Her name on his lips made Angel feel nauseous.

"Luckily, I'm not attached to an overbearing asshole. I can wear whatever I want. No one else has complained about my attire. Etienne, what do you think?" Her voice dripped as sweet as honey as she made a small circle, showcasing her goods.

Etienne winked at her. "I think you look good enough to eat."

"Now you're just teasing me." She giggled. "I think it's getting a bit crowded in here. Come dance with me, Etienne. I promised you one earlier. Jacque, Isabella, good to see you both." Taking Etienne's arm, she pushed past Jacque's disapproving stare.

***

Jacque snatched Laurent by the arm and stormed out of the ballroom, leaving Bell behind. The room faded red as he fought to contain his rage. It was killing him to see Angel in another man's arms. Watching Fabian hold her close and sensing the attraction in her fueled his jealousy.

And the way she looked in that dress.

Except for the night in Hades when they had made love, he always saw Angel dressed down. He never witnessed her in her full glory. She was magnificent in her gown and every man wanted her. *Competition.*

"What the hell are you doing?" Laurent asked.

"I should ask you the same question. You let her come out here flirting and flaunting herself to every man! Her breasts are damn near popping out of the dress." His hands shook with anger. Placing them in his pockets, he tried to calm himself.

"Look, man. She dressed herself—not my problem. Like I peeped you earlier, she has a job to do, and you need to let her do it. Anyway, she's damn good at it. If you can't handle it, go home. The way she's dressed is the least of your worries anyway."

"What do you mean?"

"Man, for someone who reads as much as you do, you're dumber than road kill when it comes to women. You're in deep shit. I'll make sure to make the sofa for you tonight, because you'll be bunking with me."

"Why the hell would I stay with you? I'll be at Angel's."

"She's pissed at you. So pissed, she's gone into calm-before-the-storm mode. You're an idiot. Why would you bring Bell, your *ex-girlfriend?* The one person Angel can't stand?"

"Because I needed a way in. Bell knows it doesn't mean anything." Jacque raised a brow in question.

"Did you tell Angel you were coming with Bell?"

"No. Shit. It didn't even cross my mind. I just needed a way in. Fuck!" He slammed a fist into the marble column, fracturing the stone.

"Look. You got some serious beggin' to do. Bring your knee pads and a big diamond when you go over there."

"I've got to explain to her what's going on."

"Not right now. We all got to play this out the way you dealt it. She's already pissed, so no use making a scene here. Talk to her after the party."

"I'm a fuck up. I should've known to talk to Angel or just not come with Bell. Then Bell doesn't help with the smart-ass comments. I guess they'll never get along." He shook his head at his lack of forethought. It was going to take some groveling to get himself out of this one.

Jacque lingered in the hall after Laurent left, thinking about how to make this go away. As he leaned against the wall, a new guest came through the front door.

Antione was the last person he expected to see tonight, however, Jacque was happy for the lucky break. A smile pulled at his lips as he watched the maid trip as she was checking out Antione. It astonished him that women found Antione so attractive. His long lean build was frail compared to Jacque's thickness. The tussled sandy-brown hair looked as if he just rolled from the bed and a scar trailed along his jaw, a gift from the last person who tried to bring him in. Silver left a lasting impression on vamps. Unfortunately, the silver dagger ended up in the heart of the guy who gave Antione the scar.

"What's up, man?" Antione gave him a nod.

"Not much. Haven't seen you in a while. Where the hell you been hiding?"

"Around. You know how it goes. The women of this time make things so easy I have to make my own challenges. What 'bout you?"

"Just tryin to stay out of trouble."

"You still with Bell?"

"It is what it is. We're here tonight. Doesn't mean anything tomorrow." Jacque's laugh bounced off the stone floors.

"I hear there's fresh meat in town. I came to check out the new chick. Have you seen Marie's granddaughter?"

Jacque eyes narrowed at the thought of Antione near Angel. "Yeah. She's here."

"What's the verdict?"

"I wish I would've left Bell back home."

Antione punched him in the arm jokingly. "Then I'll be seeing you later. I got work to do."

Jacque followed Antione back to the party. He scanned the room for Angel and found her perched on a stool surrounded by admirers. The light shimmered off her caramel skin, creating a golden aura around her. Antione stopped at the bar, eyeing her as he ordered a drink. Jacque had to warn her.

As he headed in Angel's direction, Bell grabbed the back of Jacque's jacket. She was beginning to be more trouble than she was worth. He really should've thought this plan through before he asked for Bell's help. He snatched her arm and started to leave, but she clutched his hand, stopping him a second time. He didn't have time for her shit right now.

"What're you doing?" Bell spat under her breath.

"What are you being crazy about now? You know *this* is why we keep breaking up," Jacque answered, in an exasperated tone.

"Every time I look up, you're making goo-goo eyes at her. Do you know how embarrassing it is when people know my date wants someone else?"

"Look. You knew the deal when I asked you to bring me here. I came here for Angel. End. Of. Story." He growled into her ear and snatched his hand from her.

"It'll never work. As a human, her emotions will drain you until there's nothing left of you. And her time with you will always be limited," Bell challenged.

Pissed, Jacque fired, "A short life with her will be better than a lifetime of bullshit with you." Then turned and darted away before she could move.

Shifting through the small gathering, he watched Angel work the crowd. She reminded him of a Victorian doll sitting on her stool, delicate and beautiful, but he knew a fierce woman lay underneath the resplendent exterior. Her gaze traveled over Jacque, gracing him with a sultry smile. He couldn't tell if this was a part of the show or if she forgave him. She gave Antione the same smoldering stare, making him curse under his breath.

A DJ replaced the quartet at some point while Jacque was away. The modern music transformed the ball into a feverish dance club. The DJ slowed the pace down with "Brand New Luv" by Robin Thicke.

Inhaling some courage, he asked, "Can I have this dance? For old times." Everyone waited for her answer.

Antione nudged him with his elbow. "You beat me to the punch, young."

"You're not going to embarrass me in front of all my boys? Are you?" Jacque said half-jokingly.

"What happened to your date? I hate to cause any trouble between you two." Her words were like daggers of ice piercing his heart.

"There's always trouble between me and Bell."

A roar rose from the crowd at Jacque's statement.

He waited with his hand outstretched, hoping she wouldn't refuse.

She took his hand and he led her to the middle of the room. "For old times."

Sweeping Angel onto the parquet floor, he took in the sweetness of her fragrance. Her arms circled his waist and rested on his lower back. Her breast pressed against him, making his temperature rise. They swayed to the rhythm of the music. She floated like a cloud in his arms. He wanted to pick her up and sneak her away to one of the bedrooms upstairs made available for just these situations. Instead, he opened his eyes to remind himself where he was. Maintaining his control was paramount.

He lowered his lips to her ear. "You're magnificent tonight."

She pulled away. "Glad you approve. Bell's pretty, too. You two look good together."

"You have to let me explain. I just don't have time now."

"Whatever, Jacque."

He felt her body stiffen. "Look, babe, I'm sorry. I should've told you about her. It's not what you think."

"Is there a reason you asked me to dance? I won't talk about us here."

Jacque pulled her tighter, trailing his hand down her spine. "Antione's here," he whispered.

"What!" She spun her head searching the crowd filling the dance floor.

"Shhh. He the guy who made the crack about me beating him to the punch. He came to meet you."

Angel finally met his gaze. "What do you mean?"

"You're a big attraction. He came to check out the new game in town." Jacque held her in place even after the song ended. The DJ kept it slow. "Here I Stand" blared through the speakers.

"What should I do?" she asked, trying to break his embrace. His arm gathered her snug to him, not allowing her to leave.

"Our best bet is you making him your new friend. Get close to him." His wishes contradicted his words. "*Please* be careful. He's more dangerous than he looks." Jacque brushed one of her curls out of her face. Instinctively, he bent down and kissed her. Before he could stop her, Angel shoved him and brought a stinging blow across his face. The crowd gasped as she turned on her heels and stomped away, leaving Jacque alone on the dance floor.

Chapter Thirteen

Satisfaction and sorrow existed in a single heartbeat.

Angel's breath weighed heavily in her lungs as she flung open the French doors and relished the sanctuary of the gardens. His unexpected kiss gave her the opportunity to remove herself from the situation. The longer she stayed in his arms, the more her defenses yielded. Every time she was close to him, her survival instincts went faulty. His lips could make her forgive any transgression. She couldn't afford to make any more mistakes when it came to Jacque.

"Angel, what's going on?" Marie asked, as she stepped on to the veranda.

"Sorry, *Grand-mère*," she answered, wiping the tears from her face. "Jacque said Antione is here. Freaked me out."

"So all the fuss was about Antione?"

"Not all of it. Some of it is Jacque being an asshole."

Marie peered back into the house through the French doors. "Which one is he?"

Angel spotted him at the bar. "Oh, there he is." She pointed to the dangerously handsome stranger. He looked as if he should be in leather with a crotch-rocket between his legs — the quintessential bad boy.

"Oh, he's different, isn't he?" Marie voiced her admiration. "I wonder what brought him out? I heard he's been discreet for centuries."

"Jacque said I was the reason he was here. He came for me."

"Why? Do you think he knows you're after him?"

Angel sucked her teeth and shrugged her shoulders. "I don't think so. He claims he needs a new conquest. I guess I'm it."

Marie shook her head. "Men and their games."

Antione's gaze met Angel's. She diverted her eyes, embarrassed to be caught staring. "Let's go in." She took Marie's arm and opened the doors.

At the bar, Angel squeezed between Antione and a cute blond. She flagged the bartender, brushing her breasts against Antione's arm. He gave her a sideways grin, which crinkled the scar along his jaw. Angel cringed, remembering the damage that once adorned her own face.

"Hello, lovely." His syrupy-sweet voice was like candy.

"Hi, I don't believe I've had the pleasure." She extended her hand to him.

Antione covered her small hand with both of his and speaking in the same singsong voice announced, "You're as heavenly as your name."

She gave him her pageant smile, bright and wide. "It's not fair you know my name, but I don't know yours."

"I'm sorry, my sweet. I'm Antione." He dropped his head until his eyes met her cleavage.

"Nice to meet you, Antione." She gave a slight curtsey and pressed closer into him when the blond behind her rested his hand on her ass. Everyone at this party was a bit touchy-feely.

Reaching around Angel, Antione tapped Blondie on his shoulder. "I think the lady would like you to take your hand off her."

"Let her tell me herself." The blond jerked Angel to him by the strings on the back of her corset.

Antione's fist flew by the right side of her face and connected to Mr. Grab-ass's chin. Blondie shook off the punch and lunged at Antione. Angel spun to get out the way. Before she could remove herself from the scuffle, Blondie's shoulder clipped her and threw her on the floor. Her head slammed into the marble floor. Before she could move, several guys were by her side assisting her up. Accepting Laurent's and Etienne's hand, she smoothed her skirt as she got on her feet, trying to hide the gun in her boot.

The room spun. Angel tightened her grip on Laurent to steady herself. As she regained her focus, she looked up in time to watch Antione ram a silver spike into Blondie's heart. Mr. Grab-ass dissipated in a puff of black smoke before he could hit the ground. Dusting off his jacket, Antione ran a hand through his hair and searched the crowd to find his prize. He would be dazzling, if he weren't a homicidal maniac.

Antione slid close to Angel, placing his hand at the small of her back. "I'm sorry about the disturbance, Etienne."

"Not a problem. I would've done the same if I were with Angel."

Antione tilted her chin to search her face. "Are you okay, my sweet?"

"I'm fine. My head hurts a bit. I'm tough. I'll survive." She smiled at him. "I think I'll have Laurent bring me home. But I owe you one. Can we do dinner tomorrow or I guess it's actually tonight?"

"Dinner sounds lovely. May I pick you up at nine when the sun is completely down?"

"Perfect. Again, thank you." She reached over and kissed Antione's cheek. "Laurent, have you seen Marie?"

"She left about an hour ago. The car took her home," Laurent replied.

"Oh. Okay. Can we leave then? My head is killing me."

"Of course."

Etienne escorted them to the door.

Angel reached over and kissed him on each cheek. "Thanks for inviting me. You have a lovely home."

"I apologize for the rudeness of my guests. It seems you bring out the animal in men. I can understand the attraction and the need to be territorial. Please don't let tonight stop you from coming back." Etienne's sincerity rang true.

"I'll be back anytime you'll have me. Just call."

***

Angel jumped into the limo. Jacque grabbed her, securing Angel to his side. Laurent slid in after her, shutting the door, blocking out the nosey onlookers. Angel moved to the seat on the other side of the car, her brown eyes glimmering with rage. As Jacque broke away from her glare, he thought, *I'm in deep shit*.

Some things aren't as simple as they seem when you first think of them. He should've thought through his plan a little better. Even though Bell knew the situation, he still had to listen to her shit after kissing Angel on the dance floor. *Women! They're more trouble than they're worth sometimes.* The situation with Bell was easy. He didn't care if she was pissed. But he had to figure out a way to make it right with Angel.

The ride to Angel's was quieter than a monastery full of monks who had taken a vow of silence. Jacque kept his mouth shut. There was no need for Laurent to witness his begging. His friend would snatch his man card. When the limo stopped, Angel hopped out before the driver could open the door. Jacque jumped out after her.

Laurent wedged out the car door as though he was dodging bullets in a war zone. "Do you want me to wait for you?" he asked cautiously.

"No need to wait. He's leaving with you," Angel spat out, fumbling with her keys.

"I'm not leaving until we talk," Jacque answered, taking the keys from her and opening the door. "Don't worry about me, man. I'll see you later. Come by around noon."

"All right. I'll make the sofa for you just in case. You know where the spare key is." Laurent got back in the car, shaking his head.

***

She ran into the house; the rage welled inside of her, consuming her. Salty tears fell to her lips. She knew a life with Jacque would end in misery and pain. Opening herself up to him had been a mistake. Angel's downfall was she needed him, needed love, and needed to live the lie even if it only lasted for a moment. The undeniable passion Jacque evoked clouded her judgment.

Weariness weighed her down like an anchor as she climbed the stairs to the bedroom. She didn't have the energy to fight vampires, Lucifer, and Jacque. She prayed he would leave. Instead of leaving, Jacque silently followed her up the stairs. His silence drove her insane.

Once inside the bedroom, she turned to face him. "What do you want?" she asked as she plopped on the bed.

"I want to explain. I know how it looks. I wasn't *with* Bell." His eyes pleaded for her to understand.

"Then what do *you* call it when someone shows up to a party with their ex, or is it current girlfriend, on their arm?" Her head pounded as she waited for the answer.

Silence.

His brows furrowed as if deep in thought. *What was there to think about? It was a simple question.*

Finally he spoke. "I needed a way into the party. I knew Bell had a standing invite. I asked to come along. She knew I was there for you. She's just an ass. You know how Bell is. She wanted you to think we were together." He rattled out the statement so fast even Angel had to take a breath.

Sitting on the bed with her elbows propped on her knees, she held her head in her hands. Jacque knelt on the floor beside her, nervously playing with the bottom of her skirt. Her heart tore in two. Only logic kept her from falling apart.

If their relationship or lack thereof was this difficult now, what would happen if she lost her fight with Lucifer? What'll happen when the beautiful face he loved so much reverted to the monster she used to be? Or when age stole her beauty? Would he still want her then?

Unconsciously, she ran her fingers through Jacque's dark curls. His hand slipped under her skirt, massaging her leather-clad calf. He rolled his eyes as he reached the top of her boot and found her gun. Placing it on the floor, he pulled the boot from her foot and then the other. He held her foot in his hand, working miracles with his fingers. Her shields slipped as he massaged. This was what every girl needed after a night in five-inch heels.

His hands traveled higher up her leg, almost to his target, before she stopped him. "Please stop. Sex'll just complicate things right now. I'm still not sure how I want to move forward with you."

"Maybe it'll help you make up your mind," he answered, his voice dark with lust.

"I like you," she said, downplaying her emotions. "Right now, I like me more. I have to focus on Antione. I don't have time to worry about you and ex-girlfriends or anything else. I have to focus on staying alive. Don't pressure me to commit to anything. If you do, you'll lose." The words struggled from her mouth. She craved to have him inside of her, their bodies fusing as one. She could taste him on her lips.

"I can understand. I won't pressure you, but I'm not leaving. I need to make sure you're safe. Please allow me to stay." Next to her on the bed, the heat of his body transferred to the pit of her stomach, enticing her to retract her request.

"I won't say no to your help. I won't even force you to leave tonight. You have to promise no more sex or relationship talk for now."

His smile didn't match the sadness in his eyes. "Thanks."

"What're you thanking me for?"

He lay still on the bed, holding her hand. "Being you, being honest, and not saying no."

She released his hand, stood and turned her back to him. "Now, help me out of this contraption so I can breathe." Jacque unlaced the cinched ties of the corset. Clutching the dress to her, she disappeared into the bathroom. Reappearing with sweat shorts and a tank top, she climbed under the covers, trying to create as much separation between her and Jacque as possible. She had to find a way to let him go.

Chapter Fourteen

His brick-hard body wrapped around her like a security blanket. The morning light cascaded through the windows, warming her face. Squirming from underneath Jacque's arm, she sat up in the bed and gazed down at his sleeping face. Still wearing his tuxedo pants and undershirt, he slept soundly, his expression like an innocent child. The rays of sun created highlights in his dark curls and cast a soft glow against his skin. In this light, he resembled an angel. How ironic.

She wanted to give into Jacque, hand over her heart, except she didn't have the strength. When Jackson left, it nearly destroyed her. Agreeing to marry a man who used "I guess you've put in your time" as a line in his proposal, may not have been the smartest thing she had ever done. *Hindsight is twenty-twenty.*

It would be different this time. She was different this time. She refused to be someone's arm candy again. Jacque would have to prove his love to her before she relinquished her heart to him. Unfortunately, Angel's love life was on hold until she staked Antione and delivered him to Lucifer.

Angel scooted off the bed in an attempt not to wake him. She hated to be seen before her morning beauty ritual.

With her hair and makeup done, she quietly stood next to the bed, listening to the even pace of Jacque's breathing and resisted the urge to climb back under the covers. Angel forced herself out of the room, sneaking downstairs to the kitchen to find some Vamp Juice. Her head throbbed like someone hit her with a hammer. Guess a marble floor worked just as good.

She straddled the kitchen chair, downing thick acidic liquid when Marie came into the room.

"I heard there was a lot excitement last night after I left." Marie leaned over and kissed Angel on the cheek.

"Too much for my taste, but I got what I wanted — Antione's attention." The Vamp Juice worked its mojo, making her head feel better and her body stronger. A few extra doses might not be such a bad idea today.

"You must be careful, darling. He is very dangerous. Are Jacque and Laurent here?"

"Jacque's here. Laurent should be on his way." She grabbed another bottle of V-Juice out the fridge.

"Good. Then we can discuss a plan to defeat this Antione. I hope you're able to take him tonight. I'll have to leave tomorrow night and will not be able to assist you." Marie's eyes glistened with moisture as she hugged Angel tight.

"I'll miss you." She hid her face for fear of her own tears falling.

"Cher, I'll always be watching over you, even when you do not see me. And Faith will be here for you like always. Trust her. She'll never guide you wrong." Marie reached over and squeezed Angel's hand. "Now come. We have work to do." Angel smiled through her tears.

The light bounced off the bottles and crystals in the dining room, creating small rainbows around the room. This was magic. She pulled the bottles she needed for the protection spell and lit the incenses and candles. Marie stood behind her, watching like a dutiful teacher.

Chanting the spell over her favorite necklace from Tiffany's, Angel focused her energies. If she was going to make a protection talisman, why shouldn't it be from Tiffany's? Angel wasn't a costume jewelry kind of girl. She finished the spell and thanked the spirits. Lifting the platinum Tiffany's Petal Key pendant out of the circle of candles, she went to place it back around her neck.

Strong hands took the delicate strands of platinum from her hands and latched the necklace. She hadn't heard Jacque enter the room. The warmth of his breath licked the back of her neck, making the hairs stand on end. He smelled of soap and mint. Yearning the strength of his body, she leaned back into his arms, desperately needing the support.

"Uh hum," Marie coughed.

"Good morning, Marie." Jacque stepped away, breaking the electric current passing through them.

"We have a lot to do before tonight. You two will have plenty of time to enjoy each other once Antione is dead."

"Sorry, *Grand-mère*," Angel mumbled under her breath and blushed. She forgot they were not alone. Jacque had that effect on her.

"Jacque, will you be sparring with Angel? She needs to practice. We're done with our rituals here." There was no beating around the bush for the Voodoo Queen.

"I guess I can. I haven't spared with Angel since we were in Hades. You sure you don't want to wait for Laurent?"

"What? You afraid I'll kick your ass?" Angel cut her eyes at him, smiling a wicked grin.

"No, I'm afraid I'll hurt you before Antione gets a chance." He gave her a lopsided grin and slapped her hard on the ass.

"Oh, no you didn't! It's *on!*" She marched toward the back patio doors.

***

Jacque followed Angel to the backyard. As soon as he shut the patio door, the bottom of a sneaker caught him in his chest. He stumbled back a couple of steps from the impact. Before he could regain his composure, another blow snapped his right knee backward. Shit. She was faster than he remembered and stronger. Oddly, his pain brought him some comfort. Maybe she could hold her own if she got into trouble.

He refused to let someone half his size get the best of him, even if it was the woman he loved. *Love? Did I just admit to loving her? Shit. I did.* Another kick flew toward his ribs. Grabbing her foot, he shoved her backward. She landed in the pool and emerged from the water fuming. He was in trouble—again.

He limped to the side of the pool and jerked Angel up by the back of her T-shirt. Bad idea. Rule number one: Never underestimate your opponent.

When she cleared the side of the pool, she rammed her fist into the base of his throat and brought him to the ground gasping for air.

She screamed as she kicked him in the rib cage. He curled into the fetal position, on the ground, to protect himself. "You son-of-a-bitch! Now, my hair is ruined! Do you know how long it's going to take to straighten it?"

"You are sooooo going to pay for this!" he threatened as the bottom of her shoe met its target. She stopped kicking and straddled him, pummeling his head with her small fists. She was like an angry gnat, unleashing all its wrath. Twisting under her, he locked her arms to her side. With one fling, she landed in the pool for the second time.

Angel surfaced from the crystal blue water. She swam to the edge of the pool and pushed herself up. He tossed her a towel.

"Are we done fighting?" he asked.

"Never."

"Eventually, you have to stop being mad. I'm the one who should be pissed. You damn near snapped my leg in two." She diverted her gaze and hid her smirk behind the towel. A burning urge smoldered inside of her. Humans and their emotions, sometimes the empath thing worked to his advantage.

"You deserved it," she said as he took the towel from her and helped dry her hair.

"I deserve a lot of things. Your anger about last night is misguided. I care a lot about you and would never intentionally hurt you."

"Only crazies and psychopaths intentionally hurt others. The rest of us get caught up in unintentional bullshit or friendly fire, if you will. We both have a lot of baggage. Let's take things slow and figure out what we're both willing to give." Her voice trailed off.

Wrapping his arm around her shoulders, he gathered her close to him, smelling the mixture of her shampoo and chlorine. He kissed the crook of her neck, causing her to shiver in his arms. He wanted to keep her there forever. He would have to break through her defenses first. It might be less work if he could stop making mistakes. Thinking about the consequences of his actions was not at the top of his radar. It was something he had to work on.

He kissed the trail from her collarbone to just below her ear. The delicious apricot and pear fragrance of her perfume intoxicated him. A flash of yearning pulsed in her blood. She wanted him as much as he did her. He brushed his lips to the base of her neck and draped the towel around her shoulders. Eventually, the wall she built around her heart would crumble. Until then, he would wait. He sensed her need to be loved. And he was just the guy to do it.

Laurent leaned against the doorway. "Am I interrupting something?"

"Always," Jacque mocked.

Angel stood, wringing more water from her hair. "Good thing you're here to save him from the beat down I was about to inflict on him. The asshole threw me in the pool."

"Yeah. The scene I witnessed looked like you were killing him," Laurent joked. "Jacque, what's up with the bruise on your neck?" He nodded toward the damage.

"She's vicious. What've you been teaching her?" Jacque answered as his hand went to the spot just above his collarbone.

Laurent winked at Angel. "I'm an *excellent* teacher."

"And modest, too." Her giggle was refreshing, like lemonade on a hot day.

Laurent punched Angel in the arm as she passed him to answer the phone. He had a way with women — winning their trust. They opened up to him, felt comfortable with him. Jacque was surprised Laurent hadn't settled down yet. He wasn't the player type, yet seemed to go through women like Jacque went through socks. Guess he hadn't found the "one" yet.

***

Angel's giggle echoed off the stone floors. She was entertained by whomever she spoke with. Propping against the kitchen wall, she cradled the phone against her shoulder, twirling a wet strand of hair around her finger, nervous habit.

"No. No. It's okay. I don't mind you calling. I should've thought to give you the number myself last night. Everything got so crazy. How nice of Etienne to give it to you." Angel chatted with the other person.

Jacque straddled a stool and watched her charm. With her behavior, it could only be a man on the other end of the line. Every woman knew how to get to a man. It must be something they passed down through the generations like a secret recipe.

"It was a good time until Blondie pawed me. I appreciate how you took care of the problem for me. I guess a girl doesn't have to worry when she's with you." Her voice was light and flirty. Something he wished she saved for him.

"Oh, I can't wait to go out tonight either. It should be fun." She hugged the phone closer to her mouth. "You are so bad!" she snickered, causing Jacque to get out of the chair. Jealousy tightened the muscles of his jaw.

He pressed his body close to hers, making her jump. She gasped into the phone as his hand slid under her damp shirt, feeling the quiver in her stomach. As he caressed her breast, he trailed his tongue down the back of her neck. Angel melted into his chest, leaning her head back and closing her eyes for a brief moment. She opened her eyes, slapped Jacque's hand away, and refocused on her conversation.

"Nothing's wrong. I just felt a chill. What time again?"

Jacque caught her earlobe between his lips. "It's heat not a chill," he whispered.

"Um. I think my grandmother's calling me. I'll be ready at nine. Do you know the way to the house?" Jacque was back under her shirt, pinching her nipple, causing her to moan. "No. No. I'm fine. Look. I've *got* to go. See you tonight. Okay."

When she hung up the phone, he spun her around and ravaged her mouth. His tongue toyed along the line of her luscious lips, beckoning them to invite him in. She sucked in a breath, giving him access to her sweet wetness. As his tongue explored, he relished every crevice of her mouth. She gave in and responded. Her tongue tangled with his. Breaking down her barriers, her body shuddered in response to him as their tongues intertwined in sweet passion.

Circling her arms around his neck, she beckoned him to her. She went limp in his arms when his mouth drifted to the cleavage escaping the low V-neck of her T-shirt. He caught the neckline in his mouth, nudging it down to expose her caramel breast. Then he caught her nipple between his teeth through the red lace of her bra, winning a shuddering gasp from Angel. Lapping at her hardened nipple like a lollipop through the red lace bra, he was rewarded by the raspy call of his name.

"What the hell! Do I have to throw a bucket of water on the two of you?" Laurent yelled as he entered the kitchen. "You're like dogs in heat. Get a room or something."

Angel stiffened in Jacque's arms. He kept a tight hold. His lips gently covered hers, slowly brandishing his mark on her, giving her something to remember him by whenever she was with another man. She belonged to him. Sooner or later, she would accept it. He would make sure of it.

Chapter Fifteen

Angel loved the Emilio Pucci design even though it looked as if a box of Crayolas threw up on her. The bright blues and yellows of the form fitting dress gave her a tropical vibrancy. To finish off the ensemble, she pulled her hair back into a slick ponytail garnished with yellow and white Dendrobium Orchids. The strappy, blue custom-made Emanuel Ungaro heels served a dual purpose — complimenting her outfit and the silver plated four-inch stiletto made a great stake.

Her yellow Michael Kors Zuma Leather Satchel weighed a ton with all her weapons inside. She had to carry a larger purse than she liked. The dress left no room to hide any weapons. Laurent's tailor designed special hidden pockets for her gun and daggers in the lining of her larger purses. Damn, the purse was heavy when fully loaded.

Jacque slouched on the red leather sofa, concern plastered on his face. She promised to be careful. It didn't comfort him. She understood his fear. Her lunch churned relentlessly in her stomach. Her hands felt like a damp mop from the sweat. Inside, she was a tight knot of anxiety. On the outside, she painted on a brave face.

"Someone should call the color police on you," Laurent shouted from the bar, trying to break the tension in the room.

"Oh, shut up. What the hell do you know about fashion?" She stuck her tongue out at him.

"You look ravishing. Actually, too good. Where's your weapons. I know they're not in your dress. You're barely hiding body parts in that thing." Jacque's eyes roamed over her disapprovingly.

"They're in my purse. Don't worry. I'm a big girl. I can take care of myself." She attempted make light of the situation, but it didn't quite come through.

"Famous last words. Where's he taking you?"

"Emeril's Delmonico and then to Utopia." *How much trouble can I get into at a public place?* She figured she could do the deed and stake him when he dropped her off for the night. It could replace the good night kiss.

"We'll be around in case you need help. Don't try anything stupid. Antione's dangerous and smart. He'll kill you if he figures this out before you can stake him."

"Yeah, yeah. We've been over this a thousand times today. I get it." She played off her nervousness. Jacque made things worse with all his warnings.

He guided her down on the sofa. His petal soft lips grazed the curve of her neck. "I can't lose you. I *won't* lose you. Stay alive. Understand?" For the first time, she understood and accepted the depth of Jacque's feelings for her.

The doorbell caused everyone to jump. Standing, she straightened her dress and shooed Jacque and Laurent out the patio door. She touched the diamond key pendant around her neck and prayed the spell worked before opening the front door.

Wearing a dangerous grin, Antione consumed her with his eyes. "You like?" She turned slowly, allowing him time to soak in her image.

"I've never seen anything more beautiful in all my two-hundred fifty years. I'm indeed a lucky man." Offering his arm to her, he escorted her to the waiting limousine.

She slid into the seat with Antione so close, she felt the cool clamminess of his skin. His hand brushed against her thigh and sent a disturbing wave of queasiness to the pit of her belly. The feeling was danger masked in excitement.

His arm dangled around her shoulder as it rested along the back of the seat. When he drew her near, the knot in the pit of her stomach contracted. She wanted to slap his hand away, but instead forced a smile on her face.

Angel felt like a prostitute, using her body to pay for her beauty. Luring men into a trap to kill them and deliver them to Lucifer. Who cared if they were evil? Was being beautiful worth all this trouble? The grass on this side quickly started to brown.

"Ms. Dias, what brings you back to New Orleans?" His voice was harsh and grating.

"I missed home. No matter how long I stay away, New Orleans will always be home to me," she answered truthfully.

"You were lovely on the cover of *Vogue*."

She cut her eyes to him. She didn't trust him, and he apparently felt the same way about her. She thought only women Googled their dates. "Huh, you found my issue?"

"I was curious. I did some research."

"Did you now? And what did you find?"

"Not much more than I already knew. I was very interested to read about your horrible car accident. I can't say those photos did you any justice." He ran a finger along the line where her scar once resided. "You must have an excellent surgeon."

"You know, you French can work miracles." She pulled away from him. The reminder of her prior affliction made her jaw tense, and his hands on her made her feel dirty.

The ride to Delmonico's was taking longer than usual. She peered out the window to get oriented and didn't recognize her surroundings. Delmonico's was in the heart of the French Quarter on Saint Charles Avenue. They were crossing the Greater New Orleans Bridge, heading away from the Quarter.

Panic rose in her. She pushed it back. Remaining calm was vital to her survival. She crossed her legs and turned to Antione. "Where are we going? The restaurant is the other direction."

"Restaurants are so crowded. I wanted you all to myself tonight. Forgive my selfishness." The bitter sweetness of his tone had a sickening effect on her.

Crossing her arms across her chest, she stared at him. "Where are we going?"

"To my place."

Her lips pierced into a thin line and glared at him. "I'm not sure how I feel about going to your house. I'm not a sleep-with-you-on-the-first-date kind of girl."

"I have no interest in sleeping."

"Then what is it you think we're going to do?"

"Dinner, my dear. I invited you to dinner. No need to be alarmed."

"I don't like surprises." She watched the scenery out the window, noting where he took her. Last thing she needed was to be stranded in the middle of nowhere and not know how to get out.

Antione went silent. Angel prayed. She might have lost some of her clout when she made a pact with the Devil, but she prayed anyway.

After crossing the river, she guessed they were on RT90 heading toward the I10. They drove quite some time, until the car turned down a small lane and a gorgeous plantation house appeared before them. She recognized it from a tour she took when she was in school called "The Great Plantations of the South" tour.

The moon cast a silver-blue glow behind the antebellum-style mansion. One might think it romantic if she wasn't planning to kill the man who brought her here. Antione studied her every move. He suspected something. She didn't know how much he knew. She would play along until she staked his cold, undead ass.

"Is this your place?" she questioned, wanting to break the silence between them.

"It's been in my family for generations. I grew up here. The family lost it to the North in the Civil War. Once I regained my hold in the world, I purchased it back and restored it to its original glory." He almost sounded nostalgic, until an undercurrent of hate seeped through his words.

"It's beautiful. Can't wait to see inside."

The car came to a halt on the circular drive. The chauffeur opened the door and helped Angel out the car. Antione took her arm and strolled into the house. She absorbed her surroundings, hoping Jacque and Laurent followed them from the house. With her luck, they probably decided to go play pool and get drunk.

Inside the house, the grand hall reminded her of a scene from *Gone with the Wind*. At times, she felt like she and dear sweet Scarlet were kindred spirits. Tonight, she recognized all Scarlet's glaring flaws, self-centeredness, stubbornness, and jealousy, which weren't much different from hers. If she got out of this alive, she was definitely going to make some changes in her life.

Her heels clicked on the wide-plank pine floors as he showed her to the parlor. The navy blue silk draperies provided a stark contrast against the butter-cream walls. Taking a seat on the plum colored settee, she clutched her purse to her side.

Antione opened the doors of a antique armoire. "Would you like a drink before dinner?"

"Sure. A martini would be great." Maybe a drink would take the edge off. Her heart pounded so loud she swore he could hear it.

He mixed the drink with expertise. Setting it down on the coffee table, he took a seat next to her. Antione took a swig of his whiskey and ran the cold, moist glass up her exposed thigh. She wished she picked a different outfit. Her dress provided little coverage and sucked when it came to fighting.

"Would you like me to take your purse for you?" he asked staring at her breasts.

"No, no. It's fine. You know a girl and her purse is hard to part." She clutched it to her side on the settee.

"Very well then. Are you comfortable?" The ice-filled glass slid along her arm, making her shiver involuntarily.

"Oh, sure." Her voice trembled. She had difficulty hiding her disgust. Maybe he would mistake it for lust. Either way things were going badly for her.

Antione downed his drink. Standing, he snatched Angel by the hand, dragging her out the room.

"What the hell are you doing?" She yanked her arm from him, but his fingers only dug deeper into her flesh. "Let me go!" She dug her heels into the floor trying to slow him down.

"Shut-up, bitch. You come here flaunting yourself and now find some modesty?" He smashed her hard against the banister. Angel's shoulder cracked, sending searing pain down her arm and back.

"What're you talking about? Have you lost your mind?" The glassy haze in his eyes answered her question.

"You sluts are all the same. Taunting and teasing, then pulling away. If you want no to mean *no*, then you might rethink your wardrobe. If you act like a whore, you should be fucked like one." Madness raged in his voice. With each word he spoke, he fell deeper into his own insanity.

She bounced off the steps like a rubber ball as he dragged her upstairs. Clawing for the railings with her free hand, Angel tried to get away from his iron clasp. She kicked and flailed with little success. Blood dripped down the side of her face when her head slammed into the top step. Everything faded out of focus and then she floated into the darkness.

Chapter Sixteen

Angel awoke to a hellish nightmare. Dangling from the ceiling by a chain with her feet barely skimming the floor, her eyes adjusted to the darkness. Her wrists were chaffed by the cuffs, and her arms felt as if they might pop out the sockets. The pain in her shoulder radiated down the right side of her body. Looking down, she sighed in relief to see her clothes were still on. The only thing missing were her shoes — potential weapons. Antione was no dummy.

Breathing was a challenge as she twisted on the chain. Her lungs struggled to expand, most likely from the injury she'd gotten from being dragged up the stairs. She lifted her head and glanced around the room. She had landed in a scene from a bad BDSM movie. A large round bed sat in the middle of the room, covered with a red satin comforter. On the long black lacquer dresser, an assortment of whips, gags, and restraints lay waiting to exact their punishment.

Light filtered through the door as it creaked open, and Antione slithered into the room. The chains rattled as a tremor ripped through Angel's body as she watched him inch closer to her. Fear penetrated her core as he picked up the leather whip when he passed assorted torture devices. His eyes still held the crazed manic expression from earlier in the night. She flinched as he ran the hilt of the whip down the front of her torso, lingering a moment in the valley between her breasts. Bile raised in her throat when he trailed the cracked leather handle along the hem of her dress then between her legs. The shackles cut into her wrists as she swung back, trying to escape Antione's repulsive touch.

"I'm glad to see you're awake, my dear," he sneered.

"What're you planning to do to me? You sick, dead fuck!" Fear and rage exploded inside of her. "Let me down from here!"

"We haven't had a chance to play yet." The straps of the leather whip seared like electric eels as they wound around Angel's calf. Her scream bounced off the empty walls as she arched back in pain.

"You can kiss my ass," she growled, pulling herself up on the chains. "When I get down from here, you'll regret ever touching me." Tears streamed down her face, a mixture of anger and torment. The leather tendrils of the whip coiled around her throat this time, drawing blood.

"You'll be the one with regrets, my dear. You'll regret the day you decided to make a deal with Lucifer." Retrieving a pearl-handled dagger off the dresser, he slashed the dress off her body. It fell in a pool of color to the floor.

The lust grew in his eyes as he watched her swing from the chain in her bra and thong. Repulsed, she wanted to cover herself, instead she kicked at Antione. He snatched her by the ankle and pressed the dagger down her calf, forcing her to stop fighting. The cold stainless steel blade traced a path up her thigh. He halted at her lace thong, waiting, for what she didn't know. Angel closed her eyes, prayed and hoped for mercy.

Time had run out.

Waiting to be rescued was no longer an option. If she wanted to live, it was left up to her to find a way. As she gazed around the room, she caught a glimpse of the moon through a small slit in the black curtains. The answer revealed itself. Focusing through the pain of Antione slicing small slits into her arm and the grotesque moisture of his tongue licking the dripping blood, she found the motivation to call upon her powers.

She tilted her head back, letting out a roar, and called the elements. Thunder rumbled in the sky and a bolt of lightning flashed behind the curtain. She summoned the lightning to her, feeling the surge of electricity. Antione sensed the intense energies and backed away.

Sparks flew as lightning struck the chains suspending her from the ceiling. The metal gave away upon impact. Angel dropped to the floor. Her body hummed as the electricity surge through her veins. He froze like a statue. Energy flowed from her fingertips, blasting Antione and forcing him to the ground. As he lay convulsing on the floor, she ran.

Turn back and finish him, the words echoed in her mind, but fear pushed her to keep moving. Escape was the goal, to get as far away as possible. The pine planks felt rough against Angel's bare feet. Stumbling down the stairs, she made it to the front door. As her hand reached for the knob, her head snapped back as Antione snatched her by her ponytail.

She swung around and landed a right hook to Antione's jaw, but he didn't flinch. Fisting another handful of her hair, he yanked her to him. In a futile attempt to survive, she shoved, scratched, and kicked, trying to inflict harm to the crazed vamp. *Must get to my purse.* She had to get to the parlor, to her weapons.

Her teeth sank into Antione's arm. He recoiled in pain and brought the back of his hand across her cheek. Angel tumbled into the wall on the other side of the foyer. Gathering her strength, she darted into the sitting room, hoping her purse was still there. At the entrance of the parlor, he tackled her from behind. A human could never outrun a vampire. She would have to fight.

Angel threw punches, not caring where they landed. She backed into the room. Her purse sat on the settee. As she dived for the sofa, he caught her around the waist. Antione trapped her against him. He jerked her head back, grazing his fangs along her jugular. Before he plunged the pointy canines into her flesh, the front door burst open, distracting him.

Relief washed over her when Jacque plowed through the door with Laurent following close behind. Antione clutched her tighter to him and spun to face the intruders. Relief shifted back to fear. Jacque stopped, his breathing labored, his face contorted, and rage glowing red in his eyes. His strong legs stood slightly bowed, the moon cast a silvery-blue aura about him as he gripped his broadsword so tight his knuckles stretched taunt and white. Tonight, he was a demon, her demonic Prince Charming, coming to her rescue.

"You move another inch, and I'll tear her throat out," Antione threatened and ran his tongue along her neck.

The heat of Jacque's anger radiated throughout the room. "You fuckin' hurt her and you'll pay for the rest of eternity." Laurent stood poised behind him, his cool blue eyes turned fire engine red.

Antione's fang pierced her ear. She gasped from surprise and pain. "Eventually, I'll land in Hell anyway. This way, I take a guest with me." He slowly slid her across the parlor, adding distance between them and Jacque.

"*Nique ta mère.* They were right to string you up by your neck when you were human." Jacque never took his eyes off them. "But some idiot vampire decided he was hungry and didn't get to finish his meal before they came to bury you. You've continued raping and killing for the last two hundred and fifty years. It stops today."

"Ah. They all wanted it, even our Angel here. What self-respecting woman dresses like a whore to go out on a date? Look at her." Antione jerked Angel hard against him, while he continued to back toward the windows. He ran the dagger down the front of her, stopping at her navel.

They were at an impasse. She waited for an opportunity to escape. Antione held the knife pressed firmly to her abdomen limiting her options. As they backed away, Jacque matched every step Antione took. A low, animalistic growl escaped him as he prowled in a semi-circle, balancing the weight of his sword in front of him. Laurent flanked the opposite side, closing in on them.

Due to keeping an eye on Jacque and Laurent, Antione stumbled over the settee. Angel seized the opportunity. She rammed her elbow into Antione's side. With all the force she could muster, she slammed her head back into his chin. Once he released his hold, she jumped out of reach. As she rounded the settee, Jacque's sword sliced the air, slashing Antione's chest and striking the arm of the sofa. Unable to dislodge his weapon, Jacque pounced on Antione like a tiger attacking an antelope.

Fists flew in a tangled mess. Angel struggled against Laurent as he pulled her away from the battle. Jacque powered a blow, throwing Antione to the other end of the room. Antione picked his dagger off the floor. He rushed at Jacque, tackling him to the ground. Antione fought with the ferociousness of a rabid animal. Moonlight glistened off the blade of the dagger. A howl pierced the night. Horror penetrated her heart. Jacque collapsed to the floor with the dagger jutting from his chest.

The screams echoed in Angel's head until she realized they came from within her. Her heart pounded out of her chest, threatening to explode. She lunged out of Laurent's arms and ran to Jacque's side. The threat of loss enflamed an inferno of rage inside of her and escaped in a bellowed call to the spirits. Revenge powered her actions.

The winds shattered the windows in a shower of glass and wood. Lightning incinerated the settee. Everyone but Angel stood petrified in awe. She plucked Jacque's sword from the floor. She savored Jacque's lingering energy and wrapped both hands securely around the hilt. Antione turned to run, but ice crystals encased his legs, trapping him in place.

"See you in Hell, motherfucker," she hissed through her teeth as she swung the sword above her head, bringing it down in one swift defining blow. The blade sliced through his neck as easy as a hot knife through butter. When Antione's head rolled to her feet, she kicked it away in disgust.

The sword fell heavy from her hands. Angel ran to Jacque as he lay on the floor, blood pooling around him. She knelt down beside him, pulled him onto her lap and brushed the curls from his face. Cupping his face, she kissed him softly.

"Hey, babe." He smiled up at her. "Nice. You took his head in one swing."

"I learned from the best." She trembled as she kissed his forehead, forcing a grin.

"Sorry I didn't get here sooner." A tear fell from the corner of his eye.

"You got here just in time." She wiped the moisture from his face. Her breathing became ragged as the tears flowed freely.

"*Ma chère*, don't cry. Did he *hurt* you?"

"No. He didn't have a chance. I got free before...." She wiped her tears falling on Jacque's face, hating herself. Always a day late and a dollar short. As he lay dying in her arms, Angel realized she loved him.

Laurent kneeled next to her, placing a firm hand on her shoulder, providing his support. "Hey, dude. You look like shit."

The pain in his eyes, betrayed the lightheartedness in his words. Jacque's laugh turned into a cough, spewing blood onto the floor.

"Look, buddy. Hold still," Laurent ordered in a hushed tone. "I would remove the knife, except I'm afraid it might do more damage. I'm gonna go for help. You'll be fine." The futility of the situation was evident on his face.

"We all know there's no need to go for help. It's too late." Jacque twined his fingers through Angel's, kissing her hand. "Hey, man, take care of her for me." He closed his eyes and smiled. "Now, just let me be with my Angel."

A tear slid down Laurent's cheek. His blue eyes still held a hint of red. Standing, he kicked Antione's head so hard it flew out the window. He turned and exited the room, leaving them alone. Angel gathered Jacque in her arms, holding him to her breasts. She brought her lips to rest on his. The sweet, metallic taste of his blood brushed the tip of her tongue. He tensed at her touch.

"Babe," he whispered. "Promise me you'll take care of yourself. I don't want you ending up with Luc. Promise me." Exhaustion and fear penetrated his calm demeanor.

She would tell him anything at this moment to alleviate his anguish. "I promise."

"I know this is bad timing, but I need you to know I love you." His voice was barely audible. "You know, it's the first time I ever said those words to anyone." He gazed at her with peace and contentment.

"Yeah, really bad timing. Don't worry. If it was any other time, I wouldn't have believed you." She fingered his dark curls. His angelic smile broke her heart.

"What a pair we make." His breathing slowed, becoming more labored. She tasted his lips again, lingering, not wanting to let him go. Her pain ravaged him. He answered her kiss with the same passion.

Flames burst all over Jacque's body. *Déjà vu.* The heat seared her arms, yet she refused to let him go.

"You can't have him!" she screamed at the fire consuming them. Laurent ran into the room, prying her arms from around Jacque. Laurent dragged her from the room crying and kicking as she watched the flames engulf Jacque until he was no more.

Outside, Laurent held her close to him, sharing her grief. He wrapped a coat around her as she sat on the steps in her bra and panties. Misery seeped through her pores. Exhaustion beat her down as Laurent picked her up and placed her in the car. She curled in the passenger seat, closed her eyes, and searched for Jacque in her dreams.

Chapter Seventeen

Pain and agony woke her from her nightmares. She lay still on the bed, her body sore from the prior night's torture. Tears fell. She thought she'd run the well dry last night. Throughout the night, she replayed his death over and over in her mind, praying it was only a dream. Now, awake in the daylight, the nightmare became a reality as she lay alone in the bed.

A knock came at the door. "Sweetie, are you awake?"

"Yeah. Come in." Angel wiped her face with her T-shirt and sat propped against the headboard. Her sister padded into the room, balancing a large tray in her arms. The smell of chicory and beignets drifted through the room. The tray also held a large bottle of the magic elixir, which Angel desperately needed. Faith set the tray on the nightstand, stood at the edge of the bed, and held Angel's hand.

Unable to maintain her emotions, Angel cried out, "He's gone. He's really gone." She flung herself into her sister's arms.

Faith stroked Angel's back, gently rocking. "I know...I know."

"It's my fault. If I hadn't made this stupid deal with Lucifer, Jacque would still be alive."

Faith tilted her chin, forcing Angel to face her. "You listen to me. Jacque was here because he wanted to be here. You didn't ask him to come, and no one made him go with you."

"I know. He didn't do this because it was his job or he was asked. He did this, because he loved me and wanted to keep me safe." The depth of Jacque's sacrifice pained her. She wasn't use to someone putting her before their needs.

"Hey, sis. Jacque left this world protecting the one he loved. What greater sacrifice can someone make? He'll be fine."

"I'm not sure if demons who work for the Devil get a reprieve."

"Huh. The Devil himself was once in God's good graces. Actions turn a person away from God, not birth rights. Jacque seemed to be a good man. Had to have been to make you love him." Faith pushed the wavy locks out of Angel's face. Her sister's touch always soothed Angel. She was the calm in Angel's chaos. Faith kissed her on the top of her head and left her to her breakfast.

She downed the bottle of Vamp Juice and bit into the beignet. The neon light of the clock blinked 12:47 p.m. The day was halfway through. As much as she wanted to climb back under the covers and hide, she knew she had to face the world. Angel crawled out of bed and slogged to the bathroom. Fifteen minutes later, she reappeared dressed in jeans and a black T-shirt. This was the first time in five years she emerged from her morning ritual without any makeup. She didn't want to disrespect Jacque's memory with pomp and showiness. Her exterior matched her mood.

***

Laurent slouched on the sofa with his shoulders hung low. Angel leaned over and hugged him, absorbing his misery. He flung his arm around her neck, pulling her closer, his head pressed to hers. Once he released her, she hopped over the back of the couch and slid beside him.

"I'm surprised to see you." His voice was tired and weak.

"I can't hide upstairs forever. And someone apparently has to take care of you, because you look like crap. What'd you do? Just sit down here all night?" She knew the answer before he answered. He never left.

"Where else was I supposed to go?" He played with the fringe on a pillow, lowering his eyes to his lap.

"Home. Get some rest. It was a rough night. You need some sleep." Her hand covered his and she leaned on his shoulder.

"No shit, right? I got to make sure you're safe. If the word spreads you killed Antione, others might come after you. They'll know you're working contracts."

"Great. The man I love is dead, I have to work for Lucifer, and *now* other Supes will start gunning for me. My life couldn't suck more if I actually tried." She ran her fingers through her hair.

"You loved him?" Laurent gazed at her compassionately.

"Yeah. I loved him. Doesn't do any good to admit it now." She diverted her eyes, not wanting to share the pain reflected in her heart. It was too soon, too fresh.

"He loved you, too. I think it's the first time he ever loved anyone. It was hard for him, especially to love a human." She closed her hand around Laurent's and squeezed hard. He was a good friend, both to Jacque and her.

Buzzing inside Angel's purse broke the silence. She snatched it off the floor and dug around for the dreaded BlackBerry. She unsheathed it from the case and read the message.

From: Luc Devlin

Condolences

June 25, 2010

I'm so sorry for your loss. I know you and Jacque were close. Sometimes bad things happen to good people or demon is more correct.

You did a fine job of delivering Antione. He arrived safely.

*Since you did such a fine job, I have your next assignment. Your new target is **Laurent Lacoste**. I'm sure you know who he is and where to find him. You have one week to deliver him to me.*

Forever yours,

Luc

Sorry bastard! He was punishing her, taunting her. Enough. She refused to play his game. She clicked reply on the BlackBerry and typed two words–*Fuck You*. Then hit send.

Angel had just fucked herself. She prepared for the worst. It no longer mattered to her. There wasn't much else Lucifer could take. If it came down to being his slave and hurting her friends, she would rather live out her days in hell.

Heat scorched her skin and flames licked her face. Lucifer was revoking their deal. This was an undeniable possibility. She knew the price and was willing to pay it. Agonizing pain seized her from inside out. She felt the scars and burns reappear down her face. Laurent froze in horror as he watched her transform.

"What the hell is going on?" His eyes were wide with amazement. The flames subsided and she righted herself.

Pulling her hair to hide her face, she smiled at Laurent. "This is the real me. At least it's the me left over after the accident."

His voice was soft and comforting. "This is how you ended up with Luc."

"Yeah. Messed up, right? I sold my soul to be beautiful again. I know it's shallow. I've depended on my looks all my life. I didn't know what to do without them." A pang of shame twisted in her belly.

"Why's Luc pissed at you? I have to assume it's bad if he took back his deal."

"I refused my next target."

"What the hell for? I would've helped you," he answered sincerely.

"I highly doubt it since my target was you." She raised her brows as she watched his expression.

He paced the length of the sofa. His eyes grew redder with each step. "Has he lost his mind?" She swore the tribal tattoos banned around Laurent's biceps transversed to a different design. Jacque had the same tattoos. It must be branding of some sort.

"This is the Devil we're talking about. And I kinda told him, 'fuck you.' I've got to work on my anger issues." She needed to calm Laurent down. She wanted him rational. They had to figure a way out of this shit. Her mistakes were kicking her in the ass. This time she had to get it right. She had two choices, take down the Devil or end up in Hell.

The next time he passed, she snatched his hand and pulled him down to the sofa. She needed to think and the pacing was driving her crazy. He was her only back up. Marie was back in the Underworld. Jacque was gone. She knew a handful of other Supes, but they had no reason to assist them. Without her alluring sex appeal, she couldn't even attempt to entice their alliance.

"Look, Laurent. We got to figure something out. Luc's gonna come for us, well at least me. I don't know about you. I'm not planning on sitting around and waiting for him to kill me." The words tumbled out of her so quickly she had to take a break. "My sister always told me, 'Never let'em get the first lick. You might not get back up.' I'm not planning on letting Luc get the first lick. You in or out?"

"You want to fight the Devil?" The surprise in his voice succumbed to hysterical laughing.

"Hey. Are you making fun of me?" She crossed her arms across her breasts.

"I know you're all bad ass and stuff, but really.... You think *you* can *win* a fight with the Devil?"

"Why not? It's about time someone stands up to him. What do I have to lose? I rather die fighting than running."

"Oh, wow. Now, I understand what Jacque saw in you. This much fight in a human is hot!" Laurent fell back as she punched him in the arm. "Shit, that hurt."

Pouting, she stood to leave. "Oh, forget it."

"Don't leave. You know me. Always got jokes. But you're right, we got to hit Luc before he gets us. Only thing is we're gonna need help. And lots of it."

"Yeah. I figured, but who?" she muttered.

"I guess it's a good thing I'm here then," a voice called from the backyard. Both Angel and Laurent turned to see who entered the house.

Shock choked the words in Angel's throat when she saw Isabella step from behind the foliage. Why was Isabella here? Angel didn't have the energy to fight anyone else. Isabella was the last person she wanted to see right now.

"What're you doing here?" Angel asked suspiciously.

"I know shit hit the fan, and I figure you guys needed some help. Here I am." Isabella waved her hand down her body in a Vanna White move.

"Why the hell do you want to help me?"

"For one, it's not just you. You're sitting next to *my* brother. And two, you're not the only one who loved Jacque," Isabella announced more to the floor than to Angel.

"I guess I should say thank you. We could use all the help we can get."

Awkward silence filled the room, until Faith came out the kitchen with iced tea. Angel picked up a glass and held it to her face. The coolness of the ice tempered the frenzy of her anger and fear. Bravery wasn't one of her strong suits. She mastered acting brave in order to mask her fear. She was like a chameleon, changing her exterior to protect herself from danger. Today, she summoned her courage for Jacque.

"Faith, you said you've conjured *Grand-mère* before. Do you think you can do it again?"

She took a sip of tea and put the glass on the marble table. "I think I can. Why do you need Marie?"

"We have big trouble. I pissed off the Devil. It was fight or run. I picked fight." Angel shrugged it off.

Faith set down the tray and inhaled a deep breath. "Good lord, girl. What is wrong with you? I swear you're more like Mom than you're willing to admit."

"He wanted me to kill Laurent. I'm not letting him rule my life anymore."

Finally, Faith noticed Angel's face. "Aw, shit, I'm so sorry." She pulled Angel's hair back, studying her face. "At least he didn't make it worse."

Isabella gasped in horror, her gaze steadying on Angel. "What did he do to you?" The words slipped from her lips in a hush tone.

"Lucifer didn't do this to me. This is why I was indebted to him. A stupid-ass drunk driver hit me, and this was the result," Angel explained. "Don't drink and drive, boys and girls." She choked.

Silence stung like a slap in the face. Everyone studied the floor. Angel refused to let this ugliness incapacitate her again. The scar wasn't going to define her this time.

"Okay, we have work to do." She broke the lull. "Faith, you see if you can get Marie up here. Laurent and Isabella, find anyone and everyone willing to help us. I'll start with Etienne. I don't know if he'll help. Can't hurt to ask." She barked orders like a general. She had a newfound purpose, making Lucifer pay for stealing her chance for love.

Chapter Eighteen

Dealing with the preternatural world was like trying to break into a high school clique. Everyone thought their group was the best and no one wanted to mingle with the others. Angel's new job was creating a Supe United Nations. This job took more self-control than her in a Jimmy Choo store. Diplomacy wasn't one of her strengths. Angel realized she was short when it came to things she was good at.

Laurent worked the soldier angle, gathering as many of Jacque's loyal soldiers as he could find. Isabella welded a black book only to be topped by the D.C. Madame, working it with the same divisiveness. Faith managed to materialize Marie for the second time. Angel suspected Faith possessed more power than she let on. Etienne also agreed to help. Apparently, Lucifer pissed off a lot of people. Go figure.

The house buzzed with activity. The living room served as a makeshift war room. Sitting at the large glass and metal desk, Angel poured over Etienne's report outlining each group's costs and criteria for participation. She understood why so many of the Supes were rich. Alliances didn't come cheap.

Someone leaned on the doorbell. Angel hopped up from the black leather executive chair and ran for the door. *Whoever was at the door best be on fire.* Snatching the door open, she readied for her verbal attack.

"Is there a problem?" she snapped, peering at the two strangers on her doorstep. Two beautiful specimens of male stood watching her curiously. "Oh. Sorry. Can I help you?" She rested against the door.

"Are you Angel?" the taller dark-haired one asked.

She backed away, never taking her eyes off them. "Yeah, who's asking?"

"We've been sent to help," the blond responded in a lyrical melody. The aroma of melting chocolate drifted through the air. Strangely, it came from the two standing in front of her. *Delicious.*

"Sent here to help who and for what?" Her eyes narrowed, waiting for the answer. Strangers represented danger.

"To help you defeat Luc."

"Who sent you?" She stumbled backward into the safety of the house, pulling the door in front of her. She thought about running, but their magnetizing beauty drew her to them. Their tantalizing smell made her stomach growl.

"The Big Guy."

"Who the hell are you? There's others here with me. I'm not alone," she warned.

"Sorry. We didn't mean to frighten you. I'm Michael and this is Raphael. We're here for the battle." The dark-haired one, Michael, eyes sparkled at the mention of battle.

"Are you *Punk'n* me?" Her voice climbed an octave. "Hey, Laurent! Get out here. Ashton Kutcher sent a couple of angels to punk us."

Laurent appeared behind her faster than she expected. "Oh. Wus up, Michael. Raphael. What're y'all doing here?" The casualness of his tone made Angel do a double take.

"We heard you were going to battle. Wondered if you needed a hand. The Big Guy gave us permission to participate if we wanted. Raphael and I thought we'd see what's cracking. Gabe backed out. Last time we fought Luc, I think he got spooked." Angel stared at the hunky archangel standing at her door. A bead of sweat glistened down his radiant face, a three-quarter length suit in New Orleans, especially during the dead of summer, never a good idea. An angel and a demon stood at her front door talking like two boys from the hood. After the scene registered in her mind, she giggled hysterically.

"The Bible was right. Interesting. It's really *them?*" She gave Laurent a sideways glance.

"Yeah, they're who they say they are." He shook his head at Angel in amazement. "You accept vampires, demons, and werewolves. When it comes to angels you have a problem believing. I swear you need to use Bell's peroxide sometimes."

"Shut up, Laurent. I just wouldn't expect them to help *us.*"

"They'll help anyone who's fighting Luc. It's some kind of sick game to them."

"Can we come in?" Raphael finally asked.

She opened the door wide and moved out the way. "Sure." The angels had to angle their bodies to squeeze through the door.

Isabella flew around the corner, her blonde hair fanning about her and lips set in a sultry smile. "I should've known when I smelled cookies someone let the angels loose. Nice to see you again, Raphael. It's been a while." Her smoldering eyes explained the prior was more than a casual meeting.

"Bell, good to see you again. Maybe, this time will be as good as the last." The angel reached out, running his thumb along her chin.

"We don't have time for this right now." Michael gave Raphael a menacing glare.

The pair shrugged off their coats, revealing feathered masterpieces tucked against their backs. The wings protruded from their shoulder blades and the tips reached the bend of their knees. The feathers gleamed a brilliant white. Angel resisted the urge to touch them.

"What're you guys doing here?" Isabella questioned.

"Battle of course. And we're instructed to offer Angel a gift. The Big Guy extends you a boon for relinquishing your deal with Luc." Raphael smiled at Angel, intensifying the aroma of molten chocolate.

"A gift? What kind of gift?" Laurent asked before she could interject.

"He knows you sacrificed a lot when you turned down Lucifer. He's willing to restore your appearance as Luc did." Michael studied the seating around the room and settled on a leather ottoman beside the sofa.

Her heart rejoiced at the offer, and then broke again. She no longer had a reason for her beauty. The one man she wanted to seduce with her beauty no longer existed in her world. She couldn't care less about how she looked, but it could come in handy during negotiations.

"Do I have any other options?"

"Isn't beauty what you were seeking from Lucifer? Your need for beauty is the reason we battle." Michael's dark brows contracted in confusion.

"I've realized my obsession with physical attraction has been a problem. I have something I want more. Can I ask for something else?" She waited, holding her breath in anticipation.

"I can submit the request. I don't know what the answer will be. What is it you seek?"

"I want Jacque back." Everyone stared in disbelief.

Michael almost whispered as if he didn't want God to hear. "You want him to resurrect a dead demon?"

"Yes." She smiled at the angel, picturing Jacque's face. "I want the dead demon."

"What if he no longer wants you in your current condition?"

The thought hadn't crossed her mind. At this point, she didn't care. Jacque deserved to live. This was her chance to do the right thing for a change. "It doesn't matter."

"Understand you are declining the opportunity to regain your looks. Once I submit your alternative, the original gift is void." He gave her a second glance, searching her eyes. She met his stare and nodded her head. "I will send your request."

Michael pulled out his BlackBerry and sent the email.

**

Fear gripped Angel. In her current state, she resembled a monster in a horror film. How would she ever compete with the flawless perfection of the supernatural females flaunting themselves in front of Jacque? Even in top form, she barely met their standards. Insecurity gripped her. She prepared herself for rejection.

They worked on aligning the divisions. Assessing the strengths and weaknesses of the little army amassed, they developed a strategy. Michael was an expert strategist. Isabella and Raphael huddled in the corner debating weapons. Laurent worked on the budget at the desk in the corner. Angel stared out the window, praying silently for Jacque's return.

She rested her head on the arm, curling into a ball in the club chair. She studied the cracks in the worn leather, tracing the path with her finger. It seemed an eternity since Michael sent the request. She checked the clock and only an hour had passed. Laurent hauled the ottoman in front of her chair, showing her compassion. The tears burned her eyes. She tilted her head back to keep them from falling.

"Hey, there's no crying in war." He wiped a tear slipping down her cheek. "What's going on?"

Angel hugged her knees. "Sorry, I know I'm a downer."

"Yeah, a big one. You know I'm available if you need to talk. I'm your friend, Ang, and will do anything to help."

"You've been a great friend. I needed one. Most of the people in my life have been there, because they wanted something from me. It's strange to have people who care about you and want nothing in return." She turned her gaze back outside. The moist heat created a hazy mist in the air. Louisiana summers were notorious for the humidity.

"Tell Dr. Laurent what's going on." He chuckled.

"I'm afraid of losing Jacque again."

He swatted her shoe. "What're you talking about?"

"Look at me. If Jacque comes back, he'll never want to be with someone like me." Her head hung low and she closed her eyes, appreciating the darkness.

"He loves you ,Angel." Laurent took her hand in his. His words gave her hope.

"Yeah, we can remake the *Beauty and the Beast*, only I'll play the beast." She graced them with her fake smile reserved for bad jokes and unwanted advances from a boss.

"You're being ridiculous. We've had this conversation before. Give Jacque more credit."

"The last guy I loved ditched me while I was in the hospital, because of this face. My own mother can't stand to lay her eyes on me like this. I've known Jacque for a minute. I'm supposed to trust he can see beyond this?" She peered up at him with questioning eyes, begging for the truth.

"Your mother and the other guy are idiots. You're a good person. You have love to share. Look at all these people here to help you. It doesn't matter to us what you look like."

"Okay, half of these people you're paying ungodly amounts of money to help. The rest just like to fight or have some kind of vendetta against Luc."

"They wouldn't back you if they didn't believe in you. We're risking our lives for you. You have to be special for people to be willing to die for you, regardless of the money."

"It doesn't matter. The request will probably get denied anyway. I knew it was a shot in the dark, but I had to try."

"See that's why people love you. You risked your shot at something you deemed important for the possibility to get Jacque back even though you believe he won't want you. You're something else, Angelique Dias."

Her smile was genuine this time.

The doorbell interrupted the conversation. It was like Grand Central Station around here these days. She wiped her face and left to answer the door. Hopefully, it was the pizza. Keeping food in a house full of supernatural males was like finding a $9.99 sale on Pradas. Impossible.

When Angel opened the door, her heart stopped.

Chapter Nineteen

Angel opened the door just as Jacque decided to kick it in. Her amber tresses hid her face. The sight of her eased his pain. He thought he had lost her forever. Somehow a miracle plucked him from the gates of purgatory and dropped him on her doorstep. Yeah. Purgatory. He never expected to end up there; demons usually went straight to Hell.

As soon as she stepped within reach, he scooped her into his arms, holding her tight to his chest. Her body stiffened and she pushed back. Then realization hit, a brilliant smile broke across her face, and she circled her arms around his waist. Shaking with tears, she mumbled incoherently into his chest. He inhaled her sweetness and kissed her hair, unable to let her go.

He brushed back her dark waves to take in her beautiful face. The image of her large coffee colored eyes and pouty lips stayed with him as he waited for his judgment. She let go of him and looked the other away. Her head dropped, shoulders shook, and she sucked in air between the sobs. She pushed against his stomach, trying to escape his hold. Confused, Jacque held her tighter. Her hair cascaded around her face, blocking his view.

"Angel, baby. What's wrong?" he pleaded. This wasn't the welcome he expected.

"I don't want you to see me," she murmured through her tears.

He turned her to face him. "Why? What's going on?" She jerked away and dipped her head lower. He wanted to see her, to get lost in her eyes. She was an easy read. Her emotions laid on the surface waiting to explode.

She held strong when he tried to tilt her face to him. "You're not going to want me anymore when you see me."

He hugged her, feeling some of the tension ease from her body. "I will always want you. I love you."

"You love someone who doesn't exist anymore."

"Okay, Angel. What hell are you talking about?" Frustration resonated in his voice.

She slowly pulled back her hair and chocolate orbs stared at him, watching him expectantly. The horror tore him apart. A gaping scar mangled the right side of her face. The deep gash cut a path from her temple to below her jaw line. The scar pulled at her skin, slightly deforming the shape of her right eye. Who could do such a thing? Then the answer was evident. Words escaped him. The pain in her eyes as she watched him hurt worse than the dagger that pierced his heart. She tore herself from his arms and disappeared into the house.

Jacque felt the sorrow and turmoil boiling like a cauldron inside of Angel. Was this what she gave up to bring him back? Ignorantly, he stared at her in horror instead of comforting her fears. Every time he opened his mouth or, this time, not open, he hurt her. His track record sucked. He had to fix this. Making things right with Angel was becoming a full-time job for him.

He hurried down the hall to the living room. The room went silent when he entered. Bell called his name under her breath. Before he could take another step, she threw herself into his arms. Bell's tears wet his shirt as he stroked her back to soothe her crying.

"I thought you were lost to the Pits forever." She clung tighter. He wanted to pull away from her and find Angel. He sensed her need to be close to him and stayed a bit longer.

He let go of Bell and stepped back, unlocking her arms from him. "No, I ended in Purgatory then someone plucked me out of there and here I am."

"You can thank Angel. She made a huge sacrifice to get your no-good ass back," Laurent called from the kitchen.

"I noticed. I think I messed up." He took another step back, trying to put some distance between him and Bell. She hovered close as if he might disappear.

"What the hell you do? She's really messed up right now."

Jacque eyes fell to the floor in shame. "I was just surprised when I saw her face."

Laurent rubbed his temple as he sat in the club chair in the corner. "Shit. You *are* a dumbass! She got messed up in a car accident. She came to Luc 'cause she was trying to get her beauty back. Then, he wanted her to take me out and she refused. He forfeited the contract."

"I knew something heavy brought her to Luc. She refused to tell me what. How the hell did she get me back?"

"The archs are here, well Michael and Raphael. They offered to return Angel's beauty. Instead of helping herself, she traded it to get you back. I guess the Big Guy approved her request." Laurent shook his head as he recounted the story.

"Fuck. Did all hell break loose when I left? I thought you were supposed to be taking care of her." Jacque's eyes flash red with anger.

"Man, we're at war now. The shit has hit the fan!"

"I guess I have a lot of catching up to do."

"First you need to go and make things right with Angel." Laurent pointed up the stairs.

***

Angel stopped at the top of the stairs and watched the scene below as the reality of her situation blossomed in front of her. Isabella ran into Jacque's arms. He gathered her lovingly, soothing her shock just as he did with Angel. Only he gazed upon Isabella's face with admiration, not horror. The sharp talons of jealousy ripped a hole in her thundering heart.

She waited for him to come to her. He didn't move. He lingered with Isabella hovering close, talking to Laurent. She tried to prepare herself for this situation. She understood the possibilities. The pain still tore at her sanity. She thought he loved her, therefore could see past the monster she had become. His betrayal far outweighed Jackson's. She didn't love Jackson. He did her a favor when he left. Foolishly, she fell for Jacque, giving her heart to him.

Angel sighed, studying Isabella's delicate features, the fairness of her blonde hair and blue eyes. Her petite figure highlighted Jacque's massive frame. They were a dance of contrasts, painting a picture of contradicting beauty. She admired them with envy.

He turned, heading toward the stairs, prompting her to dart into the bedroom. She didn't need or want his pity. Locking herself in the bathroom, she faced her worst enemy, the mirror. As she stared at her reflection, she came to terms with her fate. This monster was her burden to bear forever. It was time she embraced her destiny.

Angel picked up the black band and gathered her hair high on top her head in a ponytail, her face fully visible for the first time since Lucifer stripped her of his gift. She traced the ridges with her fingertips, saying goodbye to the Cover Girl face of her past. Digging deep, she mustered up her courage and went back into the master bedroom.

Jacque stretched out across the bed with his hands tucked behind his head waiting for her. The massive bulk of his body made the king-sized bed shrink in size. Her eyes roamed over the broadness of his strong chest, catching the ripple of muscles as he watched her cross the room. The ridges of his ironclad abs showed through the tight T-shirt. His torso tapered at his waist, flowing into the powerful build of his legs. She licked her lips unintentionally. She was a lioness ready to pounce on its prey. The desire boiling inside of her reminded her how much she missed him.

Instead of reacting to her instincts, she ignored Jacque, forcing herself away from the bed. *Must stay strong.* She went to the dresser and opened the top drawer, pretending to search for something. The bed moved and she sensed Jacque's heat. She froze, holding her breath. If he touched her, she wasn't sure she could maintain her pretense.

He swept her hair across her shoulder and his lips hovered at the base of her neck. The warm moisture of his breath made the hairs on her nape sway like reeds in the wind. Her knees trembled as soft full lips whispered a kiss just behind her ear. She released the breath she held. He wrapped an arm around the front of her, melding her to him. Angel closed her eyes, basking in his seduction.

"I'm sorry," he implored, the words caressing her cheek.

She tried to escape his grasp. "I don't want your pity."

"I feel a lot of things for you. Pity is not one of them. I'm sorry I did this to you." He leaned his weight in on her, cocooning her in his arms.

She shook her head and answered, "You didn't do this. This was done long before I met you."

"But you could've changed it. Actually, you had changed it until I messed things up."

"Jacque, I shouldn't have made the deal with Lucifer in the first place. I got a second chance to make things right, to do the right thing."

"You saved my life." A kiss brushed against her temple.

"I took your life when you tried to help me. I gave you back what was rightfully yours." She touched his arm and grazed his jaw with her lips.

He spun her around to meet his gaze. Immediately, she diverted her eyes to the floor. With a finger under her chin, he lifted her face to his. "I meant what I said at Antione's."

She looked up at him with hood eyes. "Help me remember."

"My, how easily we forget." He smiled and ran a finger along the scar, gently stroking her face. "I love you."

"Look at me. How can you love this?" No longer able to bare the intensity of his stare, she buried her face in Jacque's chest.

"I see everything about you, even the things you fail to see about yourself. There's nothing monstrous about you. You're my Angel." He played with a strand of her hair.

Once again, he lifted her face, slanting his lips on hers. The urgency of his passion lit like wildfire through Angel. His tongue darted in and out of her parted lips, begging her to respond. She moaned against him, her mouth opened, welcoming the sweet taste of his eager lips. Her tongue met his, twining in desperate desire.

Chapter Twenty

Banging interrupted their kiss. Angel regained her composure and removed herself from Jacque's hold. The banging became louder.

"Hey, y'all in there?" Bell's voice called from the other side of the door, sounding as annoying as she did when they were kids. "Helloooo. Anyone home?"

He snatched open the door. "What do you want, Bell?" Bell's eyes gleamed with mischief. "Just want to tell y'all we have company. Etienne is downstairs for Angel, and your parents are here."

"What do you mean 'my parents?'" Angel piped up.

"Shit, Bell. You didn't call them, did you?" He glowered, waiting for her answer.

"I thought they would want to know you're okay. And they can help. You know they got clout in the Underworld. I'm trying to get a hold of my mom, too."

Angel sunk onto the bed with an exasperated expression glued to her face. "Who *are* your parents?"

"You would've had to meet them sooner or later. I was just hoping for later." He shot a glance at Bell. "My father is Leviathan, one of the seven Princes of Hell. My mom is Isis."

Her eyebrows crinkled in a question. "The Egyptian goddess Isis?"

"Yeah. She has a lot of titles. Some call her one of the four protectors. She has too many to name all of them."

Angel flung herself back on the bed, her arms flopping to her sides. "Fucking great. Not only do I have to meet your parents looking like this. Your father's a goddamn prince and your mother's a goddess."

"Hey, your grandma's a voodoo queen. Maybe it'll win you some points." Bell stifled a giggle, straightening quickly when Jacque growled. "Look. I'll go back down and keep everyone entertained. Y'all gotta come down. I have to catch up with your mom anyway. It's been a while since we talked." The glare Angel shot Bell could frighten Medusa solid.

Jacque gathered Angel off the bed. She slumped in his arms in protest. He laid his full weight on her and ground his pelvis into her. Kissing the hollow of her neck, he felt her quiver underneath him.

He whispered softly in her ear, "We can stay here, and I can make you forget my parents are downstairs. Eventually we have to go down, and when we do everyone will know why we were delayed."

She squirmed under him and pushed at his shoulders, trying to escape. He tasted her lips hungrily before freeing her. The fire in her eyes made him want to keep her trapped in bed, ravishing her body.

She rolled off the bed and ran to the closet. "You're such an ass. I should've left you to burn in Hell."

"What're you doing?"

"Changing. I can't meet your mom in jeans."

"It doesn't matter. Let's just get going." He dragged her from the closet. "Oh. I apologize in advance for my mom."

"What do you mean?" she asked.

"You'll see," he said, guiding her down the stairs.

***

Voices floated up from the living room, sounding like a party brewing. She took in a deep breath before descending down the stairs. When they reached the others, she resisted the urge to run and hide. Jacque's hand at the small of her back comforted her and acted as a brace keeping her steady.

A statuesque woman poised beside the armchair. Her flawless radiance glowed under the setting sun. She spoke with authority and grace. She and Marie chatted like ladies of the court. This was Jacque's mother and to Angel's pleasure, she stood as far away from Bell as physically possible.

The men huddled by the bar, drinks in hand. She wouldn't have had a problem identifying Jacque's father, even in a crowd. Both men had emerald eyes with the intensity of an exploding star. They reminded her of an NBA star mixed with a WWE wrestler. Jacque took the best his parents had to offer and combined them into a spectacular specimen of a man. Demon, she corrected herself.

The conversation died as she and Jacque entered the room. His mother came to him and embraced him. Even as he towered over her, she still exuded power and strength. Angel noticed a softer side as Isis's love for Jacque shone in her eyes. Angel could only dream of having the same kind of love from her mother. The goddess released her hold, but held his hand like she thought he might escape. Angel knew the feeling well.

Jacque's father, like most men, refused public displays of affection. He slapped Jacque across the shoulder as if to say, "He's my boy." Angel envied the interaction. Her mother could care less about her, and she never knew her father. All she knew was the memory of her father burned a hole in her mother's heart every time she looked at Angel.

Jacque moved to stand behind her. "Mom, Dad. This is Angel."

His mother examined every inch of her, narrowing her dark brown eyes in scrutiny. "Yes, we've heard a lot about you. Jacque seems quite taken with you."

Angel backed a little closer to Jacque for protection, from what she didn't know. "It's nice to meet you both. I... I just wish it was under better circumstances," she stammered like a babbling idiot.

"This is a mess you've created here." The words stung like salt in a wound.

Jacque came to her defense. "Mom. Cut it out. This isn't Angel's fault. You know how crazy Luc is."

"At least she had the decency to get you back from Death."

Angel fought her tears. She couldn't break down in front of this woman. She refused to give her the satisfaction.

"Watch how you speak to my granddaughter," Marie interjected. "She didn't mean for any of this to happen, and she risked everything to save your son. You will treat her with some respect." The two ladies challenged one another.

Lightning flashed through the horizon. Power surged through the room. "I owe no mortal respect. I would watch how *you* speak to *me!*" Angel couldn't decipher which woman caused the bolt.

"Okay. Timeout." Jacque stepped in the middle of the two, making a T-motion with his hands. "Mom...don't disrespect Angel. She's important to me."

Her heart sang. For the first time in her life, someone other than Faith took up for her. Love surrounded her.

"I'm not sure what to call you. Goddess? Isis? Ma'am? I'd never hurt Jacque on purpose. I know I've caused a lot of problems. It was because I refused to be used by Lucifer again. I wasn't going to turn Laurent over to him. Now I have to pay a price. This is not a price I asked anyone else to contribute to." It took all her determination to face Jacque's mother. She was an intimidating presence, one used to being worshipped.

"You have fortitude, young one. You might be just what my son needs. Balance. We shall see. Now, how can we assist with this situation with Luc? He is really getting out of hand. Someone must put him back in his place."

Isis turned with a swish of her dress, dismissing Angel. Isabella cursed under her breath. Hugging Angel close to him, Jacque relaxed. Angel smiled. Round one went in her favor.

Angel beamed with a confidence she had never experienced before. She held her head higher. Not even on her most beautiful days on the runway was she filled with this kind of joy. For the first time in her life, she respected herself and expected the same from others. The people in the room cared about her and not her beauty or money, just her.

Now her life was worth living, she had to figure out a way to salvage it. This battle with the Devil wasn't going to be simple. She was clueless beyond knowing how to entice people to help. She would leave the logistics and strategy to the military people. *G.I. Jane*, she was not.

"Etienne, how many others have agreed to help?" she asked, talking about the one thing she understood.

"We have a few covens of vampires and witches. The rougarou or werewolves have agreed to join. Luc has been after their pack leader for centuries. They will be strong allies. We have a few rogue Supes who offered to help at a price."

She slid back into the club chair, twirling a strand of hair. "We're going to need more help if we plan to beat the Devil."

"The legions belonged to me for a long time. I know some of my soldiers will help us." Jacque sat on the arm of her chair. She leaned her head to rest on his side.

"I talked to some of them and they agreed. I'm sure more will join once they know you're back," Laurent chimed in.

"I know Ra, Amun, and Ma'at will help. They owe me a favor, and Lucifer is not their favorite person. Your father will gather as many demons as he can get to join the cause. Call us when you have everyone assembled and ready to discuss strategy." With those words, Isis and Jacque's father vanished.

"We may be able to get some more help," the archs announced, putting on their coats.

"Okay, for right now we work on gathering as many as we can to fight. Etienne, can you secure a place large enough for all of us to meet? Let's say in three days." Angel waited for his reply.

"Sure," Etienne answered.

"Okay, we have a lot of work to do in a short amount of time. Let's get this party started." She stood, taking Jacque's hand. Everyone disbursed, leaving her alone with Jacque.

***

Rising, Jacque gazed down at Angel. Her weariness reflected in her smile. Jacque figured standing up for herself was a challenge for Angel, one he doubted she'd been successful at many times before. Although she took a giant leap, insecurities lurked in the shadows of her mind. He needed to take things slow.

He picked her up and her arms circled around his neck. She rested her head against his chest. Her sweet aroma wafted to his nostrils, teasing his senses. Her scent had followed him, kept him company in the bland nothingness of purgatory. He carried her to the bedroom, lowered himself on the bed, and cradled her in his arms. She peered up with cocoa eyes and brushed the backs of her fingers down his cheek. The heat of her touch seared his skin. He caught her fingers in his hand and brought them gently across his lips. He released her hand and ran his thumb along her bottom lip, feeling its petal-soft texture. She quivered under his touch as her hands explored the planes of his chest.

He wanted to surround her in his love and secure her in happiness. He hadn't realized how broken she was, even before her accident. She came into herself today. His duty was to make sure she didn't disappear again. This was new territory for him. He spent years trying to knock Bell down off her self-made pedestal. The women of the Underworld were born with an extra dose of self-esteem, building someone up was going to be different.

He loved her dark hair cascading around her face. Untying the black band holding her hair, he grinned, watching her shake her hair loose from the ponytail. Playfully, he threw her to the mattress, rolling on top of her. The sparkle in her smile softened him like a soothing melody. He trapped both her hands above her head, kissed the base of her neck, and tasted the skin along her collarbone.

"Let me go." She squirmed.

"Make me." His tongue lapped the swells emerging from the deep V-neck of her tee. He gathered both her hand in his left and used the right to slide her shirt up over her head, exposing perfect breasts shielded by thin purple lace. He flicked his tongue at her right nipple through the material, watching it harden instantly.

Chapter Twenty-One

A small moan escaped her lips. Traces of electricity lingered behind when his lips moved on to their next target. It was blissful agony to be in Jacque's arms again. He pinched her nipple between his lips, causing her to arch against his mouth. Angel wanted to resist him. Her body committed mutiny against her reason. The loving expression in his eyes as he gazed upon her face, even with the hideous scar, caused her defenses to shut down. She neither wanted nor needed his pity. His love, she craved like a junkie needing a hit.

Her mind teetered on the brink of ecstasy and self-doubt. Angel closed her eyes, not wanting to recognize fear or disgust if she searched his face. Large, rough hands traveled down her body, coming to rest between her legs. He worked his thumb along the seam of her jeans. The friction sparked her desire and her hips to roll in response. She wished the fabric would disintegrate under his fingers.

She opened her eyes and watched him pop the latch of her bra, allowing her breasts to spill out of the lace. He suckled the round mound into the lush warmth of his mouth. The fury of his fingers working through the seam of her jeans caused an insatiable throbbing between her legs. Jacque maneuvered expertly around her body, never once looking into her face, eliminating the need to be repulsed.

Her body tensed. She wanted to stop; she was too far gone. She needed this release, even though her mind dreaded the surrender. It would never be the same between them. He would always view her with remorse and sympathy. A charity case she was not. She didn't want him staying with her out of misplaced obligation. Unconditional love was Angel's goal, and she wasn't settling this time.

Jacque unfastened her belt and unzipped her jeans. Her hips pushed off the bed, allowing him to shimmy the denim down her legs and throw them on the floor. The hardness of his manhood pulsed inside the dark denim of his pants as his eyes roamed her body, drinking in her long bronze legs and purple lace thong. The pressure of his fingers kneading their way up her thighs made her wetter with each touch.

A finger slipped under the lace thong and ran down the scalloped edges lying against her pelvis, meeting the moist heat of her passion. His knuckle skimmed her folds, making her melt into the bed. When his fingers trailed back to the top of her thong, Jacque ripped the thin lace from her body and tossed it aside. Angel lay exposed in every way possible.

"Oh God, I've missed you so much," he grunted as he nibbled on her neck. "I would face death a thousand times if this was my prize at the end." He circled his thumb over her center. She bit the inside of her lip to keep from crying out.

Angel recovered from the writhing agony of his touch and lifted his chin to meet her gaze, wanting to see the words on his face. Jacque pushed up to kiss her lips. Smiling, she answered, "I missed you, too."

His mouth slanted over hers, and her tongue darted through eagerly parted lips, tangling with his, in untamed lust. The sweet taste of mint surged through her. She allowed her mind to give into the moment, wanting to savor his pleasure and release her worries for now.

His body ached for her. The undulating throb of his shaft beckoned to be inside her moist folds, yet he waited. This was about Angel, not him. She lay splayed before him on the bed with her dark hair haloing around her, the color a stark contrast to the ice-blue of the duvet. Her smooth honey-brown skin glowed under the light. He traced a trail between her breasts, over the taunt muscles of her stomach, to the patch of fine hair between her legs. When he slid two fingers into her wet core, his shaft grew harder, threatening to explode.

As his fingers caressed within the hot moisture, his lips followed the same trail his hand forged earlier. He relished her shuddered when he placed a kiss just above where his fingers stroked a steady rhythm inside her. For too long he imagined the taste of her, wanting to bring her the pleasure she deserved. Angel's cry, as his tongue found her spot, echoed in his head, sensuous and ardent. When her leg wrapped around his neck and her hands fisted his hair, drawing him farther into her, his mind succumbed to elated delirium.

The intensity of her reaction encouraged him to continue. He slid Angel to the edge of the bed and went to his knees on the floor. She tried to push back against his shoulders with her feet. Jacque locked his arm across the narrow expanse of her waist, trapping her in place. Her hips rolled with each thrust of his fingers and flicker of his tongue. Her moans were as mesmerizing as a siren's song, enticing him to finish his mission — his mission of delivering her undeniable satisfaction.

Her plea was low and sultry, like a hot breeze. "Jacque. P-please!"

He stopped ravaging her to ask, "Please what? Tell me what you want." His stroking fingers never missed a beat.

"You're driving me mad. I need you inside me. Now." Angel's delicate hands gripped the covers, heels dug into the mattress, and the dark lust in her eyes lured him to her.

His shaft jerked at her words. He slid out his jeans and pulled his shirt over his head. Jacque positioned himself between her legs and rubbed the tip of his cock against her swollen sex, fighting the urge to thrust deep into her wetness. Her hips tilted, coaxing him to take her, the torment almost unbearable.

"Is this what you want?" he teased, pulsating against her.

Her head sank deeper into the covers. "Oh God, yes." The throaty hunger in her voice ended his baiting. He could no longer resist penetrating her.

He guided himself into her tightness. Her sex melded around him like a velvet glove. The hot, wet chasm of her desire enthralled him. He slid in and out, increasing his pace, as she met his thrust with force, begging for more each time. Unable to control himself, he held on to her hips and sank his full length into her body, faintly hearing her scream as she came for him.

"Oh shit, Ang...." His words faded into his climax.

Jacque's weight grounded Angel as he collapsed on top of her, his breath heavy in her ear. His heart pounded so hard it vibrated against her chest. She ran her fingers through his burnished curls, brushing them away from his face.

She wiped the sweat from his brow and kissed him on his forehead. He held on to her as if she might fade away.

Angel longed to give in to the temptation of this moment, to stay frozen in bliss, never to wake. Angel refused to have her heart broken again. Too many obstacles stopped her from building a life with Jacque. He might not see them today. It was left to her to save them both from the pain and agony of a bad break up down the road.

The beautiful chiseled lines in his face showed his Egyptian heritage as he lay with his head between her breasts. He laced his fingers through hers and kissed the back of her hand. He rolled to his side and lazily traced his index finger across her body. He explored every nook and cranny of her body, always avoiding her face. Only once during their lovemaking did he bring his eyes to meet hers, the moment inevitable. Blame was not a viable option in this situation. Most days she could barely stomach her own reflection. Why should she expect him to?

"What do you want to do for the rest of the night?" he whispered against her ear.

Angel gathered the sheet around her and leaned forward, allowing her hair to fall into her face. "I've got a lot to do to prepare for the meeting. I also have to finish the books. I've been trying to keep track how much money is being spent. I need to make sure I pay people back some day."

"Who do you have to pay?"

"Laurent and Etienne have been bankrolling the operations. I got a little money put away. Nothing close to what this thing is costing. Who knew supernatural alliances would cost so much?"

"Don't worry about it. I'll pay them back."

She shot him a murderous glare. *First, he pities me and now he makes me feel like a whore. This is going downhill fast.* "The hell you will! I don't want to owe *you* money."

"Why would you owe me money?"

"I've got you in enough trouble. I can't accept your money. I can just imagine what your mother would think." She cringed at the thought of his mother's reaction.

"Angel, you're talking crazy. Why wouldn't I help you?" He sat up, facing her, as she turned her back to him.

"I appreciate your offer. I don't want to owe you either. You're not obligated to me. It's not like we're married or anything. Hell, technically, we're not even dating." She shot him a smug look over her shoulder, cringing at the anger contorting his face.

His nose flared and a flash of crimson caught in his eyes as he flung his legs over the edge of the bed. "What're you trying to say?"

"I don't know. Shit's all messed up right now. I don't need to worry about a relationship, too." She focused her attention back to the wall across the room.

"Then what was the sex about? You usually fuck people you don't want a relationship with?"

"I just got caught up in the moment. I shouldn't have slept with you." She thumbed the bottom of the scar, just above her chin.

"Angel. You're making me crazy. One minute you save my life and we're making love, the next you tell me you can't focus on a relationship. What the fuck?"

She felt his eyes burn holes in her back. She refused to look at him. If she saw his face, dove into the depths of those emerald pools, her conviction would fade. "I think it'll be best if we just be friends right now. There's more important things to worry about than hashing out a love affair. I can't juggle all of this."

He turned her around, forcing her to face him; his expression filled with rage. "Fine. Remember this conversation next time you change your mind. Or when you want someone to sex you up, don't knock on my door. I don't have time to play these games with you."

"Don't worry. I wouldn't dare knock on your door. And if I need someone to fuck, there are plenty of other options," she lied. Anger drew a tear to the corner of her eye.

"This is exactly why I stay away from humans! You're all fuckin' nuts." He pulled on his jeans and threw his shirt over his shoulder. Storming out the room, he slammed the door behind him.

Chapter Twenty-Two

Jacque's feet punished the stairs on his way down. Fury boiled in his blood like volcanic magma. She was driving him mad, probably on purpose. He slammed his fist into the mirror-covered wall, hearing then feeling the shattering glass. *Maybe I can't save her. She might be beyond my help.*

The pain she harbored must be great to inflict this kind of misery on herself. He sensed her conflict when she told him she didn't want a relationship. She sacrificed herself for him. Love wasn't an emotion he easily identified. However, he and Angel shared a strong connection. Yet whenever he drew near, she pushed him away.

By the time Jacque reached the kitchen, his hand had healed. He poured a glass of vodka, downed it, and poured another, debating his next move. Should he go back upstairs and try to force Angel to understand they belonged together, shake her until she gave into him? As attractive as it sounded, the prior argument drained him. He had no more fight left today.

A collection of keys hanging by the door caught his attention until a voice behind him made him jump.

"Are you trying to move the keys telepathically?" Marie took a seat at the small kitchen island. Faith sat next to her. Both women glared at him as if he committed a crime.

"Look. I didn't do anything. She broke up with me, or rather explained we were never dating in the first place." He poured another drink. He needed more encouragement if he had to defend himself to these two women.

"We know she's pushing you away. She's scared. A lot of people have hurt her." Faith's light brown eyes glistened with sadness. Jacque sensed she cared deeply for Angel. "I've tried to protect her. It hasn't been enough. Our mother has a way of seeping under Angel's skin and poisoning her thoughts."

His heart weighed heavy as he pulled his fingers through his hair. "I don't know how to help her," a broken voice he recognized as his own replied.

Marie shook her head. "*Mon pauvre bébé.* She's really done a number on your heart. Who knew demons could love?"

"I'm not sure if it's love. All I know is I would die a thousand times to take this pain from her." His stare gripped hers, sharing his turmoil.

"That, *ma chère*, is love," Marie explained.

"Don't worry. She loves you, too," Faith added.

"How do you know? I feel like a ping-pong ball. One minute she's loving me, the next she's telling me to go to hell."

"Women. What did you expect? If she didn't love you, she wouldn't have foregone the one thing she felt was most precious to her." Faith shared a faint smile. "She gave up everything she felt was important to get you back, not knowing whether you would even want her. Her sacrifice is the epitome of love."

"Why is she giving it all up now?" he blurted, pounding a fist into the granite, shaking the island.

"Fear does strange things to people." Marie poured a small swallow of gin into a glass and sipped it, as only a lady would do. "You must stay strong for the both of you."

Both the women stood, sharing a loving glance at him. They each ran a hand along his arm in support or in sympathy, Jacque wasn't sure which. Once they left the kitchen, he grabbed the keys to the car. Escape was first and foremost on his mind right now. He needed something to take his thoughts away from Angel. *Boy's night out, time to find Laurent.*

Jacque studied the cars in the garage. Automobiles changed drastically since the last time he was Topside. It couldn't be *too* different though. The last car he drove was a 1930 Ford Model A. This one, sitting shiny and red, was called a Carrera. A shield sporting a horse and the words Porsche was inlayed into the hood. He liked the style.

Inside, he inhaled the aroma of leather, adjusted the seat as far back as it would go, and turned the key in the ignition. The engine purred very different from the sputtering of the Model A. He evaluated the various levers and pedals. They all seemed familiar. He had watched Laurent as they rode around town before his unfortunate demise. He followed the H, shifted the stick into the top slot on the far left, and hit the gas. It jerked and stalled. This was going to be harder than it looked.

The ride to Laurent's was a rough one. After several stall outs and a few people giving him the finger, he made it to St. Charles Avenue. He knew the middle finger wasn't a gesture of pleasantries. With all his blunders, he could understand the others' frustration with his lack of driving skills. Putting the car in neutral, Jacque yanked up the parking brake. He needed more practice before going back into traffic.

Laurent answered the door on the third ring.

"What the hell you doin' here?" He peeked around the door to see if anyone else was with Jacque. "How the fuck you get here?"

"Um. I drove." *I guess my subpar performance constitutes driving.*

"Drove what man? You haven't driven since they invented cars."

"You're hilarious. I drove Angel's car."

Laurent stepped out of the house as if looking for someone to jump from behind the bushes. "You could've killed someone. Where the hell is Ang, anyway?"

Jacque kicked the front step, leaving a mark on the white paint. "Long story."

"You fucked up already? I only left you a couple of hours ago."

"Like I said, long story. One I don't feel like discussing right now."

Opening the door, Laurent waved him in. "All right. You wanna come in or we gonna stand out here all night?"

"Let's go out. I need a drink and feel like having some fun. It's been a while since I've been up top. Show your boy where the fun is." He slapped Laurent on the back.

"Look, man. You gotta stop hitting me," Laurent mumbled, rubbing his arm. "What kind of fun you talkin'? This is New Orleans. You can spit and hit fun."

"Let go to this Utopia place."

"You sure you wanna go there without Ang?"

"Angel has decided not to be in a relationship. And tonight I have, too. Get your shit and let's go. You're driving." The fact Angel refused him ate at Jacque, yet he hid this weakness in front of Laurent. He was a demon, and they didn't pine away at a loss of a female.

"No shit! Think I want to ride with someone whose last ride was a Model T?"

"It was a Model A," he called as Laurent disappeared into the house.

***

Across the street, a long spiral line formed to get into the club. Jacque was impressed by the business the club seemed to draw. Laurent went to the front of the line chatting with the bouncer. After a few words, the velvet rope came down to the jeering comments of a few farther down the line. Laurent always had a hook-up.

The club pumped with music and people. Nothing like this existed in the Underworld and definitely not the last time he was Topside. The human world had become a freer, less inhibited place. The scene was something straight out of a music video, something he watched on BET; the excitement of music and the mob invigorated him. Very different from the formal balls from his last time on Earth. The women's choice of clothing in this era, or lack thereof, had an alluring effect on him, except when Angel wore it. He wanted to keep her hidden for his eyes only.

He and Laurent leant against the bar and ordered two Grey Goose on the rocks. Jacque gulped his drink and turned to watch the crowd. Scantily clad women gyrated to the beat of the music. A few noticed him watching and added to the sensuality of their movements, not afraid to show their interest. *Love this place. No wonder Luc is bored. This world is a throwback to Sodom and Gomorra.*

With an empty glass staring him in the face, Jacque ordered another one.

"Hey, man. You better slow down. I'm not carrying you outta here," Laurent said, eyeing the pretty blonde vamp in the corner.

"Hopefully, I won't be leaving with you." Jacque tipped his glass in the direction of the dark-skinned Fae giving him the dance show.

"Don't do anything stupid you can't take back. I know you love Ang."

"Whatever. I'm tired of playing her games. I'm tired of dealing with females, period. It's time for Jacque to have a little fun for a change." *Am I really referring to myself in third person? Yes, I am. What the hell is in this vodka?*

"Okay. Do as you like. Don't come crying to me when you sober up and realize you're a dumbass."

Jacque downed the second drink and motioned for another. "You just worry about you. I'll take care of Jacque." *Again with the third person. Shit.*

"I'm going to see if I can round up some company for myself. You're on your own, playa." Laurent slid down the bar towards his prey.

***

Angel lay across the bed, weighing her actions. Had she made a mistake pushing Jacque away? The hurt in his eyes tore at her reasoning. No. She did what was best for both of them. Now she had to do what was best for Angel.

It was time to stop hiding out, ashamed of her appearance. Her face was a tad bit distracting, but the rest of her was intact. A supermodel knew how to accentuate her assets and Angel knew how to work it. Guys never looked at her face when she had the "gurlz" on display.

She jumped out of bed and headed downstairs. Her grandmother and Faith sat in the living room drinking. The scene was almost comical. Angel hopped over the back of the couch and slid down between the two women.

She kissed them both, asking, "What are my two favorite ladies doing? Hanging out on a Saturday night?"

"Just having a cocktail and catching up," Faith answered.

Angel started to stand. "Sounds like fun. I'll get a glass and join you."

Marie pulled her back down. "*Non*, you are too young to stay here. I would make Faith go, except she's not ready yet. You should be out in the streets enjoying your youth."

Angel pouted like a child, crossing her arms in front of her chest. "Yeah. But I don't have anyone to go out with."

"What about your friends you used to talk to before you went to New York? Jasmine and Natasha still ask about you. Why don't you call them?" Faith reached over, handing Angel the phone.

"I haven't spoken to them in almost a year."

"Just try."

A smile danced on Angel's lips. "I'll call. If they bail, then I can sit and get drunk with y'all, right?"

"Ladies do not get drunk," Marie snickered.

Angel searched through her contacts, finding the girls' number, and made the calls. She was pleasantly surprised when the both girls agreed to go out. They even sounded excited to hear from her. They agreed to meet at her house in an hour.

Thrilled to see her childhood friends, the welcome entailed a lot of hugging, kissing, and screaming. They were in high school all over again. All four years the group was inseparable. Then came modeling and Jackson took her away from them. She cherished the fact neither girl acted as if anything was different about her. They saw Angel and not her scars.

"Miss I'm-hiding-out-for-a-year, where are we headed?" Jasmine asked.

Angel glanced from Jazzy to Nat. "I don't know? Where y'all wanna go?"

"Somewhere different. I'm tired of the some ol' thing all the time," Nat whined.

Angel questioned her choice before she offered it up. She shouldn't get her human friends involved in her supernatural world. Other humans went to Utopia and nothing happened to them. The Supe clubs weren't much different than any other she'd been to. "Hey, I know a place. It's hot. You'll have fun."

"Okay," they answered in unison.

They took Jazzy's car to Utopia. Angel was surprised to find her car missing when they went to the garage, even though they wouldn't have fit in it anyway. Jacque must've borrowed her car. He better take care of it. It was the hottest car she ever drove; she loved it, almost as much as her shoes.

She beamed as she thought about Jacque. She already regretted her decision to push him away. Perhaps she'd talk to him in the morning and apologize. He'll probably bunk at Laurent's for the night. She didn't blame him. She had been an ass tonight.

They parked on Bourbon, a block down Conti. Angel thought back to the last time she was on this street, again she wore unpractical shoes. She was going to pay for it at the end of the night. Tonight she had no one to carry her to the car.

Angel pouted and folded her arms across her chest when she saw the size of the line. Her friends frowned, too. As she was about to suggest going somewhere else, Angel spotted Etienne coming up the block.

She waved to get his attention. "Hey, Etienne!"

His smile radiated in the darkness. "*Bonsoir*, my Angel. You're looking lovely tonight."

"Thanks, can you get us in?" she requested, giving him her puppy dog eyes.

Etienne admired her friend, winning disapproval from his entourage. "How could I not escort such beautiful women? Who are your friends?"

"This is Jasmine and Natasha. My very best friends." She nodded to each girl. "Girls, this is Etienne, a new friend."

"Nice to meet you both. Hopefully, you all will save a dance for me tonight."

Angel gazed at him, sweet and teasingly. "Of course."

"Where's Jac?"

"I couldn't tell you and couldn't care less," she lied.

"Are you still seeing that asshole?" Jasmine interrupted.

Angel followed Etienne to the front of the line. "Not Jackson. Another asshole."

Chapter Twenty-Three

The club was jumping. The girls huddled close together to weave through the crowd. Etienne invited them to sit at his table in the VIP section at the far end of the club. Once they got to the table, the runway-model-thin waitress took their order. She narrowed her dark brown eyes as she studied Angel and her friends. It made Angel second guess bringing them to a Supe club.

Jasmine's grey eyes sparkled with excitement. Her shiny black spiral curls bounced as she bobbed to the music. Natasha scanned the crowd smiling each time she caught a glimpse of a hot guy, which was often.

Jazzy pointed to the dance floor. "Now, he's *fine!* Shit. He looks to be taken."

It only took one glance for Angel to identify the hottie Jazzy pointed out. Jacque was in the middle of the dance floor with some frail girl, who looked as if she might pass out from hunger, rubbing her body all over him. Rage burned inside of Angel's chest as she watched the two slither to the music, teasing and toying with one another.

"There are plenty of other options tonight. No need to waste time on someone already taken." Angel clenched her jaw as she took another look back at Jacque. *He took our breakup well, moving on to his next target. Guess I didn't make such a bad decision after all.*

Etienne brought another round of drinks to the table plus some new faces. Angel wondered who the three new guys were and didn't mind having to get to know them better. The one in the middle was taller than Jacque with hazel eyes, highlighted with golden flecks. His chest muscles strained through the tight tee and tapered down to what Angel swore was a twelve pack of abs. His brown hair complimented his light eyes. He was clean-cut like a marine, odd for a Supe.

She purred toward the sexy hunk of man in the middle. "Etienne, who's your friends?"

"I'm hosting some of our out of town guests for the meeting next week. These are the Boudreaux brothers from Lake Charles. They're with the rougarou pack," Etienne introduced. The girls were confused for a second. Luckily, good looks hid the most glaring flaws sometimes. Jacque was the poster boy for hidden flaws.

The hottie in the middle reached for Angel's hand, brought it to his lips and said, "It's a pleasure to finally meet you. You're more beautiful than Etienne explained." His smile belonged in a Crest commercial.

Angel didn't care at this moment about the sweet lies men told. She needed the compliment and accepted it greedily. "Thank you. And what should we call you, besides sexy?"

"I'm Damon. This is my brother Albert. And our baby brother Henri," he said, his eyes never leaving her face. This was what she wanted from Jacque. For him to look at her, *all of her*, with unadulterated admiration.

"It's nice to meet you all. These are my friends, Jasmine and Natasha." The music thumped harder. Angel recognized the song. "Rude Boy" by Rihanna.

She downed her drink and hollered, "Ladies, it's time to party! Let's dance."

"Do you mind if we join you?" Damon asked.

Grabbing Damon's hand, she headed to the dance floor. "I'm game if you are. Let's go."

***

Although the petite Fae grinding against him embodied sex, Jacque was bored. This made the third dance and he was ready to call it quits. As he told his unyielding partner he was retiring to the bar, a familiar voice rang through the music. As he scanned the club, he spotted her holding some dude's hand, leading him to the dance floor.

The sting of jealousy pierced his heart as the animal following behind her admired the sway of Angel's hips in the much too small dress. The purple scrap of cloth she wore barely covered her ass and cut across the swells of her breast to tie across one shoulder. Just seeing her made Jacque's pulse quicken, sending the wrong message to his new friend.

Jacque debated whether to leave or stay on the dance floor. He wasn't sure if Angel saw him yet. He decided to stay for a better vantage point, wanting to make sure Angel was safe. At least that's what he told himself.

When the group got closer to the dance floor, he was able to sense the beings. The females were human. The males were werewolves. What the hell was Angel doing hanging out with weres? Those mutts were dangerous. Then Jacque realized they came with Etienne.

Angel weaved through the bodies, writhing to the music, with the big dog in tow. She stopped only a few feet away from Jacque, giving him optimal view of her movement. Every time her body brushed against the wolf, murderous images flashed in his head. When she slithered her body down the front of the male and turned to grind her ass into his crotch a low growl rumbled in Jacque's chest. He swore a smile played across Angel's lips as if she heard him.

This was the longest song ever. He sighed in relief when it finally ended. Jacque led the Fae back to the bar and deposited her with her friends. He ordered another drink and found Laurent at Etienne's table. Angel and the wolf stayed on the dance floor, making Jacque cringe. The music slowed down and *his* woman latched herself onto this stranger when she should be with him. He fought every urge to go and retrieve what belong to him.

"I told you you'd regret this." Laurent took a swig of his drink.

"Shut up," Jacque hissed as he watched the wolf's hands roam down Angel's back. Anger coursed through Jacque's body, causing the veins in his neck to bulge.

"It sucks to be you right now. She's pissed. She saw you with the Fae. And I'm a dude and can tell you the rougarou is serious competition."

Laurent just doesn't know how to keep his mouth shut.

Another growl escaped as the dog cupped Angel's ass. "Shit. What don't you understand about shut up? I know I fucked up."

"I want to make sure you understand. I'm going to mention it once again. I told you this was a bad idea." Laurent slapped Jacque on the back, hard. "Hey, who're the hot chicks Angel's got with her?"

"Oh, she said those were her friends," Etienne answered.

"And you let them go with the rougarous without calling me over? I thought we were bros?" Laurent joked.

Etienne's voice held a hint of disappointment. "I wasn't sure you were interested in humans. Anyway, the Boudreaux brothers arrived, I made introductions, and the ladies grabbed them up and took them for their pleasure."

"Man, Jacque, you fucked it up for all of us," Laurent spat in disgust.

Etienne eyed Jacque. "This is your fault? You upset Angel?"

Laurent leaned on the railing, studying the dance floor. "Yep."

Etienne gazed at the girl on the dance floor. "Then you need to fix this. I have my eye on the exotic dark-haired one Angel brought."

"I'm not stopping either of you from getting a girl. My female problems don't extend to y'all. Angel's still speaking to you fools." Jacque leaned back in his chair propping his black Kenneth Cole loafers on the table. "If you don't have game, don't blame me."

***

Guys like Damon existed in fantasies, the poster boy for tall, dark, and handsome. He had a bad boy vibe going on like he rode out of a scene from *Biker Boyz*. As much as Angel wanted to be into him, she wasn't. When Jacque left the dance floor, she almost did the same, until she realized he still watched them from the table, *her* table. She wasn't ready to confront him yet.

Angel felt uncomfortable dancing to the slow song and resisted the urge to slap Damon's hand when he palmed her butt. She couldn't decide if he was a werewolf or an octopus. Any woman would kill for the attention of a man like Damon, which was evident by the lingering stares from the other females in the club. Angel's heart was already spoken for, only she messed it up with her insecurities.

Anger and sorrow glinted in Jacque's eyes. She couldn't bear to see him hurt, even when she inflicted the pain. As soon as the song stopped, Angel led Damon back to the table. Jazzy and Nat made it back also. They smiled, enamored with Jacque as he flirted and wooed them. He was a charmer.

Angel, feeling mischievous, threw her arms around Laurent and smacked a big kiss on his lips. "Fancy meeting you here."

Laurent's blue eyes sparkled. "Oh, you're feeling it tonight, aren't you? How many drinks have you had?"

"Not enough. Be a good boy and get me another."

"What're you drinkin'?"

"Whatever you bring. Oh, wait. Can you get something for Jazzy and Nat, too?"

"Not a problem, cause you *will* introduce me when I get back."

"Of course." She kissed him again and sat on Damon's lap by accident.

Before she could move, he circled his arm around her waist, holding her hostage.

When a deep rumble erupted out of Jacque, the girls jumped away. Both Etienne and Laurent stepped between Jacque and Damon. After struggling with Damon, Angel managed to remove herself from his lap. Once released, she took the seat next to Jazzy.

Laurent held his hands to Jacque's chest. "Hey, man. Help me with these drinks."

"Fine." Jacque fumed as he stalked toward the bar.

Everyone left at the table remained quiet for a moment. The crazy Zydeco beat of the music added to the frenzy.

Damon raised a brow. "Angel, is there something you forgot to tell me?"

"I didn't forget. I just haven't had a chance to tell you yet."

"Like to tell me now?"

She shrugged her shoulders playing it off as nothing. "Jacque and I use to date and we kinda broke up earlier tonight."

"I don't think y'all are broke up yet. At least not in his opinion." Damon's Cajun accent grew stronger with his frustration.

"It's hard to let go of all of this." She waved her hand down her body.

Damon's low roar shook the table. "Oh, you are trouble. Maybe more trouble than I'm willing to tangle with."

She gave him a half-grin as relief washed over her. "It's your loss."

Jacque reached across Angel's shoulder and placed the drink on the table. His mixture of musk and heat was as intoxicating as the liquor. She brushed off the instinct to press her lips against his neck as the hair along his collar tickled the side of her face.

"I got you a chocolate martini." His breath caressed her ear. "Hope you like it."

"I love anything chocolate," Angel answered as Jacque pulled up a chair and sat behind her. The closeness of his body felt both right and uncomfortable at the same time. The girls eyed her, silently demanding the dish. They would force the whole story out of her later or at least the closest version to the truth Angel could divulge.

"So, Angel, we bought drinks. Now you owe us introductions." Laurent flashed a smile at Nat. She easily affected men with her golden skin and sandy-brown hair. She stood as tall as Angel, only with a slimmer less curvy build. They loved her for runway work. Nat beamed her perfect white smile back at Laurent, mesmerizing him with her Creole beauty.

"Laurent, these are my two very best friends in the world, Jasmine and Natasha. We all grew up together. Nat and I even ran off to New York together to start our modeling careers. She still does a lot of stuff in Paris and Milan."

"It's a pleasure to meet you, ladies. And I hope we'll be seeing more of you." Laurent spoke only to Nat.

"Angel, you've been holding out on us," Jazzy interjected. "You've been hiding out with all these handsome men and keeping them all for yourself. Not cool."

"Luckily there's enough to go around." Angel winked as Etienne brought a chair and squeezed in between Jazzy and the youngest Boudreaux boy. She chuckled at the boy's frown. Even as a girl, Jazzy held a power over men.

Although Jacque was quiet, his presence surrounded Angel. He played with a strand of her hair, twirling it around his finger. She turned to him and asked, "Where'd your friend go?"

He dropped his eyes to the floor before he answered, "What friend?"

"The one you were dancing with when I came in." A hint of anger bit in her words. She hated men who played stupid, and Jacque was far from stupid.

"She's not a friend. Just someone who wanted to dance."

"Huh, you two looked very comfortable with each other."

His gaze finally met hers, pleading for forgiveness. "Just dancing."

Etienne broke into the conversation. "That is a stunning dress you're wearing tonight."

"Thanks." Angel turned to look at him. "Something old I had at the back of my closet."

"The only thing more beautiful is the woman wearing it." Etienne winked at her.

No matter how farfetched, Angel appreciated the compliment. "You always know what to say to a girl."

"E is correct. You are truly breathtaking tonight," Damon offered.

"Thank you so much." She appreciated his flattery. She wasn't sure if it was to please her or piss off Jacque. Maybe a combination of both.

Jacque glared at Damon. "You need to keep your eyes to yourself, dog."

"Maybe, it's you who needs to remember where his attentions should be." Damon growled.

This is going to be trouble, Angel thought.

Chapter Twenty-Four

If Jacque scooted any closer, he'd sit on top of Angel. He needed to claim her, to show the big dog she belonged to him. As he played with her hair, he sensed conflict inside her. She was still open to him, wanted him.

The music slowed, Laurent and Etienne asked the girls to dance. Jacque wanted to use the opportunity to hold Angel close.

He leaned forward, brushing his face close to Angel's. "May I have this dance, *ma bien-aimée?*"

She gazed into his eyes. "I'm your beloved now? Why should I dance with you?"

Jacque ran the backs of his fingers down her cheek, feeling her shiver under his touch. "Pleeease." She bit her lip and gazed up at him with surrender in her eyes. Angel gave him her hand, letting him lead her to the dance floor.

Once on the floor, he pulled her tight to him. The strawberry smell of her shampoo enticed him to burrow further into her neck. Her hips ground into his to the slow rhythm of the music. His hands trailed down her back, coming to rest at the curve just above her firm ass. He released a breath when she laid her head against his chest and relaxed.

Her touch was agonizing. He wanted to whisk her away, but feared pushing too hard. As they danced, he whispered, "I'm sorry."

She lifted her eyes to his, smiling. "Me, too."

He engulfed her with his massive body and kissed her softly. Her mouth parted in a groan and his tongue entered its sweetness. He deepened the kiss as they circled languidly on the dance floor. He was home.

Shots rang out.

Jacque spun them around with his back facing the direction of the gunfire, trying to protect Angel. The heat of the bullet set his arm ablaze. It caught him in the shoulder. Another entered just below his rib cage, radiating pain throughout his torso. When the second shot hit, Jacque realized something was wrong. Angel went limp in his arms.

Gunfire continued to zip past him, coming from all directions. *Shit. Who brings guns to a Supe club? Swords and daggers are expected, but guns?* Jacque picked Angel up and sprinted for the back door. Laurent and Etienne grabbed the other girls hot on his trail. The wolves jumped the railing, charging in the direction of the initial shots, hunting for the gunman.

Outside, Etienne shoved everyone into his limousine. Jacque slid in behind the girls, laying Angel on the seat beside him. Blood covered the front of her dress. He couldn't tell how much was his and how much actually belong to her. He ripped the dress from her body. The bullet hit her in the chest, most likely lodged in her right lung.

"Is she okay?" the dark-haired one screamed, kneeling on the floor of the limo.

"She'll be fine," Jacque answered.

"She's not breathing."

To hell with the humans being there, he had to save Angel. "Etienne, I need your help. She needs blood," Jacque pleaded with him. With her head in his lap, he bent down, kissing her temple and whispered, "You're going to be fine. I promise."

Etienne took her wrist to check for a pulse. "I think it's too late. I don't hear her heart."

"It's not too late. Just do it," Jacque demanded.

Etienne slit his wrist with his claw and put it to Angel's lips.

Jasmine tried to yank him away. "What the fuck are you doing!"

"I'm trying to help her." Etienne held Jasmine at arm's length to shield himself from her flailing hands. Laurent trapped her arms, dragging her back in the seat.

Angel wasn't drinking.

Natasha sat on the floor next to Etienne. "Move back. Maybe I can help."

Natasha covered Angel's heart with her small hands and closed her eyes. A bright light radiated from Natasha's hands. She chanted in a language vaguely familiar to Jacque. The energy in the car increased as her chants grew louder and faster. She skimmed her hands all over Angel's body, and the light grew brighter. After an explosion of energy escaped Natasha's body, she collapsed onto the floor. Laurent gathered her into his arms and cradled her against his chest.

The group waited in silence.

Angel moaned his name as her eyes fluttered under closed lids. She was alive. Jacque gathered her close, raining kisses on her face.

"Jacque?" she murmured.

He brushed the hair from her face and pressed his lips on her forehead. "I'm here, babe."

"What happened?"

"Too long to explain now. We've got to get you girls outta here."

"Everyone else okay?"

"Yes. Etienne is gonna take y'all back to your place to get your grandmother and sister, and then you all go back to his place. Okay?" She closed her eyes and tried to refocus on his face. "Why?"

Jacque caressed her cheek and ran a finger across her lips. "Just do what I say for once. I don't want any of you to stay at the house or be alone." He smiled down at her oval face.

She pushed up on her elbows, trying to sit up, but failed. "Where're you going?"

"Laurent and I have to go find the shooter. We'll meet y'all back at Etienne's."

"Be careful. And you better come home." Her gazed captured his, the intensity in her eyes showed she meant her words.

Jacque winked at her. "I always do." There was no need to tell her about him being shot too since his wounds had already healed. "Etienne, you take good care of these ladies." Jacque hesitated, laying Angel's head on the soft leather.

Laurent settled Natasha in the seat. The healing spent her.

"I'll protect them with my life. They'll be safe once we're back at my place. I have several guards and many of the visitors have started to come into town. Do you want me to send help here?" Etienne pressed his lips in a thin line, creasing his brow.

"No, we should be fine with the weres. Hopefully, they've already caught the gunman. Do you have a place we can hold him for questioning?" He fingered another strand of Angel's hair. He hated leaving her. He had to find the shooter to ensure her safety.

"Yes. Of course. Just bring them back to St. Charles."

"Why is no one calling the police? Have y'all all gone crazy?" Jasmine questioned, frantically looking around and eyeing her friends. "They need a hospital and we need to talk to the police."

"Jasmine. Angel and Natasha will be fine. They'll explain everything once they're a little stronger. Until then, I need you to trust us and stay with Etienne." Jacque reached for her hand to calm her down, but she snatched it back.

"Don't fucking touch me!" She trembled from fear.

"Look, handle her, man," Jacque said, nodding toward Jasmine. "We got to get back inside." He gave Angel his shirt and hopped out the car with Laurent right behind him.

Chaos ravaged the club. Tables and chairs lay toppled on the floor. Shards of broken glass hung from shattered mirrors. Supes sat scattered about the club; some wandered, searching for friends. A few had been caught in the crossfire. They would all heal, unlike Angel and her friends who were human. At least two of them were human, he needed to find more about Natasha when he returned to Etienne's.

The Boudreaux brothers had the petite Fae Jacque danced with earlier in the night trapped on the DJ stage. He and Laurent went to investigate.

Jacque hung on the rail surrounding the stage. "What's up? We leave you alone for a minute and you manage to trap a little Fae."

"Fae or no. She's the one who shot you and Angel," Damon answered.

Laurent hit Damon with a sideways grin. "Get the fuck outta here."

"Why the hell are you shooting up the place?" Jacque questioned, the sharpness in his tone identified his irritation.

Her voice cracked when Jacque's hand wrapped around her throat. "I don't have to tell you shit. I hope your little human's dead."

"You don't know who you're playing with, you little slut." He snatched her by her arm, causing her to wince. "You'll tell me everything by the time I'm done with you." Jacque's eyes flared red and heat emanated from his skin.

"Fuck you, demon," she seethed.

With one swift movement, Jacque snapped her neck. "Take her back to Etienne's before she heals."

Damon picked her up and threw her over his shoulder. His brothers followed him out the front door.

"Hey, who the fuck is gonna pay for this mess?" Alana asked as she sauntered up to Jacque.

"Sorry, Lana. It was the little dark-skinned Fae who shot up the place. Send the bill to them." The Fairy Kingdom had plenty of loot. Why shouldn't they be held responsible for the damage caused by one of their own?

"Jacque, every time you come to one of my clubs my place gets wrecked. I'ma have to ban you from my place if you keep this shit up. Lucky for you, I rarely see you anymore." Alana had run clubs since the early 1900's. She was one tough woman, not taking any shit from anyone.

"Hey, I told you I didn't start it." Jacque backed away, putting up his hands in protest.

"Laurent, keep your friend out of my club. Why do you think I told Etienne he couldn't use it for the meeting? You demons are too much trouble."

"You know you love me, Lana. You'll miss me until I come back Topside." Jacque planted a big kiss on her cheek.

"If the Fairy King stiffs me on this bill, I'ma come lookin' for you."

"It's a deal. Love ya, babe. We gotta bounce. Gotta get info out of this stupid Fae."

"I'll see you at the meeting then," Alana called as they scurried away. "You're coming?"

"Yeah, the rest of panther pack is coming from Baton Rouge. Tired of Luc fucking with us every few hundred years. It's getting old."

"Thanks, babe. Catch ya then," Jacque called over his shoulder, in a hurry to get back to Angel.

Chapter Twenty-Five

This must be what it felt like to be hit by truck. Truck or bullet, it didn't really matter. They both hurt like a motherfucker. She sat next to Etienne wearing Jacque's shirt, which covered more than her dress. Her chest hurt and her head throbbed as the bright lights of Bourbon Street entered the car.

Etienne's driver parked in front of her house and Etienne ushered them inside, using as much of his long lanky body to shield them as possible. Nat snapped out of her comatose state halfway to the house. Jasmine went numb, not saying or doing much of anything. She aimlessly followed Etienne's orders.

Marie and Faith rushed into the living room when Angel and the others entered the house. Horror distorted their faces as they stared at the group.

"What the hell happened tonight?" Marie inquired.

"Long story, *Grand-mère*. We have to get our things and get outta here. I'll explain later." Angel ran to the kitchen and grabbed two bottles of Vamp Juice. She tossed one to Nat when she returned back in the room.

"What the hell is this?" Nat scrunched her nose as she cracked open the bottle and took a whiff.

"You don't want to know. Drink it. It'll make you feel better. I know you used a lot of energy saving me. And yeah, you'll be explaining how you did it later."

"Okay, ladies. I need you to gather all *essential* items as quickly as possible. We need to get out of here." Etienne began packing the items in the dining room, all the potions, ritual items, and spell books. Marie and Faith went to pack Marie's bags. Angel grabbed Nat and flew up the stairs.

She threw open the closet doors, debating what to take.

"Nat grab the biggest suitcase you can find and make sure to get every designer shoe you can manage to carry. If nothing else, everything over five-hundred dollars must come with." Angel snatched her Louis Vuitton off the floor and shoved clothes into it. "I'll take care of clothes." Four suitcases later, she and Nat struggled down the stairs. Angel said a sad goodbye to those items she left behind.

Etienne shook his head in frustration. "Ladies, I said 'essential.'"

Angel clutched her bags to her. "I don't know how you roll, but all this is 'essential,' unless you plan to replace five years of collecting designer shoes."

"Okay, the driver will put everything in the car. Come on, we have to leave."

Everyone shuffled into the limo. Exhaustion tackled Angel like a linebacker. She rested her head on Marie's shoulder as Faith patted her leg.

"What happened?" Marie questioned again.

"I'm not sure of everything. We were at the club dancing. Then someone started shooting. Jacque and I got hit. I woke up in the back of this limo."

"Who would be shooting at you?"

Angel yawned and stretched her arms behind her head onto the back of the seat. "Jacque and Laurent went back into the club to find out more information. Hopefully, they'll have something when they meet us at Etienne's."

"Let's hope they are safe and will return soon." Marie forced a grin.

"The rougarous were there helping, too. I hope they're fine. I have no more bargaining chips up my sleeve. Jacque better be fine!"

"Now, Nat, please explain what the hell you did to me. I'm not complaining, just *what the fuck?*" Angel kicked her friend's feet, drawing a smile from her.

"Her family is all witches. One of the most powerful in this country rumor has it," Faith answered.

"Faith, you've known all this time?" Nat's voice was a bit nasally.

"Yeah, the spiritual community is a small one. We try to watch out for any strong powers. They can become problems in the future."

Nat's excitement was evident by the glow in her hazel eyes. "Then what're you guys? Are y'all witches, too?"

"No, not witches. This is our grandmother, Marie Laveau." Nothing more needed to be said.

Nat looked from Angel to Marie and back to Faith. "Oh. Oooh!"

"What's your power child?" Marie interjected, allowing Angel to curl into her side.

"Healing is my innate power. I have some gift of sight, too. Do you guys have powers?"

"Some do. Angel and Marie both call upon the elements for their strength," Faith replied. She had kept so much from Angel. Hopefully, this was the end to all the surprises.

"I'll be damned. All this time and neither of us knew." Nat shook her head in disbelief.

Angel chuckled at Nat. "I've learned a lot of things in the last few months."

"You're all fucking freaks!" Jasmine screamed, reaching for the car door. Etienne grabbed her around the waist to stop her. It was a lot to swallow in one night, and Jazzy's staunch Catholic background worsened the situation.

Angel fidgeted in her seat, playing with her hair. This night of fun with her friends had gone so wrong, like too many other things in Angel's life. Vanity forced her to think she couldn't survive without physical beauty. Her selfishness brought destruction and wrecked havoc to everyone's life. Angel reminded herself to seriously evaluate her priorities when she got everything straightened out.

The beautiful homes of St. Charles Avenue remained as beacons of a bygone era. Angel slid to the edge of her seat as they neared Etienne's home. As they pulled into the driveway, she noticed Laurent's car. When the limo stopped by the front stairway, she jumped out, not waiting for the driver to open the door.

She sped up the stairs and burst through the front door.

"Jacque!" Her voice trembled as she called out for him. "Jacque!"

"Good God, woman. Where's the fire?" His silky tone soothed her as soon as she heard him coming up from the basement, which was a rare find in a home in New Orleans.

She slammed into Jacque, grasping his face, as she kissed him hard. His strong arms held her tight, lifting her from the ground. Seeing his face, she exhaled. She was wound so tight she could snap, knowing he was safe gave her relief. She stretched on her tiptoes and sealed her lips on his. He answered her urgency as her tongue explored the salty sweetness of his mouth.

Laurent pushed against Jacque to clear the basement doorway. "Hey! Cut it out! I keep telling y'all. I'm gonna turn the hose on you."

Angel tore her lips from Jacque's, but remained close to him. The warmth of his body comforted her. She took his hand and started toward the parlor. The others entered the house and headed in the same direction. Etienne carried Jasmine fireman-style into the room.

Angel brushed a curl out of Jazzy's face. "What did you do to her?"

Etienne laid Jazzy on the settee on the far side of the room. "I just convinced her she was tired and needed to sleep." He placed a pillow under her head and smiled down on her with sympathy. Etienne's gentle handling proved to Angel he wouldn't hurt Jazzy.

"Okay and you're just now thinking of hypnotizing her? You couldn't zap her when she started calling us freaks?"

"She kept fighting me when I tried to get her out of the car. I didn't know how you'd feel about me messing with your friend's mind. I finally got desperate. Couldn't think of any other option."

"Jazzy has always been a handful. Hopefully, she'll calm down."

"I could erase everything she saw tonight if you want."

"Let's wait and see. We have other things to worry about right now."

Everyone found a seat. Marie, Faith, and Nat occupied the sofa flanking the fireplace. Laurent and Jacque opted for the armchairs. Angel settled herself on Jacque's lap. A tingle traveled up her spine as he stroked her back. Etienne rang a bell and a tall dark-haired man came out and took drink orders.

The doorbell rang and a small blonde girl announced the Boudreaux brothers. Etienne greeted his guests, offering a seat. He ordered the small girl to have more chairs brought from the other room. Damon grimaced as he passed Angel and Jacque. Jacque pulled her closer and kissed her shoulder, marking his territory.

Damon took the seat across from them. "I'm glad to see you're well, Ms. Angel."

"Thanks, Damon. I'm glad y'all made it back fine."

His smile gleamed and his eyes sparkled as he gazed at her. "Yes, it's been an exciting night. And I'm sure there's more to come."

"Thanks for your help. We put the Fae downstairs. She had some interesting things to say after some convincing," Jacque interrupted.

Damon's eyes never left Angel's face. "Really, who was she trying to kill?"

"Angel." Laurent's answer was simple and to the point.

"The bitch you were dancing with? Why would she want to kill me? I never met her before," Angel said.

"Apparently, Luc put an open contract payable to the first person who brings you in." Jacque tightened his grip on her as she began to tremble.

"A contract on me? You mean there's going to be random crazies out there trying to kill me?" She struggled to remain calm.

"What's the bounty?" the youngest brother asked.

Jacque's continuous petting subsided her shaking. "It's open. Luc offered to wheel and deal on all open contracts if Angel's brought in. Those with the worst deals with Luc will most likely be the ones who'll come after us first."

"What're we going to do?" Her voice sounded small and tired in her head.

"We continue the plan we started. And fight anyone we encounter in the meantime," Damon answered.

"Exactly," Jacque agreed then looked to his friend. "Until we find another place, do you mind if we stay here, E?"

"Not at all. It'll be a bit crowded since I have a few more guests than usual due to the meeting. We can make it work." Etienne rang the bell again. "Ladies, I have two rooms upstairs for you. They each have two double beds so you'll have to share. Jacque, there's a small room on the third floor you can have. It's not fancy. I'll make sure the help makes it suitable."

Angel rushed across the room, squeezing her arms around him. "Thank you for all your kindness, Etienne."

Faith's voice was soft, nudging. "Angel?"

"What?" she asked, settling back on Jacque's lap.

"What about Mom? Do you think she might be in danger? Should we get her, too?"

Angel tried to keep her mother at arm's length. Elise brought out the worst in Angel, pointing out all her flaws, which was the last distraction she needed. "Aww, hell! I forgot all about her. I hate to do it. I guess someone has to go get her."

"It's going to be difficult to explain everything to her. I've never told her anything I found out about our family. I'm not sure how she'll take it." Faith frowned, wringing her hands in her lap. Mother caused everyone worry.

Angel laid her head on Jacque's shoulder, exhausted. "As long as something is in it for her, she'll be fine. I apologize in advance to everyone for my mother. If you thought Jazzy was a handful, you haven't seen anything yet."

"I'll go get your mother if you like," Damon volunteered. "If you think she'll come with me."

She smiled at his kindness. By the tick in Jacque's jaw, she figured he wasn't as appreciative. "Thanks, Damon. She's my responsibility. I won't put her off on anyone."

"We'll go get her, babe. We need a bigger car than any of us brought." Jacque tapped her butt for her to stand.

"You can borrow my S500," Etienne offered. "Only if Angel drives."

"What the hell? Have you been talking to Laurent?" Jacque raised a brow.

Etienne tossed Angel a set of keys. "No, I remember the last time you came Topside. It's been a while, and I don't want my car ruined."

The laughter ringing through the room masked the tension of the danger they all faced. Angel left to retrieve the one person she desperately tried to leave behind.

Chapter Twenty-Six

Angel parked in front of the brightly colored house she knew so well. The dim light of the television glowed through the window. She imagined her mother sitting on the floor with her popcorn, watching *Pretty Woman* for the millionth time. Saturday night was always chick flicks, wine, and snacks. To be such a beautiful lady, her mother rarely had any dates. If she did manage to solicit a date, it was only the one, never a second. It would take a special kind of man to deal with her mother.

Jacque came around and opened Angel's door. A hot and muggy breeze stifled the air. She checked her hair in the car window and smoothed her dress before turning to the house. She flinched when she saw the scar running down her face. Her mother was going to have a field day when she saw Angel was flawed again. Jacque hung his arm around her shoulders for support. She appreciated the gesture as she sucked in a deep breath and prepared for battle. As they strolled up the brick path to the front door, Angel snuggled closer to Jacque, absorbing his strength.

"Mother." Angel stuck her head in the living room.

Elise jumped when Angel called out. "What the hell are you doing here?" Elise's long limbs lengthened as she stood, transfixing a provocative grin on her face when she caught sight of Jacque.

"We came to get you. You have to come with us," Angel huffed, putting herself between Jacque and her mother's line of sight.

"What the hell happened to you? Why is your face messed up again?" Elise turned on the overhead light to get a better view.

Angel held up a hand to shield her eyes from the light. "It's a long story. Please grab some stuff. We need to go."

"I'm not going anywhere until you tell me what's going on. And why your hideous face is back again. How're you gonna go back to work if you look like a monster?"

Angel placed a hand on her hip, digging in her heels. "Mom, get your shit and come on. We have to leave, and I don't have time for your nonsense right now." Her mother never made anything easy. Angel wished she could just leave her and forget the past.

"Watch how you talk to me! I'm your mother. You *will* respect me."

"Again. I don't have time for this. We're in danger and have to go. And when you start acting like my mother, I'll treat you like my mother. Until then, get your shit and come on! Or else I'll leave your ass here, and you can fend for yourself."

"What kind of danger?" Elise questioned.

The pressure of Jacque's grip got stronger. She glanced up at him, seeing the concern in his face. Before Angel could answer, Jacque stepped between the women. "Ms. Dias or can I call you Elise?"

She batted her lashes and gave him her fake come-hither smile. "Oh, Elise is fine."

"Elise, there's a lot of danger. I'll be happy to explain everything once we're in a safe place. Please pack your things. I'll feel better by ensuring you're secure somewhere else." The silky reassurance in his voice could entice steel to bend.

"Oh, of course. Let me go upstairs and grab a few items and I'll be right down." Elise looked down her nose at Angel and left the room. Angel dreaded being back in her mother's grasp, allowing her access to her life, especially this life.

Twenty minutes and a large suitcase later, Elise reappeared. Jacque relieved her of the bag, garnering a bright smile. Angel swore her mother brushed her breast against Jacque's arm when he took the suitcase from her. His expression gave no clue if she did. Classic Elise. She'd been hitting on Angel's boyfriends since she was in high school. Always just toeing the line of inappropriate, but never crossing over. None of them had been as hot as Jacque nor were they old enough for consent. Angel would have to keep a close eye on her mother.

"Nice car." Elise ran her hand along the shiny black finish. "Is it yours? I didn't catch your name, sugar."

The idea of being trapped with Elise was insufferable. Angel wanted to make it short and sweet. "Jacque. His name is Jacque. And no, it's not his car. We borrowed this from a friend." She wished her grandmother was still alive to serve as a buffer. When they were all in the car, Angel hit the gas.

"Jac, what do you do?" Elise probed.

Jacque took a moment to think about the answer. "I guess you can say I'm a military consultant right now."

"Ooohh. Sounds exciting. Are you from New Orleans?"

"No. Farther south." This drew a giggle out of Angel.

"Farther south? Like Houma or Morgan City?"

"Something like that." This time it was Jacque who was amused.

"How did you meet my daughter?"

"We have a mutual friend."

"Mom, stop being nosey," Angel snapped.

Elise traced the lines of Jacque's seat, grazing the tips of her fingers across his shoulders. "I'm just making small talk. Getting to know our fine friend here. Jac, are you seeing anyone?" Jacque shifted in the seat to escape her slender fingers.

Angel caught the movement and ground her teeth. "Mother, I'm warning you!"

Jacque gave her the most innocent smile laced with an undercurrent of mischief. "I'm sorry, Elise. Yes. I *am* seeing someone. I'm dating your daughter."

"Why?" The shock in Elise's face was evident.

"What do you mean 'why?' She's a beautiful person, and I care about her."

"Look at her," she announced, pointing to Angel's face.

Angel gripped the steering wheel until her hands turned white.

Jacque rotated in his seat and met her mother's stare. "Yes, I see her. Apparently much better than you do." He turned back around and played with the radio.

Angel had a new alliance to buffer her mother's attacks. Only one other person ever shut her mother up, her Gran. She reached over and caressed Jacque's hand, thankful for his support. When she went to pull her hand away, he grabbed it, keeping it in his hand. She understood at that moment Jacque loved her.

***

Jacque held Angel's hand in his, providing her the security she needed to face the horrid woman, she called her mother. He understood the reasons behind Angel's insecurities once he met Elise. Breaking through the walls built by her mother would be a difficult task. He had to make Angel understand her own self-worth. The silence was a welcomed retreat from the stinging words Elise dished out ignorantly.

The heat rose with the emotions trapped within the car, pulsing in the back of his head. Angel's pain twisted his heart, while Elise's disregard invoked both sadness and anger. He couldn't imagine the self-loathing it took to despise your own child. Elise deserved her seat in hell for the way she treated Angel.

Angel reached Etienne's house record time. She drove as if she were in the Indy 500. "Get out," she barked to her mother.

"Nice place. Is it yours, Jacque?" Elise lingered close enough to him she stumbled when he stopped.

Jacque grabbed the bags and started up the stairs. "No. It's a friend's."

The small blond opened the door before they even rang the bell. Elise absorbed her surroundings with a look of contentment. Jacque placed the suitcase at the foot of the stairs and caught up with Angel as she entered the parlor. He slung his arm around her shoulder, cuddling her close to him, ensuring both Elise and Damon got a good view.

Elise's surprised expression brought Jacque amusement.

"You're back safely and with another beauty on your arm. Jacque, you're a lucky bastard." Etienne graced Elise with a small bow, and she rewarded him with a magnificent smile. He garnered his attention to Marie, who sat primly on the settee in the corner. "I must say you have a fantastic bloodline."

A confused Elise recovered quickly. "Why, you're too kind. I have to assume this is your home?"

"Yes, I'm Etienne." E brushed his lips on the back of her hand.

"Faith, I didn't expect to see you here. I should've known you'd be taking care of your sister."

"I can't say I've missed your humor, Mom. I hope you didn't give Angel any trouble." Faith sipped her drink and glared at her mother over the rim of the glass.

"Why would I give her trouble? She has a talent for finding her own trouble. Have you seen her face lately?" Elise jerked a thumb toward Angel, rolling her eyes.

Faith snorted. "I see you're still vying for the Mother of the Year award." The ever diplomatic Etienne jumped in the middle. "Elise, can I offer you a drink?"

"Yes, I'll take a Crown Royal on the rocks. Someone needs to tell me what the hell is going on."

"I'll make introductions while you wait for your drink. These guys are the Boudreaux brothers. You know Nat and Jazzy. And this is Marie Laveau, your great-great-grandmother." Faith watched Elise's expression, as did everyone else.

"Y'all shitting me, right?"

"*Non chère* It's the truth. I'm your great-great-grandmother." Marie's smile turned to a grimace.

"They're all crazy, Ms. Elise. The girls think they're witches and voodoo queens and dead people. Who knows what the guys think. They're a bunch of freaks." Jazzy perched on the settee. Etienne's spell must have worn off. Angel sat next to her friend to calm her down.

All the emotions in the room roared inside Jacque, making his stomach turn. This was the problem with humans, always flaunting their emotions, especially the women. Emotional overload had a sickening feeling.

The butler brought Elise's drink, and she downed it in one swallow.

"Elise. The important thing is there are people trying to kill Angel. They'll do anything to get to her. You ladies aren't safe by yourselves. You need to stay where we can protect you," Jacque explained, as he sank into the seat next to Angel.

"You always seem to find trouble, don't you, girl?" Elise's honey-colored hair bounced as she shook her head. Take away the hardness around her mouth and the void in her eyes, she would be a stunningly beautiful woman. The poison of hate stole her youth, aging her prematurely.

"It's not her fault." Jacque cut his eyes at Elise, wanting her to shut up. Unable or unwilling to read his queues, she continued yapping.

"Who she piss off now?"

"The Devil."

Elise was the only one who found it humorous. "I'ma need another drink," she said when she realized no one else thought it was a joke.

"I think we all need to call it a night and reconvene in the morning." Jacque helped Angel to her feet. "Jazzy, are we gonna to have to put you out again, or are you gonna cooperate?"

"We'll take care of her." Marie took the girl by the hand, patting it lightly. "She'll be fine."

"Mom, you're with us." Faith nodded toward the stairs.

"Where's Angel going?" Elise questioned.

"With her man, I assume. She's the only one here with one. No need for her to suffer because of the rest of us." Marie winked at Angel. "Good night, *chère*."

The quiet was welcoming. He and Angel left the rest of the group on the second floor, continuing to their room on the third. Looking around the room, Jacque realized it must be one of the servant's quarters. He wondered which servant was inconvenienced in order to get the room. He had to remember to make it up to them. The compact size of the room created an air of cozy comfort. The double-bed seemed tiny compared to the king-size one he slept in at home. He lay across it watching Angel rummage through her bags. The bed shrunk as his body filled the space, making it seem even smaller than it actually was.

Tonight revealed many things about her he wished he could take away. Her mother's behavior explained a lot about Angel's insecurities. She was Elise's creation, and somehow he had to find a way to undo the damage.

Angel's smile caused his heart to race. She clutched her gown as she teetered on the edge of the bed. "Thank you," she said, her warm hand running across his arm.

"What're you thanking me for?" He leaned on his elbow and brushed a wayward curl from her face. The gratefulness and love inside her glowed in her aura, fulfilling his heart.

"For helping me with my mom. I know she's a handful."

He leaned back and grinned, thinking about his own mother. "Oh, she's nothing. Trying having a goddess for a mom."

"She doesn't really mean a lot of the stuff she says. She's had a hard time with my father leaving and all. My Gran said she was never the same after."

Her happiness cocooned around him, surrounding Jacque with warmth. "Babe. No matter what someone does to you, you should never treat your child as she treats you. You deserve better. I hope you know she's wrong."

"I know. It's just hard sometimes to block her out."

"Think of me as your shield." He lightly kissed the curve of her shoulder. Her heat pulsed through him awakening his desire.

She leaned back into him, allowing Jacque to gather her close. He tucked her protectively into the contours of his chest, pressing his face into her hair. She shivered in his arms as he trailed light kisses down her neck, and his hand fondled her breast. Her body went lax, releasing the weight of the night's events and surrendering to his will. With his face in her hands, she captured his bottom lip with her teeth and then freed it with a light flick of her tongue. Her mouth covered his with hungry passion, searching for fulfillment.

Jacque answered with his own demanding need. He stopped to catch his breath and gazed into the chocolate brown pools smiling up at him. He trailed quick kisses down her scar; she stiffened and she tried to turn away. His steely grasp detained her from moving. Showing her he loved every part of her was important.

"You're beautiful," he whispered.

The fast beating of Angel's heart thumped loudly. She laid against his chest. Jacque drew her closer, kissing her forehead. Fire followed Angel's touch as her hand trailed down his arm. His resolve weakened as her lips grazed the base of his neck.

He rose, lifting Angel from the bed, and carried her to the small bathroom. He turned on the water and began to remove her clothes. He drank in the glory of Angel's body as she stepped into the steaming shower. The perfection of Angel's breasts and taut roundness of her ass caused him to harden.

He stripped and joined her. The hot stream of the shower washed away the anguish of the day. He grabbed the soap and wrapped his arms around Angel, lathering the suds over the swells of her breast and the flatness of her stomach. The feel of her wet, naked body created a pulsating arousal in him.

As he washed lower, skimming his hand between her legs, she moaned and backed into him. His hands explored the curves of her body as the water rinsed the soap away. He ran the lather over her breasts, feeling her nipples tighten under his thumb. Jacque leaned over her and slid his hand down her flat stomach and between her thighs, discovering the heat within the folds of her sex. The moisture of her mouth mixed with the wetness of the water as she lapped at the spot just behind his ear. He groaned against her as his fingers glided into her.

Angel moved against his palm, moaning his name. She removed his hand reluctantly and turned toward him. Her moist pink lips slanted on his as she stretched to reach him. The water created a moist heat as her breasts rubbed against his chest. He cupped the firm round cheeks of her ass and lifted her off the floor.

Her legs encircled his waist and his cock grew even harder between them. He longed to be inside her, to be a part of her. Jacque leveraged Angel on the shower wall as his tongue explored every expanse of her mouth. Angel ground her sex down the length of his shaft, causing him to release a low growl.

His mouth found the soft mounds of her breast. He sucked hard on the supple flesh and brushed his tongue across the pinkish-brown peak. Angel panted as her rhythm increased. He grazed her nipple with his teeth. She stiffened at the sharp pain of euphoria surged through her nervous system. In her heightened arousal, she ground herself into his hardened shaft. He rubbed the tip of his crown into the sinful pleasure of her wetness, but stopped her from taking him into her. His thumb danced slow circles around the center of her desire, until she begged for relief.

With the hot stream of the shower washing over them, he held steady against the wall and thrust deep inside her. Angel bit down into the top of his shoulder, sending sheering bolts of ecstasy inside of him. Her tightness gripped him with every thrust. He battled to maintain control as she countered his movement, making him want to explode.

Angel angled herself to stroke the length of his erection.

"Make me come," she groaned hotly into his ear, tangling her fingers in his hair.

A tremor tore through him at the urgency of her words. He pushed harder, penetrating deeper inside of her. Their pace increased to a frenzied hunger.

"Oh God, don't stop!" Angel's nails dug into his arms. The pleasure of pain pushed Jacque closer to his climax.

With her back pressed hard onto the tile, he stroked until he felt the warmth of her release surround him. Her tongue flirted with his earlobe and down his neck. A quiver of satisfaction encouraged his release. Stoking deep inside her, he shuddered into his own orgasm.

His arms looped under hers and came to rest against her shoulder blades, trapping her to him, not wanting to disconnect. The water had turned icy. Jacque took her lips once more shivering, partly from the cold, mostly from the ecstasy she delivered.

He moved to escape the chill of the shower and smiled at her. "You're going to be the death of me."

"Already been there and got a souvenir. Let's try to avoid it in the future." She kissed him and quickly refreshed herself in the freezing water.

Chapter Twenty-Seven

Angel fondled the warm body tangled around her. She lay listening to his breathing and basting in the joy of being loved for once in her life. With closed eyes, she prayed for this dream to never end.

She snuck out the bed and found her ice blue BCBG top and a chocolate brown skirt to match. She opened the suitcase stuffed with shoes and grabbed a pair of chocolate Michael Kors with a four-inch heel. Her outfit was comfortable, yet dressy enough for a house full of guests. Frumpiness was not an option when unknown guests were involved.

She brushed the hair from Jacque's brow and kissed his forehead. She resisted the urge to crawl back in bed and wake him with a more compromising greeting as a reward for last night's performance. They would never make it downstairs if she did.

The house was bustling. Angel hummed the chorus of "Brand New Love" by Robin Thicke as she descended the stairs. Boisterous conversation floated from the back of the house from what she assumed was the kitchen. She followed the smell of coffee and bacon until she found the other ladies sitting around the kitchen table.

Angel beamed at the eclectic group gathered before her. "Morning, ladies."

"You look much happier this morning, *ma chère*," Marie pointed out with a devilish glint in her eyes.

She winked at Nat and stole a piece of toast off her plate. "I have to admit I'm in a good mood."

Nat giggled, taking a bite of the other slice of toast. "I wonder why."

"We all heard why. I guess y'all forgot others were in the house with you. I wasn't aware I raised such a trashy daughter." Elise poured a cup of coffee.

"Mother, don't worry. You didn't raise me at all. You have no fault or reward in anything I do. At least not anymore."

Nat interrupted the bickering. "I'll be trashy if it gets me a man who looks like Jacque. Tell me where I sign up." All the women laughed, except Elise. Even Jazzy cracked a smile at Nat's admission.

Angel poured some coffee and grabbed a piece of bacon off Faith's plate. Bacon had been a guilty pleasure when she worked the runway. Once or twice a month, she allowed herself to eat like a regular human, otherwise it was low carbs, high protein, and zero sugar. She appreciated not having to watch everything she ate for a change.

She hopped on a stool at the granite counter and examined the kitchen. It was rarely used, nothing unexpected in a house owned by a vampire. This was probably the first time someone actually cooked in it. Although Etienne didn't have a use for the kitchen, he didn't skimp in its design.

"Jazzy, how're you doing this morning? I'm sorry I got y'all mixed up in this." She waited for her reaction.

Jazzy fidgeted in her chair a bit before answering. "Your grandmother explained a lot to me last night. I'm still not comfortable with it. I guess y'all are telling the truth. You know I was raised in the church. These things just aren't acceptable."

"I understand how you feel. I promise we're not bad because we're different. Not all the Supes are bad, just like all humans aren't good. I'm not gonna say there's not *really* bad ones out there, but there's good and bad in everyone."

"What the hell are Supes?"

"Beings with supernatural powers."

"Okay, I understand about you and Nat's families. What about all these guys? Are they like y'all?" Jazzy leaned across the table, eager to hear Angel's answer.

"I guess my grandmother didn't tell you everything. *Please* don't freak out on me again. I promise the guys here with us are good and will never hurt us."

Jazzy had her infamous tell-me-now-and-stop-bullshitting look plastered on her face. "What're they?"

"Jacque and Laurent are demons, as in born and raised in Hell. Etienne is a vampire. And the brothers are rougarou or werewolves. You'll be meeting a lot of other Supes, too, in the next couple of days." Angel sipped her coffee, savoring the aroma.

"And all these people running around here helping? What're they?"

"I'm not sure. Some I think are human, some not. I can't tell you anymore."

Jazzy's brows creased in toward the bridge of her nose, wrinkling her forehead as if she was working hard to figure out the pieces of the puzzle. "You mean to tell me demons, vampires, and werewolves are all real."

"Yep, I know, threw me at first, too."

"Son-of-a-bitch. Now, we have to re-evaluate our whole way of thinking, don't we?"

Angel reached over and hugged her friend. Jazzy was Catholic to the core. She was also the most logical-minded person Angel ever met. Things would work out just fine. This day was getting better by the minute.

"Good morning, ladies," Etienne's deep voice called from the doorway. "Would you mind pulling the blinds for me?"

Angel raced to the windows, pulled the blinds, and drew the heavy curtains.

"I thought vampires couldn't come out in the day," Jazzy asked cautiously.

"I'm glad to see you're better, Ms. Jasmine. I was quite concerned about you last night." The smoldering gaze he sent Jazzy almost made Angel melt.

"You still didn't answer my question." Her friend held her stance, crossing her arms over her chest.

"I'm quite old, *mon petit*. We grow stronger and more tolerant with age. Although I wouldn't venture outside in the full sunlight, I can wake and move about the house with ease."

"Shit, again with the re-evaluating my information. I guess garlic's out, too." She giggled at her own statement.

"Etienne, how're the plans for the meeting coming along?" Angel asked.

Etienne leaned against the doorframe. "I've moved it up. It'll be tomorrow night. I think we should move fast with the new developments."

"Okay. Good idea. Is there anything we can do to help?"

"Yes, if you don't mind. There'll be many guests starting to call about housing arrangements. I have a list of the hotels available to accommodate the various groups. If you ladies wouldn't mind fielding the calls, I would greatly appreciate it."

"No problem."

"Also, you'll have to make sure each of you have the appropriate attire. These meetings are formal occasions."

"We have to wear formal gowns to a meeting?" Nat chimed in.

"It's customary." Etienne answered to the floor.

Jazzy gulped the last of her coffee and said, "We need to go shopping."

"I assumed as much. I have three guards who'll accompany you when you're ready to go out."

As she rose, Angel dusted the crumbs of toast off her lap. "Okay, ladies, let's get ready to head out. I'll go up and let Jacque know we're leaving. And we'll go find something suitable to wear. I hate off the rack. I guess we have no choice at this point."

"You ladies will be fabulous in anything." Etienne smiled as he surveyed the women. "You know this is the first time anyone has actually used the kitchen except caterers. It's nice to sit in here and chat. I hope you ladies take your time finding a new place to stay." He bowed, with a slight dip of his head, and disappeared from the room.

In the hall, Angel froze when she met Jacque coming down the stairs with Isabella hanging off his arm. Isabella's high-pitched voice dug into her like nails on a chalkboard. Heat rose in Angel's stomach, a mix of anger and nausea. She wanted to run and hide or slap Isabella; it was a tossup at this junction.

Everyone observed Jacque as he descended the stairs with the little blond beauty. They volleyed from Jacque to Angel, waiting for fireworks, but none came. She refused to put on a show.

"I see you finally made it out of bed." Her voice was as sultry as a warm sea breeze as she spoke to Jacque, ignoring Isabella.

He kicked the stair with the back of his heel, looking everywhere but in her eyes. "I guess I was more tired than I expected."

"I'm sure you were. We all heard what made you tired last night," Nat threw at him with sarcasm. Nat was Angel's new champion.

Isabella batted her lashes and gave the crowd a prom queen smile. "Ahh. I remember those nights. Some days you'd sleep til noon." Jacque nudged her in warning.

"Nice to see you're back to your usual self, Isabella." Angel glared at her.

"Always, I see you've acquired an entourage. Who are the new additions to your crew?"

"Friends." Angel never took her eyes off Jacque. "Jacque, we're headed out to find something to wear to the meeting. Just in case you noticed I'm gone, I wanted let you know." She turned her back on him, grabbing Marie's arm. *Why do I keep ending up in the same place with him? Always landing in the middle of him and Isabella.*

"Wait, I don't want you out by yourselves. I'll come along."

"Don't bother, Etienne provided three guards for us," she scoffed.

"You're not a bother. I'm coming."

"Whatever," she called over her shoulder.

"Great! I need to find something, too. I'll come with," Isabella chirped.

Angel bit the inside of her lip and tightened her grip on Marie. Faith squeezed her hand tight in warning, trying to subside her anger.

Jacque quickened his pace to catch up to Angel. He pulled her away from Marie and to the side, allowing the group to pass. "I'm sorry," he whispered.

"This is not the time for this," she snarled, resisting the temptation to punch him. Not only was he flirting with Isabella, he embarrassed her in front of everyone.

"She caught me coming down the stairs. I didn't even know she was here." He pleaded his case, beseeching her to forgive him.

"You didn't seem to mind her draping herself all over you."

"I didn't even pay her any mind. It's Bell. She flirts all the time."

Angel poked a finger into his chest as she spoke, increasing the pressure with each word. "You and your *not thinking* is becoming tiresome. You need to start thinking, especially when it comes to her."

"Look. I'm sorry. Won't happen again, even though nothing happened this time."

"Nothing happened, but you embarrassed me in front of my family and friends. What do you think my mother will have to say about this?" Angel felt the tremor in her lip and inhaled deeply to regain her composure. She needed to stop crying over every little thing. There was no crying in supernatural warfare.

274

"What the hell does your mother have to do with this?"

"She'll tell me she knew you would cheat with someone prettier. Someone like me could never keep a man. Shit, maybe she's right."

"Now, you're talking crazy."

"Like I said, whatever. Now is not the time to discuss this." She started to head toward the car when Damon called her name.

Damon ran to catch up with her and Jacque. "Hey. Where are y'all headed?"

"Shopping," she answered with a smile.

"Mind if I tag along?"

"Of course not. The more the merrier," Angel responded in a singsong tone as she slid into the back of the limo. Jacque pushed Damon aside and hurried in behind her. Damon took the open seat across from Angel, eyes twinkling and a grin seeping across his face, landing in the deep crevices of his dimples. It was going to be an interesting day.

Chapter Twenty-Eight

The shopping trip became an exercise in patience and a battle of wills. Isabella flirted. Angel restrained from strangling her. Jacque avoided comments from the ladies. Damon took advantage of every opportunity to outshine Jacque. It was an exasperating experience, plus Angel wasn't pleased with the dress she settled on buying.

The rest of the day entailed answering phones and arranging accommodations for the arriving guests. The housekeeper remained busy answering the door. By mid-afternoon, Angel collapsed on the sofa from exhaustion. Nat and Jazzy were already lounging in the parlor chatting.

"Man, I never thought I would be happy to not talk on the phone." Nat licked her lips and rubbed her throat. Nat was all about drama.

"Nope. Not something I expected to come out of your mouth," Angel responded, kicking off the pumps.

"It's crazy to know all these creatures live in New Orleans as if we didn't have enough human freaks," Jazzy added.

Angel stretched back on the pillows and propped her feet on Nat's lap. "Yeah, I know, but you get use to it. Most of them look normal. You'd never know they were different."

Nat's eyes sparkled with excitement. "Are they all as hot as the ones we've met already?"

"I don't know. I haven't met an ugly one yet. It's kinda depressing being surrounded by so many beautiful people," Angel answered.

"Welcome to the world we lived in being your friend for so many years. What's the deal with Laurent? He seeing anybody?" Nat was a sucker for blue eyes.

"I don't think so. I'll see if we can seat you together at dinner. You can dig for more info. Remember, he's a demon and they play by different rules than we do."

"You don't seem to mind dating one."

"Jacque and I have more problems than an Amish girl trying to get beads at Mardi Gras. Every other day or hour, we're arguing."

"And whose fault is that?" Again with the don't-give-me-your-bullshit look.

"It depends. Y'all saw him with Isabella. She's a huge pain in my ass."

"Because you let her. Jacque's your man and you need to let her know it. Getting mad and not speaking to him isn't doing anything except giving Ms. Peroxide a way in."

"It's hard for me to think straight when it comes to Jacque and Isabella."

"And what's up with you and Wolverine?" Jazzy interjected.

"I don't know what you mean." Angel tried to hide her smile. "I met him when y'all met him. Damon's a nice guy."

"Oh, no. Dimples has the hots for you. And he's waiting for his chance. Jacque better watch himself, because Damon is delicious!"

"It's nice to have a backup plan. Especially one who looks like he belongs in a Calvin Klein underwear ad." Angel blushed, thinking about Damon with his clothes off. "Hey, dinner is going to be at the La Fleur Plantation tonight. We should go up and get ready."

"What's up with the Supes getting dressed up all the time? Don't they have any casual occasions?" Jazzy was a jeans and T-shirt kind of girl.

Angel arched a brow as she thought about the question. "I guess they all came up in an age where things were more formal. Most of them are at least one hundred years old."

"Okay. Gross. Talk about robbing the cradle." Jazzy's smile lit up her face. Angel was glad to have her friend back.

"Most of them have been frozen in their twenties and thirties. If you think of it in those terms, it's less weird. You'll get use to it."

"I don't know."

"Whatever, Jaz. You dated the guy who was, what, forty-five? Now, *talk about gross*, he was old enough to be your father. Go upstairs and get dressed. See y'all at five." Angel pulled Nat off the sofa and pushed her friends toward the stairs.

***

Everyone met downstairs to leave for dinner. Three limos waited outside. The night air clung like a warm damp cloth against Angel's skin. The ladies all climbed into the first available car. Jacque slid into the seat next to Angel. The emerald-green stripes in his tie accented his eyes and brought out the dark blue of his suit. She smiled at him despite herself.

The car drove slowly through the gates of the La Fleur Plantation. The statuesque columns and ornate architecture of the 1800's seemed appropriate for the group gathered tonight. The car slowed to a halt, and the driver came around to open the door.

Angel was surprised to see how many other guests had already arrived. Jacque offered his arm and escorted her into the main hall. Entering the mansion was like entering another era. She loved the opulence of the old plantation. The grand ballroom on the right was set for their dinner.

As they entered the purple and gold wallpapered room, Etienne greeted them.

"Wow, Etienne, this is beautiful." She brushed a kiss to both his cheeks.

"Not as beautiful as you and these lovely ladies behind you." He caught Jazzy's gaze, causing her to blush.

"There must be a lot of people coming tonight."

"Yes, many people have already arrived."

"Let me know if you need help with anything."

"No, no, don't worry yourself. The staff has everything under control. You've helped enough today. Please relax and try to have some fun tonight."

Etienne took his leave to welcome more guests. Jacque led them to their table and seated all the ladies. Isabella sat four tables away. Angel smiled and waved as she glanced back longingly. Isabella recovered quickly. She drew closer to the dark-haired vamp sitting next to her, faking her interest when he whispered in her ear. A hint of jealousy seized Angel as she watched Isabella work the crowd with her beautiful face and dazzling smile.

Jacque startled Angel out of her daydream. "Babe, do you want a drink?"

"Oh, sure. A Grey Goose Cosmo is fine."

"Ladies?" Jacque questioned the others and took their orders.

He was only a few steps away when Isabella stood, making her way toward Jacque. Nat kicked her under the table, reminding her of their earlier conversation. Angel hurried to catch up with Jacque before Isabella could dig her claws into him.

Isabella slid next to Jacque and gave Angel a smug grin. "Aren't you just fetching tonight?"

Jacque scooted to the right, not daring to stand too close, understanding the fire in Angel's eyes.

"I see you're already working the room," Angel returned, wedging her body between them and placing her hand in the crook of Jacque's arm.

"Just seeing what's new."

"Try to stick with the single guys. We don't want any trouble tonight." Isabella shrugged. "If a woman can't keep a hold of her man, he's free game."

"You have no class," Angel scolded.

"I had enough to keep your man for almost fifty years."

"Not enough to get him back."

"Oh, it's still early in the match, honey. I'm not down for the count yet." The hussy winked at Jacque.

Angel raised her hand to strike a blow, but Jacque caught it in mid-air, swiftly positioning himself in the middle of her and Isabella. "Look, enough from both of you. Bell, is there something you need?"

"I thought you'd like to know Luc contracted Xavier. It's getting ugly." Isabella frowned and pouted her lips as if he hurt her feelings.

"Shit, how'd you find out?"

"My mom called me this afternoon. She accidentally found the contract."

"Who the hell is Xavier?" Angel stared at the two, demanding an answer.

"Xavier is a hit man and my older brother." Jacque's voice was a combination of fear and reverence.

"I didn't know you had a brother." Angel reached over and laced her finger through his. The pain in his eyes raised a knot in her throat.

"I haven't seen him in a couple centuries. We're not close. We have different mothers."

"We've got to be careful. You know Xavier's crazy." Isabella's hand played with Jacque's sleeve. The intimacy of the gesture disturbed Angel as she examined their interaction. Their bond was strong. She understood why the relationship had been ongoing for fifty years. It was going to be hard to compete.

"We'll get everyone together after dinner and let them know." Jacque's grip tightened on Angel's hand. "I really need a drink now. Let's hit the bar."

***

Jacque's stomach churned all through dinner. The air in the car was suffocating. Angel's emotions gnawed at him, her worry and fear throbbed in his head. The ride to Etienne's felt like an eternity.

As soon as they reached the house, Jacque raided the bar. The vodka burned its way down his chest, hiding the pain brought to the surface from hearing about his brother. Last time Jacque saw Xavier, he ended up with a broken leg, three broken ribs, and several stab wounds.

Xavier's powers were much stronger than Jacque's. He'd honed his shifting abilities to surface at will. Jacque could only shift under extreme emotions or if he maintained complete focus. Even then, he barely controlled what he shifted into. Jacque spent a lot of time and energy learning to control his emotions because of his inconsistencies. Most demons didn't have those problems; emotions were like second thoughts they pushed away easily.

Angel arranged herself between his legs as he straddled the barstool. Her lips brought warmth and ease as she brushed them along his chin, coaxing his nerves to settle. Her emotions calmed which helped to bring his under control.

Her dark eyes met his. "Hey, what's going on?"

"Nothing. My brother's just bad news."

"How bad can he be?"

"The last time I saw him we fought because he hit my mother." Jacque clenched his fist, remembering the outline of Xavier's hand imprinted on his mother's cheek.

Angel's arms encircled his waist, providing him a safety net to discuss a topic he avoided for centuries. "I'm so sorry."

"Xavier has a lot of power. He's good. Shit, better than good at what he does. He's most people's last resort. The person you call when nothing else worked."

"There's only one of him. There's no way he can get through all of us."

"He's strong. I couldn't take him. It took me two weeks to heal from our fight."

"You're more experienced. You were the commander of the legions. And we got everyone else to help."

Jacque appreciated her support. He was the man, the one who was supposed to be doing the saving. "He's like a supernatural special ops soldier. You never know when he'll strike. You and the others can't *ever* be alone. Okay?"

She played with the curls at his nape. "Of course. When are we ever alone now?"

"No, I'm serious. Don't leave the house without me. Promise."

"Sure."

"And none of the others either. He doesn't care who he hurts."

She pushed the hair back out his face and kissed him again, this time on the lips. The sweet taste of Moscato and chocolate lingered in her mouth. He drew her near, ravaging the plush softness of her lips.

"Hate to interrupt." Isabella's voice jarred him out of his rapture. He forgot about the others in the room. After filling everyone in on as much information he had about Xavier, they retired to their rooms.

The group would be on high alert until Xavier was caught.

Chapter Twenty-Nine

Preparations for the meeting were in full swing. It was two hours away and five women getting ready was a challenge. They took over the left wing of the second floor as their dressing space. As Angel finished her hair, the maid entered the room carrying a large box.

"*Pour vous, Mademoiselle.*" Angel's French was limited, but sufficient enough to understand the package was for her.

"Oh, thank you. Do you know who sent it?" Angel questioned, taking the box from her.

The woman shook her head, never making eye contact with Angel. "*Non*, just delivered to the door. No card."

Angel set the box on the bed and the others gathered around. Nat pushed Angel towards the box. "Open it!"

"Okay. Geesh. Gimme a minute." She lifted the lid and removed the delicate paper lining the box. Inside laid the most exquisite dress Angel had seen in a long time. She spun around like a little girl, holding the lavender and silver creation against her.

Cecelia fingered the tissue paper thin overlay of silver netting on the dress. "Oh *cher*, it's beautiful. You're such a lucky girl. Jacque's a very thoughtful boy."

"I can't believe he got this for me. It must've cost a fortune."

"Shit, I'm gonna have to find me a hook-up at this meeting if this is the kind of gifts monster's give," Jazzy commented as she twisted her long black hair.

Angel wiggled into the dress with the help of Marie. She dug out the silver Valentino pumps from her suitcase. It was the perfect combination.

The ladies checked themselves in the mirror one last time and went downstairs. Isabella lounged against the bar in her blood-red gown, resembling the devil Angel knew she was. As much as Angel hated to admit, Isabella was gorgeous.

"I feel honored to be surrounded by such beauty," Etienne announced proudly, extending his arm out to Jazzy. She hesitated a moment before taking it.

"Where's the rest of the guys?" Angel asked, disappointment written on her face.

"They went ahead to check security and make sure everything is okay."

"Oh, okay," she answered, her dissatisfaction more pronounced. She wanted to thank Jacque for the dress.

"We have the guards who'll follow us." Etienne and Jazzy led the way to the car.

***

The bellman for Le Pavillon hotel opened the car door. Etienne exited, and helped the women out the car. The four guards flanked them as they moved toward the lobby doors. The main entrance was a flurry of activity. Cars arrived with elegantly dressed people. The women looked ready for New York Fashion Week, the men, a photo shoot for a tuxedo ad. Angel absorbed her surroundings, enjoying the atmosphere of posh luxury.

Angel and the other women poised under the portico and chatted as they waited for Etienne to speak with some guests.

"Hey, who's the fine brother over there?" Nat asked, pointing to a stunning brunette who stepped out of a stretch SUV.

Angel met his gaze and hauntingly familiar green eyes stared back at her. "I don't know." She spun around to ask Isabella, only to find her up to her usual games, pushing up on some hottie beside the gilded doorway.

"Aw, shit, he brought a whole frigging harem with him. I guess he's a lost cause." Jazzy scouted the crowd for a new target.

"I'm sure you'll find somebody if you really want. If you open your eyes, you'll realize you already have someone."

Jazzy put her hand on her hip and tilted her head to look at Angel. "What do ya mean?"

"I mean Etienne. He's had the hots for you since I introduced you at the club."

She contemplated the idea, dimples forming as her lips turn up into a smile. "Ya think?"

Angel scanned the crowd, trying to find someone she knew. "I know."

"He's not bad looking. Shit, he's fine. I'm still not sure about the non-human thing, plus he's a vampire. Kinda creeps me out. Maybe someone who won't want to drink my blood will be easier." She giggled.

"I doubt he'll try to drink your blood."

"Hey, the cutie from the car is coming our way," Nat whispered.

A gnawing sensation ached in the bottom of Angel's stomach. Something was off, but she couldn't pinpoint the problem.

"Evening, ladies." The gorgeous specimen of man bowed, greeting them with a dazzling smile.

"Hi." Angel returned his greeting as the entourage of beauties closed in on him.

"You must be the Angel I've heard a lot about."

"Oh." Heat brushed her cheeks. "Why, yes. And you are?" The heat transferred to her belly, creating an uncomfortable burning sensation.

"It saddens me you don't know who I am. I would've thought someone might have told you about me." His face was expressionless, devoid of emotions.

Angel strained her eyes past the stranger. He stood as tall as Jacque, which not many men could say. She scanned the crowd for Etienne or someone she knew. The guards watched from a short distance. They didn't seem alarmed.

"I'm sorry. I don't think they have. I would've remembered if someone told me to look out for someone tall and good looking." The familiarity kept bothering her. She knew his face, those eyes. *Shit!*

"My brother still has to work on his strategy. I know he expected me. I've no idea why he would leave you unprotected."

A crash sounded close to the lobby doors. Etienne staggered to the wall to steady himself. Movement flashed too quickly for Angel to recognize what happened. The tall brown-skinned guard shoved her to the ground as the blade of Xavier's dagger sliced into his torso.

As the injured guard hit the floor beside her, she grappled for the gun strapped to his side. Freeing the .9mm pistol, Angel squeezed off two rounds where Xavier last stood. She dug her heels into the ground and used her free hand to push off the ground. She scanned the crowd for Xavier. She lost him. Angel hoped she didn't miss her target. The wound might not kill him depending on the location, but the silver bullets would slow him down for a while.

Angel screamed for everyone to run. The females Xavier brought with him were fierce fighters. The guards struggled to restrain them. Mayhem broke loose as Angel attempted to decipher friend from foe. Everyone under the portico joined in the battle.

The women scrambled for the limo. A brown-haired woman, wearing the blue dress, caught Faith by the arm.

"Faith!" Angel's heart pounded in rhythm with her footsteps. Angel thought about firing off a shot only stopping when the risk of hitting Faith caused her hand to tremble.

The bitch in blue held Faith around the throat, flashing her sharp fangs in a cocky smile. "I suggest you get in the SUV if you want your sister unharmed."

Angel's hand shook with fear and anger. She gripped the .9mm with both hands, trying to keep it steady. "You let her go or you'll never leave here alive."

"You have no leverage to argue, bitch. Get in the SUV."

Angel and the vampire circled one another.

The others sat in the car, witnessing the showdown unfold.

"Get the hell outta here," Angel screamed at the car. "Shut the door and go."

Marie jumped out the car and shut the door. The driver sped off, screeching the tires as he cornered the turn.

Kicking a decapitated guard out of her way, Marie picked up the sword lying on the ground. Angel focused back on the dark-haired vampire, holding her sister hostage. With one swift, blurry movement, the vampire and Faith faced Angel and Marie.

"I see you're well, Marie. The last time I saw you, they were sealing you in a crypt." The vampire tightened her grip on Faith.

Marie welded the sword in both hands ready to attack. "You always picked the wrong crowd to hang with, Susanna. Let my granddaughter go, and we can all walk away from here."

"Oh, you won't be beheading anyone today. Tell the ugly one to get in the SUV. We're going on a little trip."

Angel trembled and tears threatened to fall. "Bitch, you *will* let my sister go."

"As you wish." The light reflected off the blade as she unsheathed it from her hip. Before Angel could move, the vampire rammed the knife into Faith's back.

Faith's body slid to the ground with a pool of blood spreading around her. Angel stood frozen, concreted in place, too devastated to move.

The vampire howled as Marie ran the length of the sword through her abdomen. Angel steadied her aim, as the feeling returned to her limbs, and unloaded the clip into the vampire's pretty face. There was no need for decapitation.

Angel and Marie both fell to their knees. Angel gathered her sister into her arms. "We're going to get you help." The words choked her.

Her breathing fluctuating as she clutched on to Angel. "No, Ang. It's too late," Faith whispered.

"No. We can get some help. One of the vamps can give you blood." Angel rocked her sister in her arms. "Please, *Grand-mère*. Help her!"

"I was born a human, and I'll die a human, even if it's today." Faith closed her eyes, relaxing in Angel's arms.

Angel's tears dropped on Faith's face. "I can't lose you."

"I'll always be with you, like I've been since you were born."

Angel stared down at her sister, empty and scared. "Who'll take care of me? Who's going to love me now?"

"Oh, sissy. You have a lot of people who love you. You have to remember to love yourself. You've always had the answer to your own problems. Be brave enough to look for them."

"I don't know what you're talking about." Angel sought Marie for clarity. She only shrugged in reply.

Faith laid her hand over Angel's heart. Angel covered it with her own, wishing she could turn back time. "You went out to retrieve your beauty, never realizing it was always within you."

Marie leaned over and hugged them both. Angel shuddered as she rocked, clutching Faith to her. Faith's body went limp. Her eyes stared blankly at the dark sky. The one constant in Angel's life was gone.

The sounds of Angel's screams ripped through the night and pierced her heart.

Chapter Thirty

Jacque barreled out the lobby doors. He felt her pain before he heard her cries. Her anguish ripped holes inside his heart. He fought his way to Angel, slashing down anyone who stood in his way.

She sat with her dress sprawled on the ground, covered in blood. She held Faith in her arms, crying and rocking softly. Angel leaned her head into the crook of Marie's neck, as the woman hugged her close.

The battle ensued around them. It was a picture of calm serenity in the fury of madness. A large blond ghoul fell into Jacque. He kicked him in the small of his back, propelling him forward. Laurent caught the ghoul, ran his blade through him, and severed his head. Jacque spotted Etienne farther down the drive trying to detain a thrashing female vamp. He reached Angel's side as a young vamp lunged for them. He seized his neck, snapping it clean. He threw his remains by the potted palms.

Jacque crouched down next to Angel. "Babe, we have to leave."

"I won't leave her." She latched onto Faith's dead body

"I know you're hurting. I feel your pain. We've got to haul ass. You have to let her go." He pried her arms loose and scooped her off the ground. "Marie, come on. I'll make sure Faith gets back."

Marie reluctantly complied when Jacque nudged her with his foot. He carried Angel to a waiting car. The driver jumped when he shoved Marie into the back seat.

"We're going to Etienne's house on St. Charles Ave," Jacque barked. "But I'm suppose to wait for—"

"You have new passengers now. Drive!" he directed the driver, slapping the back of the seat.

The driver stepped on the gas. They reared back into the seat as the car took off. Jacque laid Angel's head in his lap, trailing his fingers down her face. Her body quivered with her silent tears. Marie stared out the window, lost to the darkness.

Halfway to Etienne's, Jacque asked, "Where's Elise and the girls?" In the rush to get Angel to safety, he forgot about them.

"The car took them back to the house. We got them out safely once the fight started," Marie mutter, her forehead resting on the window.

"Okay, at least they got out with no problems."

When they arrived at the house, Jacque carried Angel upstairs and laid her on the bed. He removed her dress and wiped the blood off her arms and face.

"Sorry," she whispered.

"For what, babe?"

She was fixated on the dress, her voice flat and distant. "For ruining the beautiful dress you got me."

"What dress? I didn't get you a dress." Jacque thought the conversation odd, figured her grief confused her.

"I assumed it was from you when the maid brought it earlier." Her empty eyes focused on him.

"Don't worry about the dress right now. You get some rest. I'ma check on everyone and be back."

He kissed her, lingering close for a while longer. As he left the room, a pang of jealousy washed over him, wondering who sent the dress. Downstairs in the parlor, panic kicked in when he saw the expression on Marie's face.

"What's wrong?" he inquired, taking a seat next to her on the sofa.

Nervously, she fidgeted with the silky fabric of her gown. "I can't find the girls or Elise."

"I thought you said the car brought them back here."

"We put them in the car. I assumed they were brought back here." Big brown eyes, reminding him of Angel's, met his gaze. Water welled in them, catching the light from the chandelier.

"Where else would they go?"

"I don't know? Home, maybe?"

He dreaded bearing more bad news. "I'll get Angel to call and find out."

"I don't have a good feeling about this." Marie twisted the fabric of her gown.

"I don't either. Who was around when you got to Le Pavillon?"

"I don't know. Your brother tried to take Angel when the fight broke out. She shot at him. He disappeared before we could figure out what happened to him."

Jacque jumped from his seat. "Xavier was there?"

"Who'd you think was behind this?"

"I haven't slowed down enough to think. Fuck!" he shouted, slamming his fist into the wall, cracking the plaster.

Marie waved him off. "Go get Angel."

Jacque hurried up stairs. Angel sat on the floor, in her bra and panties, with her head in her hands, her eyes red and puffy. When he stepped into the room, she pushed her hair back and wiped the tears with the back of her hand.

"Babe?" He crouched down in front of her, gently caressing her arms.

"Yeah, what's up?" she asked in a raspy voice.

"I need your help. I'ma get you some clothes and we're gonna head downstairs. Okay?"

"Yeah. What's wrong?" Angel's questioning eyes looked up at him.

He dug through her suitcase and found some sweats and a T-shirt. "We'll discuss it downstairs. Here. Put these on." He lifted her off the floor. She held on to him as she put on her clothes, her body weak, limbs uncoordinated. The fragility of her mental state was a concern. He wasn't sure how much more bad news she could handle before she broke. Jacque picked her up and carried her downstairs.

"I can walk," she protested.

He gave her a quick kiss on the lips. "I want you close to me."

She wrapped her arms around his neck and eased against him. He inhaled the lingering bouquet of her perfume tainted with the hint of blood.

Etienne, Laurent, and Damon leaned with their backs to the bar. They passed a bottle of Dewar's from one hand to the other. It must have been bad when Etienne — Mr. Etiquette — drank straight from the bottle. Isabella slumped on the sofa in her tattered gown. Her blonde hair, torn from its pins, straggled loosely about her head. The two younger Boudreaux brothers slouched back-to-back on an ottoman.

"Hey, glad to see everyone made it back." Jacque placed Angel on the sofa next to Marie. "How many did we lose?"

"It's hard to tell. I'm not sure exactly who was with us or against us. I fought anyone who fought me." Etienne tilted the bottle to his lips, grimacing as it poured down his throat.

"Yeah, everyone was fighting, even the hotel staff. Which apparently wasn't the staff. I knew they weren't human. I thought it was something special for the meeting." Laurent liberated the bottle from Etienne.

"It was Xavier," Angel piped up.

He sat on the arm of the sofa, drawing her into him, waiting to absorb the impact of the news. "Marie told us. But we got another problem."

"What kind of problem?"

"Can you call your friends?"

She rotated, breaking his hold on her. "They aren't here?"

"They never made it back," Marie uttered.

"Gimme a phone!" Angel straightened in the seat. Damon tossed her his cell. She dialed number after number with no success, tears streamed down her face. "He took everything! First my sister and now my friends and my mother."

"We'll find them Ang," Laurent promised.

Bell went to the bar to fix another drink. "Jacque, your brother has always been a pain in the ass."

"I've lost enough shit in my life. I'm getting my friends back. I even want my mother back. I don't care how fucked up she is." The anger boiled inside of her. The intensity of her emotions played every muscle in Jacque's body like the tense strings of a guitar.

"We got to find out where Xavier is hiding them and what he wants." Jacque massaged her back, his muscles loosening as she relaxed.

Angel stiffened. "Simple. He wants me."

"You're not his only target. He could've just taken you if he wanted to."

"Maybe I actually hit him and he's hurt."

Jacque pressed his fingers deep into Angel's shoulders. "I don't think he's hurt. If he's hurt, it's not bad enough for him to leave his target behind. We would've found his body back at the hotel. He wants something else."

"Angel and I will work a locate spell and see if we can find the girls." Marie's dress fell in a rustle of taffeta as she rose to her feet, the beautiful royal-blue marred by the crimson of Faith's blood.

"I'll go round up anyone left from the meeting." Etienne hit the bottle one more time.

"Can we be of assistance?" a voice called from the doorway.

Jacque was elated to see his parents. His father was a great strategist and his mother gave him reassurance. Her confidence was contagious. "We need to find out where Xavier might be hiding out."

"I hear your brother's behind this?" Jacque's father inquired.

"Luc contracted him." He kissed his mother on both cheeks. "Things don't make sense. He could've taken Angel at the hotel. He didn't."

"He's here for us, not Angel. He wants to hurt the family." His mother's hand rested in the bend of his elbow. "He's waited a long time for a way to take us without retribution. As long as we side with Angel, he has every right to hunt us."

"I don't care. I'm with Angel. You two don't have to get involved. I don't want to give him a reason to hurt you."

"I wouldn't expect anything different from my son. You would never desert the one you love. As such, we would never desert you." She honored him with a rare smile. There wasn't a lot of warm and fuzzies growing up with a goddess.

Jacque seemed to be the only one in the family affected by Xavier's hatred. His mother thought Xavier's mother beneath her, therefore he fell into the same category. Jacque's father wrote Xavier off when he put his hands on Isis. As children, Xavier used every opportunity to make Jacque's life miserable, always getting the best of him. This time would be different.

Jacque wasn't a rash teenager, trying to protect his mommy. He was a seasoned soldier, a veteran of many battles. Jacque refused to let Xavier hurt any more people he loved. He vowed to take him down.

Chapter Thirty-One

Overwhelming envy choked her each time she witness Jacque and his mother together. One couldn't call Angel's mother a nurturer. Shit, you could barely call her a mother. With Faith killed and Marie technically dead, too, her mother was the only family Angel had left. Since she didn't know her father, he didn't count. No matter how bad the relationship, Angel was determined to get her mother back.

"We're going to go see what we can find out." She looped her arm in Marie's. "It was nice seeing you again, Goddess."

Isis's expression softened, showing compassion. "We'll be seeing a lot of each other. I also bring a message from your sister. She said do not forget what she told you."

Angel halted mid-stride, shocked at the news of her sister. "You saw her?"

"Yes. The deities can walk in all worlds. It's one of the perks."

Angel's heart raced. "Can you take a message back to her?"

"She can hear you if you speak to her. They can see into this world."

Angel ran to her and threw her arms around Isis, causing her to go rigid. "Thank you."

Slowly, Isis brought her arms around Angel and the warmth of the goddess's embrace engulfed her in happiness. She expected a more standoffish reaction. Jacque's mother held her close, ending with a tight squeeze. Her own mother's touch never met her with such enthusiasm.

***

Angel and Marie scanned through the books, searching for the right spell. They originally tried the conjure spell, figuring it was safer to bring the girls to them instead of going to fight Xavier on his home court. It would've been a great idea if it worked. All it got them was one smoky room.

Jacque's face weighed heavy with concern. "Any luck yet?"

"Yeah. We used a locator spell. They're somewhere on St. John Bayou. It's an old white and green Creole colonial house. Sorry we couldn't get more." Angel rubbed her temples, trying to circumvent the forming headache.

"Better than nothing. How many green and white colonial houses could there be on the St. John? I'll have Laurent look online to see if he can narrow it down some more."

"Where're all the others?"

"Etienne is gathering everyone out at Le Fleur. Once you're done, we'll head out to meet the others."

"Let me change, grab my weapons, and I'll be down." She and Marie blew out the candles and swept up the powders.

***

The ballroom was packed with strangers. It was both a surprised and relief to see the amount of people willing to fight with them. Jacque shifted his eyes through the crowd, ready to pounce. The taut line of his lips and the tick in his jaw drew attention to his alarm. Angel sensed his distress as she clung to his arm, weaving through the crowd. Jacque's brother threw him off balance, making him question himself. The confident male she learned to love over the past few weeks was crumbling and it concerned her.

Laurent met them in the middle of the room, dragging them to the side.

"Hey, I found a place. The Ranier House fits the description. It's used as a museum now."

Jacque pushed through the crowd, holding Angel close behind him.

"Great, let's find the others."

Etienne and Damon chatted with several devastatingly beautiful women, the kind that would make Naomi Campbell jealous. The guys held on to their every word as if under a spell.

"How are you ladies tonight?" Angel flashed a smile at them, which they returned. Their smiles were like heaven.

"Much better than you, we fear. Sorry to hear about your loss," the one closest to Etienne answered. Her bronze skin and raven hair glistened in the candlelight.

"Thank you. I'm sorry. I don't know your names."

"I'm Arielle. And these are my sisters. We're the sirens."

"Oh, I didn't realize. Never mind. It doesn't matter. It's nice to meet you. We need to steal Etienne and Damon." She stood in front of the guys to get their attention. "If I can break them from your spell."

"Of course." Arielle turned her attention to Jacque. "It's good to see you again, Jacque. It's been a long time." Her words escaped like lyrical notes played by a saxophone, low and sexy.

He quickly diverted his gaze from the dark beauty when Angel flashed him a disapproving glare. Jacque seemed to be acquainted with every woman in the Underworld. She pushed the air from her lungs slowly and steered him away from Arielle.

Etienne's trance faded as they walked away from the sirens. "Do we have any more information about the girls?"

"The girls are at the Ranier House. I downloaded the floor plan from the Internet. Is there somewhere we can talk?" Laurent asked Etienne.

"Yes, we can use the small meeting room in the back."

In the back room, Laurent laid out the plans on the small conference table. The house was two stories with six rooms on the second floor and eight on the main level.

"He probably has them in the back servant rooms on the main level," Damon offered as studied the drawings.

"Makes sense. It's the most secure place," Laurent chimed in.

Jacque's hold on Angel's hand crushed her like a vise grip. "Xavier isn't predictable. We have to watch our every move. If something doesn't feel right, get the hell out." Jacque's voice came out weak. The others watched him, questioningly, as he spoke.

"How many do you think he has guarding them?" Angel twisted her hand, trying to loosen his grip.

"There's no telling. He can't fit too many into the house with us seeing them. We'll have to case the house to see what we can find out first," Jacque answered.

"Me and my brothers can go. It shouldn't take us more than a couple of hours to get back," Damon offered.

Jacque ran a hand through his dark curls, his green eyes focused on the drawing. "Thanks, while you're gone, we can determine who'll be the best people to take with us."

Angel walked around the table to gaze out the window as the guys discussed the rest of the layout and best lookout points from the bayou. Damon touched her arm, causing her to jump. "Oh, sorry, Damon. I zoned for a minute."

"You've had a hard day." He embraced her. His familiar smell comforted her. "I wanted to say sorry about your sister. I know she was important to you."

"Thanks, it's going to be hard not to have her close to me anymore." The stars twinkled in the sky, and Angel wondered if Faith was watching her.

"She'll always be close to you."

It was too soon, the wound too fresh. All Angel felt was empty. "Everyone keeps saying the same thing. I'll be glad when I start feeling it."

"I know it's probably ruined. I hope you liked my gift."

"What gift?"

"The dress. I sent you a dress." He inched closer, his body creating a shadow over her, shielding her from the others.

"Oh. You sent the dress?"

"Yes, I hope you don't mind. I knew you weren't happy with the one you bought when we were out. I found the one I sent and thought it was made for you."

"Thank you, Damon. The dress was beautiful. I loved it."

His smile beamed brighter than rays of sunlight. "All I need to know then."

"Damon. I have to be honest with you. I really like you. You're a nice guy. But I love Jacque. I'm sorry if I gave you the wrong impression." She cringed from the disappointment in Damon's face.

"I understand. Demons make bad mates. One day he'll mess up, and I'll be waiting. If you give me a chance, I'll make you happy."

"I'm sure you'll make some girl very happy. Right now, my heart belongs to Jacque. It's not fair to you to let you think anything else."

"If you change your mind, you know where to find me."

Angel kissed him lightly on the cheek. "Thanks, Damon."

Jacque cocked his head and gave her a look. She winked at him, walked back to his side, and laid her head on his arm. He brought his arm across her shoulder and planted a kiss on the top of her head. Angel's heart went out to Damon as he walked out the room.

***

Damon and his brothers returned as promised. They counted about fifty guards. Jacque created five teams, consisting of mostly vamps, shifters, and demons. All of them male.

"I'm with you, right?" Angel asked.

"No, you're staying here," Jacque ordered.

"Wrong answer."

"Angel, this is not debatable. I can't risk anything happening to you."

She poked a finger in his chest, his pecs flexing as his anger grew. Angel didn't care. She poked him again. "I don't give a shit what you say. Those are my friends and my mother. I'm going."

"You don't know what Xavier will do if he catches you. He knows you're important to me."

"I guess I'll have to not get caught then." Angel grabbed her extra clips and the sword off the table. She was amazed at the amount of weapons they amassed in such a short time.

His eyes pleaded with her as he clutched her hand. She refused to bend. It was time she defended herself for a change. She spent weeks learning how to fight and it was time for her to use it. In addition, she needed to be near Jacque. There was a void in him tonight. He needed her strength.

"It's going to be all right. You can beat him." She trailed a finger down his cheek.

Fear welled in the emerald-green pools of his eyes. "I'm not sure I can."

"I'm sure. I know you'll never let him hurt me. You're better than him."

"Why do you believe in me?"

She paused before answering. "Because I love you."

"I love you, too." He folded her in his embrace and slanted his lips over hers. She ran her tongue along his lips, inviting him to let her in. She explored his mouth with an intense hunger, hoping to release his doubt. She would lend him her strength tonight, giving him the power to do what needed to be done.

Chapter Thirty-Two

Angel's newfound confidence provided Jacque assurance and pause. She exuded a strength he never sensed in her before. He gave up on the idea of talking her out of going with him. He had to figure out another way to keep her out of trouble. The thought of Angel in Xavier's hands caused his stomach to burn. He would die a second time before letting his brother touch her.

"Look, make sure you stay close to me when we get in there." Jacque held her hand as she sat on the edge of the seat in the SUV, the door open and her feet resting on the running board.

She patted the hilt of the sword strapped to her back. "I'm always close to you. I'll be fine. Don't worry about me." She also packed a Smith and Wesson M&P .9mm fitted with specially made silver bullets, essentially silver hollow points.

"I don't like you being here. If anything happens, I want you to haul ass outta there. Don't worry about me. Just get out."

"Nothing's gonna happen. We're going to be fine."

"Still, if anything goes wrong, I want you to get out. If you need help, find Etienne or Laurent. Laurent will come through the back of the house through the garden doors."

Angel adjusted the sword to the front to sit more comfortably. "I promise if I can't handle things, I'll find help."

"I can't lose you." He shifted his body between her legs, her arms encircled him, and she laid her head on his chest. He prayed for the first time, not knowing if God listened. He closed his eyes, combing his fingers through her hair, and pleaded for her safety regardless.

"You won't lose me. We've been through too much."

Jacque pulled her out the car and stood her up, covering her lips in a slow, lingering kiss. Not wanting to let her go, he held her tight, breathing her in. Her arms wrapped around his neck and the weight of her body felt good against his.

She reached up and her lips grazed his ear. "You can beat him," she whispered.

Thought of fighting his brother caused a flash of heat and his hands to sweat. He kissed her once more and placed her on the ground. The rest of the group tried to ignore the intimate scene. The soldier in him returned and he addressed his team.

"We're going through the front. From what the Boudreauxs saw, there are five guards out front. Etienne, you stay with Angel. If anything goes wrong, get her the hell outta here. If we get separated, meet back at the vehicles. Any questions?"

No one spoke or moved.

His sword jostled against his leg as they moved towards the house. "Okay, let's go kick some ass."

***

The team crouched behind two large magnolia trees in front of the house. Jacque pressed Angel into the trunk of the tree as one of Xavier's guards passed near them. He signaled to Jean, who hid behind the other magnolia, to take the guard. Before the guard noticed, Jean materialized behind him and ran a silver dagger through his heart.

"Make sure no one uses guns until we're outted. We need as much advantage as we can get," Jacque whispered.

They could easily pick off the guards outside, but getting into the house quietly was a different story. They had two options. They could break down the door or crash through the windows. Doubtful the front door would be unlocked for them to waltz through. Jacque dragged Angel behind him as he sprinted for the side of the house. The rest of the team followed.

"I'ma kick down the door. Jean and Pierre y'all are behind me. Take down anyone you see unless it's the girls. Everyone else, you kill first and ask questions later. Understand?"

"Yes," they answered in unison.

"Etienne, you and Angel bring up the rear. We're going straight through the house to the servant quarters behind the kitchen."

Voices behind them interrupted the conversation. Two guards rounded the side of the house. Etienne clothes-lined the first one and ran his sword into his chest. While Etienne pinned him to the ground, Angel unsheathed her sword and took his head. Jacque caught the second guard and twisted his head until it came free from the body.

The team sneaked toward the front of the house. It was lit up brighter than the National Mall on the Fourth of July. Xavier expected them; there was no need for subtlety. He snatched the body of the red-haired guard from the ground and flung it into the front window, jumping in after it.

Sharp pieces of glass pierced his back as he rolled to the floor and pulled his Glock 37 .45. Jacque took out the vamp standing in the doorway. He was on his feet before Angel and Etienne came through the window. Pierre and Jean traced to his side.

Angel fired two shots in his direction. He turned in time to see a were shifting back into its human form as it hit the old wood floor. Jacque winked at his girl and headed toward the hall. Angel and the others followed close behind.

Jacque expected more resistance as he entered the narrow hallway, which barely provided walking space for his big frame. The hallway was empty. He kept close to the wall away from the stairs. Just before they reached the kitchen, fists crashed through the wall, pulling him through to the dining room on the other side.

Angel's screams echoed through the house. The element of surprise was definitely over.

Plaster and dust blocked Jacque's vision. Something with the force of a sledgehammer slammed into his jaw, knocking him back into the hole he came through. The attacker clasped Jacque by the throat and slung him to the other side of the dining room. His head crashed into a painting, and he slumped into a heap on the floor.

Angel was inside the room.

"Get the fuck outta here, Angel! I got this."

"What the hell is that?"

The creature growled. The sound moved away from him, most likely heading for Angel.

"Etienne, get her the fuck outta here and go find the girls. I'll take care of this." Jacque's sight cleared. In front of him, with its back turned to him was a pit demon. The monster stood at least a full foot taller than Jacque. He couldn't believe Luc allowed one to come Topside. Pit demons were the lowest of all demons because of their lack of reasoning abilities. They possessed brute strength and ferociousness. It only understood how to kill.

Angel fired several shots into the creature with no results. "I'm not leaving you," she shouted over the blasts.

"You promised me. Now go find your friends." Jacque took out his dagger and launched himself on the demon's back. It thrashed, trying to throw him off. Jacque's bicep trapped the monster's neck in a chokehold, and he locked it with his other arm, trying to keep from being thrown. He steadied himself enough to pierce the dagger into the base of the creature's skull.

The pit demon's massive hand stretched back, palming Jacque's head. It yanked him over its shoulder and flipped him on the ground. Jacque's back snapped, shooting electric fire down his lower extremities. As he lay on the floor with pain coursing through his body, the creature kicked him in the stomach. The cracking of ribs ensued as another foot met its target.

More shots rang out. Jean and Pierre were at his side, dragging him from the room.

"We've got to kill it or it'll keep coming after us," Jacque managed between winces.

Angel wiped the blood from the side of his face. "Okay, how do we kill it? Apparently shooting doesn't work."

"We got to pierce the base of its skull. The base of its skull is the only weak point."

"Shit, couldn't you pick something easier?"

The wall between the hall and the dining room crashed down around them. They scurried up the stairs, out of the way.

"Not really a good time to discuss this." Jacque stood on his own as his body healed.

The pit demon filled the hall with its stench of sulfur.

Jacque hurdled the rail and lunged onto the creature's back once again. The narrow hall restricted its movements. He gripped the dagger firmly and plunged it into the base of the demon's neck. As he twisted the knife, the demon fell to the floor with a loud thud.

***

Angel didn't breathe as she waited for Jacque to move. She never imagined something as hideous as the monster lying on the floor in front of her. All eight feet of its bulging body lay in a heap on the hardwood. Its charred and blistered skin peeled away from the flesh. Dark eyes sunk into the hollows of its face, staring at the ceiling. Black tar oozed from two holes in the middle of the creature's face. Angel assumed the holes represented what humans considered a nose. Jacque held on to the beast as if he anticipated it waking up, yet it remained in a rancid pile on the floor.

"Baby, you okay?" Angel scooted around the demon's blistered arm. It looked as if it had third degree burns all over its body.

Jacque pushed himself off the creature's back. "I'm fine. Come on. We gotta go. We're gonna have a lot of company soon."

Etienne was already in the kitchen. Angel followed behind Jacque. Jean and Pierre held up the rear. The clamor of fighting sounded from the other side of the house. The others must've run into some trouble. It was time to find her friends and get the hell out of this place.

"Hey, I hear them." Etienne signaled. He kicked in the oak paneled door, leading to the maid's quarter.

The metallic smell of blood filled the air. Each of the girls lay strapped to a table. Nat and Jazzy had half-healed cuts all over their bodies. Angel's mother was duck-taped to a chair, facing the monstrosity. Angel ran to her friends.

Etienne appeared at Jazzy's side and untied her, his movement gentle, as not to injury her any further. The torture of her friends devastated Angel. Her feet froze as if glued to the floor. Jacque brushed past her and helped Nat off the table, handing her to Jean.

Angel's mother screamed as Jacque ripped off the tape. Her high-pitched wails destroyed Angel's sanity. Her mother's eyes were void of recognition.

Her face showed signs of the beating she endured. Angel's vision blurred and her head swam. Jacque passed her to Pierre just in time to catch Angel before she fainted.

"Ang, babe. You need to snap out of this. We don't have time for you to freak out on us." Jacque's voice sounded far away. He held her by her arms, shaking her.

She blinked her eyes and the room came back in focus.

"I'm okay. Let's go." Her throat burned as she choked back tears.

"We're gonna go out the back and around the side of the house and back to the vehicles."

"This doesn't feel right. Even with the thing in the hall, it was too easy." She studied Jacque's reaction and saw he thought the same.

"We don't have time to question it now. Let's just get the hell out."

Putting aside her uneasiness, she focused on getting her friends to safety.

Battle raged outside. The lawn was littered with decapitated bodies. Angel couldn't tell who belonged to their team and who was with Xavier. Laurent struggled with a large dark-haired vamp. The vamp sank his fangs into Laurent's arm. Down at the far end of the lawn, Michael charged an enormous demon with red hair, the purity of his white wings decimated with blood. She hadn't realized the archs came tonight.

"Jacque, Etienne can get us back to the vehicles. You should go help Laurent and the others," she instructed. She hated leaving the others behind.

"I'm not leaving you with Xavier still loose."

"They need help. We don't need all of us to go to the vehicle."

"Etienne, give me Jazzy. I think your mother can walk. Put her down Pierre. Angel can help her. Go back and help Laurent. Once we get to the truck, I'll send Jean back, too."

Angel held her mother under her arm and supported her around the waist. She lugged her across the grass toward the road. Although her mother stumbled a few times, they made the mile trek back to the SUV. Jean laid Nat in the third row seat. Her mother sat stiff in the back seat with Jazzy's head in her lap. Jacque revved the truck, kicked up the gravel, and removed them from the harm's way.

Chapter Thirty-Three

The Escalade skidded to a stop in front of Le Fleur. Angel jumped out the SUV, before Jacque could put it in park, and ran inside for assistance. When she returned, Elise scooted out the vehicle and leaned against the side, waiting for instructions. Jacque lifted Jazzy from the backseat, giving access to Nat in the third row. The girls needed help fast.

Two weres from Damon's pack took Jazzy and Nat into the building. Jacque carried Elise, afraid her legs might give out at any moment. They went back to the conference room they were in earlier. Marie and his mother were there to tend to the girls.

"What happened to them?" Marie questioned.

"We don't know. This is how we found them. Actually, they look better than when we found them. They've been healing slowly." Angel brushed the hair out of Jazzy's face.

"Elise," Marie called.

Elise spun in a rolling chair and stared blankly out the window.

"Elise! Girl, I know you hear me talking to you." Marie blocked Elise from making another spin.

"*Grand-mère*, please. She's been through a lot tonight," Angel pleaded.

"I know, child, we have to try to snap her out of her shock."

She hung close to Elise as if she wanted to touch her, but was afraid. "Give her a little time."

"Someone go out there and get some of the vampires to donate some blood," Jacque's mother commanded. The two weres left to fulfill her request.

Jacque crossed over to Angel, hugging her from behind. She was right. Something was off. It should've been harder to get the girls, and Xavier was nowhere to be found. Xavier wasn't the lay-low type. It wasn't his nature to have others fight for him.

Angel sunk her back into him, pressing so close not even light could penetrate between them. "What's wrong?"

Jacque buried his face in her hair before he answered. "Nothing. It's just not like Xavier to not show up to a fight."

Her soft caress soothed the electricity floating like a veil atop his skin. "Maybe he was there, and we didn't run into him."

"No, he would've come for us." He placed a kiss behind her ear.

"Do you want to go back and see if we can find him?"

Jacque squeezed her tighter. "I don't want you to go back there. I'll go back. You stay here. Your friends and your mother need you."

Angel spun to face him. "No, you're not going without me."

Elise's shrill voice rang through the room. "Are you two always this sickening?"

"What the hell are you talking about, Mom?" Angel snapped.

Elise turned in her chair to face him and Angel. "Your mother and your best friends were captured and tortured all night. All you care about is this...this monster."

Angel's eyes grew wide and her nose flared. "Mom, Jacque risked his life to come and get you. You're not going to talk to him like that."

"Do you know what his brother did to your friends?" Madness glinted in her eyes as tears formed in the corners.

"What, Mother?" Angel asked reluctantly. She didn't really want the answer.

"He sliced them with a razor all over their bodies then gave them vampire blood to heal them. As soon as they healed, he did it all over again. He strapped me to a chair and forced me to watch. I heard those girls screaming in pain, not able to do anything about it. All I could do is sit there."

"Oh, Mom, I'm sorry." Angel fell to her knees beside the chair. Her forehead lay against Elise's arm.

"I'm sure you cried worse when you lost Jacque. He means more to you than your own mother," Elise spouted.

Angel's voice took a hard edge. "I don't want to fight with you."

"Tell me. Why do you love him?"

"What do you mean? He's a good man and he loves me."

"He's not a man. No matter how much he wants you to forget, remember he's a demon. Even if his mother gave him the power to feel emotions, he'll always be a monster." Elise backed away from Angel, meeting Jacque's glare. She had nerve calling someone a monster the way she treated her own daughters.

Angel stood up and followed her mother. "Have you lost your mind? What the hell are you talking about?"

"How do you know about me and my son, Elise?" Isis's eyes narrowed as she crept towards the wild-eyed woman in the chair.

Elise challenged his mother's anger. "I know more than you think. You! Always looking down on people, because you're a goddess. No one was ever good enough for you and your son."

Jacque hurled himself at Angel and pushed her away from Elise. "Stay away from her."

"What's wrong with her? What did he do to her?" she cried.

"She's not your mother," Isis answered.

Jacque kicked, Elise in the chest, sending the chair flying to the far end of the room. "Mom, take everyone and get out."

Elise morphed in front of them. Jacque envied his brother's talents. Xavier gradually replaced Elise in the chair. "What's up, little brother? Not happy to see me?" Xavier stood, cracking his neck to either side.

"I can't say I've missed you."

"Aw. That hurts, bro. All I've done since the last time we were together was think about you and your mother. And where's Father? He's usually close, holding on to your mother's skirt."

Jacque prowled around the conference table. The weres returned with the blood. He handed them each a girl instead of taking the bags of blood, as they stood staring at Xavier. "Get them out of here. Make sure no one comes back here. Mom. You, Angel and Marie need to go with them."

A wave of crimson washed over Xavier's eyes. "No, they stay. I want them to see me kill you."

"They're not staying. This is between me and you." Jacque tried to herd the group out the door.

Xavier waved the cell phone, taunting, threatening. "Angel, if you leave, your mother will die. I can make one call and she's gone."

"You're one sick fuck, Xavier. What happened to you?" Angel spat, remaining where she was, as did Marie and Jacque's mother.

"Who's to say? Maybe, if my father would've stuck around to take care of me, I would've turned out better. My mother was a lowly demoness, not worthy of the Prince. Guess Father slummed it the night he knocked Mom up. " Xavier's cackle was cold, harsh, and vacant.

"Let them take the girls out. You don't need them," Jacque insisted.

"Always the Boy Scout. Remember what happened the last time you tried to protect someone from me, brother?"

"I'm not the same boy," Jacque growled.

"Ah. What you don't realize is you haven't let him completely go yet. Your emotions have always been your weakness. You'll never reach your full potential without being able to suppress those emotions. Always thinking, regretting, feeling. Such a waste."

"I'm strong enough to kill you. Nothing else matters."

"We'll see, little brother." Xavier unsheathed his broadsword, twirling it above his head and bringing it down with both hands.

Jacque gripped his sword, his hands perspired and his pulse raced. The pounding of his heart drummed in his ear. The combination of everyone's fear and anxiety in the room churned in his belly. He circled the table, trying to steady his hands and kept his eyes locked on Xavier.

Xavier kicked the table. It flew toward Jacque. He blocked the impact with his right arm. The mahogany table splintered around his body. Pieces of wood scattered about the room.

With his sword readied, Xavier rushed Jacque. He drove the sword into the wall as Jacque spun out the way. Jacque reversed his hold on his sword plunging it behind him. The hard steel of the blade sank into soft flesh. Jacque's sword punctured his brother's side. Xavier gaped at the wound in shock. He caught a bit of the blood oozing from the gash and brought it to his lips. As he licked his fingers, a smile played on his lips.

Jacque froze.

Xavier's combat boot smashed into Jacque's right knee. Jacque fell to the floor. He stopped the second boot from meeting his head. He rolled out of the way of Xavier's sword as it impaled into the wood floor. Jacque returned to his feet and limped around a piece of the broken table.

Xavier yanked at the embedded sword. "You've gotten better, little bro. But not good enough."

"Fuck you, Xavier." Jacque stalked closer.

Xavier's lips twisted into a sinister grin. "Ah. No thanks. I might try your girl when I'm done with you."

Jacque lunged at him. His shoulder plowed into Xavier's midsection, knocking him to the ground. Jacque straddled him, raining blows into Xavier's face.

Xavier yanked out his dagger and slashed the blade at Jacque. A deep gash appeared across Jacque's torso. Jacque trapped Xavier's arm and snapped it in two. Angel sucked in a breath and distracted him for one second. The leg of the table caught the side of his jaw, and he crashed into the wall.

Angel went for her gun. Isis stopped her before she fired a shot.

"This is between Jacque and Xavier. They need to finish this," Isis said, taking the gun from Angel's hands.

"He needs help!" Angel cried out.

"This has been coming for a long time. His fear of Xavier has been what has kept Jacque from his full potential. He needs to finish this."

Xavier wound his hand in Angel's hair and snatched her toward him, causing her to shriek. "I'm tired of you trying to shoot me, bitch." He slammed her head into the wall.

Rage fueled Jacque. He dove over Angel, tackling Xavier. With Xavier's hands still tangled in her hair, she tumbled back with the brothers, her screams filling the air.

Chapter Thirty-Four

The hardwood floors felt like concrete against Angel's back. Her spine quivered, and her lower back throbbed. The excruciating agony radiated down her legs. She lay on her back, staring up at the ceiling, regrouping, hoping Xavier released her hair. Death was never something she wished upon a person. At this moment, she prayed for it.

The crisp snap of bone breaking rang in her ear. The hand trapped in her hair released its grasp. Angel dragged her body across the floor out of Xavier's reach. Marie and Isis ran to her aid.

"They're gonna kill each other," Angel choked.

"They're a close match." Isis slid under her arm, placing it over her shoulder, as Marie did the same on the other side. Together, they lugged her to the far side of the room.

"Can't we stop it?" Angel's head pounded. Lighting struck outside the window.

"Sometimes we need to let men be men." Isis lowered her into the rolling chair.

Angel's head swam; splotches of light filled her vision. The lightning intensified outside, and the wind began to howl.

"You have to control your emotions." Marie combed her fingers through Angel's hair, trying to calm her down.

"What?" Angel cast a glance out the window as thunder rumbled in the sky.

"The storm. You're causing it. If you don't control it, it will soon be in here."

Breathing deeply, Angel pushed the storm away.

Jacque picked Xavier up and slammed his knee into the small of Xavier's back. Dumping the limp body to the floor, he stumbled after the sword lying next to the rubble of wood in the middle of the room.

Xavier twitched, rolled on his side, and lifted on all four. Each of his vertebrae crackled as they rippled down his back. He arched as black fur replaced his bronze skin. Angel stared in amazement as the sleek, black panther prepared for attack. The massive cat pounced, sinking its teeth in Jacque's neck. Jacque fell forward from the momentum, dropping his sword.

Jacque's eyes burned blood-red. His body trembled under the panther, and his joints popped as they shifted under his skin. White and black fur grew in place of the glistening olive skin Angel loved.

The magnificent white beast released a fierce roar.

The women backed into the corner of the room. The two creatures circled one another. Another bolt of lightning flashed across the sky. Angel swallowed hard and exhaled the breath she was holding. *Must calm down.*

The white tiger leaped, clawing into the back of the panther and tearing down its side. The black cat snarled, latching its canines into the tiger's chest. The red of blood defiled the white fur. Long white incisors locked onto the panther's neck as they rolled on the broken scraps of the table.

Angel sprinted from the corner of room and secured Jacque's sword. She watched for her opportunity to send Xavier to his death. Her gazed locked with the white tiger. It silently pleaded with her, for what she didn't know.

Its roar shook in her chest.

The animal rolled on top of the panther, piercing its sharp claws into the beast's flesh. Angel weighted the sword heavily in her hands. Sweat dripped down the side of her face. She resisted the urge to wipe it on the back of her arm, instead stood ready to plunge the sword into Xavier's panther form.

The tiger took on a familiar form.

"Throw me the sword!" Jacque leaned the full weight of his body against the panther.

Angel tossed the sword in his direction. With one hand, he snatched it from the air. The animal swiped at Jacque, clawing him on the side of his face, four red slashes appeared. As Jacque leveled the sword, the panther shifted and Xavier lay in its stead. Jacque used the sword like a spear and drove it through Xavier's chest, pinning him to the ground.

"I underestimated you." Xavier choked, shrill and haunting.

"I told you I wasn't the same boy."

"There are times I wished things had been different between us," Xavier announced, bringing a look of surprise to Jacque's face.

Jacque's knuckles whitened around the leather hilt. "It could've been. You never allowed it."

"Finish it, brother."

"Where's Elise?" Jacque gritted through his teeth. He kicked his brother in the ribs and walked away in frustration.

Xavier's smile was cool and easy. "You asked the million dollar question."

Running out of her corner, Angel screamed, "Even in the end you're an asshole." She glared down at Xavier, twisting the sword in his chest, causing him to writhe in pain. "Don't fuck with me. Where's my mother?"

"Fuck you." Xavier closed his eyes, shutting them out.

With all her strength, Angel yanked the blade down Xavier's chest to his abdomen, gutting him. He opened his eyes, meeting her glare. His eyes were the same shade as the man she loved with all her heart. They were the same eyes except a deep sorrow lay trapped beneath Xavier's.

"Where's my mother?" she demanded. Her knuckles taut as she griped the weapon. Tears burned as they tumbled down her cheeks. Thunder clapped outside and the skies opened to the rain.

"Fuck you, bitch."

Angel pushed Jacque off Xavier. Lightning crashed through the window and hit the sword like a lightning rod. Electricity ravaged Xavier's body. As Angel concentrated, the power of the energy surging through him increased.

"Stop," Marie yelled. "If you kill him, we won't find your mother."

"Babe. You got to stop it." Jacque pulled her away from Xavier, burying her face in his chest.

When Angel turned back around, Xavier was gone. The only thing left was the sword stuck into the wood floor.

"Where the hell did he go?" she questioned.

Jacque walked to his sword and plucked it out the floor. "Fuck!"

"It smells like Lucifer's work. He saved him." Marie took her place beside Angel, placing an arm around her waist.

"How're we going to find Momma?"

"We'll figure it out. Let's see what's going on with the others. We'll go back and search the house. She might still be there." Jacque sheathed his sword.

Angel picked up her .9mm and Xavier's sword off the floor. Isis and Marie headed into the main ballroom with the others. The destruction was unimaginable. They were definitely going to lose their deposit.

Jacque towered behind her, his strong arms wound tightly around her shoulders. He smelled of heat and musk with a faint lingering of the feline. She collapsed into his broad frame. The hot moisture of his breath tickled as he nuzzled her neck. His soft lips grazed her cheek. Reaching back, she pressed his face against hers, the stubble rough and scratchy against her cheek. His touch was like fire and ice, awakening a savage desire.

"I thought I was going to lose you again." Her lips skimmed the line of his jaw. His big hands traveled down the front of her body, making her shiver with anticipation.

"I told you I wasn't leaving you."

"He'll come back for you." She shivered as he cupped her breast, brushing his thumb across her nipple. She ached for him, desperate for his closeness, yearning for their union.

"I'll be ready." His tongue danced along the back of her ear. The pressure of his teeth on her earlobe sent chills down her spine. His strength and power was an aphrodisiac, seducing her to want him more. Heat ruptured inside her, remembering the magnificent white beast.

"We can't do this now." She prayed he ignore her words.

"I can't stop." He kicked the door closed and spun her to face him. His lips consumed hers. His tongue forced its way into her mouth, greedily exploring. She returned his enthusiasm, tasting the small traces of metallic saltiness of blood.

Jacque's hands trailed down her back and under her shirt. His fingers passed over her navel and fluttered over the flat expanse of her abdomen. Her hand played with the lavish curls falling at the base of his neck as the kiss deepened.

As they stumbled backward, she hit the wall. Her shirt and bra landed on the floor with Jacque's assistance. His lips tickled her collarbone. He lowered his head, taking her breast into his mouth. His tongue flickered over her nipple. They hardened under his wicked touch. He worked his magic, extracting a moan from her.

Angel pressed further into the wall as Jacque worked his way down her body. His moist tongue teased her navel as he worked the button on her jeans. Once he unzipped them, she wiggled to help get them past her hips.

She drew in a breath when his thumb rubbed the center of her desire. He ran his tongue along crease of her thigh and groin. His fingers slipped inside her wetness and his mouth replaced his thumb. He consumed her with his sinful kiss. She ground against his palm, needing to be filled.

His mouth and fingers played her with agonizing ecstasy. The rhythmic pacing of his fingering and constant teasing of his tongue drove Angel to the brink of insanity. When she thought she could take no more, Jacque pushed her legs onto his shoulder and delved deeper into her sweetness.

She stifled her cry, her mind hazed in the delirious rhapsody as she rode the crashing waves of her climax. Jacque lowered her legs to the floor. He placed his hands on either side of her, trapping her into a kiss. Angel tasted her pleasure in his mouth.

As Jacque held her in the kiss and massaged her breast, she worked the buckle of his belt and unzipped his jeans. His shaft pulsed under the dense material, rejuvenating her desire. She pushed his jeans to the floor and folded her hand around the bulk of his manhood. As she moved along the length of him and rubbed her finger over the slickness of the tip, Jacque groaned into her hair. "I want to be inside of you."

She quickened her movements, her hand not fully circling his cock, stroking the length of it with the precise rhythm of her wrist. Jacque braced himself against the wall. Angel took his hand, guiding it back between her legs. His fingers entered the fiery abyss, matching her pace. His body compressed, bearing down on her. She answered his call by guiding his thickness along the liquid heat between her legs.

"Now," she pleaded.

Her legs encircled his waist as he entered her. Her body accepted the full length of him as he filled her completely. His hips ground into her, each thrust pounding harder, releasing the frustrations of the night. She moved with his strokes, gliding along his manhood, clenching herself around it. He built up sped, carrying them to their rapture.

With each thrust, her back crashed into the wall. She bit into his shoulder as she reached the height of her pleasure. Her release raked throughout her body as Jacque spilled his seed into her, the warm fluid mingling with her juicy aftermath.

Ironclad arms clasped her to him, so secure she could barely breathe. They stayed clinging to one another not moving, appreciating the moment.

Angel shook her head, dropping her leg, and murmured, "We got to go, baby."

"I know. But just stay like this for a second longer." If he pushed her any more, she might bust through the other side of the wall.

"We can pick this up later. People are waiting on us."

"I guess." He stole another kiss. His tongue begged her not to leave. Angel broke the kiss, brushed a wayward curl out of his face, and smiled up at him.

He let her go and tossed her clothes to her. "Come on. Let's go find your mother."

Chapter Thirty-Five

The ballroom resembled a field hospital. Supes healed faster than humans, although some wounds took longer than others to repair. Silver worked a number on most supernatural species. The smell of blood and dying flesh permeated the air, nauseating Angel. She scanned the room searching for her friends and found them helping a couple of vamps on the stage.

"I see they got you up and going." Angel hopped onto the stage.

Nat pushed the hair out of her face and wiped her brow. "Yeah. If you ever make me drink blood again, I swear I'll never talk to you again."

"Has Laurent and Etienne come back yet?"

"I haven't seen them. You should ask Marie and Isis. They're in the other room with the more injured ones."

Angel's nails dug into her palms. "Shit, this isn't everyone?"

"Naw. They've been sending more out to help and more come back hurt." Nat wiped the sweat from her forehead.

"Okay. I'll find Jacque and get back out there."

"What happened to Jacque's brother?"

Angel shrugged. "The hell if we know. He was there one minute then gone. Luc probably got him outta there."

Nat went back to Steri-stripping the gash on the vamps side. "That's jacked."

"Yep, but we got to go get this fight over with and find my mother. We'll look for Xavier later." Angel handed Nat some gauze and tape.

"You *sure* you wanna find her and bring her back?"

Angel shook her head at her friend. "Yes, Nat. She's my mother. I gotta bring her back."

"I'm just saying. I know there's been many days we wished she would disappear." Nat's quiet chuckle reminded Angel of when they were girls, whispering stories about her escape from Elise.

"Not this way. And I don't want *her* gone, just her attitude."

Jacque waved from across the room, motioning for her to come. She jumped off the stage and darted toward him. Her sword bounced against her back and rubbed the base of her neck. The injured watched as she traveled to the other side of the room. She quickened her steps to remove herself from the center of attention. Her heart broke to know she caused their pain.

"How's your friends?" Jacque asked as they walked out the ballroom.

"They'll be fine. I'm worried about Laurent and Etienne."

"Yeah. Me, too."

"We got to go back and help them."

She grabbed the keys from him since his driving was still a little unsteady. "Let's head out."

***

Body parts lay sprinkled all over the lawn. Blood tinted the green grass a gruesome shade of crimson. She hoped most of these men belonged to Xavier. Angel forced herself to try to identify them. Jacque stalked behind her with his sword drawn, cautious of her every move. She used her own sword to poke and prod the bodies in her path.

The battle was over. Only the grunts and groans of the wounded disturbed the calm. A hand grasped Angel's ankle as she stepped over a body. Her high-pitched scream pierced the silence. Jacque raised his weapon to strike. Angel grabbed him before he could administer the blow. A familiar voice called out to her, and she dropped to the ground to comfort him.

"Hey." She smiled at Damon. "You look like shit."

"It's been a bad day all around." The wet gurgle in Damon's chest distorted his words.

"Yeah, you look pretty banged up. We should get you back to Le Fleur."

"There were a lot of them. We held our own." His breathing was heavy. Angel propped his head on her lap and held his hand.

"I can see. Y'all kicked ass."

"Did Laurent and Etienne make it back?"

"We haven't seen them."

"They were in the house the last time I saw them." The light dulled behind his amber eyes. She brushed back his dark brown hair, caressing his temple.

"We'll look for them once we get you to a vehicle."

Damon looked away into the night. "It might be too late."

"You're full of shit, Damon. You'll be fine." Her throat closed as she swallowed her fear, knowing he might be telling the truth.

Jacque bent down, picked Damon up, and hauled him over his shoulder. "Let's get him back to the SUV. Someone can drive him to Le Fleur. Mother and Marie will patch him up." He gave Angel his hand and helped her from the ground.

They sprinted to the house once they turned Damon over to the group headed back to the vehicles. The lights in the house blazed bright against the night sky. Angel remembered how out of place the lights seemed the first time they arrived. It was an ambush. One they readily walked into. This time Angel refused to be caught off guard.

The house held the stench of death. The body count was high. Jacque kicked limbs and other parts out of the way as they navigated through the front hall. The pit demon still blocked the narrow walkway. Angel gagged from its fumes as they climbed over its body.

Shadows shifted in the kitchen at the end of the hall. Jacque maneuvered in front of Angel to shield her from danger. She slid the .9mm out of the holster, changing to a full clip.

"Who's there?" Jacque called out.

No one answered. The thud of wood hitting the floor caused Angel to peek from behind Jacque. He pushed her back.

"Who the hell's back there? Answer or we'll start shooting." Jacque inched his way forward.

Cans clanged on the table. Muttered curses flowed from the kitchen. "Jacque, is that you?" Laurent yelled.

"Yeah," Jacque huffed as he hurried toward the noise.

Laurent leaned on the kitchen table, a foot missing from his right leg. He used his sword as a crutch. Etienne sulked, exasperation etched in the lines of his face, behind Laurent with her mother draped over his shoulder.

"Where the hell did you find her?" Angel scrambled over to assess her mother's condition.

Etienne shifted her mother, allowing Angel to better evaluate the situation. "She was tied up and locked in the old slave quarters out back."

"What did they do to her?"

"I'm actually the one who knocked her out. She was hysterical and trying to fight everyone when we untied her." She understood the reason for the expression on his face.

Her mother always bit the hand that fed her. "Sorry about her. She's a piece of work."

"I'm fine. Laurent's the one with the problem. She whacked off his foot with a machete. I didn't realize how strong she was. I wrestled her down to the ground before she hurt anyone else."

Angel suppressed a giggle. "Oh, shit! I'm sorry, Laurent."

"I'm okay. It'll grow back. You owe me big time!" Laurent limped down the hall, holding on to the wall.

"Anything you want, babe. I got you." She laughed. His drama was in full effect.

He glanced back with a devilish grin. "You can start by getting me a date with Natasha once my foot grows back."

"I'll see what I can do."

The moon smiled down on them, casting a silvery shadow on the group. Angel reveled in the stillness of the night. It was a welcomed break after the chaos of the battle. The trek was slow going since Laurent refused Jacque's help.

Exhaustion crawled into Angel's bones. She wanted a hot bath, a warm bed, and to curl into Jacque's arms. She played with his hair as she drove. She shivered when his fingers caressed the bumpy ridges of the scar running down her face.

The madness of the day managed to make her forget about her looks. Not once did she stop to think about what someone thought and not once did anyone mention her scar. The people with her tonight appreciated her for more than just her appearance. They cared about the person who lay beneath the surface. Angel's heart warmed at the thought. Other than Nat and Jazzy, she never had real friends before.

Several cars were leaving Le Fleur as they pulled into the drive. Isis and Leviathan poised on the steps of the porch, bidding everyone goodnight. They exuded royalty. Angel waited, admiring Jacque's interaction with his mother, always respectful and caring. Even with Jacque towering over her, Isis maintained her regal presence.

She squeezed Jacque's arm. "I'm glad everyone arrived safely."

"Yeah, except Xavier got away. And he'll be back." Jacque kissed his mother's cheek.

Jacque's father smacked him on the back like a proud papa. "I heard you had the best of him, until he disappeared."

"I guess, but he gave as good as he got. He's strong."

"You're stronger, son." Isis eyes shone with pride. Something Angel never saw in Elise's eyes, not even when she got the contract with one of the top modeling agencies in the country.

"I hate I have to fight him. He's my brother and he's hurting." Jacque met his mother's gaze. "I felt his pain."

"I felt it also. He channeled his pain into hatred. I doubt anything will ever be able to break through to him, especially us."

"You have to admit, we've never really accepted him into our family."

"He has always been welcome in our home. Your father knows I tried." Her tone was stern, defensive.

"Being welcomed in the house and being accepted as family is different, Mother. You know you never accepted him as one of us."

Isis crossed her arms over her chest. "Because he was not one of us. Even as a child his hate ruled him."

"And he's always sensed your distance. You're not the only one to blame.

We all did this to him."

"I will not take responsibility for Xavier's choices." Isis spun on her heels and stomped away.

Angel recognized the hurt in her eyes. Isis had the same expression she observed in her own mother's features — guilt. *Our parents relive the regrets of their decisions as we children suffer the consequences. It's a fate we can't outrun.* Angel's mother made it a mission to find a way to admonish her accountability in Angel's flaws, never quite succeeding.

Angel pushed Jacque toward the front door. "Go after your mother." He reluctantly followed her orders.

The ballroom was almost empty. A few more seriously injured needed to be moved. Nat and Jazzy sat on the edge of the stage, chatting with Etienne. Marie bandaged Laurent's leg, in tears as he retold his struggle with Elise. Angel smiled as she took in the scene. This was her new family. Jacque returned, disrupting her moment of accomplishment. She had stood admiring her situation longer than she realized.

Jacque's lips grazed her forehead. "You ready to go get some sleep?"

"I'm ready. I need a hot shower and a soft bed."

"I can help you with your shower."

Giggling, she nudged him with her elbow. "I'm sure you can, but I need sleep and you helping would interfere with the whole sleeping thing."

"Who needs sleep?" He gave her butt a playful tap.

"All right, let's round it up and head out," Angel yelled, flagging her friends. She slid under Jacque's arm, melted into his side, and headed for the door. She wasn't sure whether to put this one under the win column. At least everyone was still alive. The war wasn't over; they still had to find Xavier. As long as he was free, they wouldn't be safe.

Chapter Thirty-Six

Jacque woke with the weight of Angel's body across his chest. Her hair cascaded in dark waves over his body. The sunlight through the window danced against her golden skin. He played with the brown tresses as he watched her sleep. He hated to disturb her. She tossed and turned most of the morning, finding rest only a couple of hours ago. The madness of the night refused to let Jacque's mind rest.

He shifted his body from under Angel. She murmured and reached out for him when he moved. The gesture made his chest swell. He wanted her in his arms forever. First, he needed to take care of Xavier.

Muted voices came from the kitchen downstairs. Jacque paused in the doorway, enjoying the smell of chicory coffee and beignets. His mother and Marie talked in hushed tones at the small kitchen table.

He kissed his mother. "What're you two conspiring about this morning?"

"Son, it's afternoon and there is no conspiring."

"Angel still sleeping?" Marie asked.

Isis poured Jacque a cup of coffee. "It was a long night, even for those of us who aren't human. I'm sure she's quite exhausted."

"Sometimes I forget she's human." He took the cup from his mother with a sideways grin.

"Yes, she's got spunk." Marie chuckled.

"Have you seen anyone else this morning?" he questioned, dipping the beignet in his coffee, earning a frown from the ladies.

Isis straightened the gold clasp in her braid. "Laurent's in the parlor. He slept down here last night. Etienne hasn't come down yet."

"All right, I'll leave you two to your whispers. I have to figure out how to find my brother." Jacque inhaled and forced the air out in one breath.

Laurent sat with his leg propped on a pillow. His head rested on the arm of the couch. Jacque's and Laurent's friendship stretched back to their childhood. They were inseparable until Laurent first tasted Topside. Jacque always thought Laurent would fall in love with a human. The Fates turned the tables.

Jacque tapped Laurent on the shoulder. "Hey, bro."

"I wondered how long it would take you to get down here. Angel's making you slow." Laurent's eyes popped open.

"You're just jealous."

"Yeah, you're a lucky SOB. I've been here over a century and haven't found *the one*. You refuse to leave the Underworld, date the same chick for half a century, and still manage to find a human to fall in love with. I can't win for losing."

"It happens when you're not looking and at the most inconvenient time." Jacque thought about the life he left behind. He lived a good existence before his world exploded into mayhem. Who wanted to only exist? With Angel, he was alive.

"What happened to Xavier?"

"I don't know, man. I think Luc got his ass outta there."

"It won't be easy to find him."

"I know. We can't sit around waiting for him to show up though."

"I don't know about you, until my foot grows back, sitting around waiting is kinda my thing."

Jacque looked down at Laurent's missing foot and burst into laughter. "Man, how did you let a little woman whack off your foot?"

"She's crazy. I'd fight ten vamps before I mess with her again. I say we sic *her* on Xavier when we find him."

"She's something. I know she's worked a number on Angel. Those scars are gonna take longer than your foot to heal." Jacque expression turned serious. Elise was like poison to Angel.

"Talking about messed-up family. Are you going to be okay with killing Xavier?"

"I don't have an option."

"I know you always wanted things to get better between the two of you."

"We were kids then. He couldn't let it go. Now I got to let him go. Anyway, I have a brother. A footless one, but a brother all the same."

"Thanks, man. Talking about fam, have you seen my sister? It's not like her to stay out of the action."

Jacque's brows scrunched together in thought. "Naw. It's strange Bell hasn't been around. You worried?"

"She can take care of herself. If she was in trouble, she would've let us know."

A sound behind them interrupted the conversation. Jacque turned to see Etienne stroll in the room. Fatigue prevailed in his features. Jacque never thought a vampire could be too pale. Etienne's pasty complexion reflected his lack of feeding due to the craziness over the last few days.

"Man, you look like shit." Laurent pushed up on the pillows behind his back.

"I feel like shit," Etienne answered.

"Thanks for all you've done for us," Jacque offered.

"Not a problem. Things were getting dull around here. There is such a thing as partying too much."

"We're going to have to pay one hell of a bill at the Le Fleur." Jacque never pulled out the Black Card before. He might have to break it out this time.

"It's fine. I own the Le Fleur. You're going to have to put it back right. You and your brother tore up the back rooms last night."

"Put it on my tab. I got to figure out how to find Xavier."

"You got everything you need right here. Those women in the kitchen can conjure anything. You have two voodoo priestesses, a witch, and a goddess. What more do you want?" Etienne poured a shot of Ciroc, garnering a questioning look from Jacque and Laurent. "It's just to hold me over until I feed. Don't judge me."

"Do what you need to do. It's just a tad early to be hitting the sauce. And I guess I do have a lot of resources at my disposal."

"I'll be glad when night falls. I have to hunt tonight."

"We'll leave you to do what you need to do tonight. I'm going to try to find a place today. I know we're crowding you."

Etienne downed the vodka. "I actually don't mind. I quite enjoy the company."

"I'm sure you do. You know Jazzy is going to be a problem. She's stuck around thus far, because she doesn't want to leave her friends. Don't forget she's scared shitless of us. Be careful with her," Jacque reminded him.

"I know. She's irresistible. Such a sweet aroma." Etienne tongue rolled over his fangs.

"Man, you can't be snacking on her. Angel'll kill me if she finds out you're taking sips from her friend."

"I wouldn't feed off her. At least not without permission," Etienne added slyly.

"Forget about it, man. Leave her alone. We should just wipe her memory when we send her home."

Etienne shook his head and downed another drink. "Such a waste."

"Are y'all done being girls?" Laurent threw a pillow at Etienne.

"Okay, let's go see what the ladies can dig up about Xavier." Jacque helped Laurent off the sofa. "We got to find this guy some crutches."

The kitchen was filled with female energy. Isis and Marie remained in their seats at the kitchen table. Angel lounged in the chair next to Marie, looking wildly sexy in her disheveled state. Her hair was pulled back into a ponytail at the back of her head, wayward strands fell framing her face. She wore no make-up, letting her natural beauty shine. Natasha and Jasmine hung out at the island, coffee in hand.

"There you are." Angel perked up in her seat.

"Hey, babe."

"What've y'all been up to?"

"Figuring out you ladies are much more useful than us men."

"I could've told you that a long time ago." She grinned and threw him a wink over the rim of her coffee cup.

"We need some help."

Angel took a sip from her mug. "Sure."

"Can you locate Xavier?"

"We'll see what we can do."

"Thanks, babe. I have to go out for a while. I'll be back as soon as I can." Jacque kissed her gently, lavishing her scent.

"No prob. We got lots to do. We'll work on finding Xavier, and we have to go back and check on some of the wounded from last night. A few had some serious injuries."

"All right. Make sure you stay with Etienne or the guards. Don't go out alone."

She caught his face, holding his gaze. "I'll be fine. You make sure you take care of yourself."

"We don't want to see your mushy shit. You got a room upstairs if you insist on ogling each other." Laurent plopped down in the chair next to Angel.

Angel smacked Laurent on the back of the head. "I guess you're stuck with us, gimpy."

"Great, I'm not gonna complain about being surrounded by beautiful women all day. Wait, where's your crazy ass momma?"

"You reminded me. I need to go check on her."

"Okay, I'll leave y'all to cater to Laurent. I should be back in a few hours." Jacque hesitated a moment before grabbing the keys to Angel's car. Driving had become more familiar, although the Porsche's manual transmission remained a problem.

Chapter Thirty-Seven

The energy from the other women surged through Angel's hands. The power emitted from Isis caused electricity to prickle up Angel's arm. She decided getting on Isis's bad side wasn't a smart idea.

A warm breeze filled the room. The flames on the candles flickered. A haze developed over the water.

Nat tightened her grip on Angel's hand. "I see something developing."

"I don't recognize it." Angel stared at the blurry picture. "Okay, we need more power. Let's focus."

Isis broke the circle and outstretched her hands toward the forming image. The currents flowed from her fingertips.

"You ladies want to help?" Isis nodded for Angel to do the same.

Angel jumped to attention, focusing all her energy on the faded image. Marie followed suit. Slowly, the picture came into view. The blood rushed to Angel's head as she realized what she watched. Her heart pounded and her pulse raced. She shut her eyes and bit the inside of her lip. Before she could stop herself, she shattered the glass bowl in a thousand tiny pieces. The women shielded themselves from the flying glass.

"*Chère*, you must learn to control your emotions," Marie chastised.

"I'm sorry, *Grand-mère*." She couldn't stop her hands from trembling. "I'm gonna kill her."

"You don't know exactly what she was doing."

"I don't care. I've had enough of her shit. Now she's mixed up with Xavier. I'm done."

"Who the hell is she?" Nat questioned.

"Isabella, remember from the other night. Jacque's ex-girlfriend?" Angel pulled a piece of glass out of her palm.

"Why would Isabella be with Xavier?" Marie stood with her hand on her hips.

"I don't know. I should've let it play out. We don't even know the timeframe or where they were. I messed up."

Nat blew out the candles on the floor. "We know Xavier is alive."

"Maybe we're taking the wrong approach."

"What do you mean?" Isis turned to study Angel.

"Instead of trying to find out where Xavier is hiding, why don't we bring him to us when the guys are ready?"

"You mean to conjure him in physical form?" Isis inquired, a sparkle of excitement in her voice. "An interesting strategy."

"Xavier would never expect us to call him to us."

"Very good. We'll tell Jacque of the plan once he returns." Isis smiled and placed a kissed on both of Angel's cheeks.

Angel wasn't sure how to handle the show of affection from Isis. She straightened her back and squared her shoulders. Her heart smiled at the thought of winning over Jacque's mother. "I still want to know what the hell Isabella is doing with Xavier."

Angel picked up the broom propped on the side table and swept the glass and powder from the floor.

"Odd. Maybe Laurent will have some insight or can talk to his sister." Marie handed Angel the dustpan.

"She better not try to help him. I swear to God I will kill her!" Angel snapped the handle of the broom in two.

"We'll figure it out." Isis furrowed her brow.

Angel dumped the glass and powder into the trash. She dusted off her jeans and headed out of the room with the others. She needed to find Jazzy and head to Le Fleur to check on the injured.

***

Angel entered into the ballroom, surprised to find it immaculate. Someone arranged everything picture perfect, back into the fairytale setting. She imagined having her wedding in a place like Le Fleur. She scoffed at her romanticism. *I can barely maintain a relationship, yet I'm standing here thinking about a wedding. What has that demon done to me?*

Isis and Marie came out of the back rooms.

"The injured are in the back. They set up cots and other supplies back there. Everyone's almost healed," Marie advised.

"Great, is there anything we need to do?" Angel strolled to the back of the ballroom.

Marie adjusted her head wrap. "No, Etienne took care of everything."

"He's one efficient man. We need to clone him."

"Interesting topic for political debate. Not only are you cloning. You want to clone a vampire."

Angel giggled. "Where's Nat and Jazzy?"

"They're chatting with some of the guys they helped last night. The guys are very appreciative and enamored with the girls."

"They've always had a way with men. Guys have been following them since we were kids."

Marie reached out and brushed a wavy strand from Angel's face. "You act as if it wasn't the same for you."

"Yeah. It always felt different for me. Like people wanted a piece of me, not to get to know me." Angel sighed.

"And now?"

"I'm comfortable with who I am. I don't care what others feel about me."

"Really?"

Staring at the floor, Angel answered softly, "Mostly. Some people still matter."

"And your mother? Does she matter?" Marie shifted her skirt and tucked the end of her head-wrap.

"Mother has issues. I've realized her faults for a long time. I just never felt good enough about myself to understand her perception was flawed."

"I hope things have changed."

"Speaking of Mother. We've got to wake her up when we get back to the house. I think we've kept her knocked out long enough."

"Such a shame. I enjoyed the quiet." Marie's sweet voice echoed off the brocade walls.

"Okay, I'm going to get the girls and Etienne so we can head back."

She found the girls chatting with two of the guys from Damon's pack. They seemed pretty comfortable being with the Supes. She expected more resistance, especially after Jazzy's initial reaction. Angel sat on the cot next to the fair-headed were.

"Hey, who's your new friends?" Angel teased.

"This is Rick and Thomas. They were pretty banged up last night. They look much better today." Nat winked at Rick.

"You must be the infamous Angel." Thomas flashed a lopsided grin.

"I don't know about infamous, but I'm Angel."

"Are we ready to go?" Jazzy asked.

"Yep, whenever y'all are ready. Have anyone seen Damon?"

"Some of the pack took him back to Lake Charles. He was pretty bad off," Rick answered.

"Oh, I'll have to go see him when things calm down. If y'all see him, tell him to call me." She placed a hand on Rick's leg, winning his appreciation. "Sure will."

"All right ladies, we got to get back to the house." Angel stood. "Nice to meet you guys."

"Back atcha." Rick's smile beamed with warmth.

***

Angel ran in the house, hoping Jacque had returned. Disappointment set in when she realized he was still gone. She went to her mother's room to check on her. She sat at the edge of the bed, debating whether to wake her or not. Finally, Angel blew the glittering dust in her mother's face and whispered the spell.

Her mother woke from her slumber. Elise glared at Angel and snatched her by the wrist. "You let them take me."

"I didn't let anyone take you, Mother. We came and rescued you."

"You left me with those filthy monsters. Do you know the things they did to me?" Elise's nails dug into Angel's skin, drawing blood.

"Get your hands off me, Mother, or those monsters will be the least of your worries." She stared into her mother's fiery brown eyes.

Elise shook as she released her hold.

"Mother, you need to come out here and eat. You'll keep your mouth shut and not say anything offensive to anyone. These people helped us. Saved you, even after you decided to cut off Laurent's foot."

"I want nothing to do with these abominations."

Angel's jaw hurt from her clenched teeth. "Fine, I'll have a car take you home, and you can fend for yourself and see how long you can stay alive. I'm tired of your bullshit."

"You dare talk to me like a child. I'm all you've got now. I know Faith is dead." Elise's expression was mocking.

"See, you're wrong. I have people who love me. They've helped me more in this short time than you have my whole life. Mother, I've finally realized I don't need you."

Elise snatched Angel by her shoulder. "You would've been nothing without me."

"No, I was empty with you. I didn't understand my true worth until now. With or without you Mother, I'll be fine. The decision is *yours*."

"You'll find out you need me. When he gets tired of looking at your ugly ass and leave, you'll come crawling back to me."

"Even if he does leave me, I'll never come back to you. You don't deserve to be called a mother." Angel balled her hands in tight fists, wanting to land one in her mother's mouth.

The sting of Elise's slap burned. Angel's patience and sympathy for her mother had run out. She no longer had the strength to fight the poison Elise continually administered. *I must cut her out of my life before she ruins me forever.*

"I'll have a car take you home. Pack your shit and be ready to go in ten minutes." Angel stormed out the room, slamming the door behind her.

Chapter Thirty-Eight

Jacque raised a brow as he pulled into the driveway and saw Elise on the steps with her bags. Something went wrong. He almost didn't want to know. He parked the car and got out. Anger oozed off Elise like toxic waste. Whatever happened left her in a tizzy.

"Hello, Elise." Jacque stopped at the foot of the steps.

"I don't know what y'all did to turn my daughter against me. I hope y'all rot in hell. Freaks!"

He regretted stopping. "Did you and Angel get into a disagreement?"

"She threw me out." Elise pouted like a child.

His instincts told him to run, instead he asked, "Why would Angel throw you out? Did something happen?"

"You don't know anything about my daughter. Just like her father, she's abandoning me."

"I'm sure it's a misunderstanding. Let's go inside and figure this out."

"I'm not going in there. If she wants me to stay, she needs to come out here and ask me." She folded her arms across her chest, staring across the driveway to the traffic on St. Charles.

"Okay, Elise. Let me go inside and talk to Angel and see what's going on."

"Suit yourself. You just tell my daughter I won't come back in until she apologizes to me."

Jacque shook his head, restrained from rolling his eyes, and went in the house. Laurent was in the same spot on the sofa as earlier. Etienne sat in the armchair with his head in his hands. He heard his mother and Marie in the kitchen.

"Where's Angel?" Jacque called into the parlor.

"Upstairs," Etienne answered.

"What the hell happened?"

"I don't know exactly. All I know is Angel told her mother to get out. She asked me to send her back to her house."

"Shit. Why's Elise sitting out on the steps?"

"I wasn't sure if was a good idea to send her home. I haven't sent for the car yet. Angel refused to let her come back in the house, so there she sits."

Jacque ran his hand through his hair. "Okay, I'll go talk to Angel."

"I'm with Ang. Let her ass go home." Laurent made a crude gesture toward the door.

Upstairs, he opened the door to the room and found Angel lying across the bed. He slid in next to her, kissing her on the nose. He leveraged his arm under her and rolled her to him.

His hand lightly traced the curve of her hip. "What's going on, Ang?"

"I've had it with her. She needs to go."

"Is sending her home alone the smartest thing to do right now?"

"I don't care. She's like poison. She can't stay here with me."

Jacque hated dividing his resources. He sensed Angel needed this. "All right. If you need her gone right now, we'll send her home. I'm sure we can get someone to keep an eye on her."

"Thank you."

"For what?"

Tears welled in her eyes. "Being on my side. I was afraid when Faith passed, I wouldn't have anyone on my side anymore."

"I'm always on your side. Even when you don't know it." He lifted her face to his and kissed her softly.

"Okay, please go send her home now. We got a lot to talk about. I'll come down in a minute." Angel rolled over on top of him, pushing him to his back, and her lips found his again.

"Keep kissing me and we won't be making it downstairs."

***

Laurent's foot fully regenerated. What little color Etienne possessed returned. Angel struggled with the estranged relationship with her mother. Her guilt tugged at her for putting her mother out of the house. She trained with Jacque to release her stress. Jacque's mother and Marie huddled in the kitchen, speaking in whispers all day. Jacque wondered what they were plotting. Nat helped develop the spell and potions needed to conjure Xavier. Jazzy decided to go home when everyone left Le Fleur.

Jacque pulled the towel off the stone bench in the garden. He wiped the sweat dripping down his face as Angel wiped his back. The sun beamed high in the sky. The New Orleans's summer was brutal, almost as bad as Hades. Jacque smiled at the comparison. Until they found Xavier, this was his new Hell.

"You sure you want to do this tonight?" Angel rubbed the towel on the back of her neck and dabbed her forehead.

"Babe, we can't wait forever. We need to catch him before he comes back for us."

"I know. I'm just worried."

Her nervousness surrounded him, throbbing in the base of his neck. "Hey, no need to worry. You guys came up with a good plan. And I know I can take him one-on-one."

"I don't doubt you." She pushed up on her tiptoes and planted a kiss on his lips.

"Hey, have you talked to Jazzy?"

"No, she's not answering her cell. Why?"

Jacque pressed his lips into a thin line. "I know she was kinda freaked out 'bout everything."

"Yeah, she was always the straight-laced one in the group. She's strong, she'll be okay."

"I have someone keeping an eye on her, too."

Angel lightly touched his arm. "Thanks."

"Your mother hasn't left the house since we dropped her off. Have you called to check on her?"

"No, I'm not ready."

Jacque picked up the water bottle and towel. "Okay. You can't avoid her forever." He snapped the towel, hitting Angel on the back of her leg.

"Ouch!" She threw her bottle of water on him and ran into the house.

Jacque entered the welcoming coolness of the room. The air hit the moisture on his body, sending a shiver through him. Standing at the kitchen sink, he downed the rest of the water in his bottle.

His mother leaned in the doorway. "Hello, Son."

"Hi, Mom. What've you been up to?"

"Speaking with your father."

"Where is Dad?"

"He's been negotiating. Trying to come to some kind of truce with Luc."

"Any luck?"

"No, Luc is very unhappy with the recent happenings. You and Angel seem to have attracted a lot of attention in the Underworld. It's been quite the embarrassment for him."

"He started it."

"Actually, your Angel started it when she went to Luc for help," Isis corrected.

Jacque hated when his mother was right, which was most of the time. "Yeah, she figured out it was a bad idea. You don't have to bring it up."

"I know. You seem to be very enamored with Angel. Where is this going, Son? She's not like Bell. She's not the kind of girl to play around with."

Jacque gripped the edge of the counter. "I don't plan to. I love her."

"The Casanova found his match." His mother's smile beamed.

Jacque returned her smile with one of his own. "It seems she's caught me."

"She'll be good for you."

"I just hope I'm good for her. She's had a hard life."

"You've already been good for her. I think you were just what each other needed."

"I guess only time will tell." Jacque kissed his mother's forehead on the way out the kitchen.

***

The sun dipped into the auburn and sienna clouds floating outside the window. The sky resembled the soft glow of a fire. Jacque focused in on the clock on the nightstand. It was seven o'clock. They had another two hours before they planned to conjure Xavier.

Jacque lay on his back and tucked his hands behind his head. He stared at the ceiling, thinking about the impending fight. He hated having to kill Xavier. His brother had problems. He also felt there was something redeeming under the pain and anger. Jacque just didn't know how to access it.

He wanted to spare his brother, but couldn't risk the lives of the two women he loved. Xavier would continue to hunt Angel and his mother until Jacque stopped him. He breathed deeply, inhaling the scent of Angel's hair, which swept over his shoulder as she scooted closer to him. She murmured something in her sleep and stretched her arm over his stomach. The softness of her touch made his stomach flutter. It awakened a growing need inside him.

Jacque gazed down at Angel. She appeared at peace in her sleep. Her beauty radiated about her. Even in her slumber, she unconsciously hid the scar marring her perfection. Angel's confidence was much stronger than when he first met her, but she still had some underlying insecurities. She was at her full glory when he first laid eyes on her, however nowhere near as magnificent as the woman he held today.

Her eyes fluttered open. She caught him studying her. "What're you doing?" she asked, her voice husky from sleep.

"Watching you."

"Exciting stuff." She pushed her hair out of her face and lay on the pillow beside him.

"What were you dreaming about?"

"You."

"Something good, I hope." Jacque rolled to his side, turning toward her.

"It's always good when I dream of you."

Jacque twirled a strand of her hair around his finger. "You'll tell me anything."

"What were you thinking about, baby? You seemed to be deep in thought."

"A lot of things. Mainly you."

Mischief flared in her smile. "Hopefully, you were planning all the naughty things you're gonna do to me."

"Always."

She giggled. "Such a bad boy."

"Angel, where do you see us?"

"What do you mean?"

"What do you want out of this relationship?"

"I want to be happy, and I want to make you happy."

"Do I make you happy?"

She reached out, running her finger along his jaw line. "More than you'll ever know."

Jacque sat up and slid off the edge of the bed.

"Where're you going?" She called after him as he disappeared into the closet.

"Hold on. I want to show you something."

"A present?"

Jacque mused at her excitement. "You're easily bribed."

When he came back in the room, Angel bounced on the edge of the bed, waiting for him. Her hair tumbled over her shoulders, her chocolate eyes shining bright. He took her hand and pulled her to her feet.

"Angel, I've never felt about anyone the way I feel about you. I've lived longer than you could ever imagine and not until I met you have I felt complete." Jacque kneeled on one knee and pulled the ring from his pocket. "Angelique Dias, would you do me the honor of being my wife?" Jacque's heart pounded in his chest as he waited what seemed an eternity for her answer.

Tears fell down her cheeks. She tilted his face to her, kissing him softly and whispered, "Yes."

Chapter Thirty-Nine

Angel blinked to adjust her eyes to the candlelight in the room. Jacque followed close behind with his fingers intertwined with hers. Marie, Isis, and Nat set everything up for the ritual.

Her heart raced from both happiness and fear. She was close to having everything she wanted. The fact it could all be taken away tonight petrified her. She gave Jacque's hand a tight squeeze before releasing it.

"Nice of you two to join us," Isis joked.

At least Angel hoped it was a joke. She crossed the room to stand by her grandmother. "Is there anything else I can do?"

Marie adjusted the candles in the circle. "*Non bébé,* everything is ready."

As she pushed her hair from her face, the light of the candles reflected in the large emerald-cut diamond in her ring.

Isis's eyes widened with question. "Is there something the two of you would like to tell us?"

The ladies stared as they waited for her to answer.

"I asked Angel to marry me and she said 'yes,'" Jacque answered proudly.

Marie hugged her, holding her tight. "Oh, Angel! I'm happy for you."

"Congratulations, I wasn't sure if this day was ever going to come. I'm happy it's here." Isis kissed her son and winked at Angel.

"Can demons get married?" Nat asked matter-of-factly.

"Can they?" Angel turned to Jacque with raised brows.

"We won't be going to get a marriage license. I guess we can have a ceremony. I just ask one thing. No churches. Not that I can't go in one. It just doesn't seem right." Jacque grinned.

Marie clapped her hands. "This is great news!"

"What's such great news?" a voice called from the hall.

Angel stomach tightened when Isabella appeared in the doorway. "What're you doing here?"

"I came to see what was going on and make sure everyone was okay." Isabella tossed her blonde hair over her shoulder.

"Where've you been?" Jacque questioned. "We've been worried about you."

"I didn't know you still cared, sugar." She flashed him a beguiling grin.

Angel wanted to slap the smile off Isabella's face. "We were just concerned something happened to you."

"Yes. We wouldn't want you to miss Angel and Jacque's engagement party," Isis chimed in. The tremble in Isabella's lips showed the impact of Isis's words.

Isabella stepped back, stumbling over her own feet. "W-w-what?"

"Yes, Jacque asked Angel to marry him. See?" Marie held up Angel's hand, showing off the ring.

"I have to go. Where's my brother?" A glaze washed over Isabella's eyes.

"He was in his room. It's on the second floor." Jacque watched Isabella, his eyes shaded with sadness. "Do you want me to show you?"

"I don't need your help. You've done enough," she scoffed, running from the room.

"She'll be okay." Isis patted Jacque's arm.

Isabella wore her pain like a badge. Angel understood the torment of rejection. As much as she wanted to hate Isabella, she felt connected to her. They shared the emptiness of loving someone who didn't love them back. For Angel, it was her mother.

"Let's get this show on the road." Nat broke the silence.

"Yeah, Jacque, do you want to go get the guys?" Angel met his gaze, which still lingered after Isabella, causing a pang of jealousy to flare in her.

"I don't think we need everyone. We should just get this going," he suggested.

"They can help you if you get into trouble." The acid in her stomach churned and her hand slightly shook.

"I want to do this myself. You have to stay out of it, too." He shot her a stern look. She expected this from him. He never planned on anyone helping.

"Okay." She didn't argue. Instead, she meshed her lips to his, in what might have been their last kiss. Her tongue explored his mouth, tasting every part of him. She drew him down to her. He wrapped his arms around her waist, merging their bodies. He softened the kiss. She listened to the thundering of his heart against her ear. He released his hold on her and stepped back. Angel cringed, never wanting to let him go.

Jacque forced himself away from her. He hated to let her go. In order to move forward with their lives, he had to finish his fight with his brother. He wanted to be rid of Xavier and marry the women he loved.

Angel, Marie, Nat, and his mother formed a circle around the symbols drawn on the floor. He unsheathed the swords he carried on his back, balancing the weight in his hands. The bronze hilts of his swords cooled the heat permeating from his hands. The sounds of Angel's chants filled his head. The lyrical softness of her tone calmed him. The serenity of her voice contradicted the turmoil he sensed inside her.

Flames roared in the middle of the white power triangle. The chanting became louder. They called on Xavier, beckoned him to appear. Lightning flashed outside. Jacque shut his eyes, listening to the rhythmic melody of the spell. The heat intensified in the room. The venom of anger and hatred infiltrated the large space.

"Hello, ladies. Fancy meeting you here." Xavier reached out to snatch Angel's arm. Lightning struck, throwing him outside the circle.

"Leave!" Jacque cornered his brother, allowing the women to escape.

"I'm surprised to see you, bro. Did you miss me?" Xavier's laugh crackled through the long, narrow space.

"I figured it was better to meet on my terms than wait for yours."

"You're smarter than I give you credit for. Father did a better job than I thought."

"Centuries of training comes in handy." Jacque crouched around the perimeter of the room.

"Too bad it all ends here." The ring of Xavier's sword echoed off the walls as he unleashed it from its steel sheath.

Jacque circled his brother, anticipating his moves. Knees bent, body tense, he readied for the attack. Xavier's growl shook the windows as he rushed at Jacque. The blade of his sword slashed through the top of Jacque's arm, and he swung the sword to his right hand, thrusting it forward, penetrating his brother below his ribs.

He leveraged the edge of a chair, rotating into a back flip. He turned in time to run his blade across Xavier's thigh. His brother picked up a vanity chair, brandishing it like a lion tamer and used it to ward off the blows.

Jacque tripped over the candles as Xavier lunged at him. He crushed the base of his skull with the hilt of the sword. Jacque tried to focus against the pain, but the advances made at him were too quick, and he winced as the blade passed through his stomach, burning like molten lava. Once Xavier drew it out, Jacque dropped his sword as he stumbled backward.

"Where're all your friends now, bro?" Xavier's eyes glowed in the darkness.

"I don't need help finishing you." Jacque regained his balance, striking with all his might. The steel of his blade sliced through flesh and bone of Xavier's left arm. He attacked again, not allowing Xavier time to retaliate. He impaled his brother to the armoire sitting on wall opposite the door. Xavier's sword dropped to the floor.

Jacque held his stomach and stumbled back. Defeat boiled inside Xavier, something he never felt before. It emerged as confusion and disgust.

"We don't have to kill each other," Jacque offered.

"Ah. There's the Jacque I know. Those fickle emotions always interfere with your good judgment."

"Why do you hate me?"

"Because you took everything from me. You had the life I should've lived."

"Father left your mother long before I was born."

"And he never looked back. He cared nothing of me." Xavier looked away.

"He cares for you. Father rarely shows his emotions."

"What does it matter? What's done is done." He used his strength to rip the sword through his torso. Jacque doubled over in anguish from the excruciating pain his brother experienced. Xavier used the downfall of being an empath to his advantage.

He fell forward on his knees.

"Put me out of my misery, brother." He bowed his head, revealing his neck.

"I don't want to kill you."

"If you don't, as long as I live, I will hunt you."

"Why? Why does it have to be this way?" Jacque labored with the heft of his sword as his brother's request weighed heavy in his heart.

"Because I don't know anything else. It's too late. I can't turn back."

"I won't do it."

His brother lifted his head and stared into Jacque's eyes. "Please."

The agony in his voice brought a knot into Jacque's throat. He wanted freedom. As Xavier lowered his head, Jacque brought his sword down, beheading his brother.

The flames lapped over the body. An inferno ensued until it all disappeared. Jacque threw his sword to the ground, dropped to his knees, and pounded his fists into the wood floor until he pulverized it. His brother was gone. The threat extinguished.

Then why don't I feel like the victor?

Chapter Forty

Angel paced back and forth down the hall, eyes fixed on the door. Every noise emitted from the room tempted her to the rush in. She resisted the urge. This was something Jacque had to do himself. She prayed he walked out of the room unharmed. An unrealistic wish.

Isis and Marie sat on the bench and held each other's hand.

"Don't worry, *chère*. He will come out." Marie pulled her down to the bench as she made another pass, wearing a groove in the floor.

"Yes, he finally has something to live for. He won't lose." Isis squeezed her hand.

She wanted to be optimistic. The sound of the fight didn't give promise.

She nervously twisted her engagement ring around her finger, waiting for the door to open. She only wanted him to come out the room alive.

Laurent leaned on the wall. "What's going on? Are they still fighting?"

"I don't know. There hasn't been any noise for a few minutes." Angel studied the laces of her sneakers.

"Has anyone gone in there to check?"

"No. He told us to stay out here until he comes out."

"And y'all actually listened this time?" Laurent pushed up against the wall. He opened the door and peeked in. Angel hovered close behind him. A shadow lingered in the darkness. She heard his soft cries of anguish.

She kneeled beside him on the floor, embracing him. Laurent waited in the doorway, silent. Isis pushed past him and rushed to her son's aid.

"Baby, are you okay?" Angel's shaky voice feared the answer. She forced Jacque to look at her. Marie slid into the room and turn on the lights. The blood splattered about the room confirmed the brutality of the fight. She moved in front of him, finding his eyes. "Are you okay?"

"I'll be fine," he managed.

"Is Xavier gone?"

"Yes."

"Dead?"

"Yes."

Isis reached out her hand. "Come on, Son. Get off the floor."

Angel rose and brushed the white powder from her jeans. Jacque staggered as he stood. She grabbed his arm to help steady him as he clutched his abdominal wound. Laurent came over to assist, taking him from Angel.

"Take him up to our room." She followed behind them.

"I'ma be fine, babe. It's not as bad as it looks." Jacque limped up the stairs.

"We'll get you cleaned and bandaged. Afterward, we can go down and meet with everyone else."

"Or we can just stay in for the night," he proposed.

"Aren't we feisty tonight? I think we should let your wound heal up first."

"Hey. Remember me? I don't need to hear this crap." Laurent chuckled.

In the room, Laurent dumped Jacque on the bed. Angel took off his shoes and pulled his shirt over his head.

"Thanks, Laurent. We'll be down once I get him fixed up."

"No prob. Oh. I hear congratulations are in order."

Her smile beamed from ear to ear. "Oh, yeah. I almost forgot about being engaged."

"Bell came by and told me. She isn't happy. I'd stay away from her for a while if I were you."

"I'll watch my back." Angel winked at him.

"You know she's not all bad. She waited for so long for Jacque to want to settle down. She just never expected it wasn't going to be with her."

"Sorry, I know she's your sister. I feel bad for her."

"You're good for Jacque. Bell and Jacque would've killed each other eventually," Laurent joked.

"Thanks. You're a good friend."

***

Jacque woke, hoping the memories were remnants of a bad dream. When he sat up and saw his bandaged midsection, he knew it wasn't a dream. Angel smiled at him from her book.

"I see the dead has arisen." She shut the book and placed it on the nightstand.

"How long have I been out?"

"A couple of hours."

He sat up, pushing his back against the headboard. "Shit, sorry, babe."

"No need to be sorry. It was a pretty bad wound."

"I think it's good now. Where's everyone else?"

"Downstairs. Waiting."

"Okay, find me a shirt and we'll go down." Moving to the edge of the bed, Jacque rested his elbows on his knees, hung his head, and examined the wood planks of the floor.

"Everything okay?"

"Sure," he lied.

"You're bullshitting me. What's up?"

"I didn't beat him."

She stopped and asked, "What're you talkin' about?"

"Xavier. I didn't *beat* him. He gave up."

"What do you mean? It sounded like Armageddon in the room."

Jacque's head dropped even lower. "In the end, he stopped fighting back. He begged me to end him."

She crawled across the bed and stroked his back, her fingers trailing down his spine. "I'm sorry, babe. I know this was hard for you."

"I had to do it, but he was still my brother. No one should have to kill their own brother."

"I know if there was any other way, you wouldn't have killed him." She slid around his body and cuddled on Jacque's lap. She brushed her thumb across his cheek and grazed her lips across his.

"Thanks for understanding. I'm not sure if my mother understands why I feel a connection to Xavier. She has gotten good at blocking out other's emotions, almost too good."

Angel walked to the bureau and tossed Jacque a shirt. "She loves you. Even if she doesn't understand, she would at least try to tolerate it. That's more than I can say for my mother."

"All right, time to go face the others. I'm sure they're all dying to talk about the engagement." Jacque wanted to focus on happier things. He gave her thigh a tap and guided her towards the door.

***

Everyone gathered out on the patio in the garden. The soft night air was a delicious retreat from the day's scorching heat. A storm approached and brought a refreshing breeze with it.

"I see you finally found your way down. I guess your wound wasn't as bad as we thought," Laurent announced.

"You're funny, Laurent." Angel tossed a look of indignation at his mock disappointment.

Isis narrowed her eyes to observe Jacque. "How are you feeling?"

"I'm good as new." He patted his belly.

"I'm glad. I'm sorry about your brother."

"Thanks. I know he wasn't your favorite person."

"He had problems, ones none of us could repair."

Angel tightened her grip on his hand and led the way to the empty seats at the table. "We don't have to worry about him anymore."

"Now the unpleasantness is over, show us your ring, dear." Marie held out her hands to Angel.

She overflowed with joy as she gave her hand to her grandmother. The beautiful three-carat emerald-cut ring set in platinum glittered in the candlelight. Angel never had anyone give her something so extravagant. She loved it, but the ring didn't matter. She would've said yes if he handed her a soda can tab.

"My God. It's beautiful, Jacque. Good job." Marie showed the ring to Isis.

"When's the big day?" Etienne asked.

"We haven't really had a chance to discuss it." Angel glanced over at Jacque. She didn't want another long engagement. She wasn't letting this one get away.

"The sooner the better," Jacque insisted.

"I would gladly do the ceremony," Isis offered.

Angel had all she ever wanted. The only thing missing was her sister. She wished Faith lived long enough to witness the dream she always envisioned for her. Love, happiness, and family.

"Thank you. We'll be honored," Angel replied. "If this is going to happen, we might as well get it done. How does everyone feel about three weeks from today?"

"I think three weeks is enough time to get everything ready." Marie looked at Isis for consensus.

"We're guys. Just tell us when and where to show up and we'll be there." Jacque took Angel's hand, kissing the tips of her fingers.

Everything fell into place.

"Angel, Marie and I have a special gift for you. Let's call it an engagement gift." Both ladies smiled like canaries eluding the cat.

"Oh. Okay."

"Come with us." They stood, waiting for her to follow. "We'll be back, gentlemen."

Angel accompanied the women to the room they used for storing their potions. Nat was already there, mixing some concoction.

"Hey, girl. Let me see the ring." Nat grabbed Angel's hand, squealing like a schoolgirl. "He did good!"

"He always does good by me." Angel was giddy from all the attention.

Marie directed her in front of the small altar. "We know you've been through a lot these last few months. You've lost a lot. We've also watched you grow into a beautiful, confident woman."

"We want to give you the gift you originally asked for." Isis picked up the potion Nat mixed. She dabbed the oily mixture on Angel's face and down her scar.

Angel flinched, not sure if she was ready for what they offered. "I'm okay with how I look. You don't have to try and do this."

"We know, dear. Your inner beauty will now be represented on the outside. You deserve both." Marie's eyes showed her compassion and love.

"How do you know it will work? I never found a spell for beauty. Believe me. If I did, I would've used it."

"This is a mirroring spell. It mirrors what is inside and reflect it out," Nat answered. "Now focus. Focus on the things you love and make you happy."

The chanting felt as if it went on forever. Angel absorbed the energy flowing from the others. She focused on the ones she loved and her happiness. The chanting stopped and she opened her eyes. Everyone stared at her, but said nothing.

"Well?" she shouted. "Did it work?"

"And if it didn't?" Isis asked.

"No harm no foul. We tried."

"Good answer." Isis passed her a mirror.

Angel studied her reflection and remembered the words her sister gave her just before she died. The beauty was always inside her; she just had to find it.

***

Jacque leaned back in his chair with his feet propped on the table. He swirled the brandy in the glass before taking a drink. He wondered what his mother and Marie planned for Angel.

"We need to get back to strategizing on how to beat Luc." Jacque stared at the amber colored liquid in his glass.

"We'll get back to it. Right now, get your wedding over with and enjoy life." Laurent rocked on the back legs of his chair.

"He'll send someone new. He won't stop until we stop him."

Intense heat engulfed the garden, causing the flowers to wilt.

"You know me well," the dark voice called from the flames.

Jacque jumped up, recognizing the voice. Lucifer leaned against gazebo post.

"You surprised me. I didn't think it would take this much work to bring you and your lady back. Don't worry. I'll make up for the trouble when I get you in my grasp." Luc walked toward them, leaving a trail of fire in his wake.

"I'll never let you hurt her. There'll be an end to this, even if I have to kill you myself," Jacque muttered through clinched teeth.

"We'll see. Until then, I suggest you watch yourself and your girl." The flames dissipated. Luc was gone.

Jacque clenched his jaw, slammed his glass on the table, shattering it in his hand.

"I guess you're right. We'll have to work out a plan fast." Etienne kicked the ashes off the patio.

"What plan are we working out?" Angel's voice drifted from the kitchen door.

"Bachelor party stuff," Laurent lied.

"Really? Aren't you a little old for a bachelor party?" Marie countered.

"How often do we get to have one? How many of us you know run around getting married?"

"I guess."

Angel's laugh rang through the garden. Jacque turned in her direction. Her beauty stole the words from his mouth. She was breathtaking.

He took her in his arms. "What happened?"

"You like? Grand-mère and your mother found a spell to return me to my old self."

Angel's flawless beauty was restored. The deep scar jutting down her face no longer existed. Confidence radiated around her and she exuded happiness. "I like you in any form." Her happiness melted him.

"Exactly why I said yes when you asked me to marry you." She hugged him tight.

"It's been a long night. I think it's time for bed."

She stretched her arms around his neck. "I'm not going to argue."

Jacque bent down and swept her off her feet.

"Goodnight everyone," he called over his shoulder as he carried her into the house, smiling at the sounds of laughter coming from the garden. "Do you know how much I love you?" he whispered against her ear.

She kissed the crook of his neck. "Not as much as I love you."

Jacque held Angel tight as he carried her up the stairs. Silently, he promised to protect her. Danger still lurked in the shadows, but he would give his life to keep her safe.

~ABOUT THE AUTHOR~

Vivi Dumas submerges herself in the dark underworld of the supernatural. To balance the analytical and logical confines of her day job, she unleashes the fiery passions of her imagination in her writing. Although she grew up an Army brat, she calls Louisiana home, but has endured the hot summers and cold winters of Maryland for the last 16 years.

Vivi can be found online at:
www.vividumas.wordpress.com
Facebook
Twitter